THE GRAPHIC NOVEL
William Shakespeare

QUICK TEXT VERSION

Script Adaptation: John McDonald
Character Designs & Original Artwork: Jon Haward
Coloring & Lettering: Nigel Dobbyn
Inking Assistant: Gary Erskine

American English Adaptation: Joe Sutliff Sanders
Design & Layout: Jo Wheeler & Greg Powell
Publishing Assistant: Joanna Watts
Additional Information: Karen Wenborn

Editor in Chief: Clive Bryant

Macbeth: The Graphic Novel
Quick Text Version

William Shakespeare

First published: November 2008
Reprinted: September 2015, September 2019, January 2023

Published by: Classical Comics Ltd

Acknowledgments: Every effort has been made to trace copyright holders of
material reproduced in this book. Any rights not acknowledged here will be
acknowledged in subsequent editions if notice is given to Classical Comics Ltd.

Images on pages 3 & 6 reproduced with the kind permission of
the Trustees of the National Library of Scotland. © National Library of Scotland.
Images on page 141 reproduced with the kind permission of The Shakespeare Birthplace Trust.

All enquiries should be addressed to:
Classical Comics Ltd.
PO Box 177
LUDLOW
SY8 9DL
United Kingdom

info@classicalcomics.com
www.classicalcomics.com

ISBN: 978-1-906332-46-4

This book is printed by Graphy Cems, Spain using environmentally safe inks, on paper
from responsible sources. This material can be disposed of by recycling,
incineration for energy recovery, composting and biodegradation.

The rights of John McDonald, Jon Haward, Nigel Dobbyn and Gary Erskine
to be identified as the artists of this work have been asserted in accordance with
the Copyright, Designs and Patents Act 1988 sections 77 and 78.

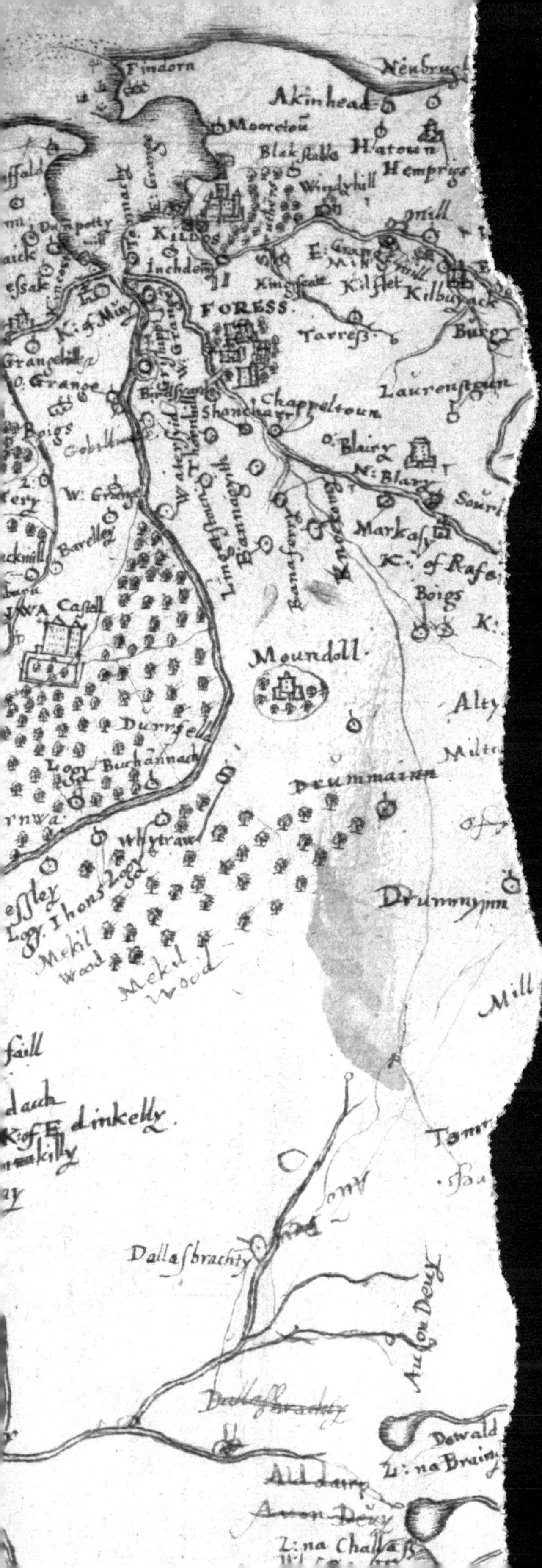
Findorn
Akinhead
FORESS
Moundoll
Dallasbrachty

Contents

Dramatis Personæ

Duncan
King of Scotland

Malcolm
Son of Duncan

Donalbain
Son of Duncan

Macduff
Nobleman of Scotland

Lenox
Nobleman of Scotland

Rosse
Nobleman of Scotland

Lady Macbeth
Wife of Macbeth

Lady Macduff
Wife of Macduff

Siward *Earl of Northumberland,
General of the English forces*

**A Gentlewoman attending
to Lady Macbeth**

Seyton
An officer serving Macbeth

An English Doctor

A Scottish Doctor

A Porter

An Old Man

Murderer 1

Murderer 2

Murderer 3

Dramatis Personæ

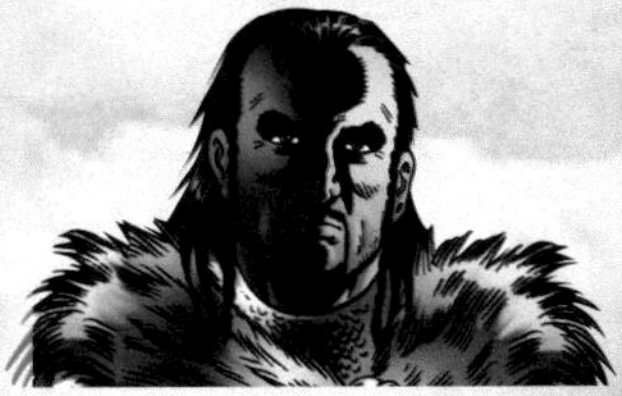

Macbeth
General in the King's Army

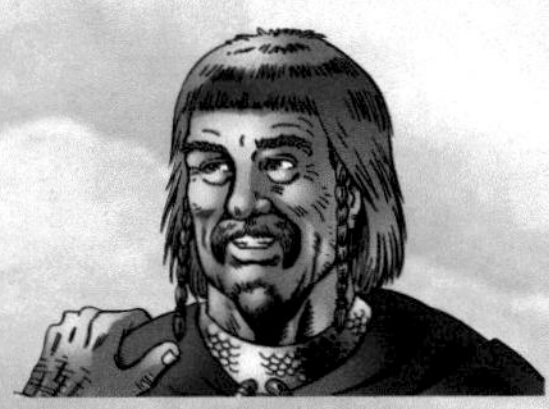

Banquo
General in the King's Army

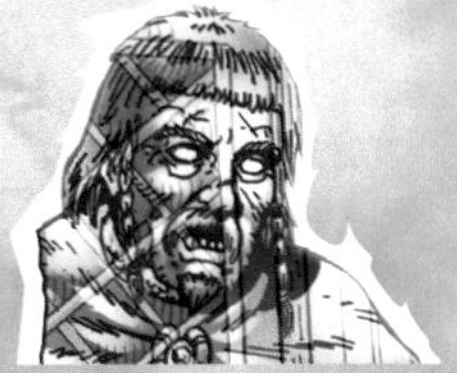

The Ghost of Banquo

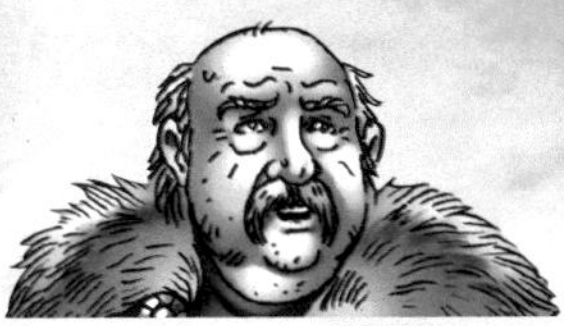

Menteth
Nobleman of Scotland

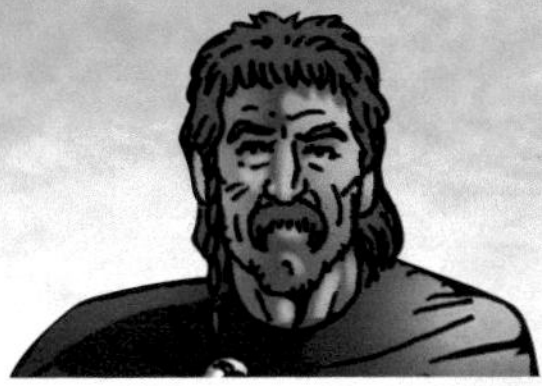

Angus
Nobleman of Scotland

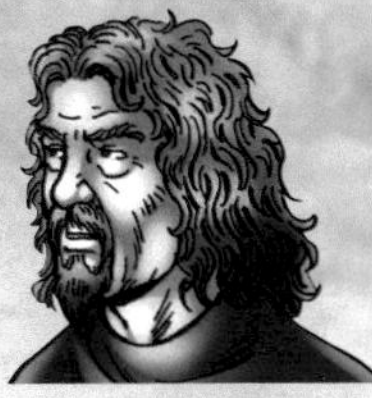

Cathness
Nobleman of Scotland

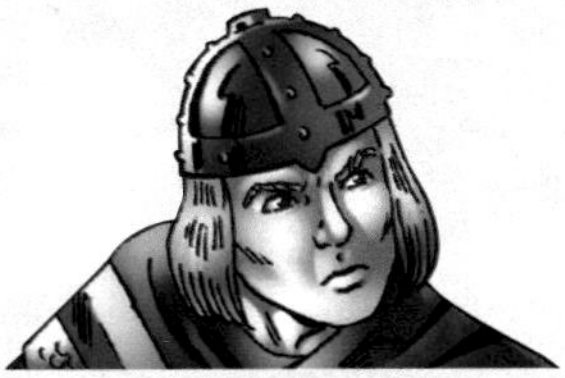

Young Siward
Son of Siward

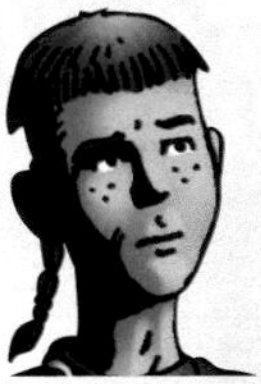

Fleance
Son of Banquo

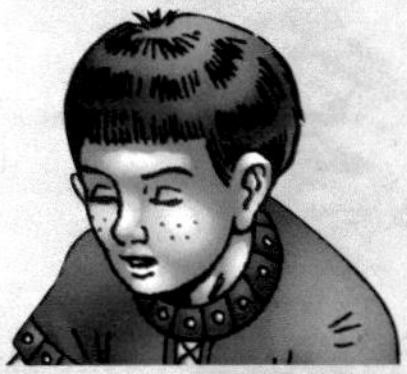

Boy
Son of Macduff

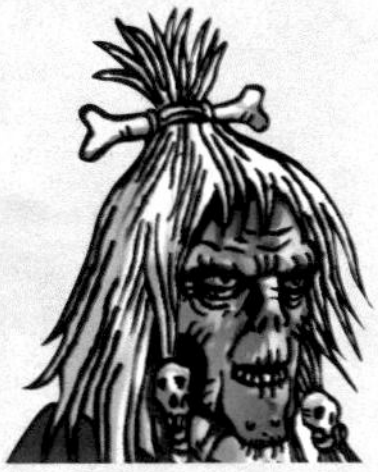

Witch 1

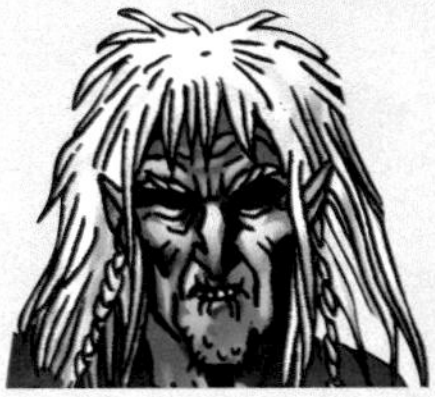

Witch 2

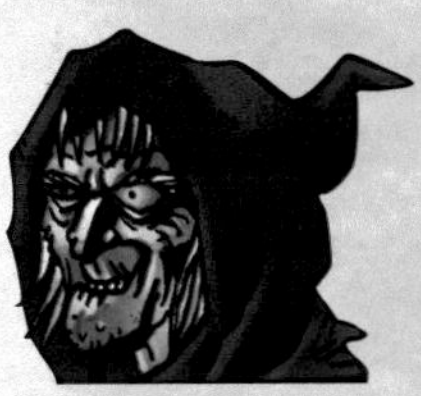

Witch 3

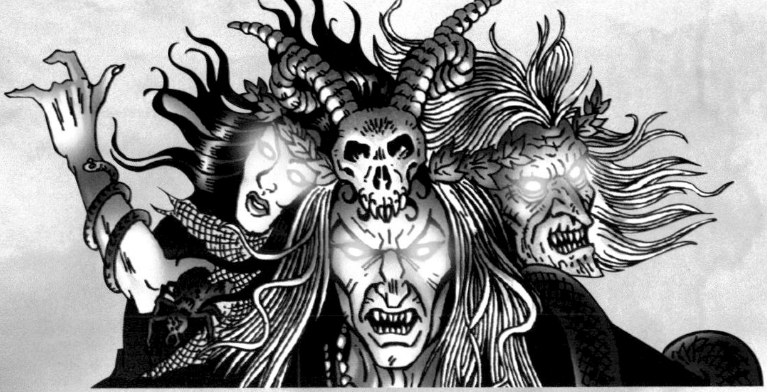

Hecate
The "Queen" Witch

and Lords, Ladies,
Officers, Soldiers,
Messengers, Attendants
and Apparitions.

Prologue

Scotland in the year 1040.

King Duncan has ruled the land for six years, ever since the death of his grandfather, Malcolm II. Duncan is a good king, but even under his kind and gentle ruling, Scotland is far from being a settled nation.

For centuries, following the departure of the Romans, the land has been split in two – with bands of Vikings in the north and tribes of Saxons in the south. It's a barbaric land. Both local tribes have strong leaders: men who rely on the strength of their sword arm for honors and often have to fight for their very survival.

But the country is changing. With the reign of King Duncan comes a rare promise of unity amongst the tribes to create a single, Scottish nation ruled by a single Scottish King. However not everyone welcomes this peace. Some chieftains want to maintain their independence and continue to rebel against the King, often joining forces with warriors from other tribes and from other countries such as Ireland and Norway; and there are even some chieftains who would like to claim the title of King of Scotland for themselves.

To defend his crown, and to maintain order in his land, King Duncan commands a powerful army, led by noblemen who are experienced in the ways of war - and the mightiest and most trusted of these noblemen is King Duncan's cousin, the Thane of Glamis, otherwise known as…

…Macbeth.

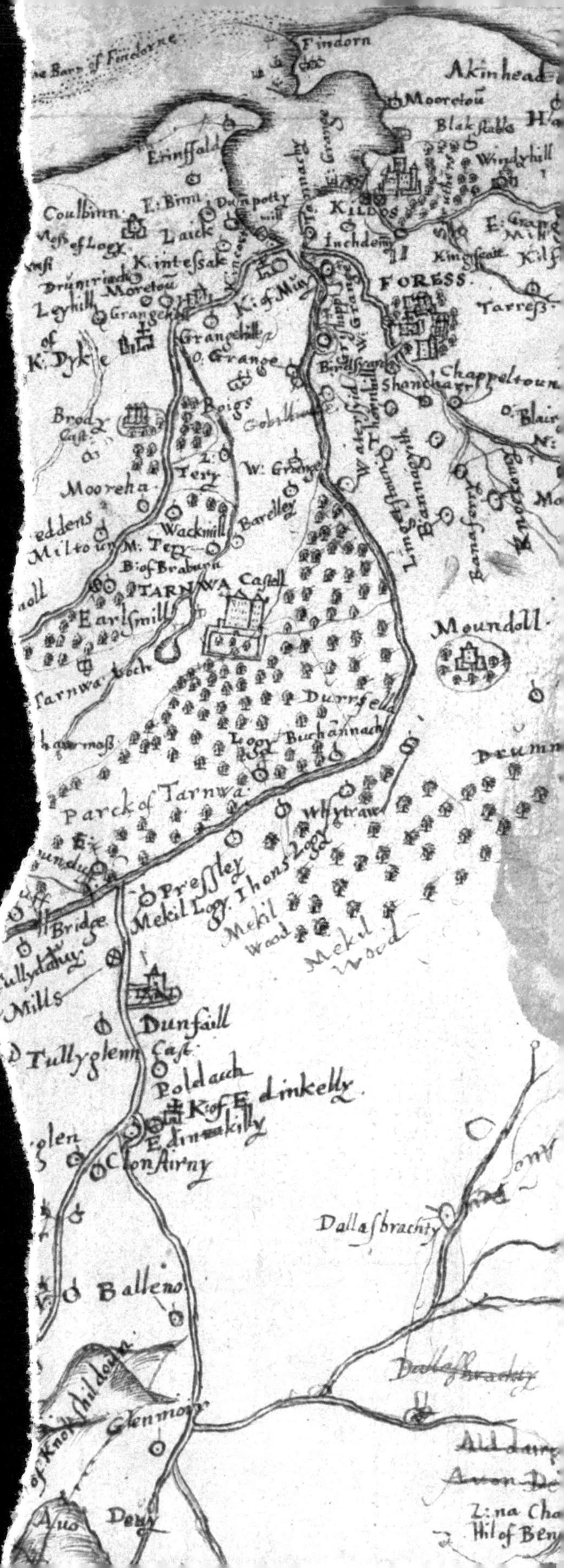

Findorn
FORESS
Chappeltoun
TARNWA Castell
Moundoll
Parck of Tarnwa
Dunfaill
Dallasbrachty
Balleno

Macbeth

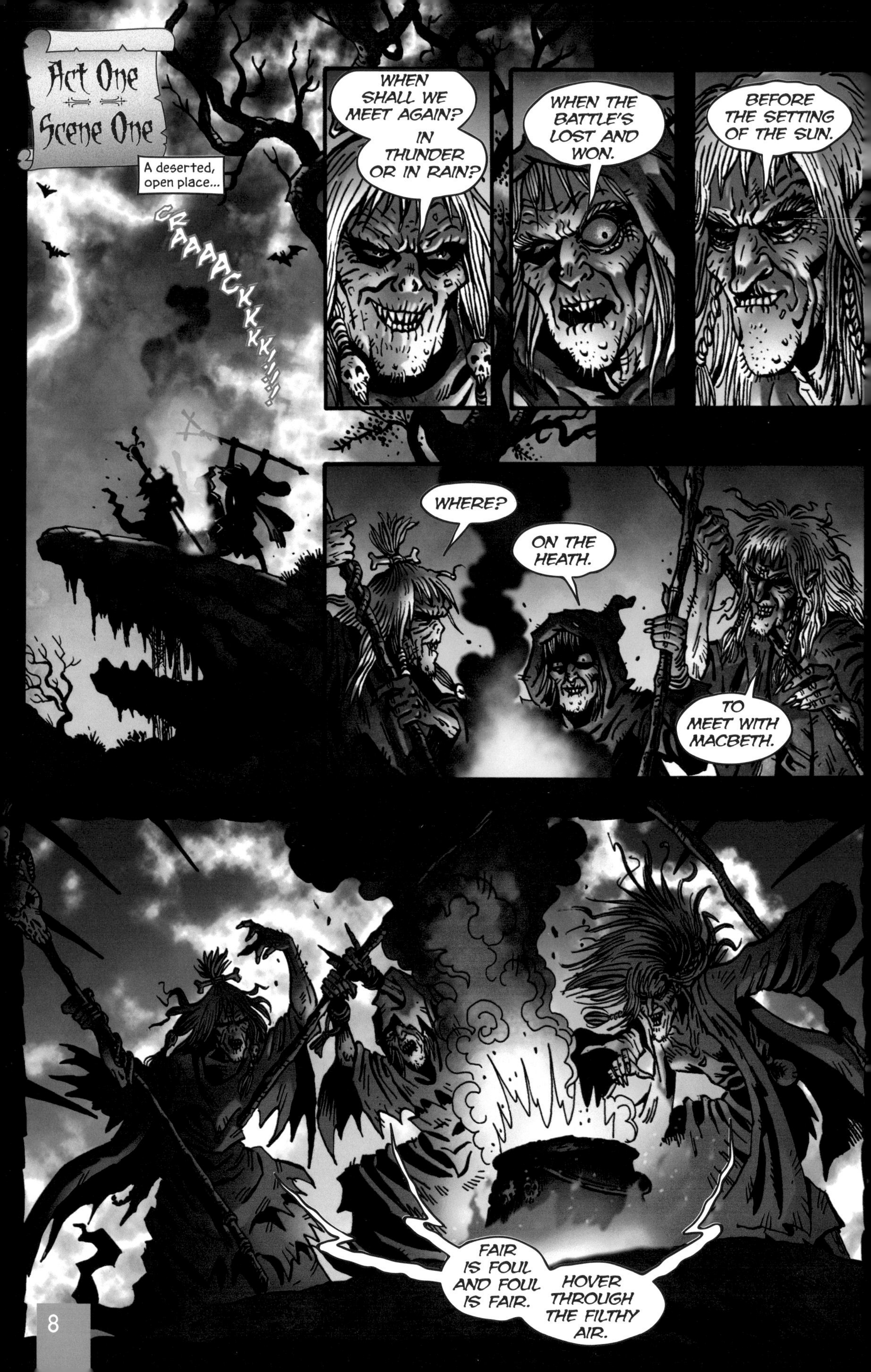
Act One
Scene One
A deserted, open place...
CRAAAACKKKK!!!!
WHEN SHALL WE MEET AGAIN?
IN THUNDER OR IN RAIN?
WHEN THE BATTLE'S LOST AND WON.
BEFORE THE SETTING OF THE SUN.
WHERE?
ON THE HEATH.
TO MEET WITH MACBETH.
FAIR IS FOUL AND FOUL IS FAIR.
HOVER THROUGH THE FILTHY AIR.

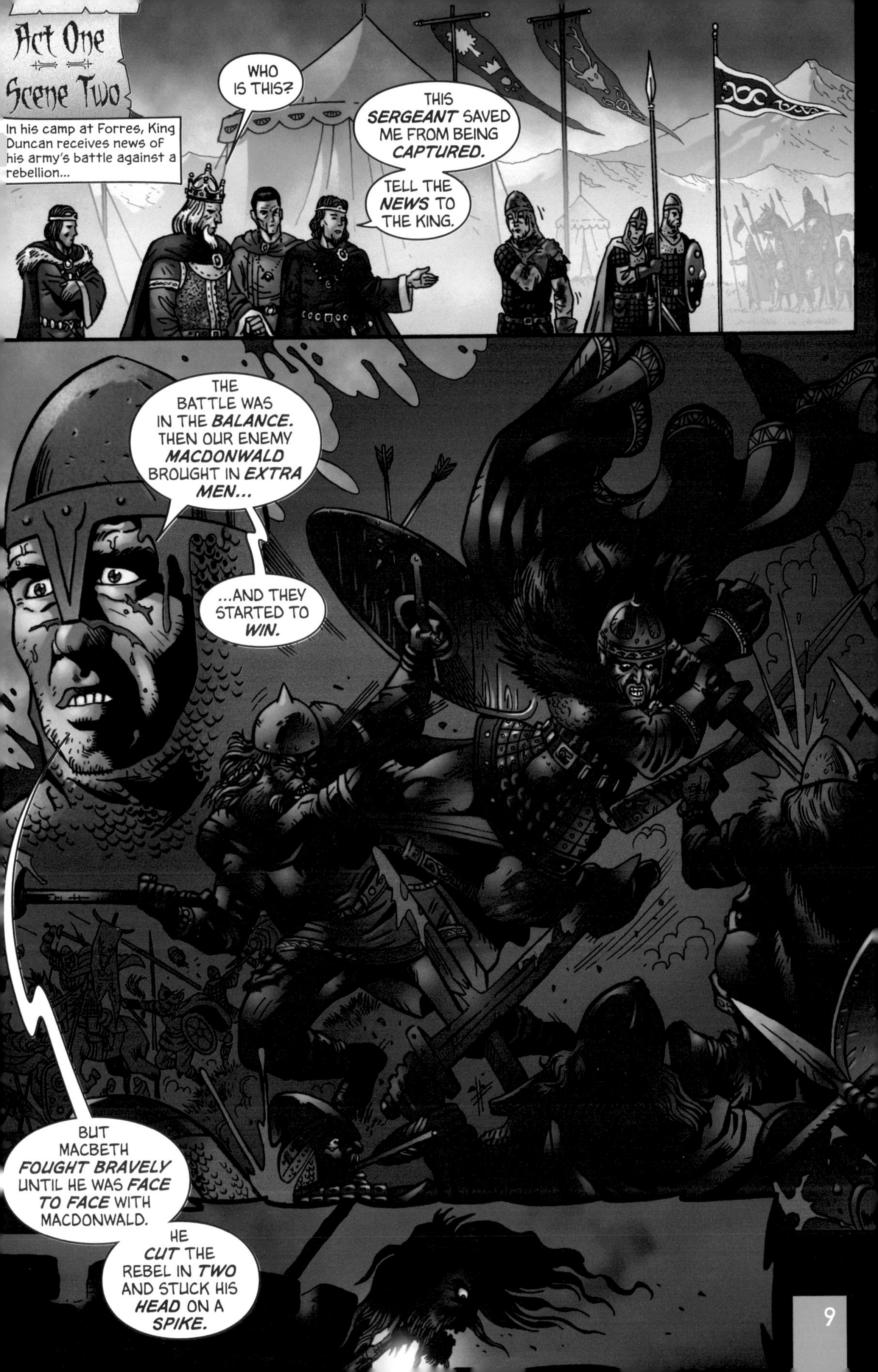
Act One
Scene Two
In his camp at Forres, King Duncan receives news of his army's battle against a rebellion...
WHO IS THIS?
THIS SERGEANT SAVED ME FROM BEING CAPTURED.
TELL THE NEWS TO THE KING.
THE BATTLE WAS IN THE BALANCE. THEN OUR ENEMY MACDONWALD BROUGHT IN EXTRA MEN...
...AND THEY STARTED TO WIN.
BUT MACBETH FOUGHT BRAVELY UNTIL HE WAS FACE TO FACE WITH MACDONWALD.
HE CUT THE REBEL IN TWO AND STUCK HIS HEAD ON A SPIKE.

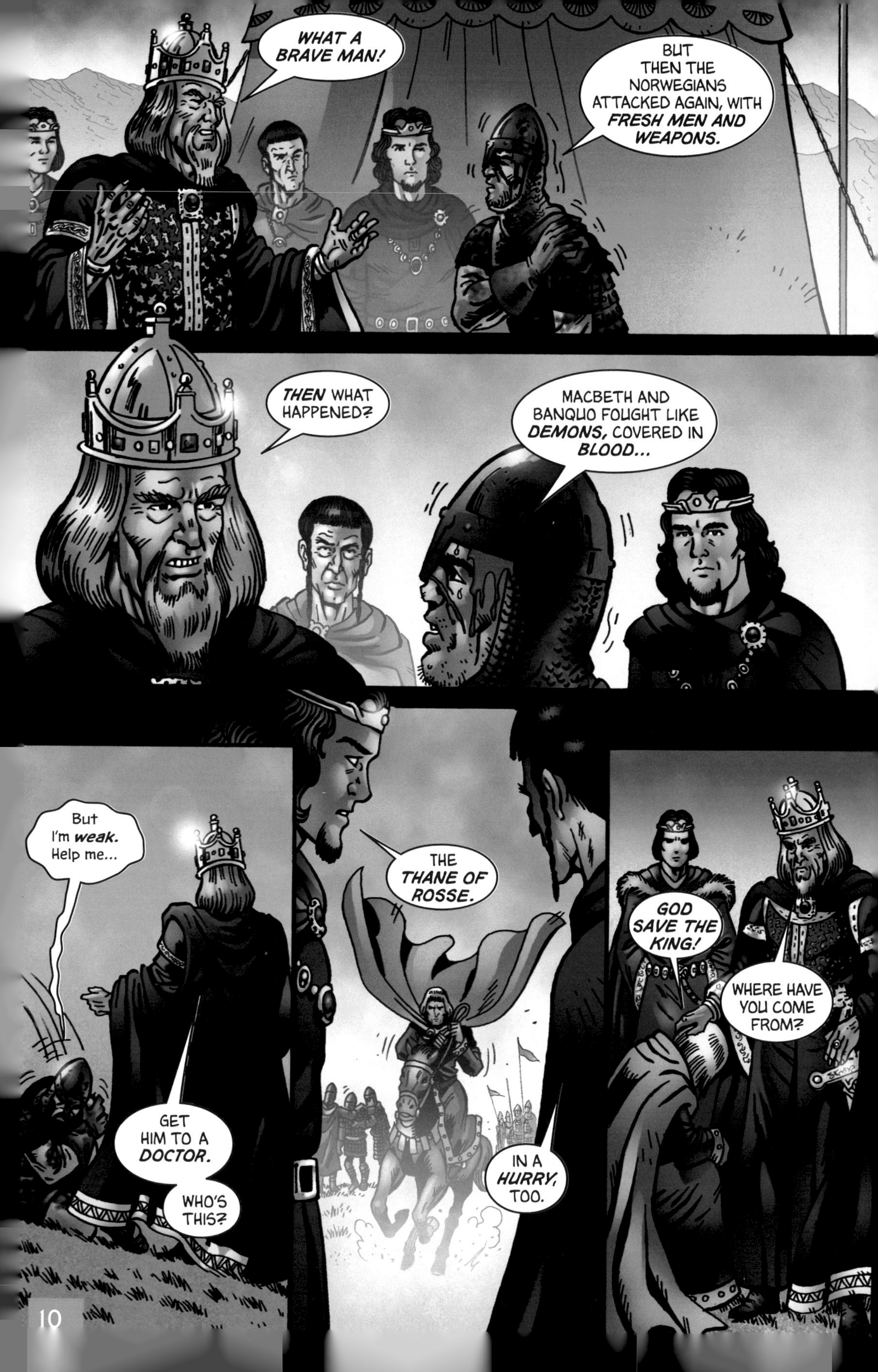
WHAT A BRAVE MAN!
BUT THEN THE NORWEGIANS ATTACKED AGAIN, WITH FRESH MEN AND WEAPONS.
THEN WHAT HAPPENED?
MACBETH AND BANQUO FOUGHT LIKE DEMONS, COVERED IN BLOOD...
But I'm weak. Help me...
GET HIM TO A DOCTOR.
WHO'S THIS?
THE THANE OF ROSSE.
IN A HURRY, TOO.
GOD SAVE THE KING!
WHERE HAVE YOU COME FROM?

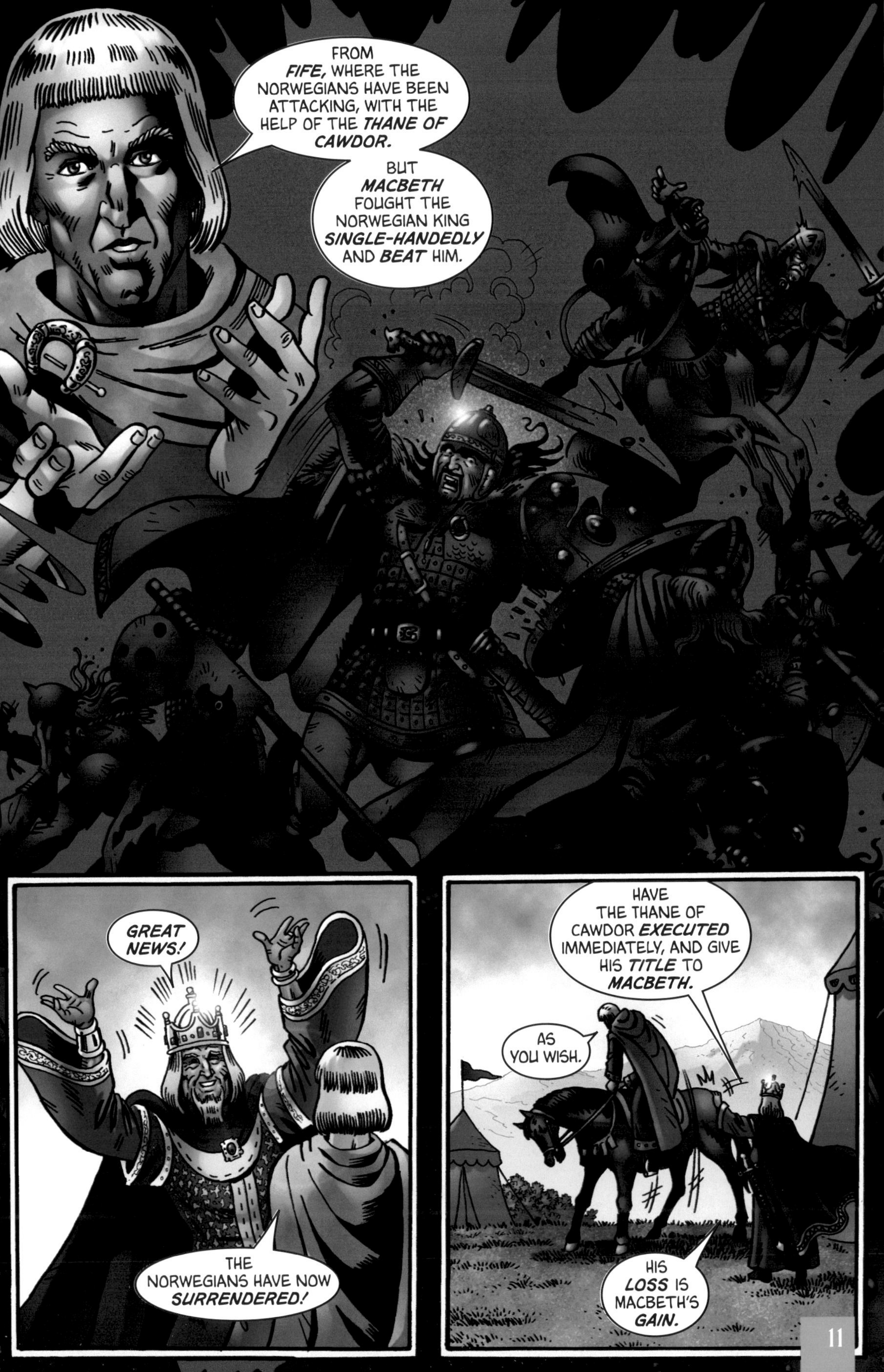
FROM *FIFE,* WHERE THE NORWEGIANS HAVE BEEN ATTACKING, WITH THE HELP OF THE *THANE OF CAWDOR.*
BUT *MACBETH* FOUGHT THE NORWEGIAN KING *SINGLE-HANDEDLY* AND *BEAT* HIM.
GREAT NEWS!
THE NORWEGIANS HAVE NOW *SURRENDERED!*
HAVE THE THANE OF CAWDOR *EXECUTED* IMMEDIATELY, AND GIVE HIS *TITLE* TO *MACBETH.*
AS YOU WISH.
HIS *LOSS* IS MACBETH'S *GAIN.*

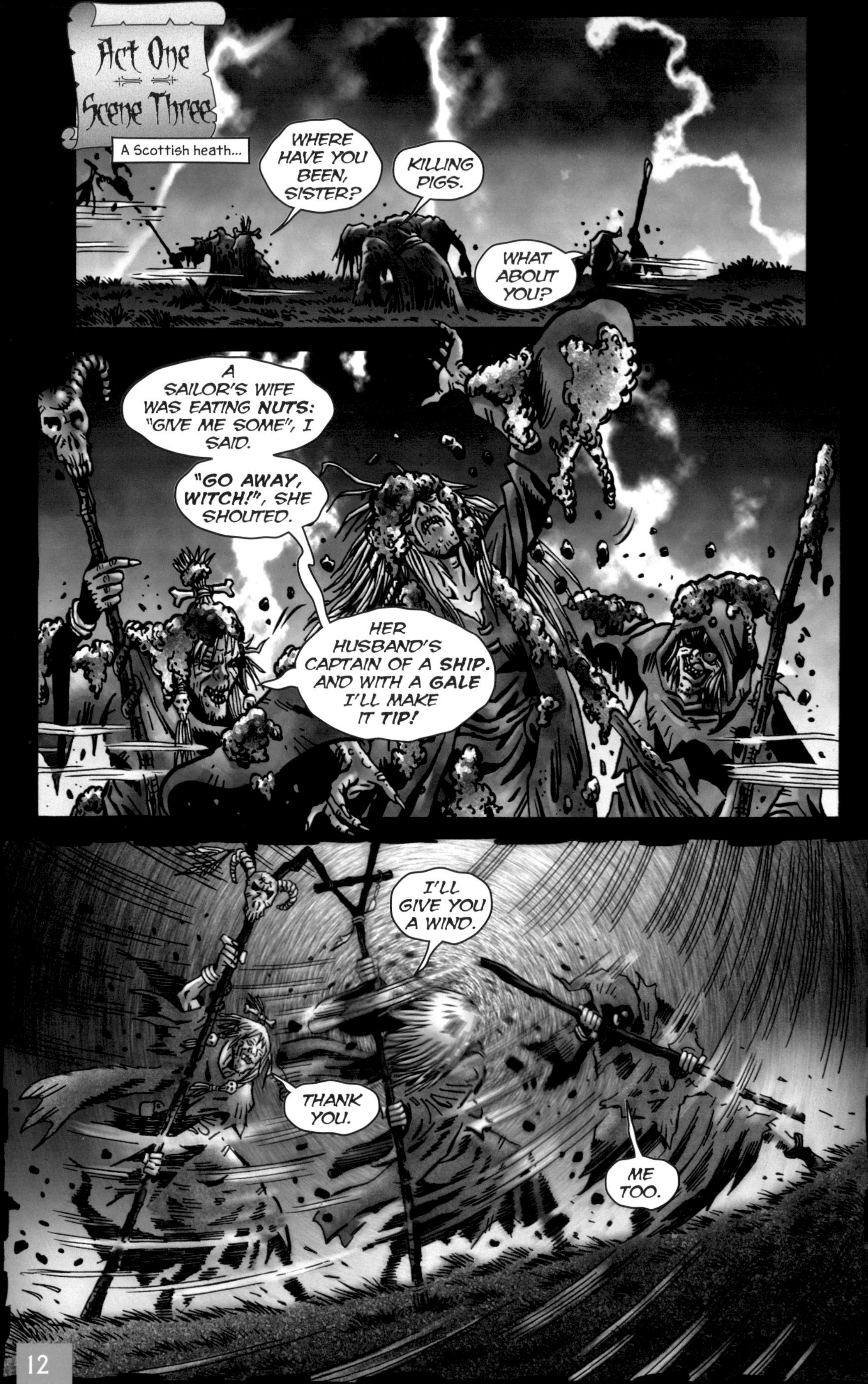
Act One
Scene Three
A Scottish heath...
WHERE HAVE YOU BEEN, SISTER?
KILLING PIGS.
WHAT ABOUT YOU?
A SAILOR'S WIFE WAS EATING NUTS: "GIVE ME SOME", I SAID.
"GO AWAY, WITCH!", SHE SHOUTED.
HER HUSBAND'S CAPTAIN OF A SHIP. AND WITH A GALE I'LL MAKE IT TIP!
I'LL GIVE YOU A WIND.
THANK YOU.
ME TOO.

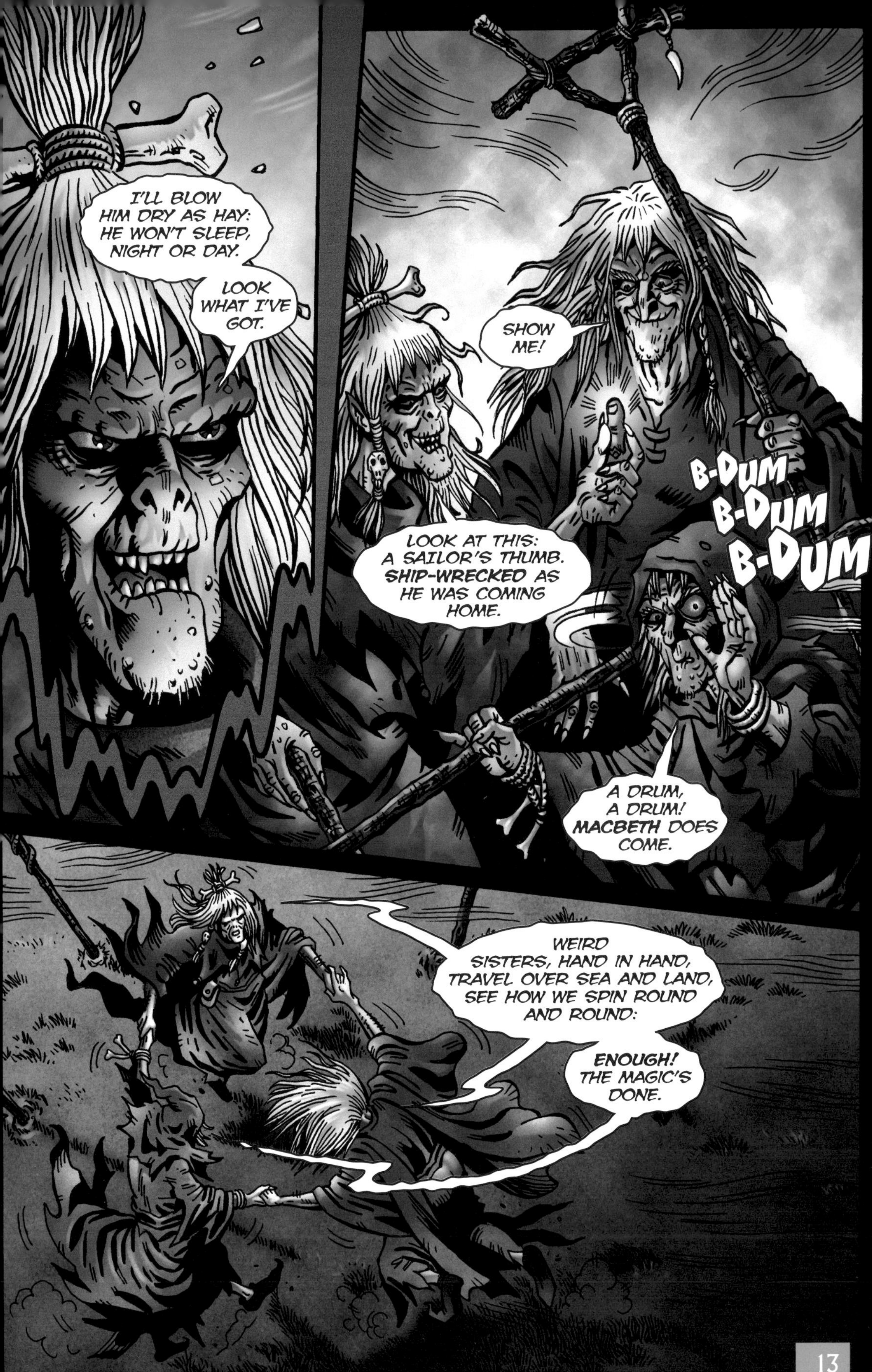
I'LL BLOW HIM DRY AS HAY: HE WON'T SLEEP, NIGHT OR DAY.
LOOK WHAT I'VE GOT.
SHOW ME!
LOOK AT THIS: A SAILOR'S THUMB. SHIP-WRECKED AS HE WAS COMING HOME.
B-DUM B-DUM B-DUM
A DRUM, A DRUM! MACBETH DOES COME.
WEIRD SISTERS, HAND IN HAND, TRAVEL OVER SEA AND LAND, SEE HOW WE SPIN ROUND AND ROUND:
ENOUGH! THE MAGIC'S DONE.

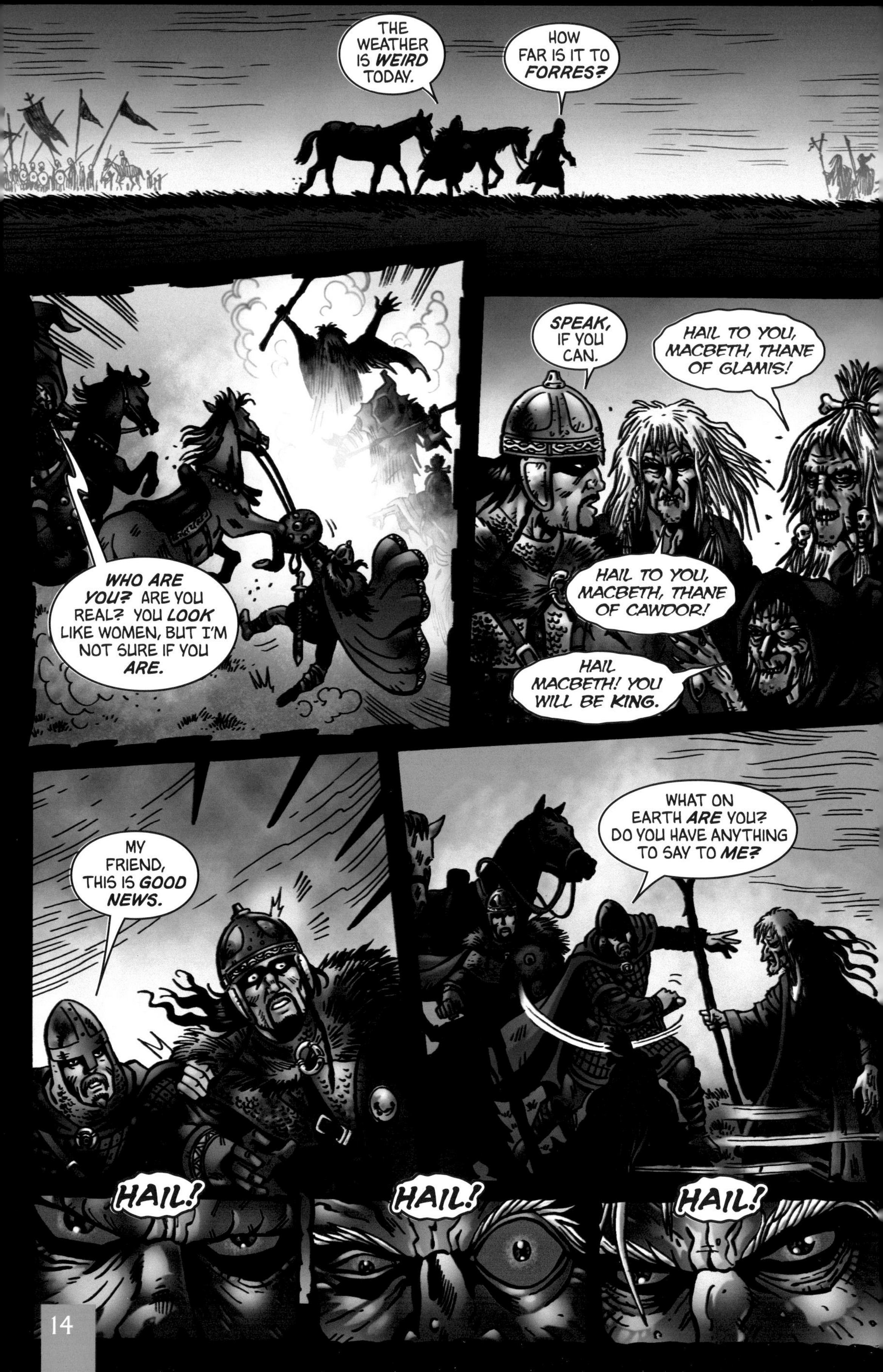
THE WEATHER IS WEIRD TODAY.
HOW FAR IS IT TO FORRES?
WHO ARE YOU? ARE YOU REAL? YOU LOOK LIKE WOMEN, BUT I'M NOT SURE IF YOU ARE.
SPEAK, IF YOU CAN.
HAIL TO YOU, MACBETH, THANE OF GLAMIS!
HAIL TO YOU, MACBETH, THANE OF CAWDOR!
HAIL MACBETH! YOU WILL BE KING.
MY FRIEND, THIS IS GOOD NEWS.
WHAT ON EARTH ARE YOU? DO YOU HAVE ANYTHING TO SAY TO ME?
HAIL!
HAIL!
HAIL!

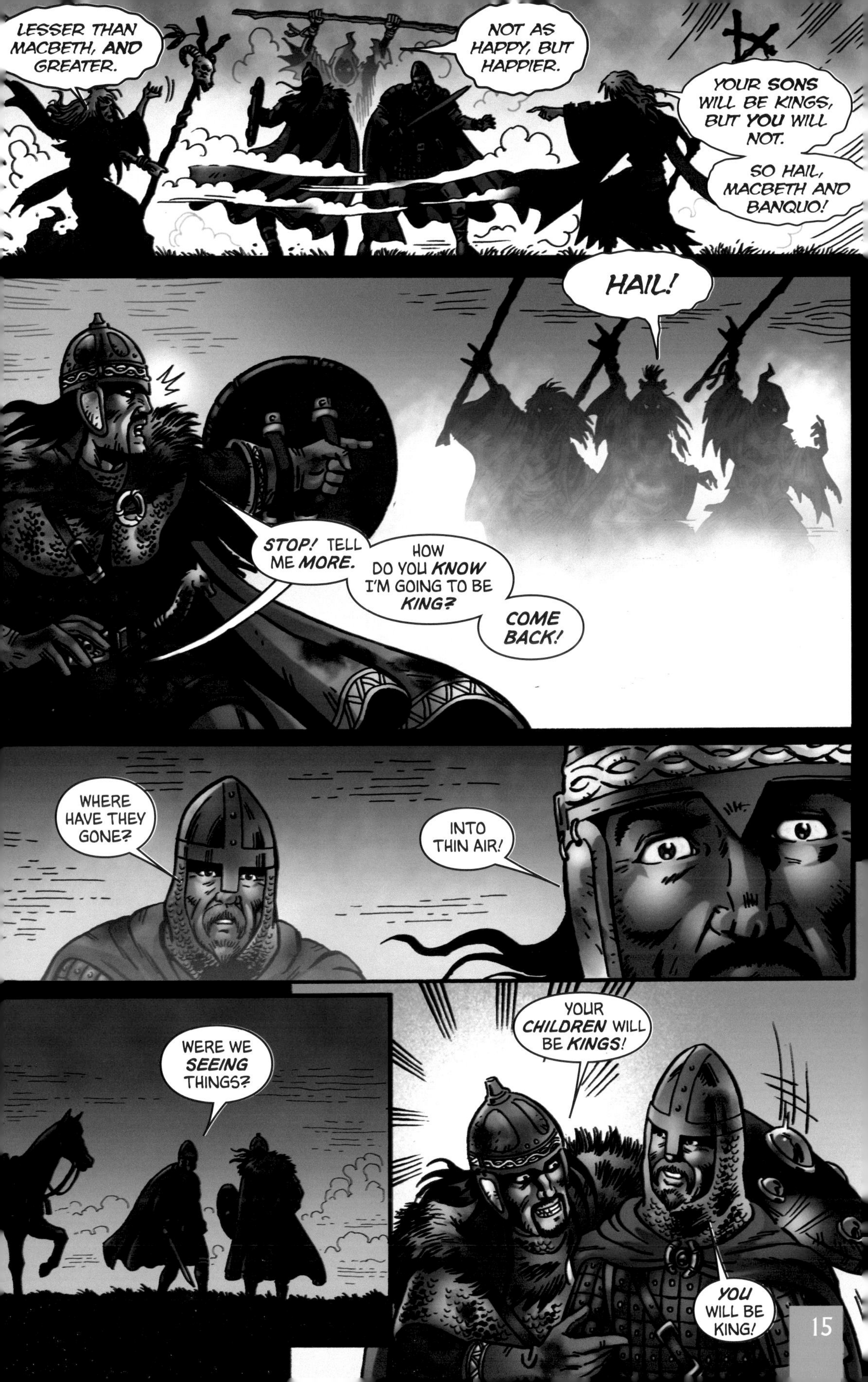
LESSER THAN MACBETH, AND GREATER.
NOT AS HAPPY, BUT HAPPIER.
YOUR SONS WILL BE KINGS, BUT YOU WILL NOT.
SO HAIL, MACBETH AND BANQUO!
HAIL!
STOP! TELL ME MORE.
HOW DO YOU KNOW I'M GOING TO BE KING?
COME BACK!
WHERE HAVE THEY GONE?
INTO THIN AIR!
WERE WE SEEING THINGS?
YOUR CHILDREN WILL BE KINGS!
YOU WILL BE KING!

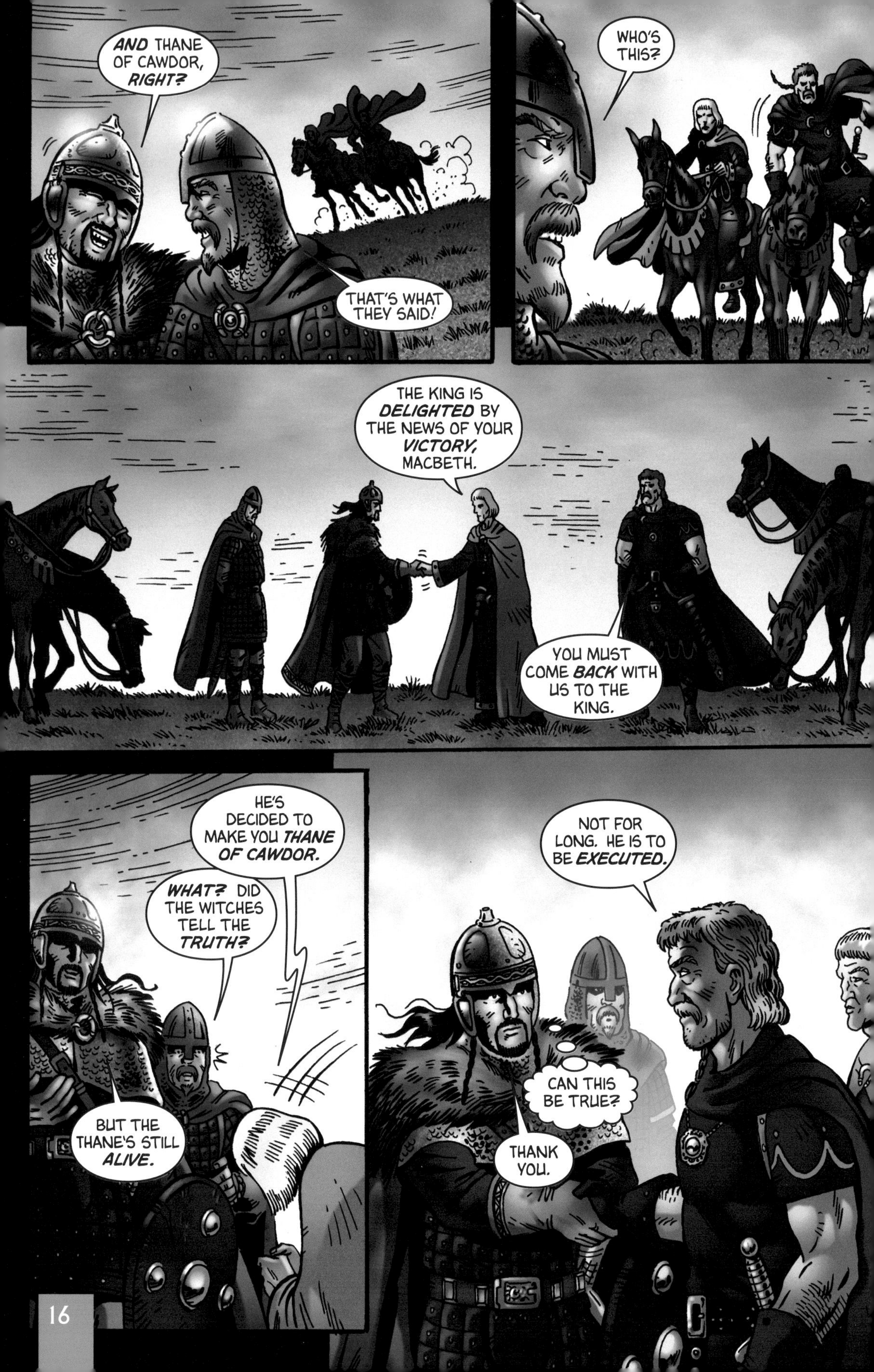
AND THANE OF CAWDOR, RIGHT?
THAT'S WHAT THEY SAID!
WHO'S THIS?
THE KING IS DELIGHTED BY THE NEWS OF YOUR VICTORY, MACBETH.
YOU MUST COME BACK WITH US TO THE KING.
HE'S DECIDED TO MAKE YOU THANE OF CAWDOR.
WHAT? DID THE WITCHES TELL THE TRUTH?
BUT THE THANE'S STILL ALIVE.
NOT FOR LONG. HE IS TO BE EXECUTED.
CAN THIS BE TRUE?
THANK YOU.

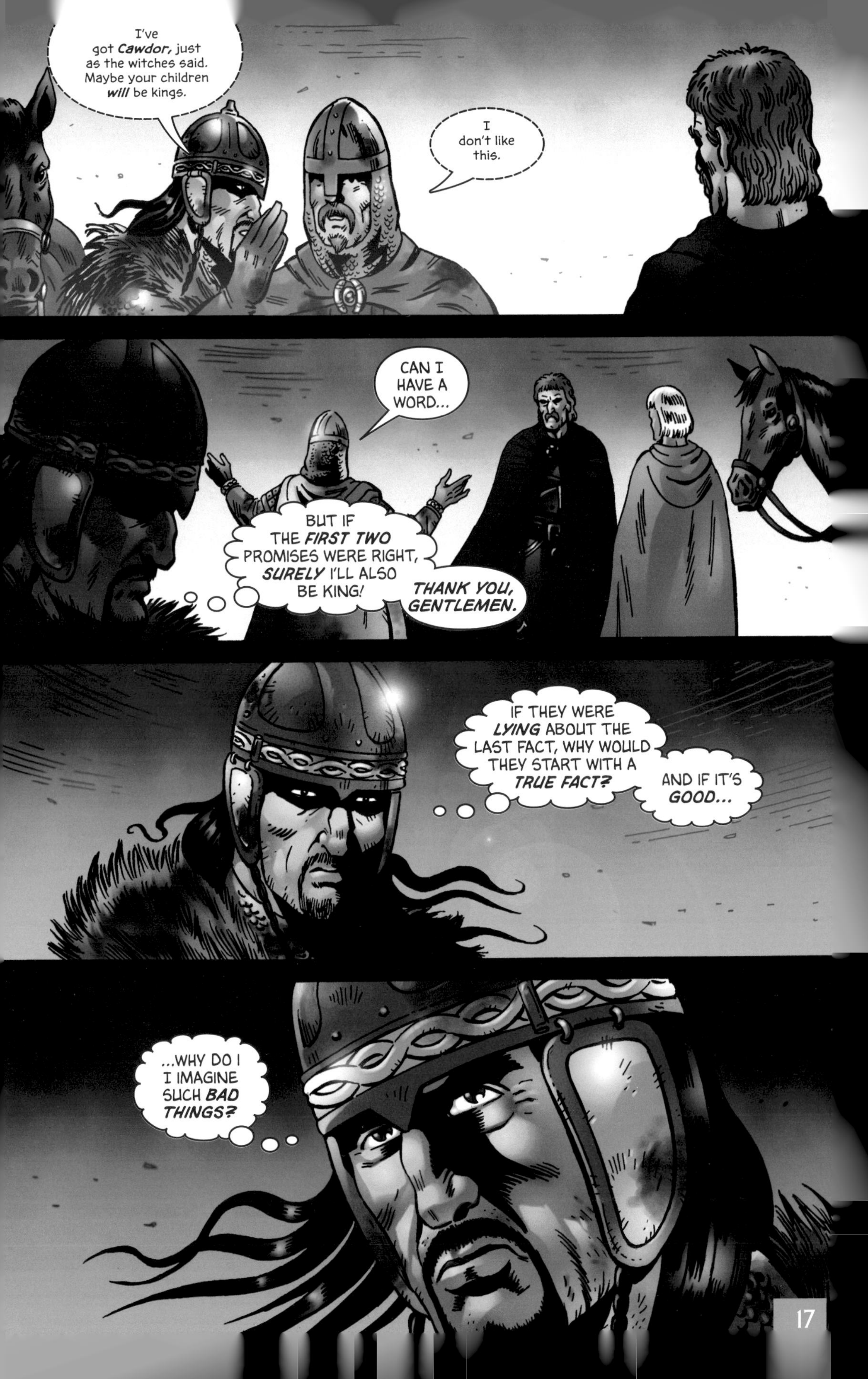
I've got Cawdor, just as the witches said. Maybe your children will be kings.
I don't like this.
CAN I HAVE A WORD...
BUT IF THE FIRST TWO PROMISES WERE RIGHT, SURELY I'LL ALSO BE KING!
THANK YOU, GENTLEMEN.
IF THEY WERE LYING ABOUT THE LAST FACT, WHY WOULD THEY START WITH A TRUE FACT?
AND IF IT'S GOOD...
...WHY DO I IMAGINE SUCH BAD THINGS?

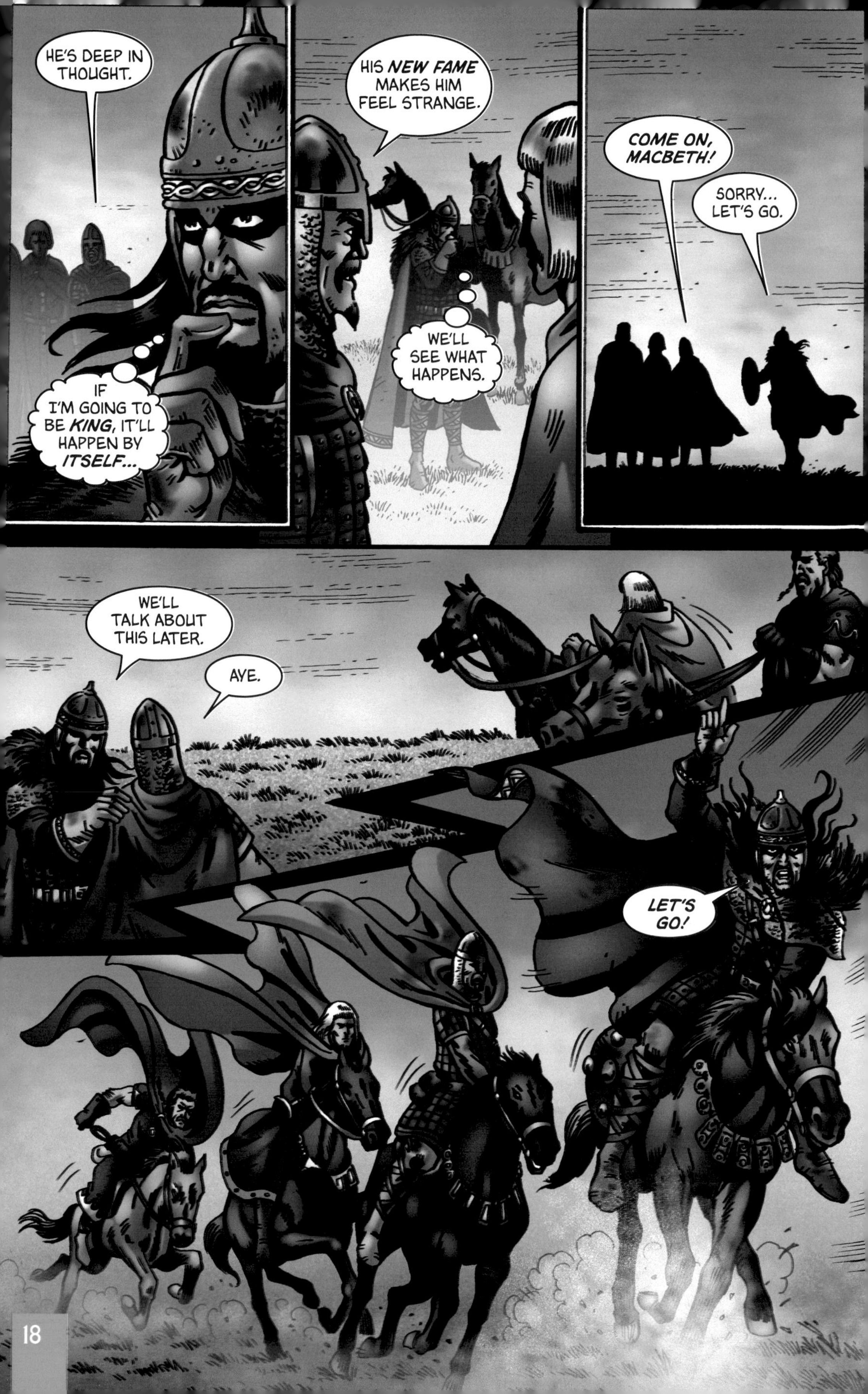
HE'S DEEP IN THOUGHT.
IF I'M GOING TO BE *KING*, IT'LL HAPPEN BY *ITSELF...*
HIS *NEW FAME* MAKES HIM FEEL STRANGE.
WE'LL SEE WHAT HAPPENS.
COME ON, MACBETH!
SORRY... LET'S GO.
WE'LL TALK ABOUT THIS LATER.
AYE.
LET'S GO!

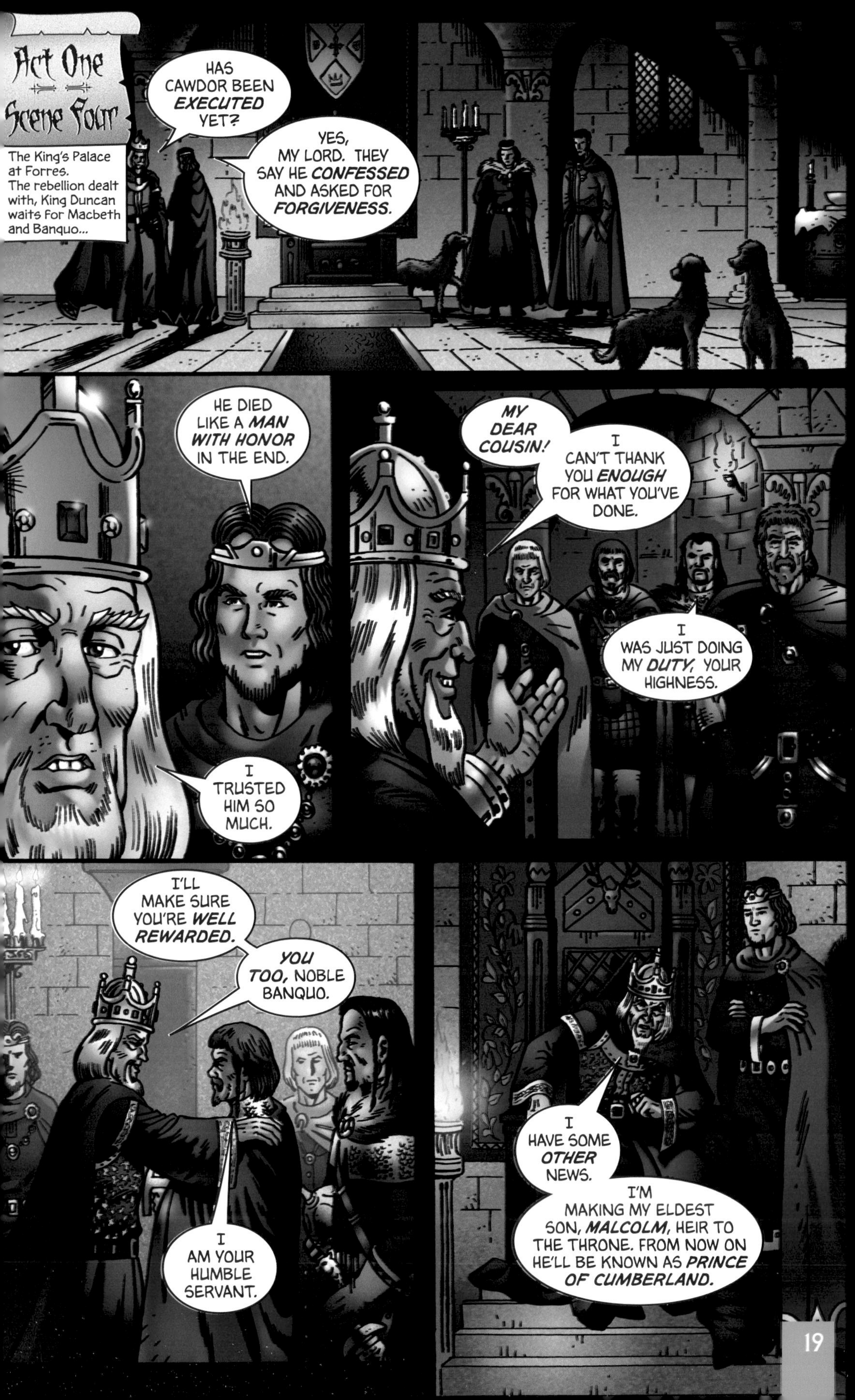
Act One
Scene Four
The King's Palace at Forres. The rebellion dealt with, King Duncan waits for Macbeth and Banquo...
HAS CAWDOR BEEN EXECUTED YET?
YES, MY LORD. THEY SAY HE CONFESSED AND ASKED FOR FORGIVENESS.
HE DIED LIKE A MAN WITH HONOR IN THE END.
I TRUSTED HIM SO MUCH.
MY DEAR COUSIN!
I CAN'T THANK YOU ENOUGH FOR WHAT YOU'VE DONE.
I WAS JUST DOING MY DUTY, YOUR HIGHNESS.
I'LL MAKE SURE YOU'RE WELL REWARDED.
YOU TOO, NOBLE BANQUO.
I AM YOUR HUMBLE SERVANT.
I HAVE SOME OTHER NEWS.
I'M MAKING MY ELDEST SON, MALCOLM, HEIR TO THE THRONE. FROM NOW ON HE'LL BE KNOWN AS PRINCE OF CUMBERLAND.

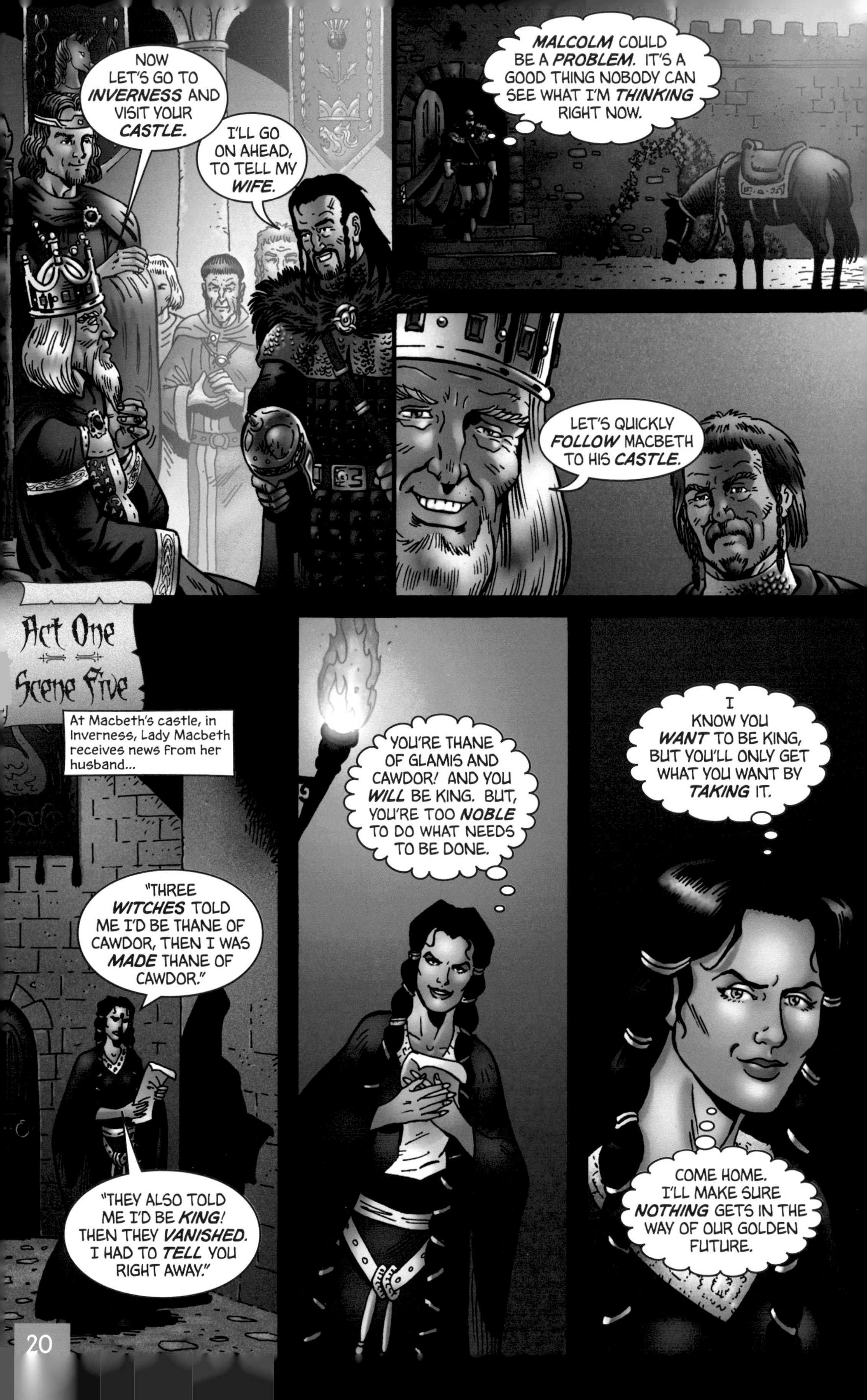
NOW LET'S GO TO INVERNESS AND VISIT YOUR CASTLE.
I'LL GO ON AHEAD, TO TELL MY WIFE.
MALCOLM COULD BE A PROBLEM. IT'S A GOOD THING NOBODY CAN SEE WHAT I'M THINKING RIGHT NOW.
LET'S QUICKLY FOLLOW MACBETH TO HIS CASTLE.
Act One
Scene Five
At Macbeth's castle, in Inverness, Lady Macbeth receives news from her husband...
"THREE WITCHES TOLD ME I'D BE THANE OF CAWDOR, THEN I WAS MADE THANE OF CAWDOR."
"THEY ALSO TOLD ME I'D BE KING! THEN THEY VANISHED. I HAD TO TELL YOU RIGHT AWAY."
YOU'RE THANE OF GLAMIS AND CAWDOR! AND YOU WILL BE KING. BUT, YOU'RE TOO NOBLE TO DO WHAT NEEDS TO BE DONE.
I KNOW YOU WANT TO BE KING, BUT YOU'LL ONLY GET WHAT YOU WANT BY TAKING IT.
COME HOME. I'LL MAKE SURE NOTHING GETS IN THE WAY OF OUR GOLDEN FUTURE.

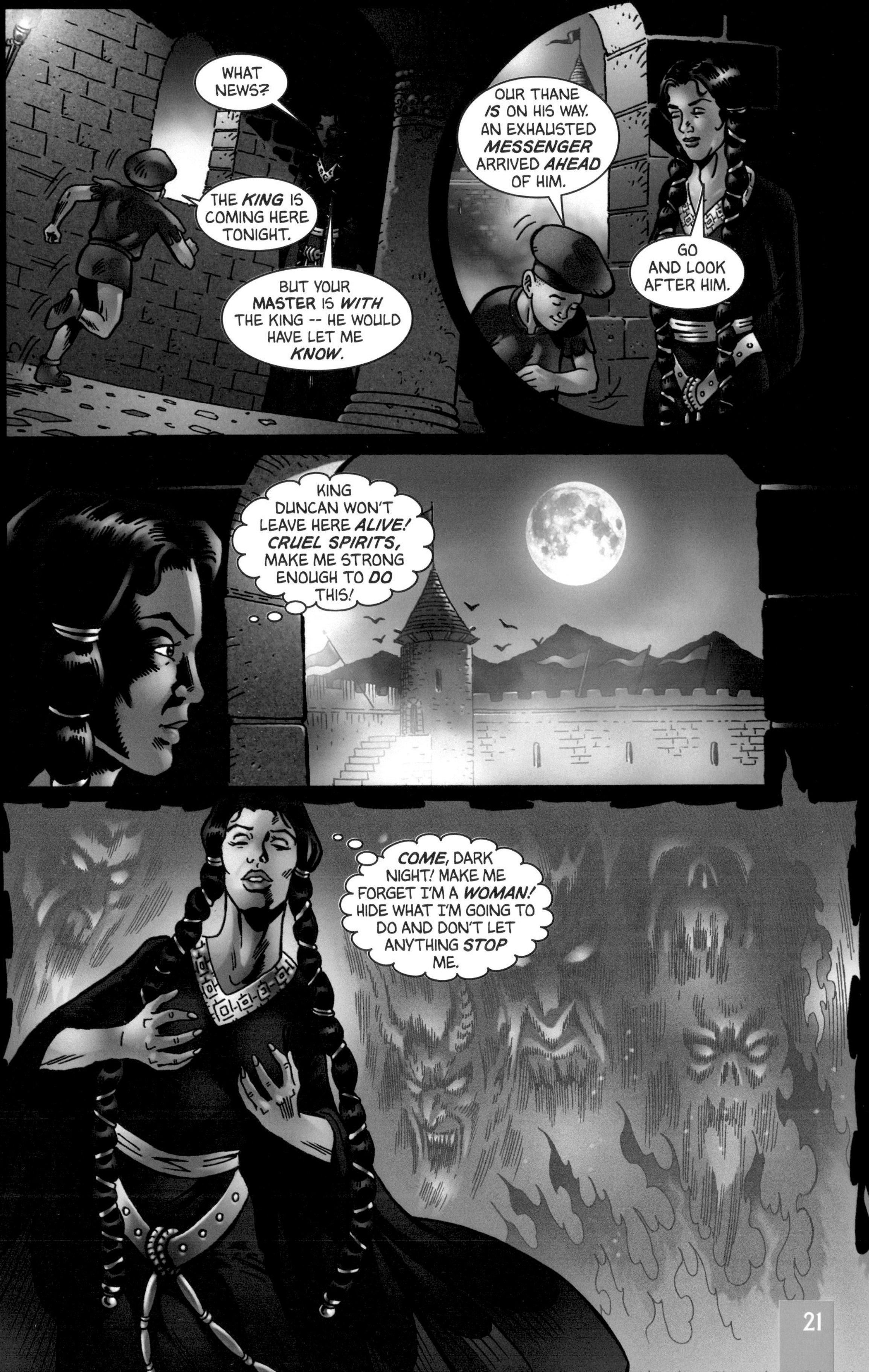
WHAT NEWS?
THE KING IS COMING HERE TONIGHT.
BUT YOUR MASTER IS WITH THE KING -- HE WOULD HAVE LET ME KNOW.
OUR THANE IS ON HIS WAY. AN EXHAUSTED MESSENGER ARRIVED AHEAD OF HIM.
GO AND LOOK AFTER HIM.
KING DUNCAN WON'T LEAVE HERE ALIVE! CRUEL SPIRITS, MAKE ME STRONG ENOUGH TO DO THIS!
COME, DARK NIGHT! MAKE ME FORGET I'M A WOMAN! HIDE WHAT I'M GOING TO DO AND DON'T LET ANYTHING STOP ME.

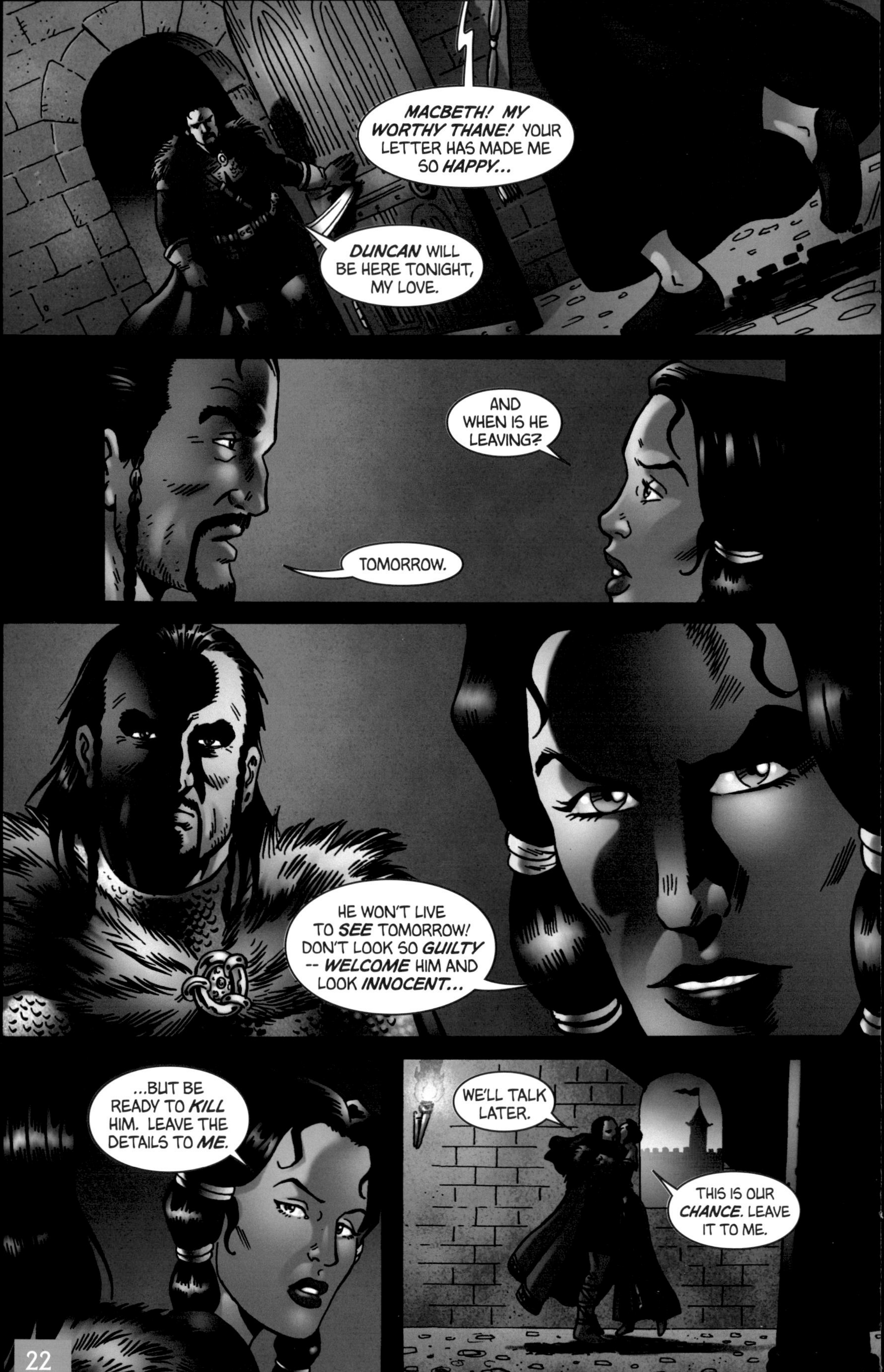
MACBETH! MY WORTHY THANE! YOUR LETTER HAS MADE ME SO HAPPY...
DUNCAN WILL BE HERE TONIGHT, MY LOVE.
AND WHEN IS HE LEAVING?
TOMORROW.
HE WON'T LIVE TO SEE TOMORROW! DON'T LOOK SO GUILTY -- WELCOME HIM AND LOOK INNOCENT...
...BUT BE READY TO KILL HIM. LEAVE THE DETAILS TO ME.
WE'LL TALK LATER.
THIS IS OUR CHANCE. LEAVE IT TO ME.

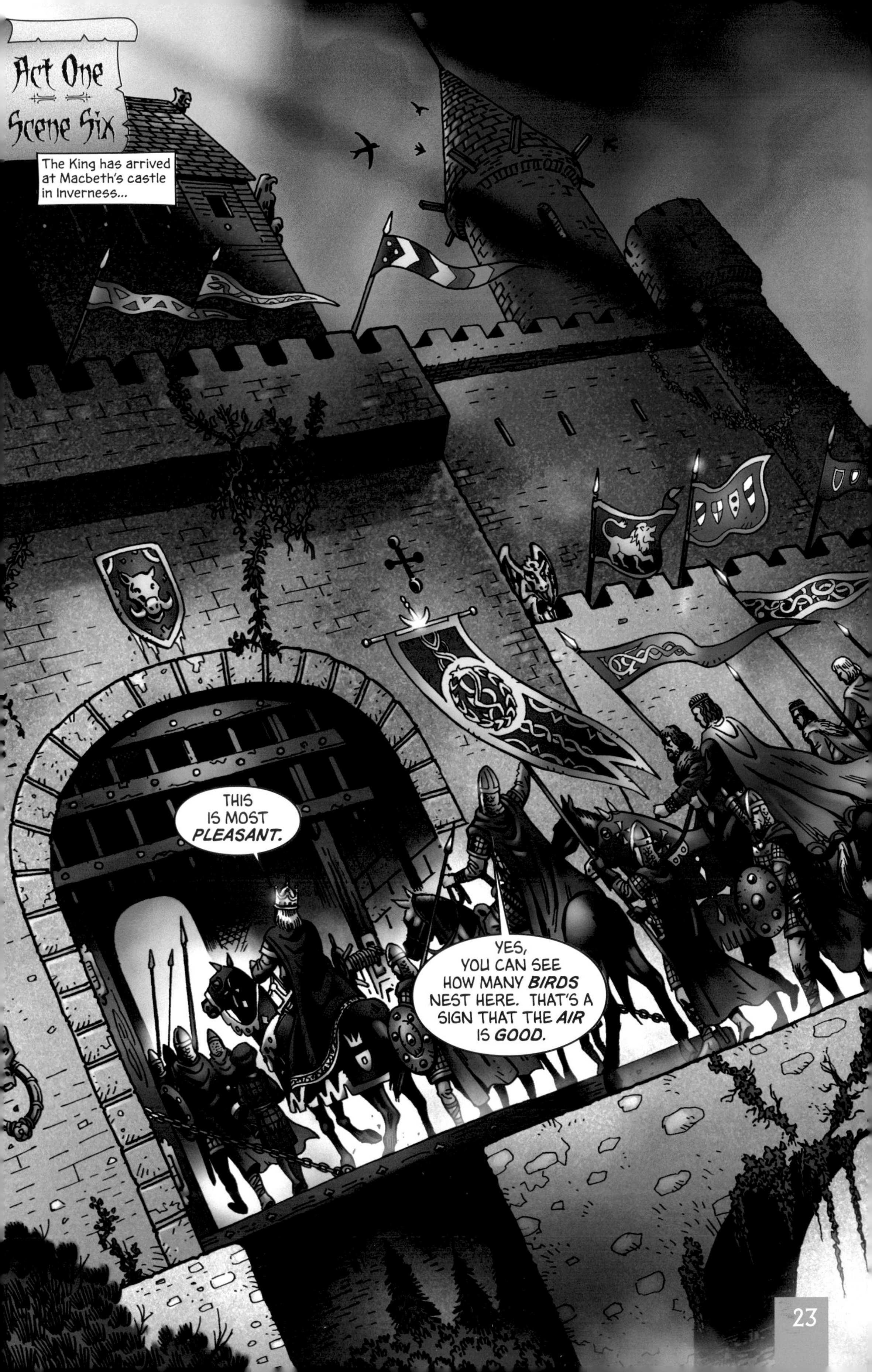

Act One
Scene Six
The King has arrived at Macbeth's castle in Inverness...
THIS IS MOST PLEASANT.
YES, YOU CAN SEE HOW MANY BIRDS NEST HERE. THAT'S A SIGN THAT THE AIR IS GOOD.

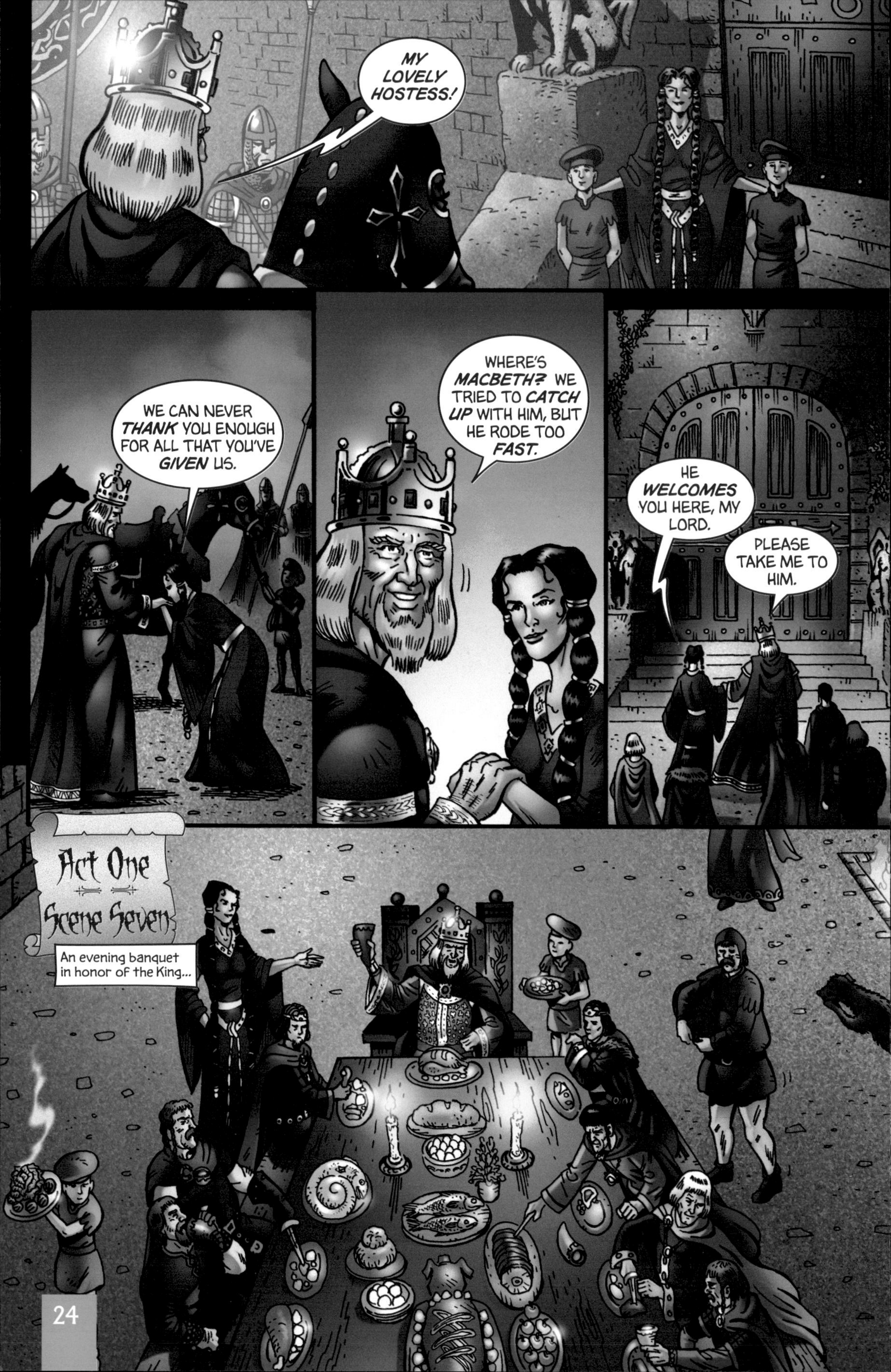
MY LOVELY HOSTESS!
WE CAN NEVER THANK YOU ENOUGH FOR ALL THAT YOU'VE GIVEN US.
WHERE'S MACBETH? WE TRIED TO CATCH UP WITH HIM, BUT HE RODE TOO FAST.
HE WELCOMES YOU HERE, MY LORD.
PLEASE TAKE ME TO HIM.
Act One
Scene Seven
An evening banquet in honor of the King...

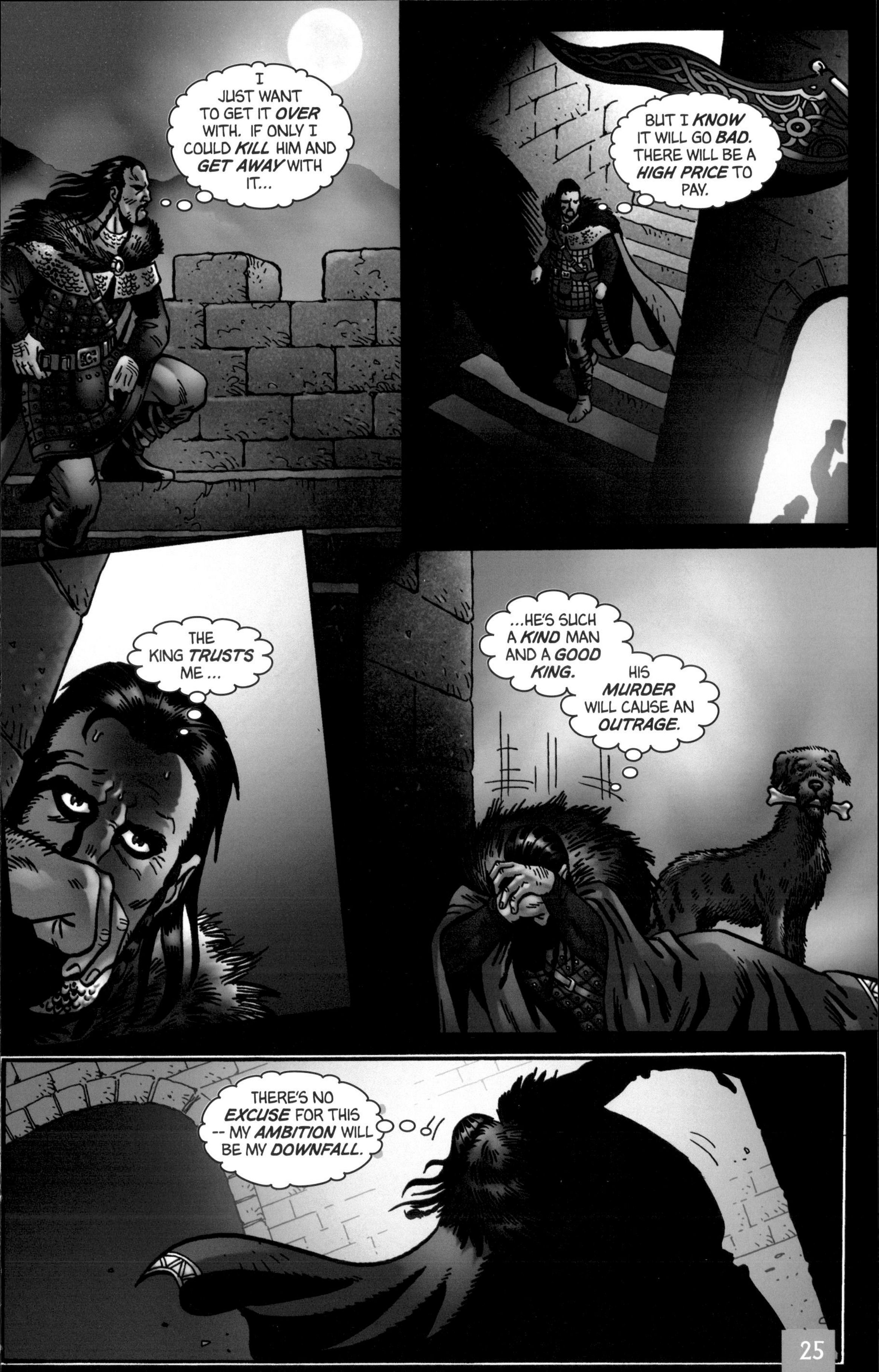
I JUST WANT TO GET IT OVER WITH. IF ONLY I COULD KILL HIM AND GET AWAY WITH IT...
BUT I KNOW IT WILL GO BAD. THERE WILL BE A HIGH PRICE TO PAY.
THE KING TRUSTS ME ...
...HE'S SUCH A KIND MAN AND A GOOD KING.
HIS MURDER WILL CAUSE AN OUTRAGE.
THERE'S NO EXCUSE FOR THIS -- MY AMBITION WILL BE MY DOWNFALL.

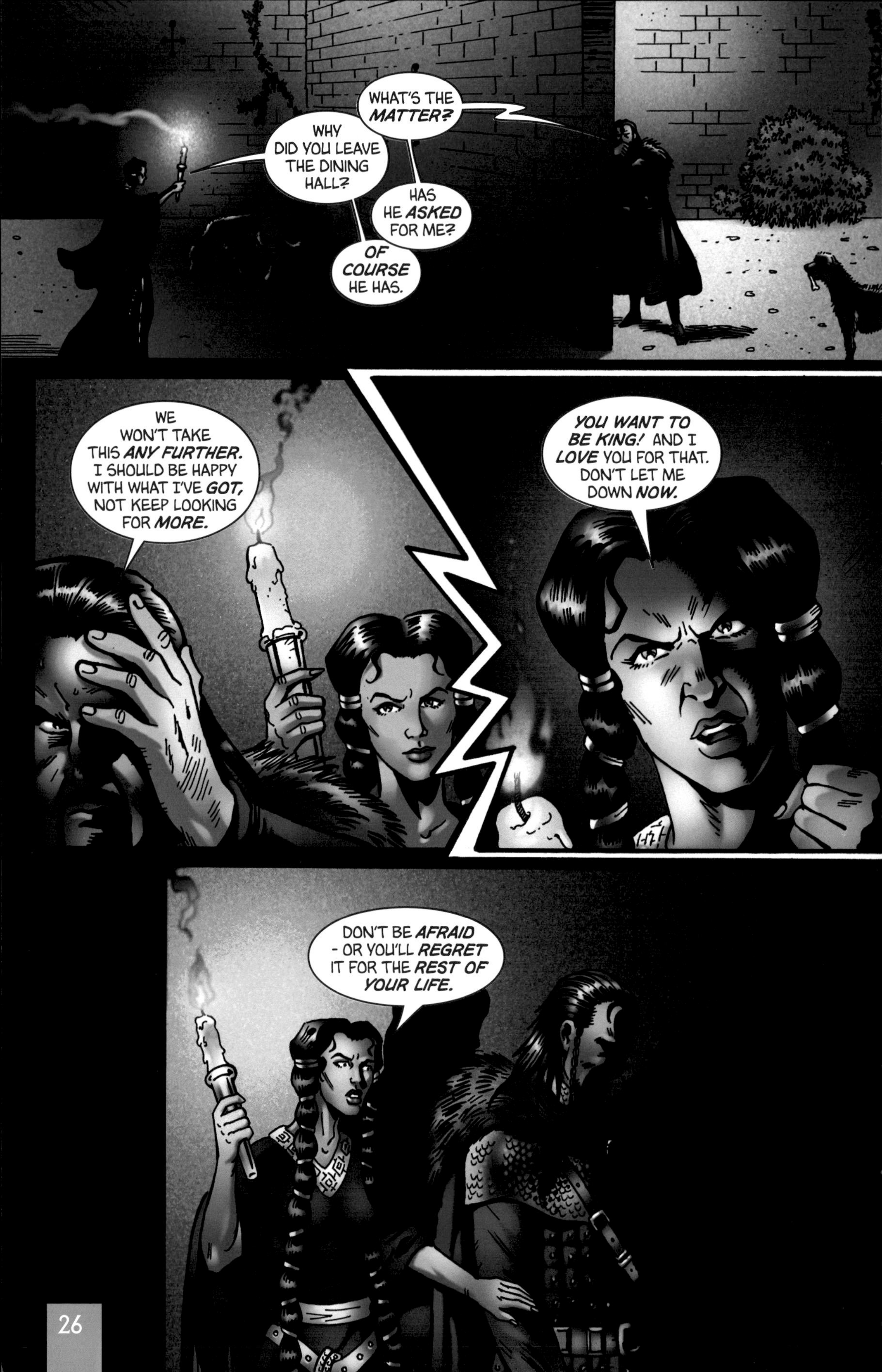
WHY DID YOU LEAVE THE DINING HALL?
WHAT'S THE MATTER?
HAS HE ASKED FOR ME?
OF COURSE HE HAS.
WE WON'T TAKE THIS ANY FURTHER. I SHOULD BE HAPPY WITH WHAT I'VE GOT, NOT KEEP LOOKING FOR MORE.
YOU WANT TO BE KING! AND I LOVE YOU FOR THAT. DON'T LET ME DOWN NOW.
DON'T BE AFRAID - OR YOU'LL REGRET IT FOR THE REST OF YOUR LIFE.

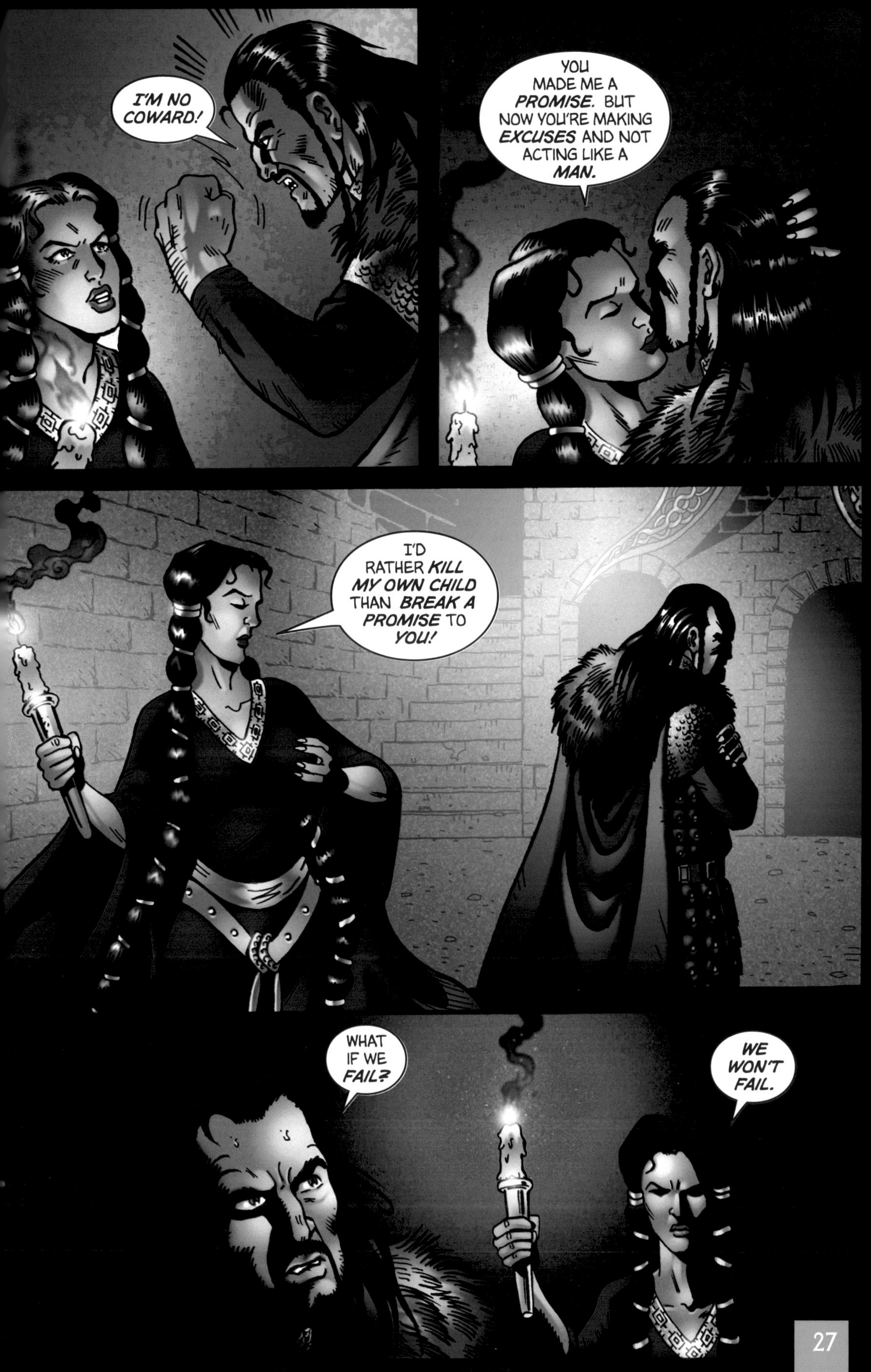
I'M NO COWARD!
YOU MADE ME A PROMISE. BUT NOW YOU'RE MAKING EXCUSES AND NOT ACTING LIKE A MAN.
I'D RATHER KILL MY OWN CHILD THAN BREAK A PROMISE TO YOU!
WHAT IF WE FAIL?
WE WON'T FAIL.

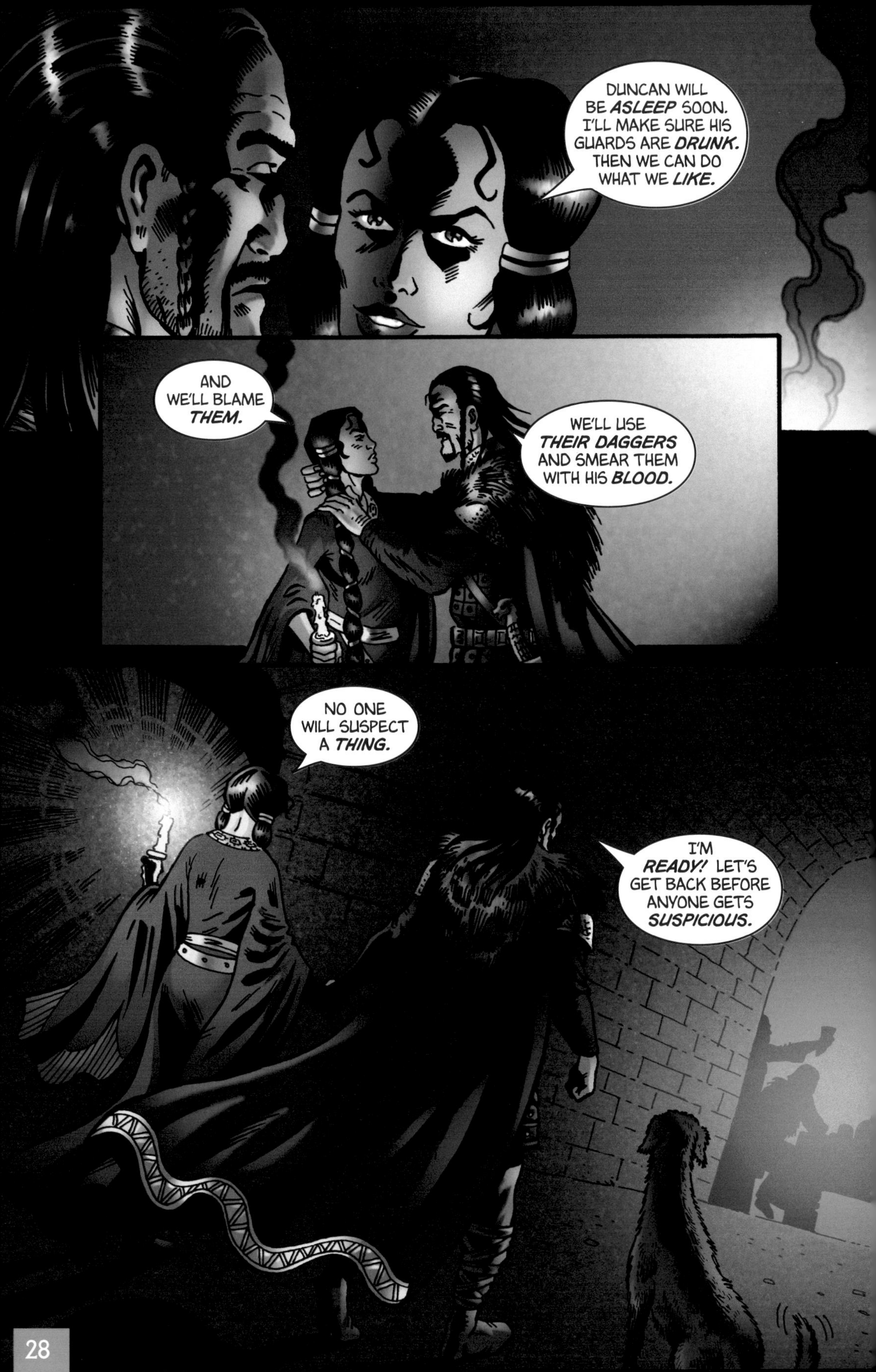
DUNCAN WILL BE ASLEEP SOON. I'LL MAKE SURE HIS GUARDS ARE DRUNK. THEN WE CAN DO WHAT WE LIKE.
AND WE'LL BLAME THEM.
WE'LL USE THEIR DAGGERS AND SMEAR THEM WITH HIS BLOOD.
NO ONE WILL SUSPECT A THING.
I'M READY! LET'S GET BACK BEFORE ANYONE GETS SUSPICIOUS.

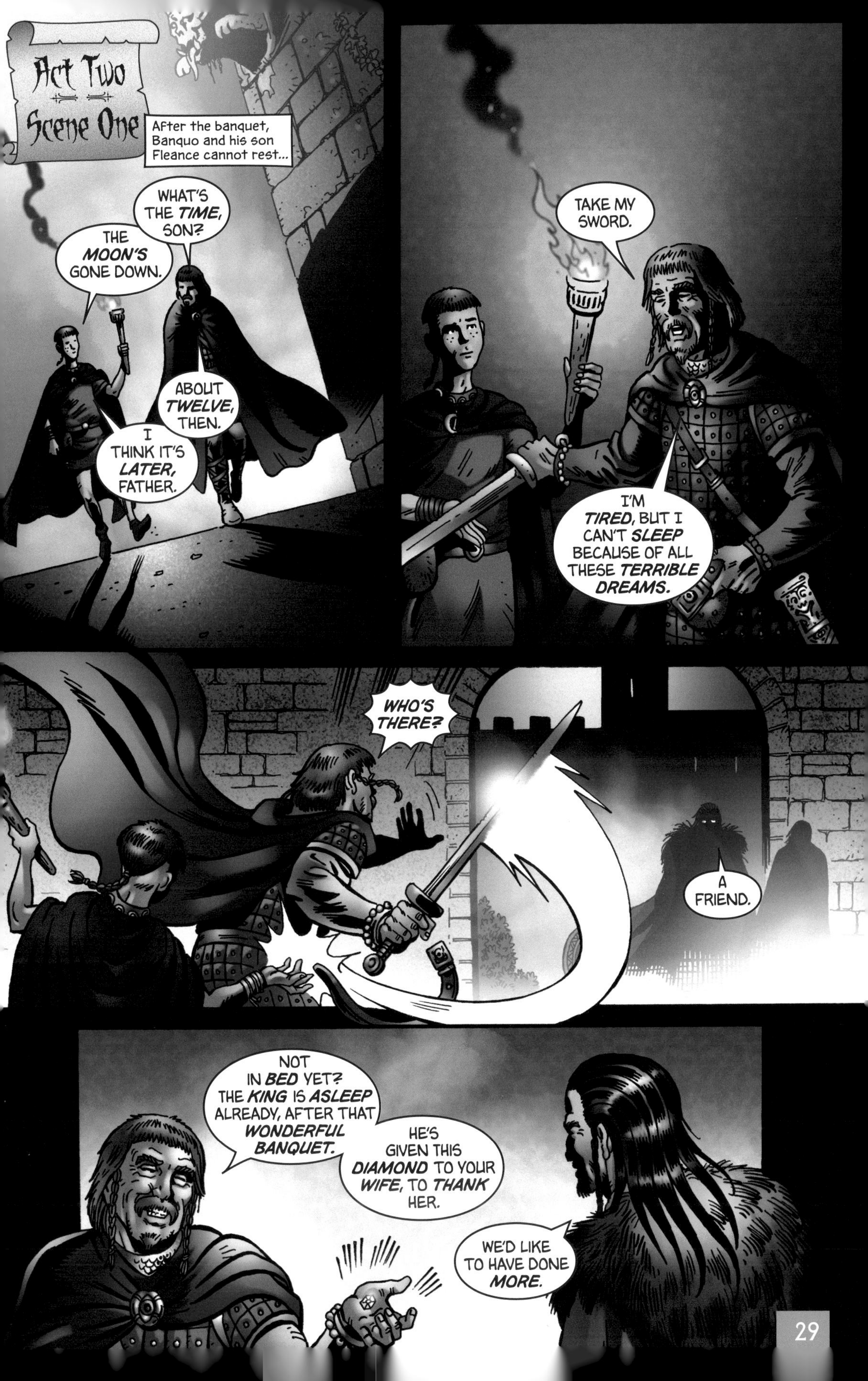
Act Two
Scene One
After the banquet, Banquo and his son Fleance cannot rest...
WHAT'S THE TIME, SON?
THE MOON'S GONE DOWN.
ABOUT TWELVE, THEN.
I THINK IT'S LATER, FATHER.
TAKE MY SWORD.
I'M TIRED, BUT I CAN'T SLEEP BECAUSE OF ALL THESE TERRIBLE DREAMS.
WHO'S THERE?
A FRIEND.
NOT IN BED YET? THE KING IS ASLEEP ALREADY, AFTER THAT WONDERFUL BANQUET.
HE'S GIVEN THIS DIAMOND TO YOUR WIFE, TO THANK HER.
WE'D LIKE TO HAVE DONE MORE.

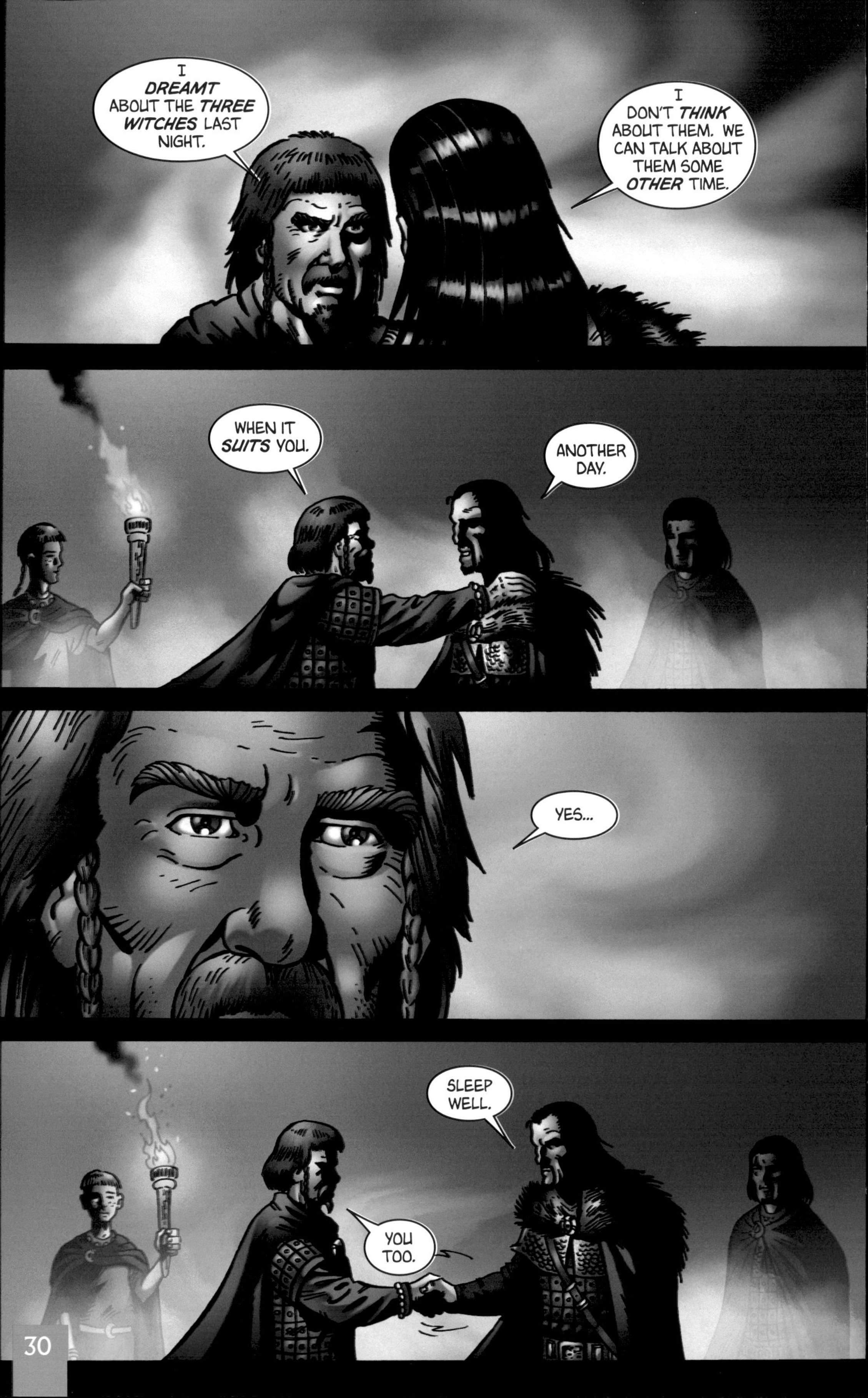
I DREAMT ABOUT THE THREE WITCHES LAST NIGHT.
I DON'T THINK ABOUT THEM. WE CAN TALK ABOUT THEM SOME OTHER TIME.
WHEN IT SUITS YOU.
ANOTHER DAY.
YES...
SLEEP WELL.
YOU TOO.

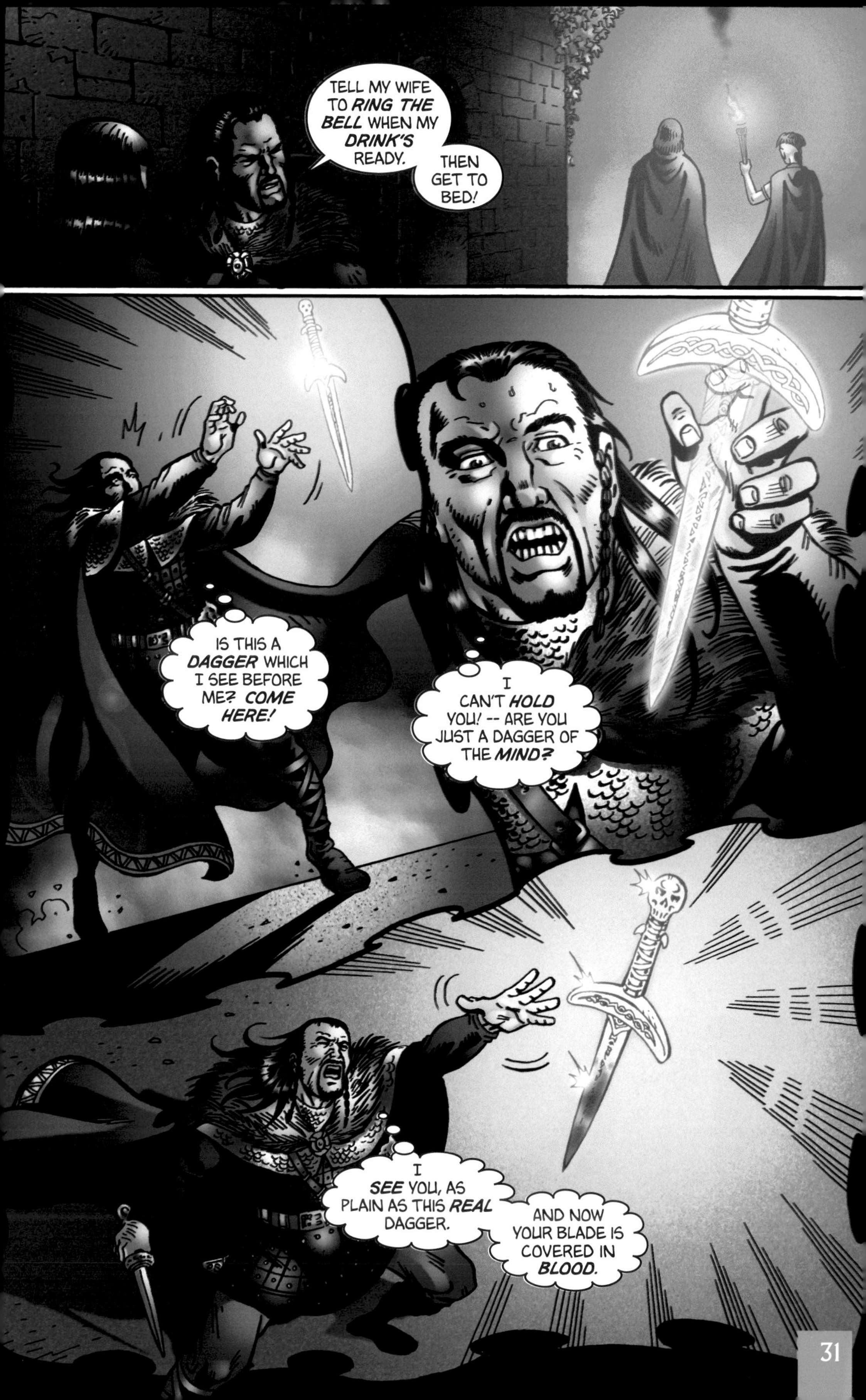
TELL MY WIFE TO RING THE BELL WHEN MY DRINK'S READY.
THEN GET TO BED!
IS THIS A DAGGER WHICH I SEE BEFORE ME? COME HERE!
I CAN'T HOLD YOU! -- ARE YOU JUST A DAGGER OF THE MIND?
I SEE YOU, AS PLAIN AS THIS REAL DAGGER.
AND NOW YOUR BLADE IS COVERED IN BLOOD.

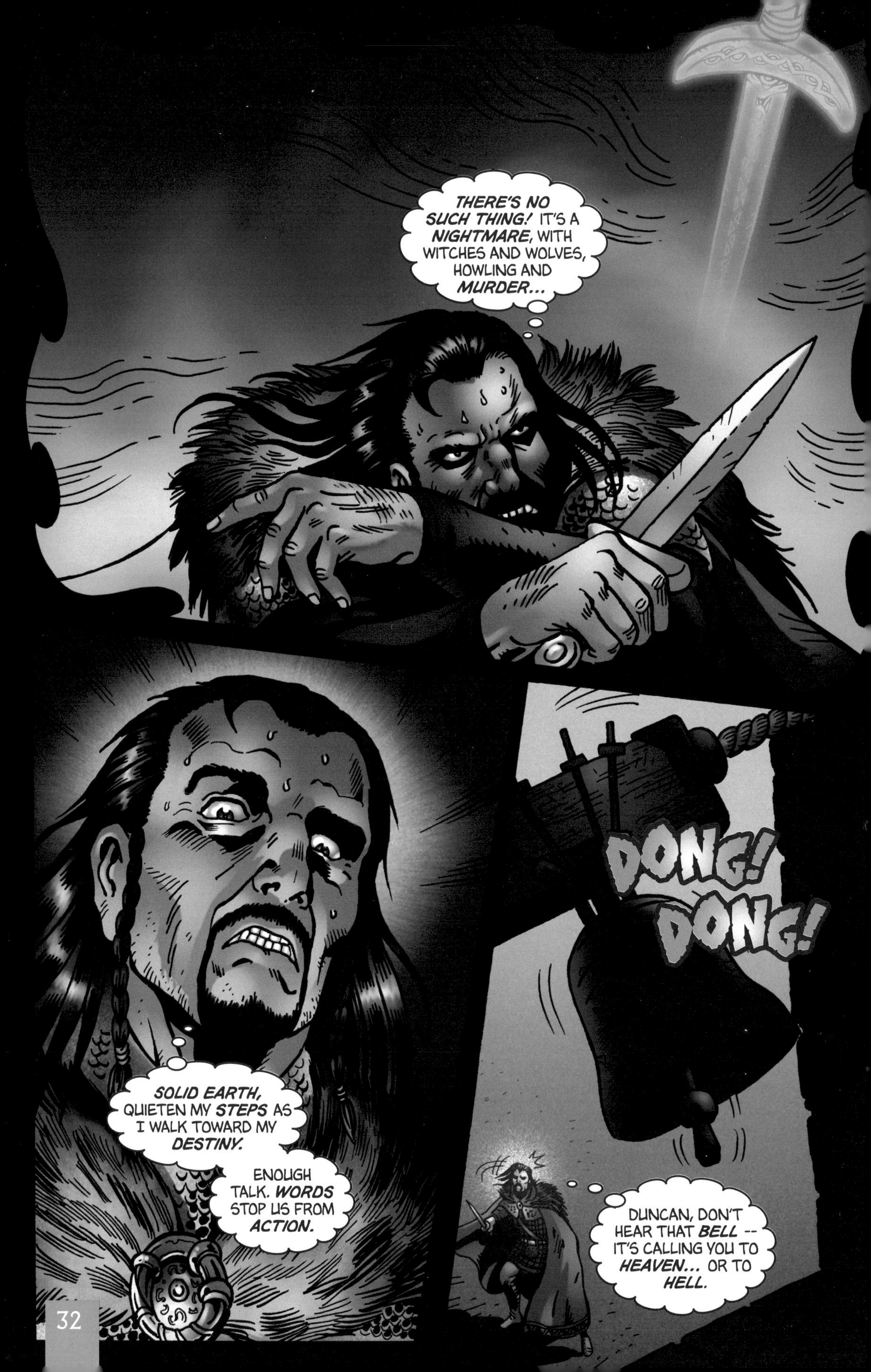
THERE'S NO SUCH THING! IT'S A NIGHTMARE, WITH WITCHES AND WOLVES, HOWLING AND MURDER...
SOLID EARTH, QUIETEN MY STEPS AS I WALK TOWARD MY DESTINY.
ENOUGH TALK. WORDS STOP US FROM ACTION.
DONG! DONG!
DUNCAN, DON'T HEAR THAT BELL -- IT'S CALLING YOU TO HEAVEN... OR TO HELL.

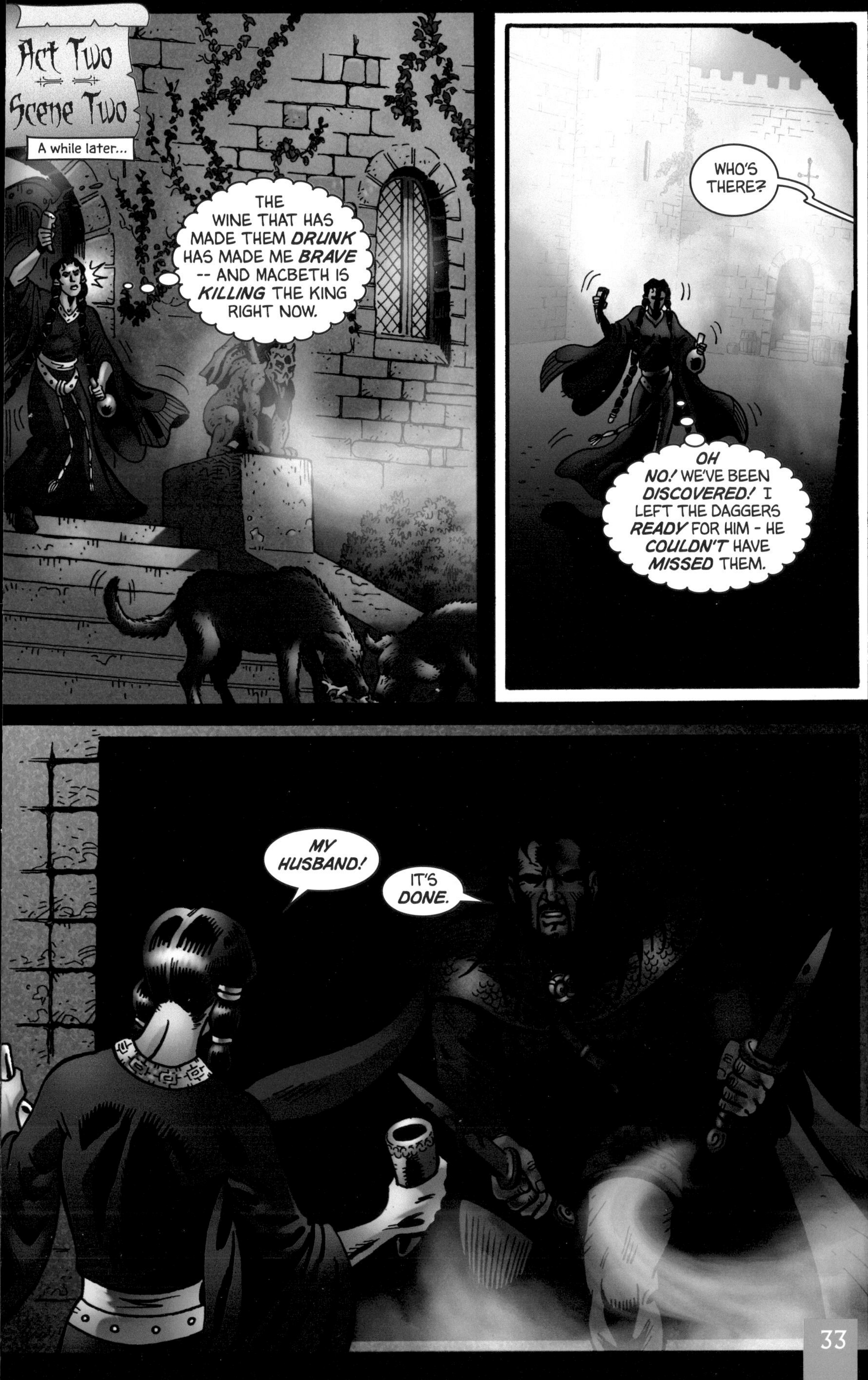
Act Two
Scene Two
A while later...
THE WINE THAT HAS MADE THEM DRUNK HAS MADE ME BRAVE -- AND MACBETH IS KILLING THE KING RIGHT NOW.
WHO'S THERE?
OH NO! WE'VE BEEN DISCOVERED! I LEFT THE DAGGERS READY FOR HIM - HE COULDN'T HAVE MISSED THEM.
MY HUSBAND!
IT'S DONE.

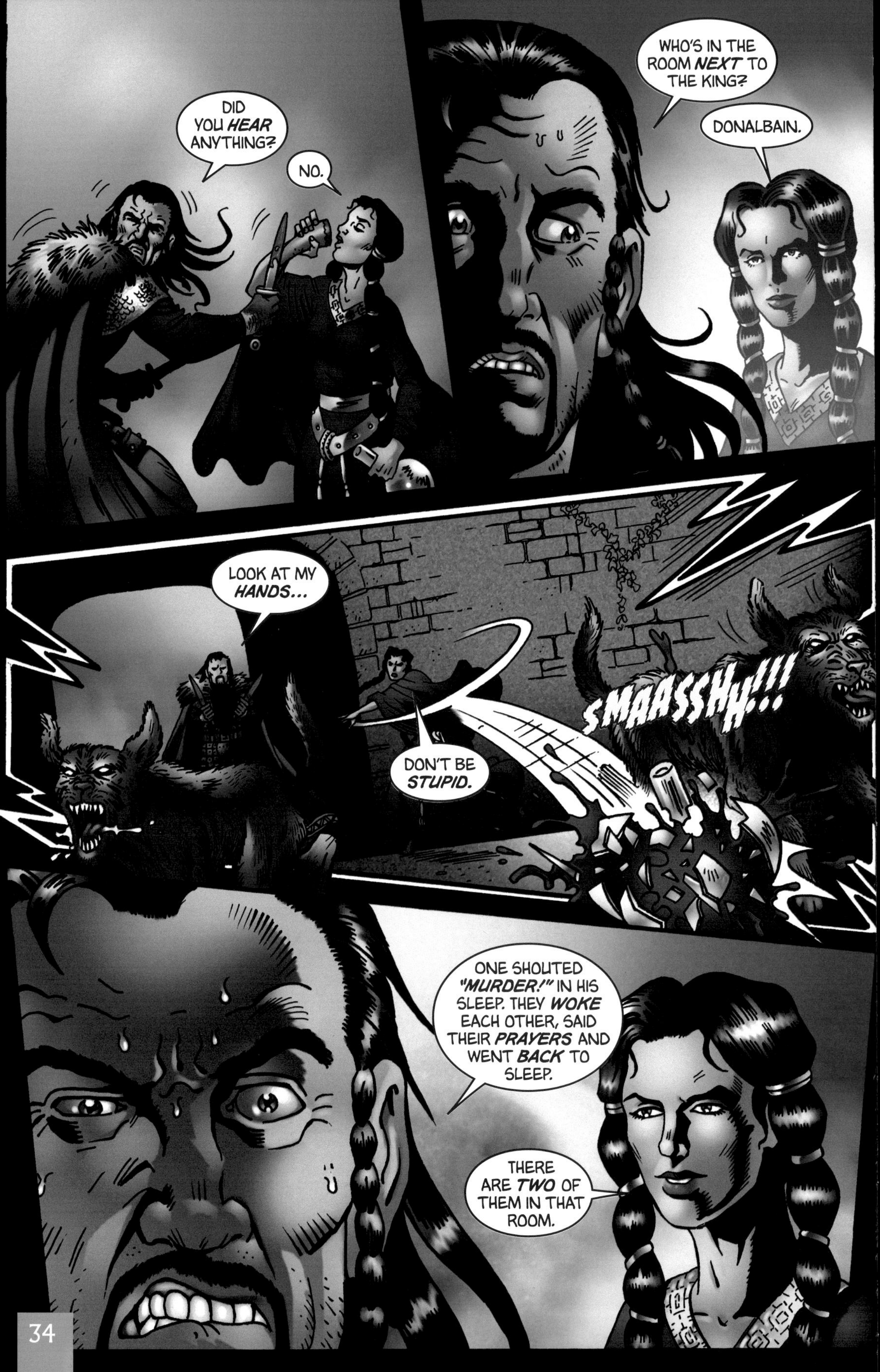
DID YOU HEAR ANYTHING?
NO.
WHO'S IN THE ROOM NEXT TO THE KING?
DONALBAIN.
LOOK AT MY HANDS...
DON'T BE STUPID.
SMAASSHH!!!
ONE SHOUTED "MURDER!" IN HIS SLEEP. THEY WOKE EACH OTHER, SAID THEIR PRAYERS AND WENT BACK TO SLEEP.
THERE ARE TWO OF THEM IN THAT ROOM.

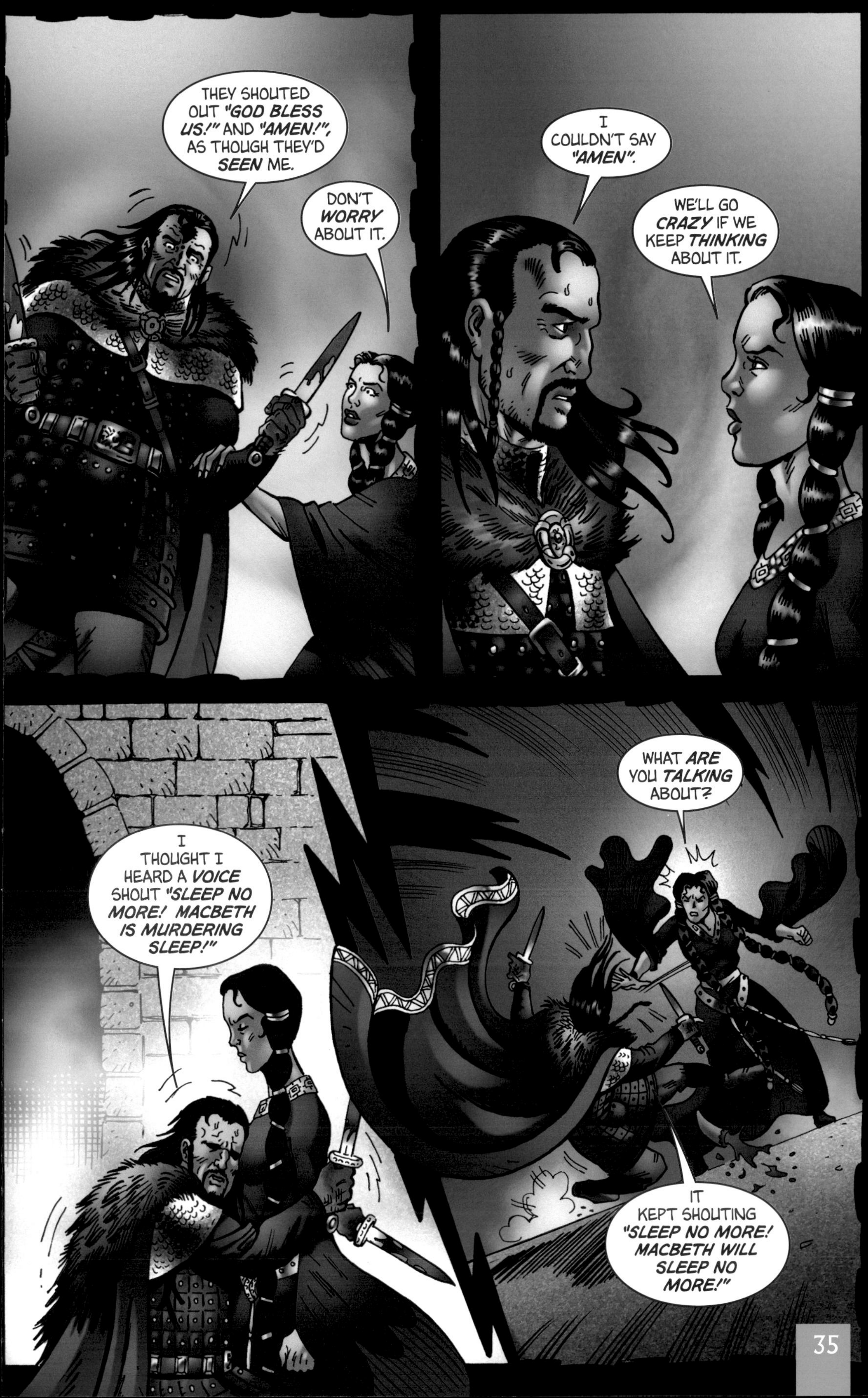
THEY SHOUTED OUT "GOD BLESS US!" AND "AMEN!", AS THOUGH THEY'D SEEN ME.
DON'T WORRY ABOUT IT.
I COULDN'T SAY "AMEN".
WE'LL GO CRAZY IF WE KEEP THINKING ABOUT IT.
I THOUGHT I HEARD A VOICE SHOUT "SLEEP NO MORE! MACBETH IS MURDERING SLEEP!"
WHAT ARE YOU TALKING ABOUT?
IT KEPT SHOUTING "SLEEP NO MORE! MACBETH WILL SLEEP NO MORE!"

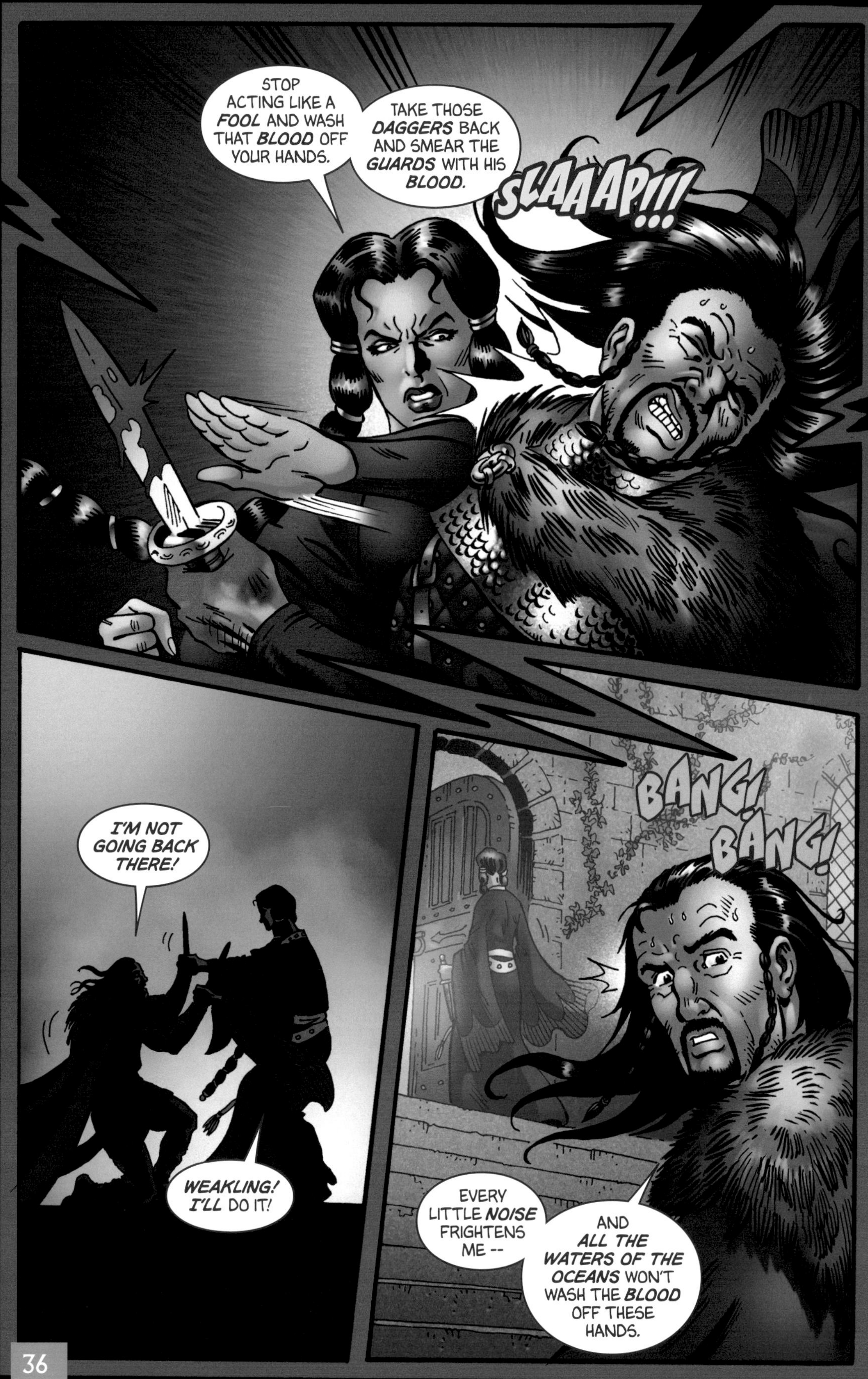
STOP ACTING LIKE A FOOL AND WASH THAT BLOOD OFF YOUR HANDS.
TAKE THOSE DAGGERS BACK AND SMEAR THE GUARDS WITH HIS BLOOD.
SLAAAP!!!
I'M NOT GOING BACK THERE!
WEAKLING! I'LL DO IT!
BANG! BANG!
EVERY LITTLE NOISE FRIGHTENS ME --
AND ALL THE WATERS OF THE OCEANS WON'T WASH THE BLOOD OFF THESE HANDS.

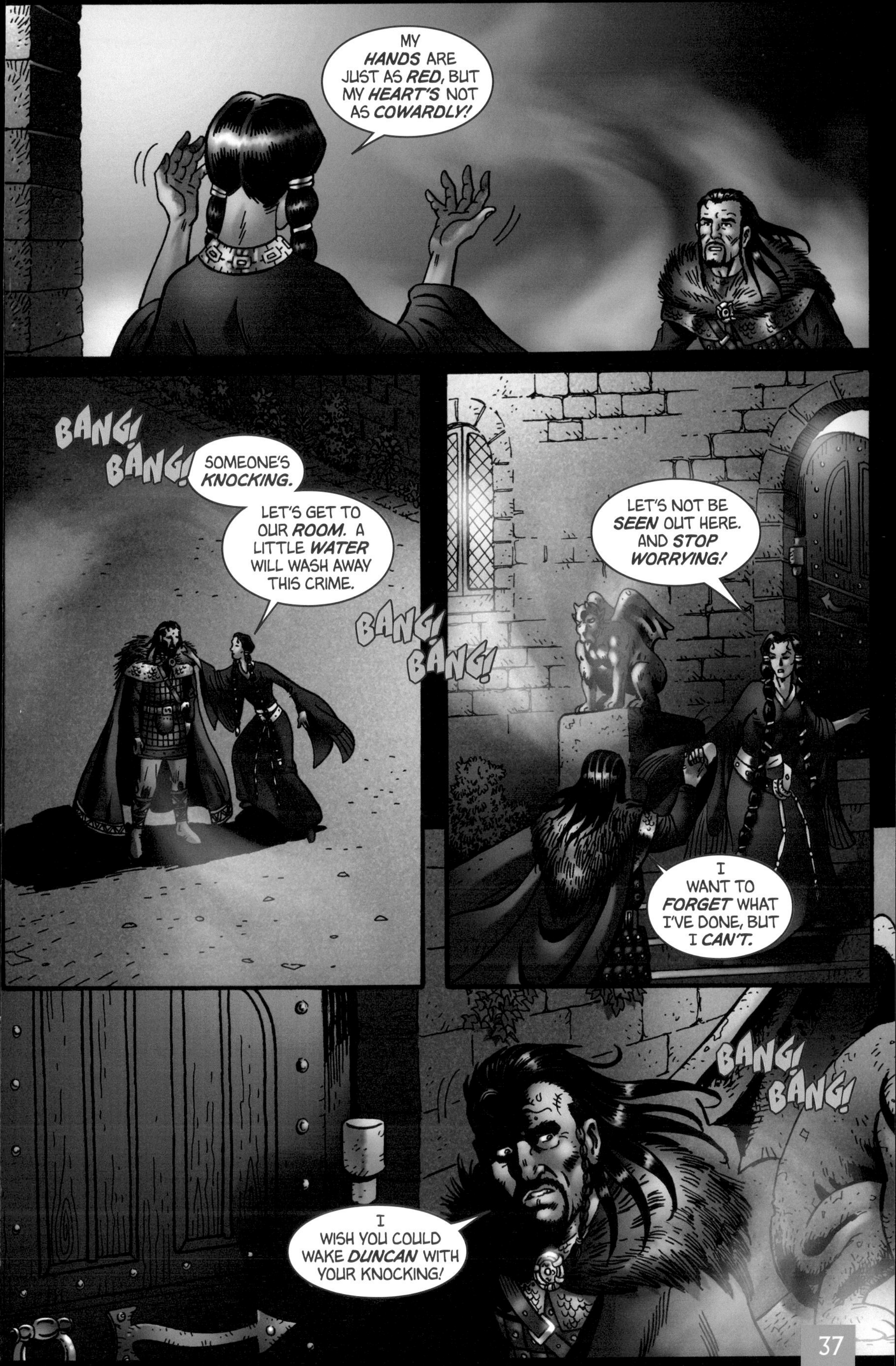
MY HANDS ARE JUST AS RED, BUT MY HEART'S NOT AS COWARDLY!
BANG! BANG!
SOMEONE'S KNOCKING.
LET'S GET TO OUR ROOM. A LITTLE WATER WILL WASH AWAY THIS CRIME.
BANG! BANG!
LET'S NOT BE SEEN OUT HERE. AND STOP WORRYING!
I WANT TO FORGET WHAT I'VE DONE, BUT I CAN'T.
BANG! BANG!
I WISH YOU COULD WAKE DUNCAN WITH YOUR KNOCKING!

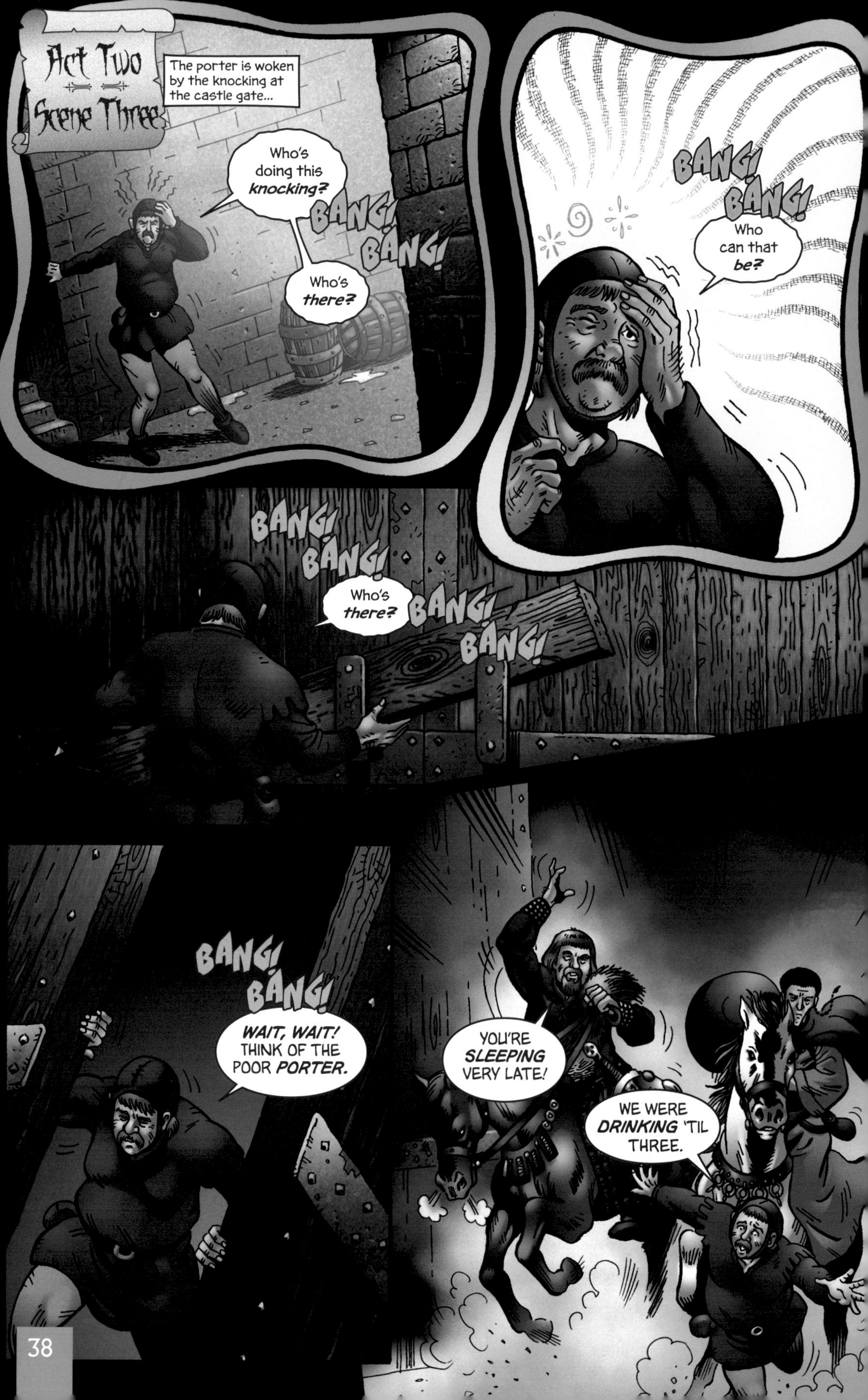
Act Two
Scene Three
The porter is woken by the knocking at the castle gate...
Who's doing this knocking?
BANG! BANG!
Who's there?
BANG! BANG!
Who can that be?
BANG! BANG!
Who's there?
BANG! BANG!
BANG! BANG!
WAIT, WAIT! THINK OF THE POOR PORTER.
YOU'RE SLEEPING VERY LATE!
WE WERE DRINKING 'TIL THREE.

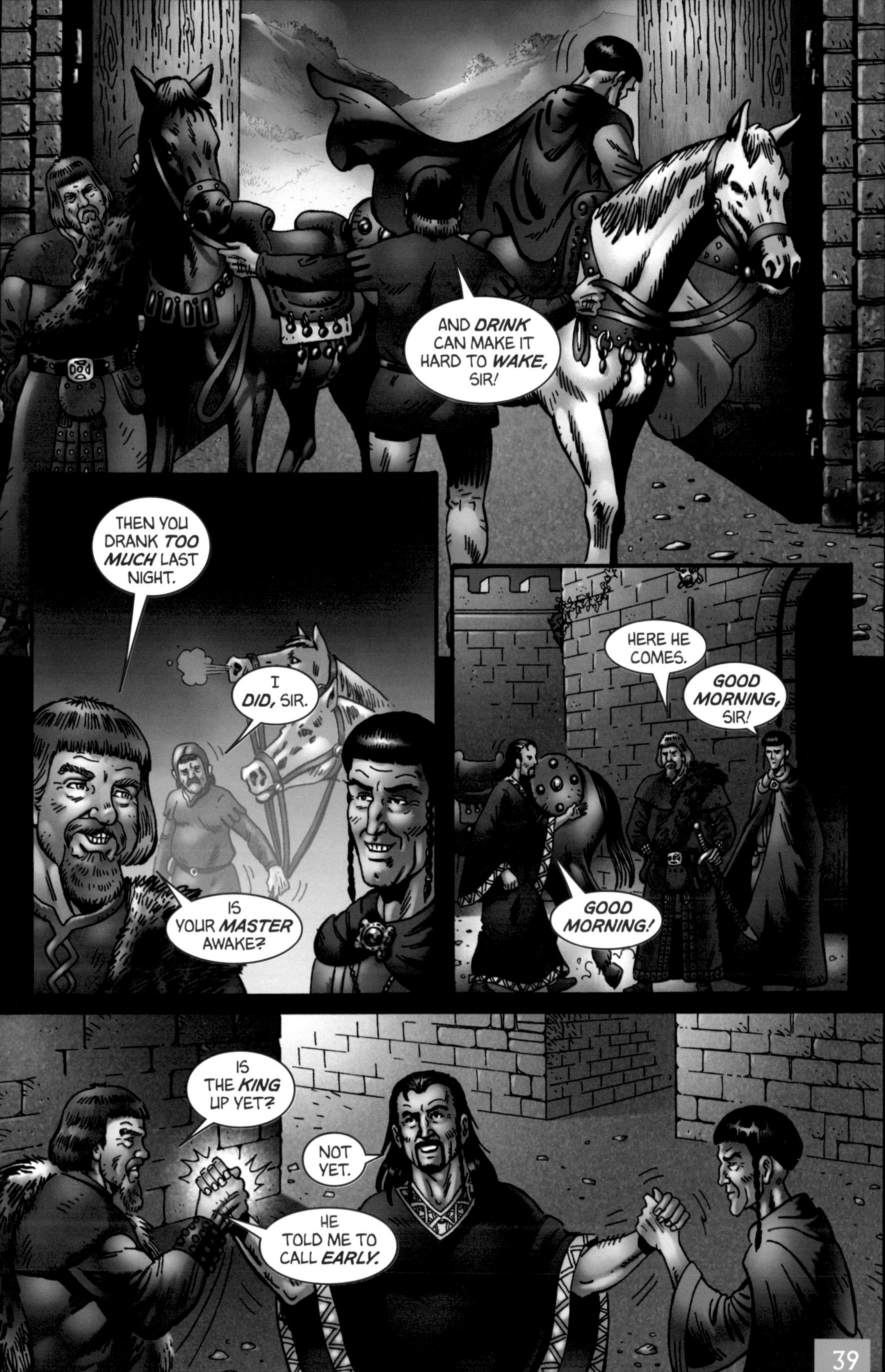
AND *DRINK* CAN MAKE IT HARD TO *WAKE,* SIR!
THEN YOU DRANK *TOO MUCH* LAST NIGHT.
I *DID,* SIR.
IS YOUR *MASTER* AWAKE?
HERE HE COMES.
GOOD MORNING, SIR!
GOOD MORNING!
IS THE *KING* UP YET?
NOT YET.
HE TOLD ME TO CALL *EARLY.*

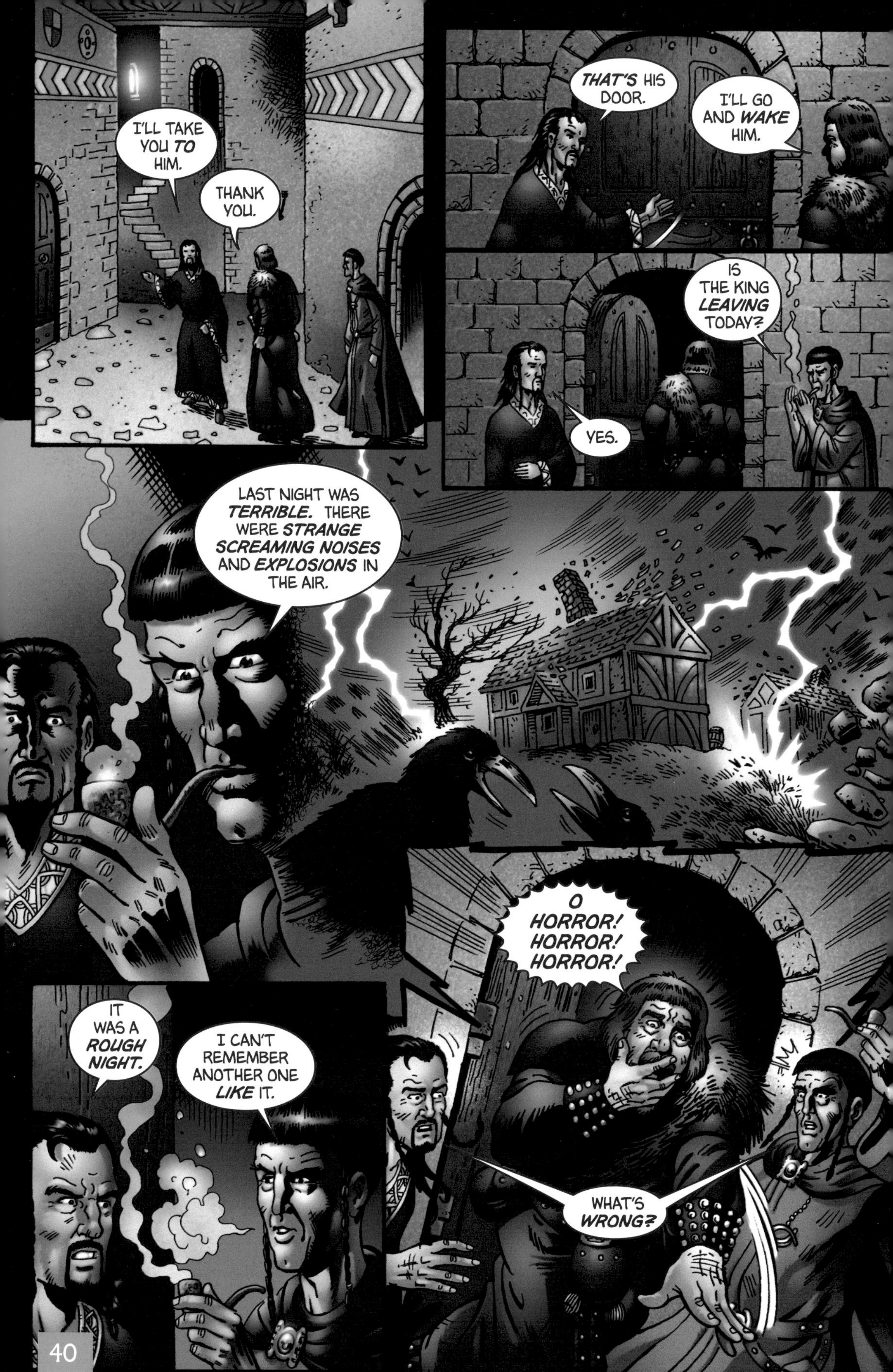
I'LL TAKE YOU TO HIM.
THANK YOU.
THAT'S HIS DOOR.
I'LL GO AND WAKE HIM.
IS THE KING LEAVING TODAY?
YES.
LAST NIGHT WAS TERRIBLE. THERE WERE STRANGE SCREAMING NOISES AND EXPLOSIONS IN THE AIR.
IT WAS A ROUGH NIGHT.
I CAN'T REMEMBER ANOTHER ONE LIKE IT.
O HORROR! HORROR! HORROR!
WHAT'S WRONG?

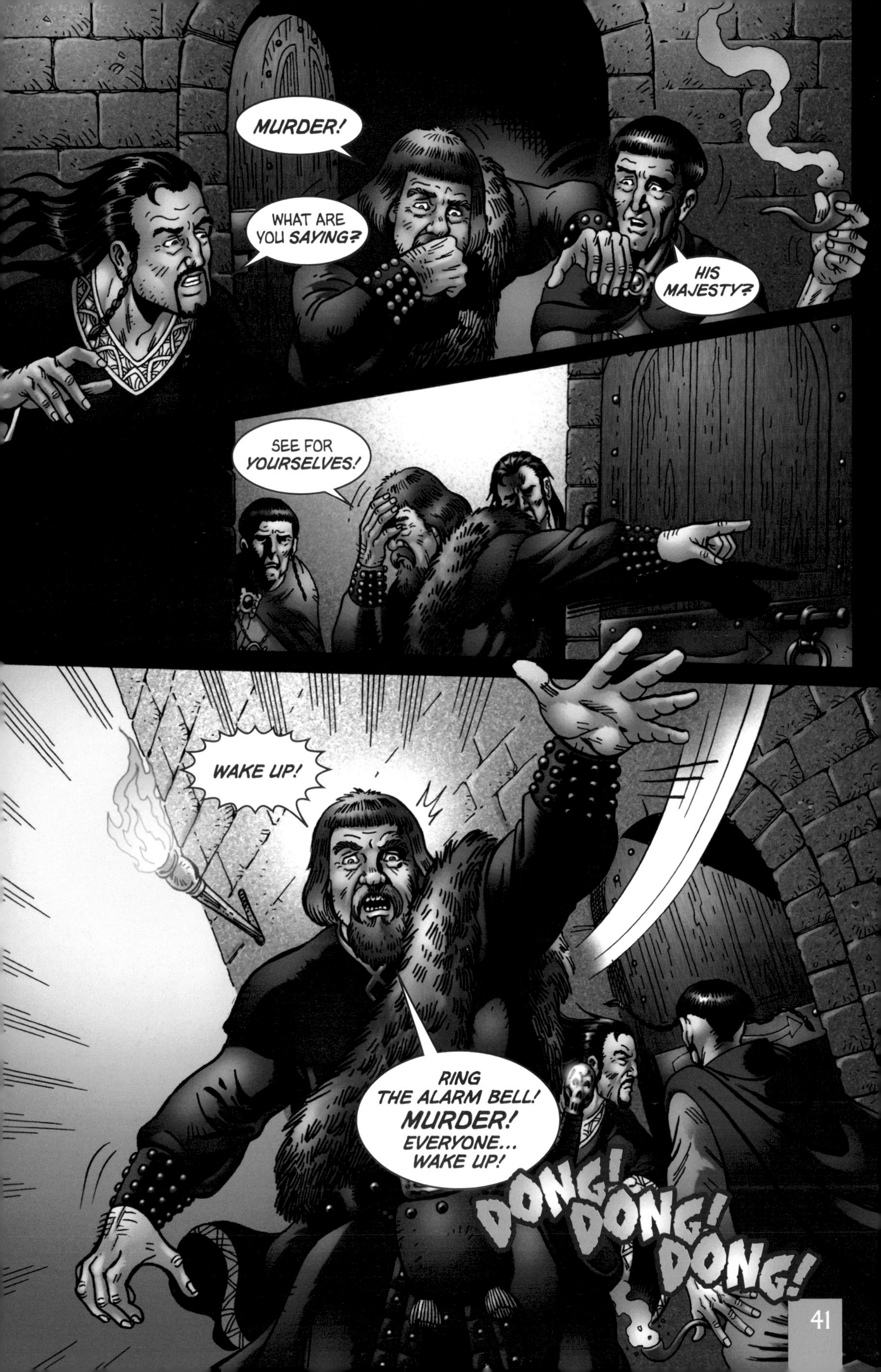
MURDER!
WHAT ARE YOU SAYING?
HIS MAJESTY?
SEE FOR YOURSELVES!
WAKE UP!
RING THE ALARM BELL! MURDER! EVERYONE... WAKE UP!
DONG! DONG! DONG!

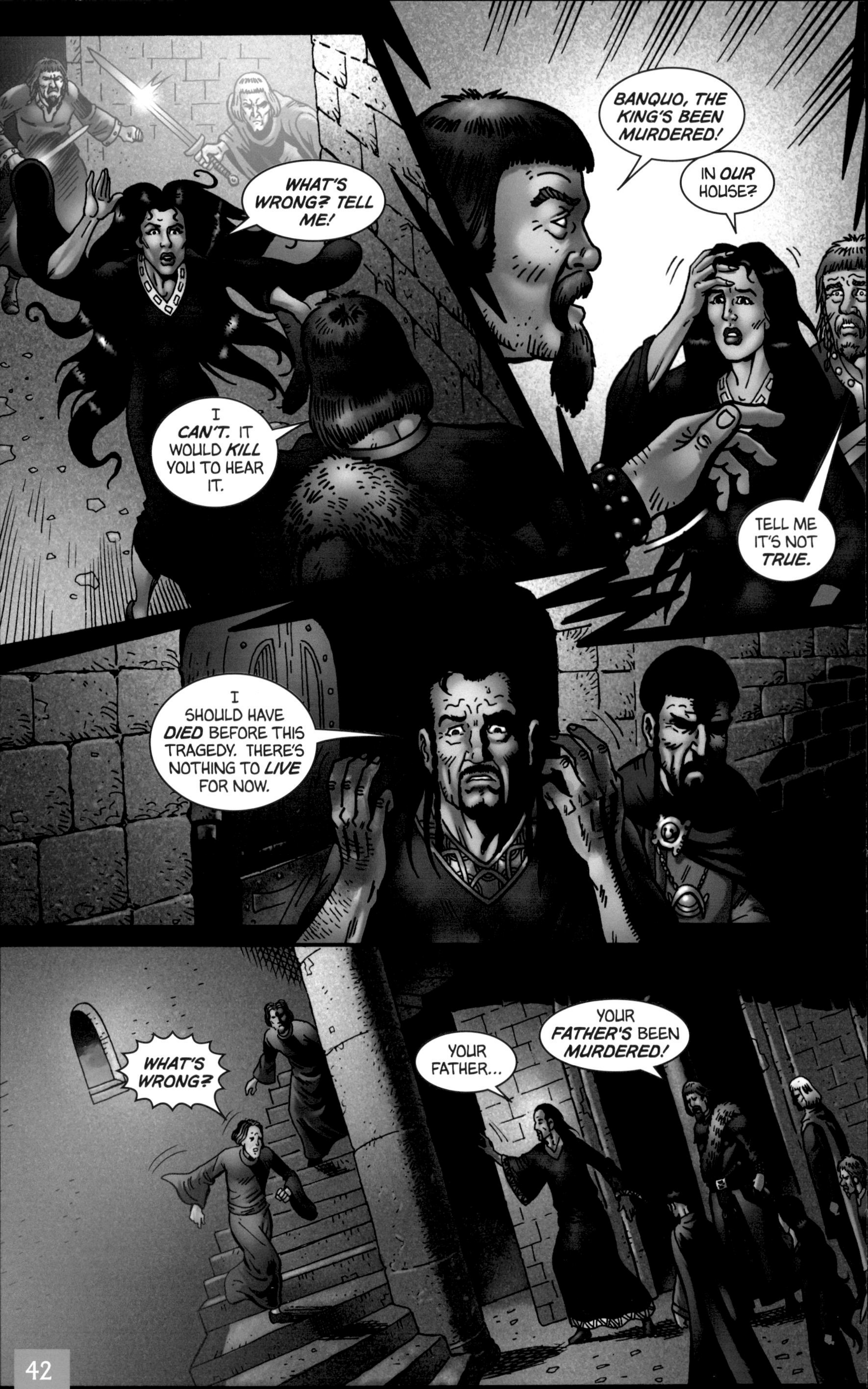
WHAT'S WRONG? TELL ME!
I CAN'T. IT WOULD KILL YOU TO HEAR IT.
BANQUO, THE KING'S BEEN MURDERED!
IN OUR HOUSE?
TELL ME IT'S NOT TRUE.
I SHOULD HAVE DIED BEFORE THIS TRAGEDY. THERE'S NOTHING TO LIVE FOR NOW.
WHAT'S WRONG?
YOUR FATHER...
YOUR FATHER'S BEEN MURDERED!

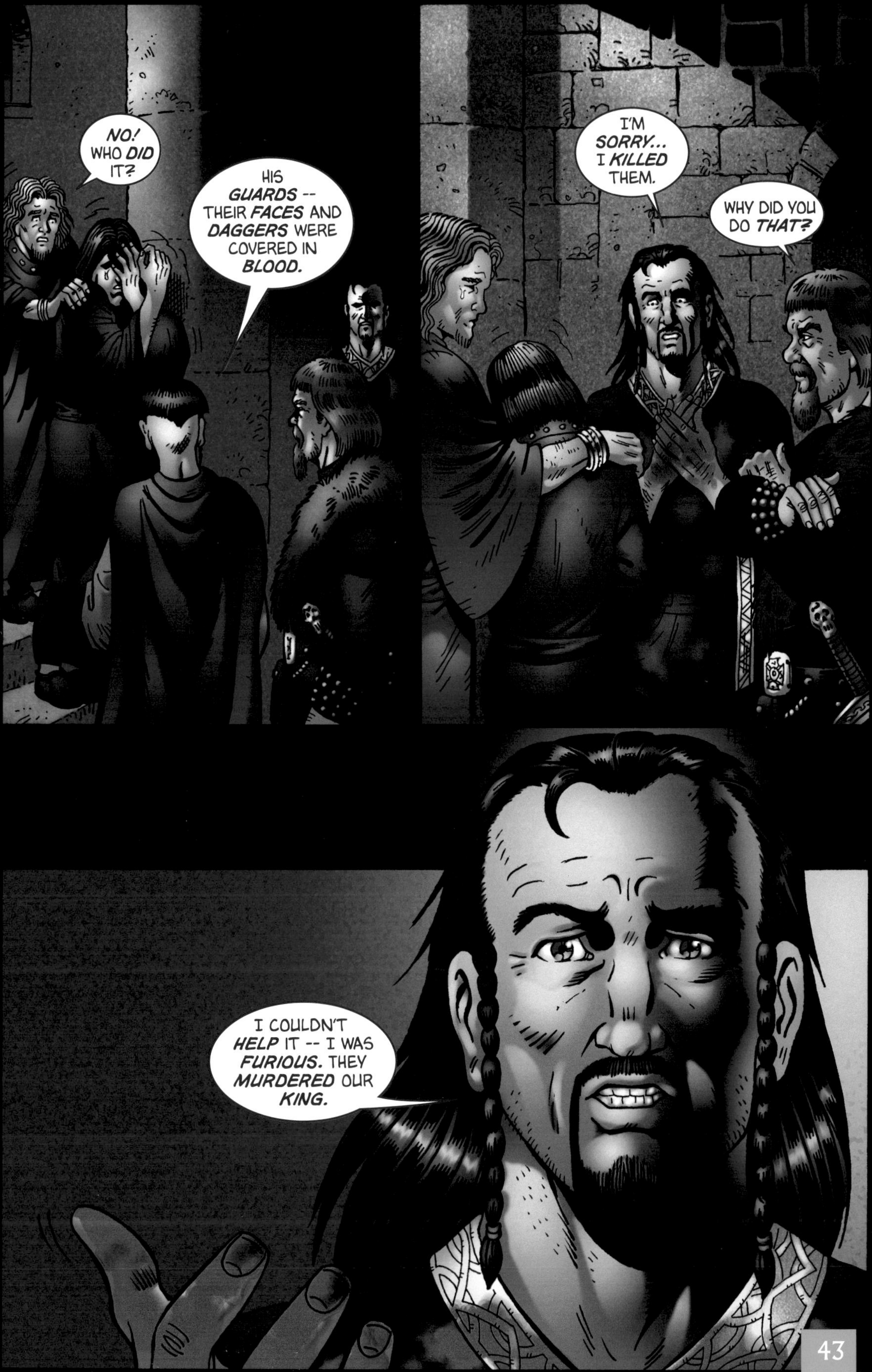
NO! WHO DID IT?
HIS GUARDS -- THEIR FACES AND DAGGERS WERE COVERED IN BLOOD.
I'M SORRY... I KILLED THEM.
WHY DID YOU DO THAT?
I COULDN'T HELP IT -- I WAS FURIOUS. THEY MURDERED OUR KING.

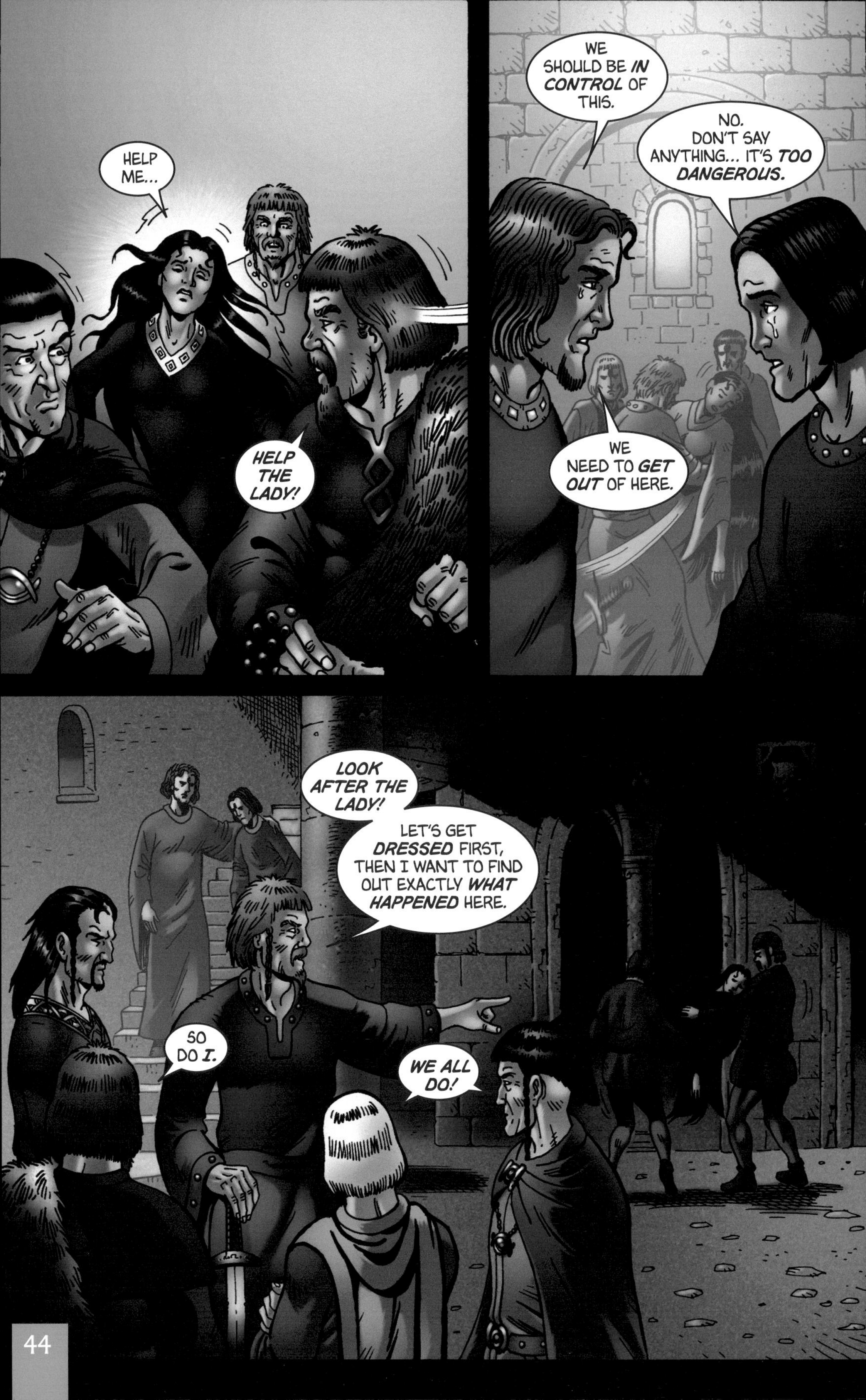
HELP ME...
HELP THE LADY!
WE SHOULD BE IN CONTROL OF THIS.
NO. DON'T SAY ANYTHING... IT'S TOO DANGEROUS.
WE NEED TO GET OUT OF HERE.
LOOK AFTER THE LADY!
LET'S GET DRESSED FIRST, THEN I WANT TO FIND OUT EXACTLY WHAT HAPPENED HERE.
SO DO I.
WE ALL DO!

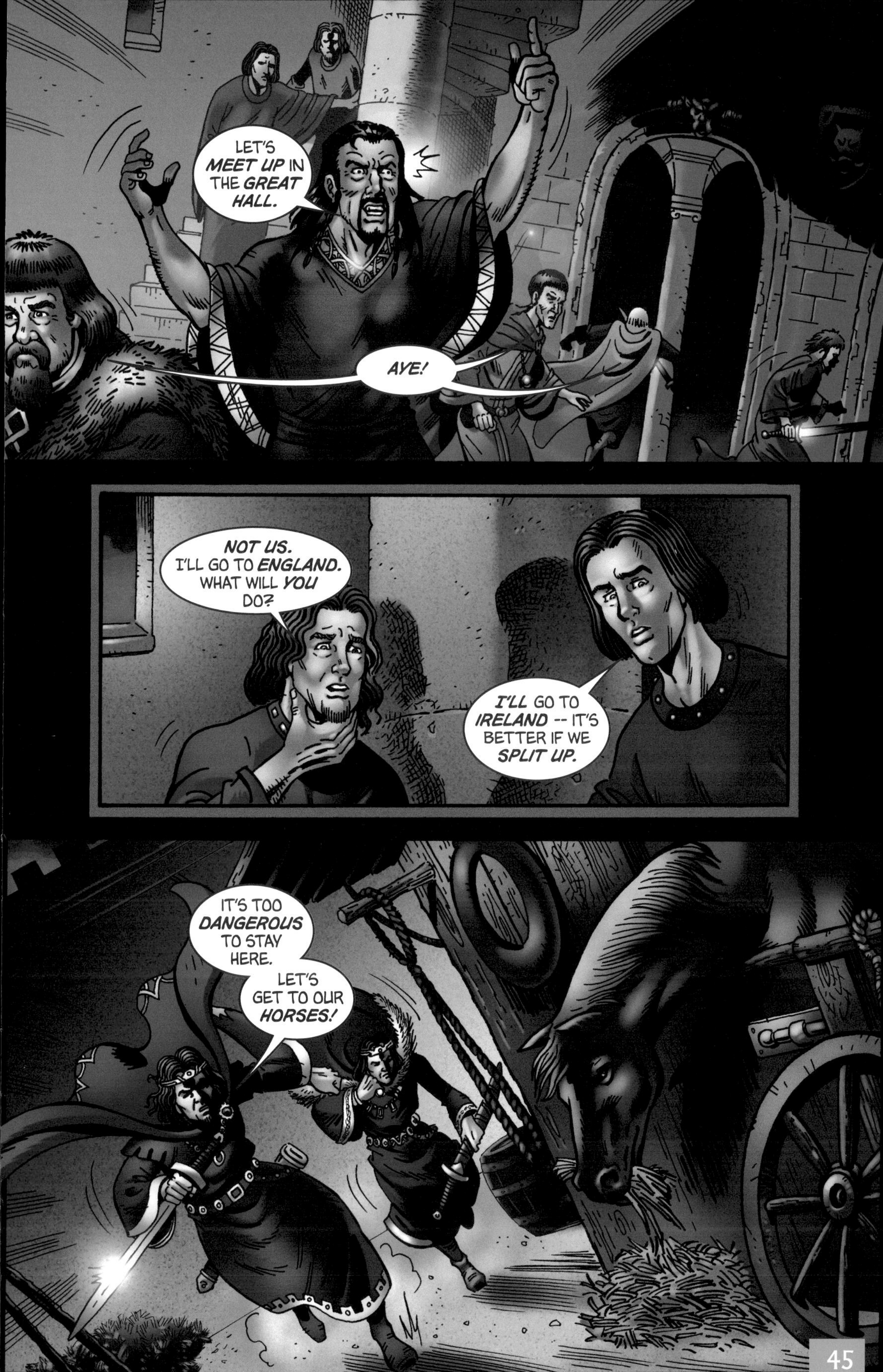
LET'S MEET UP IN THE GREAT HALL.
AYE!
NOT US. I'LL GO TO ENGLAND. WHAT WILL YOU DO?
I'LL GO TO IRELAND -- IT'S BETTER IF WE SPLIT UP.
IT'S TOO DANGEROUS TO STAY HERE.
LET'S GET TO OUR HORSES!

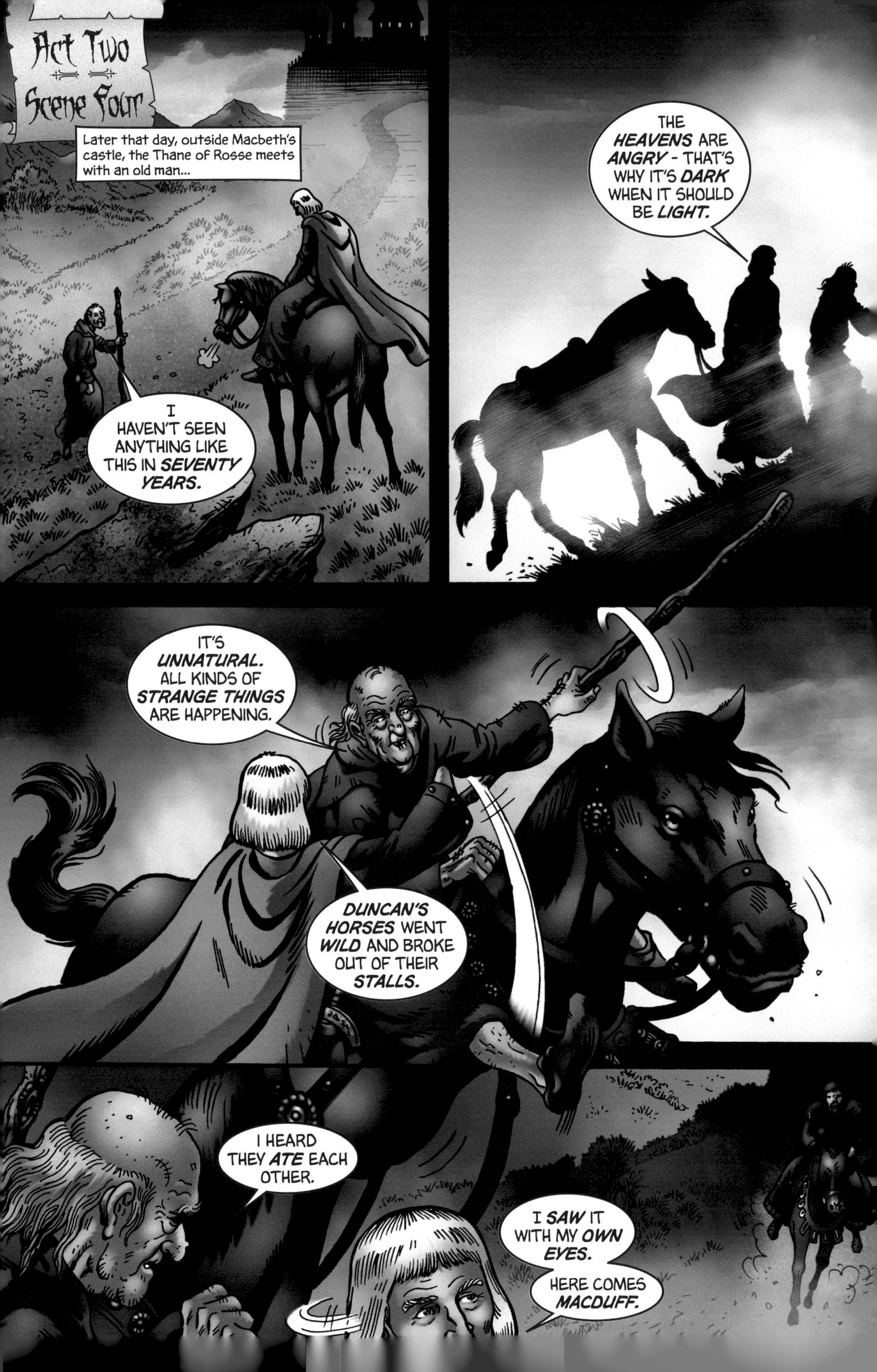
Act Two
Scene Four
Later that day, outside Macbeth's castle, the Thane of Rosse meets with an old man...
I HAVEN'T SEEN ANYTHING LIKE THIS IN SEVENTY YEARS.
THE HEAVENS ARE ANGRY - THAT'S WHY IT'S DARK WHEN IT SHOULD BE LIGHT.
IT'S UNNATURAL. ALL KINDS OF STRANGE THINGS ARE HAPPENING.
DUNCAN'S HORSES WENT WILD AND BROKE OUT OF THEIR STALLS.
I HEARD THEY ATE EACH OTHER.
I SAW IT WITH MY OWN EYES.
HERE COMES MACDUFF.

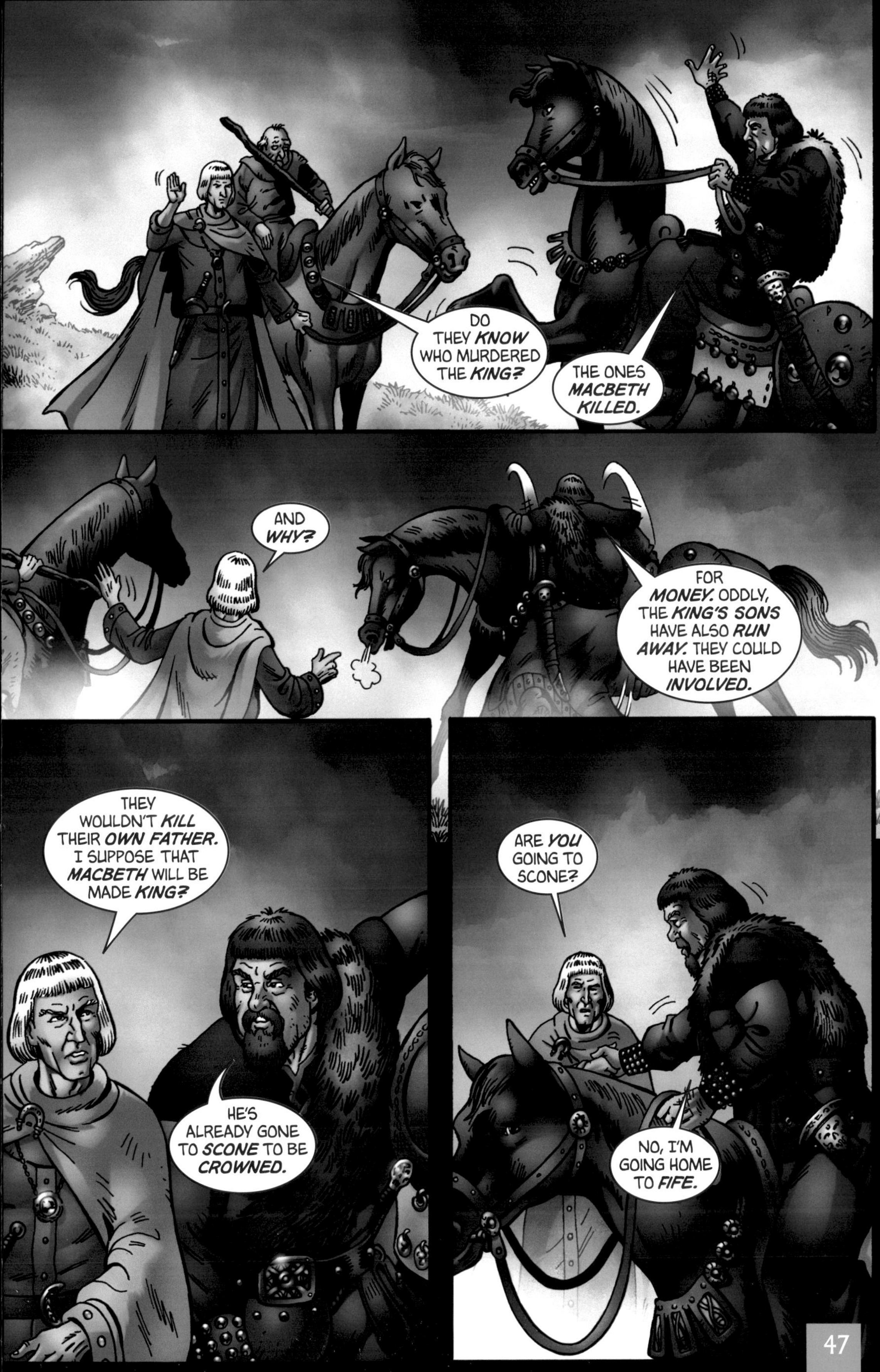
DO THEY KNOW WHO MURDERED THE KING?
THE ONES MACBETH KILLED.
AND WHY?
FOR MONEY. ODDLY, THE KING'S SONS HAVE ALSO RUN AWAY. THEY COULD HAVE BEEN INVOLVED.
THEY WOULDN'T KILL THEIR OWN FATHER. I SUPPOSE THAT MACBETH WILL BE MADE KING?
HE'S ALREADY GONE TO SCONE TO BE CROWNED.
ARE YOU GOING TO SCONE?
NO, I'M GOING HOME TO FIFE.

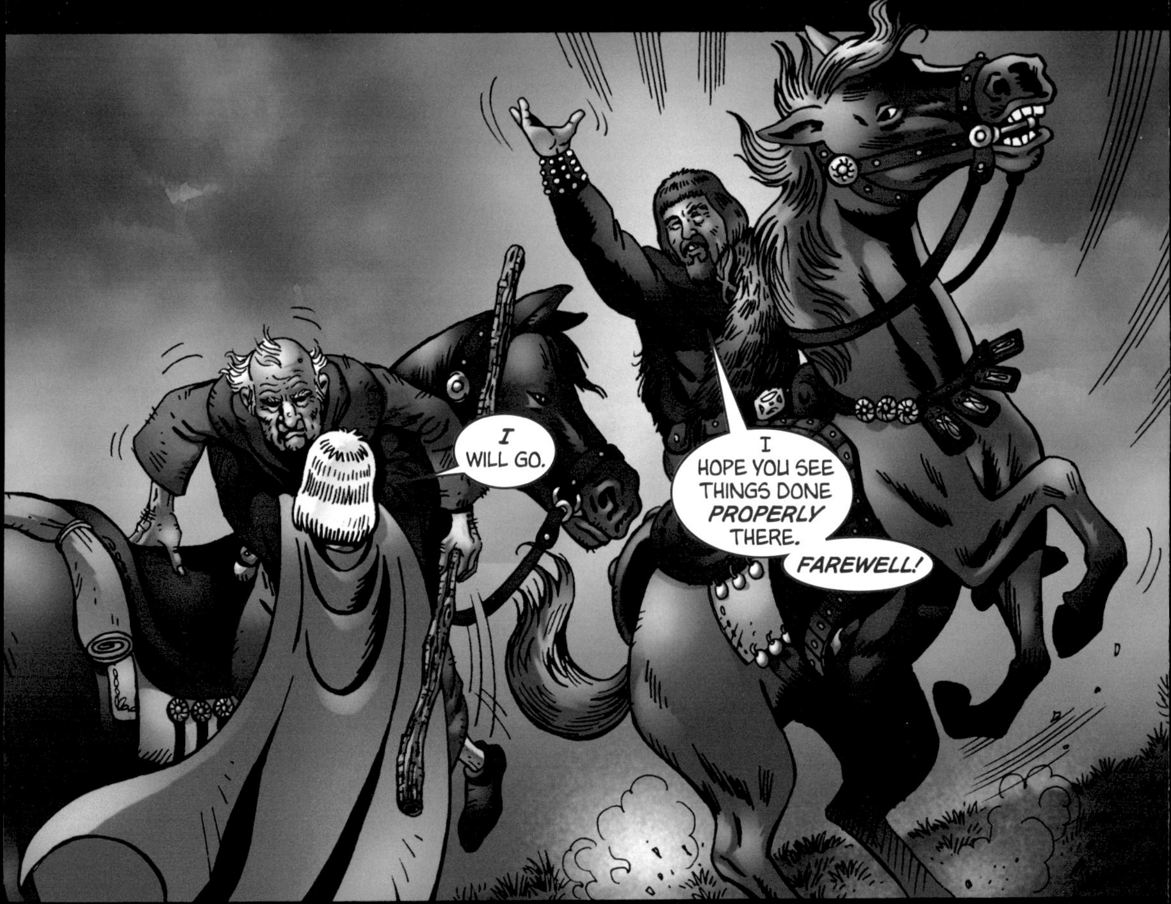
I WILL GO.
I HOPE YOU SEE THINGS DONE PROPERLY THERE.
FAREWELL!

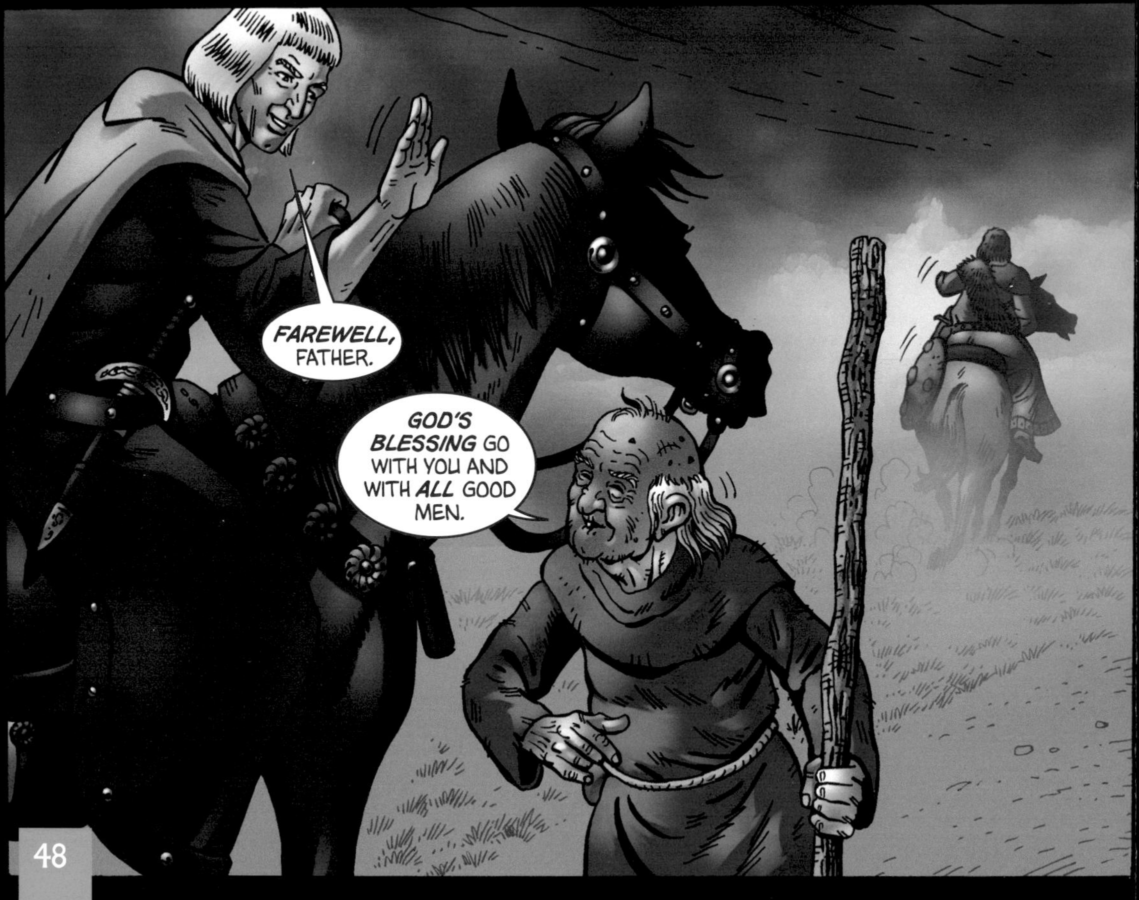
FAREWELL, FATHER.
GOD'S BLESSING GO WITH YOU AND WITH ALL GOOD MEN.

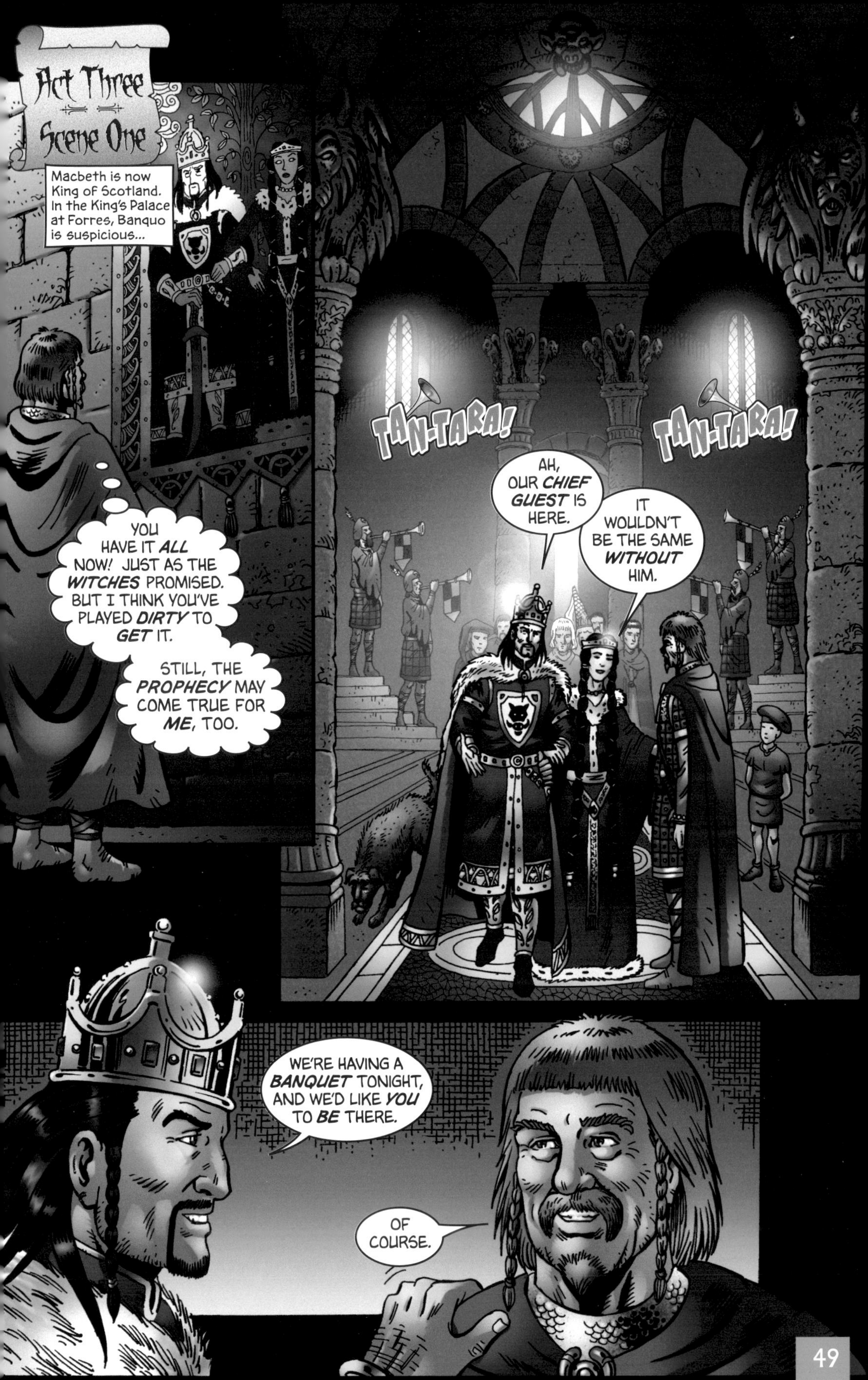
Act Three
Scene One
Macbeth is now King of Scotland. In the King's Palace at Forres, Banquo is suspicious...
YOU HAVE IT ALL NOW! JUST AS THE WITCHES PROMISED. BUT I THINK YOU'VE PLAYED DIRTY TO GET IT.
STILL, THE PROPHECY MAY COME TRUE FOR ME, TOO.
TAN-TARA!
TAN-TARA!
AH, OUR CHIEF GUEST IS HERE.
IT WOULDN'T BE THE SAME WITHOUT HIM.
WE'RE HAVING A BANQUET TONIGHT, AND WE'D LIKE YOU TO BE THERE.
OF COURSE.

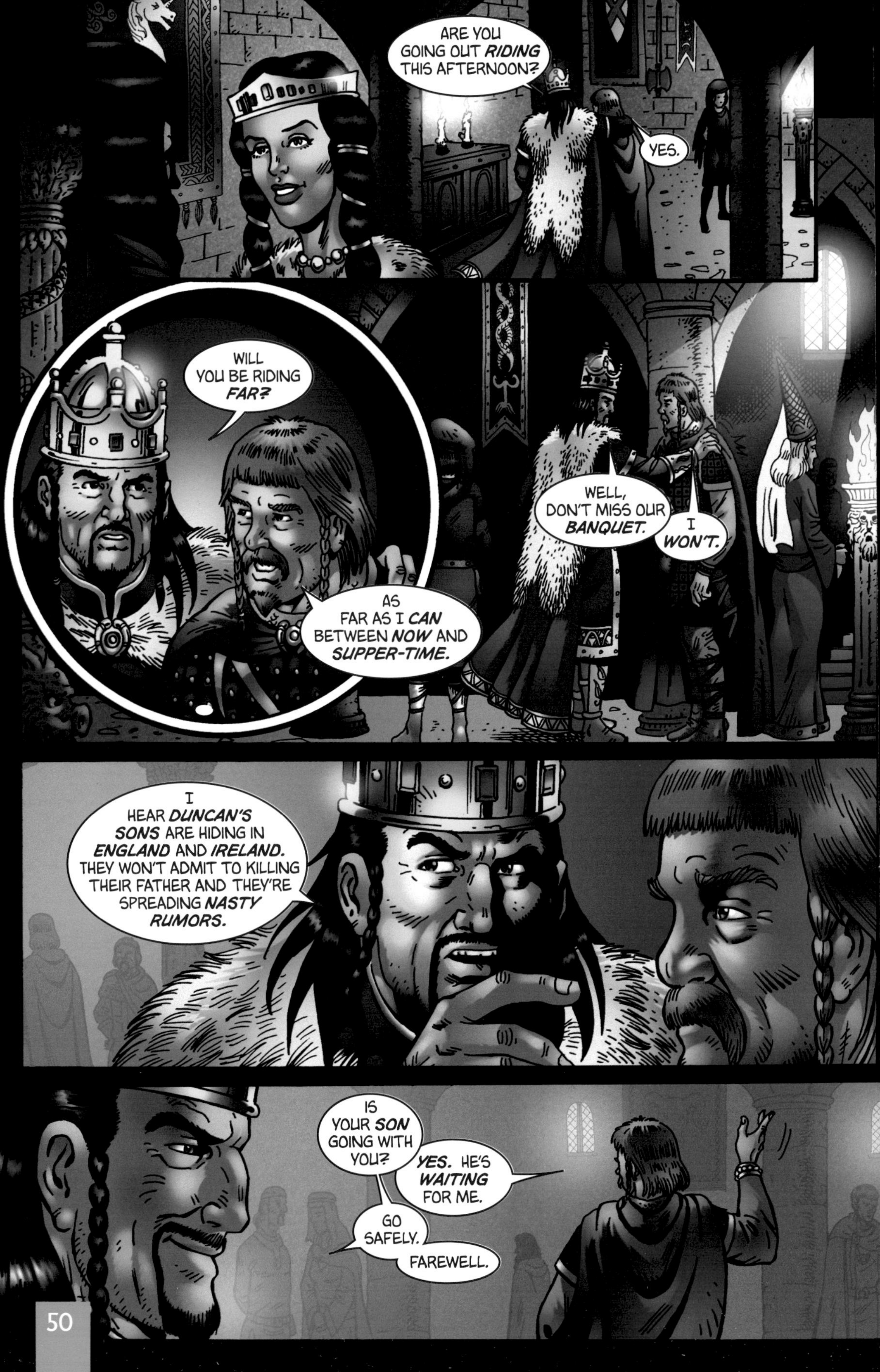
ARE YOU GOING OUT *RIDING* THIS AFTERNOON?
YES.
WILL YOU BE RIDING *FAR?*
AS FAR AS I *CAN* BETWEEN *NOW* AND *SUPPER-TIME.*
WELL, DON'T MISS OUR *BANQUET.*
I *WON'T.*
I HEAR *DUNCAN'S SONS* ARE HIDING IN *ENGLAND* AND *IRELAND.* THEY WON'T ADMIT TO KILLING THEIR FATHER AND THEY'RE SPREADING *NASTY RUMORS.*
IS YOUR *SON* GOING WITH YOU?
YES. HE'S *WAITING* FOR ME.
GO SAFELY.
FAREWELL.

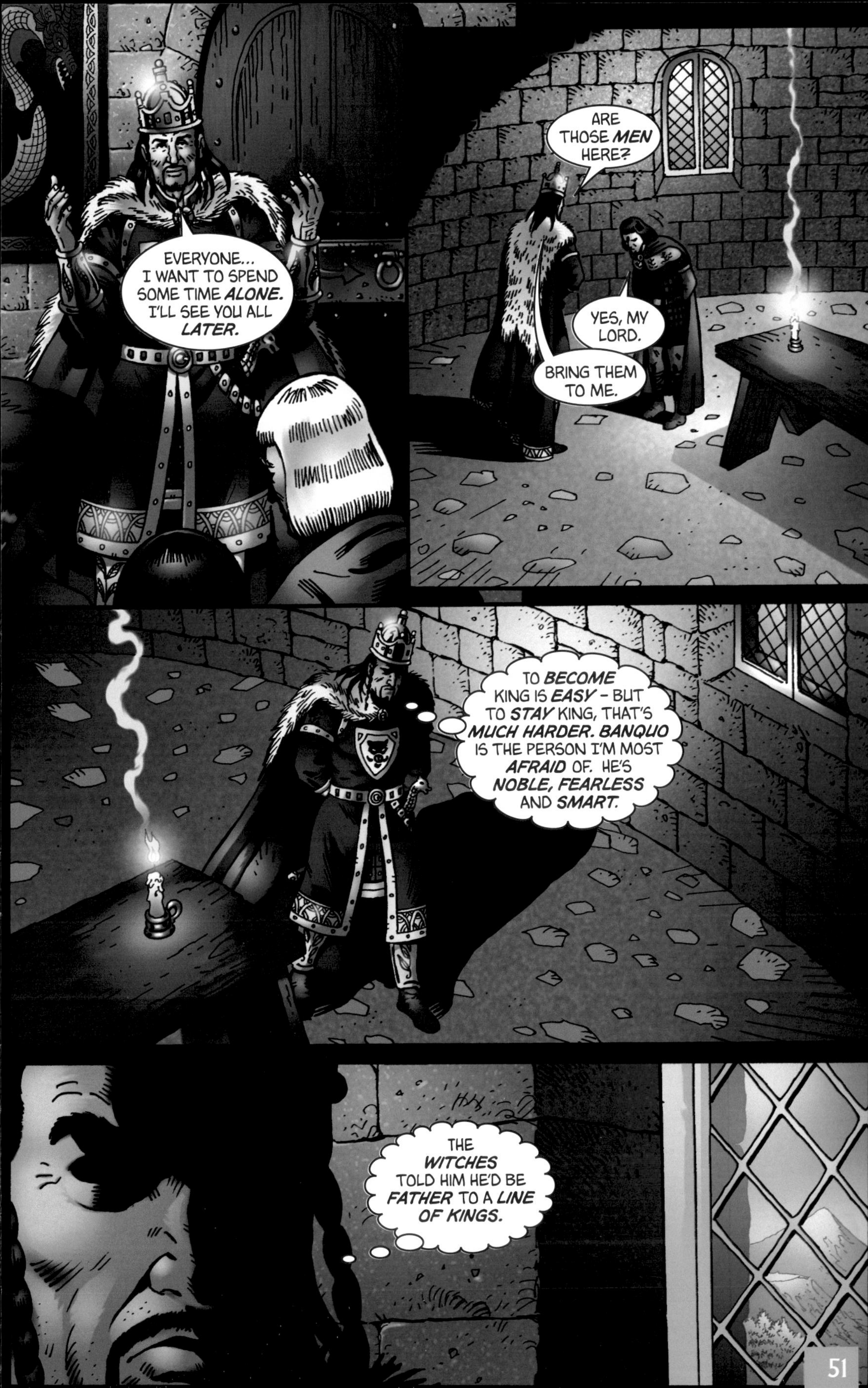
EVERYONE... I WANT TO SPEND SOME TIME ALONE. I'LL SEE YOU ALL LATER.
ARE THOSE MEN HERE?
YES, MY LORD.
BRING THEM TO ME.
TO BECOME KING IS EASY – BUT TO STAY KING, THAT'S MUCH HARDER. BANQUO IS THE PERSON I'M MOST AFRAID OF. HE'S NOBLE, FEARLESS AND SMART.
THE WITCHES TOLD HIM HE'D BE FATHER TO A LINE OF KINGS.

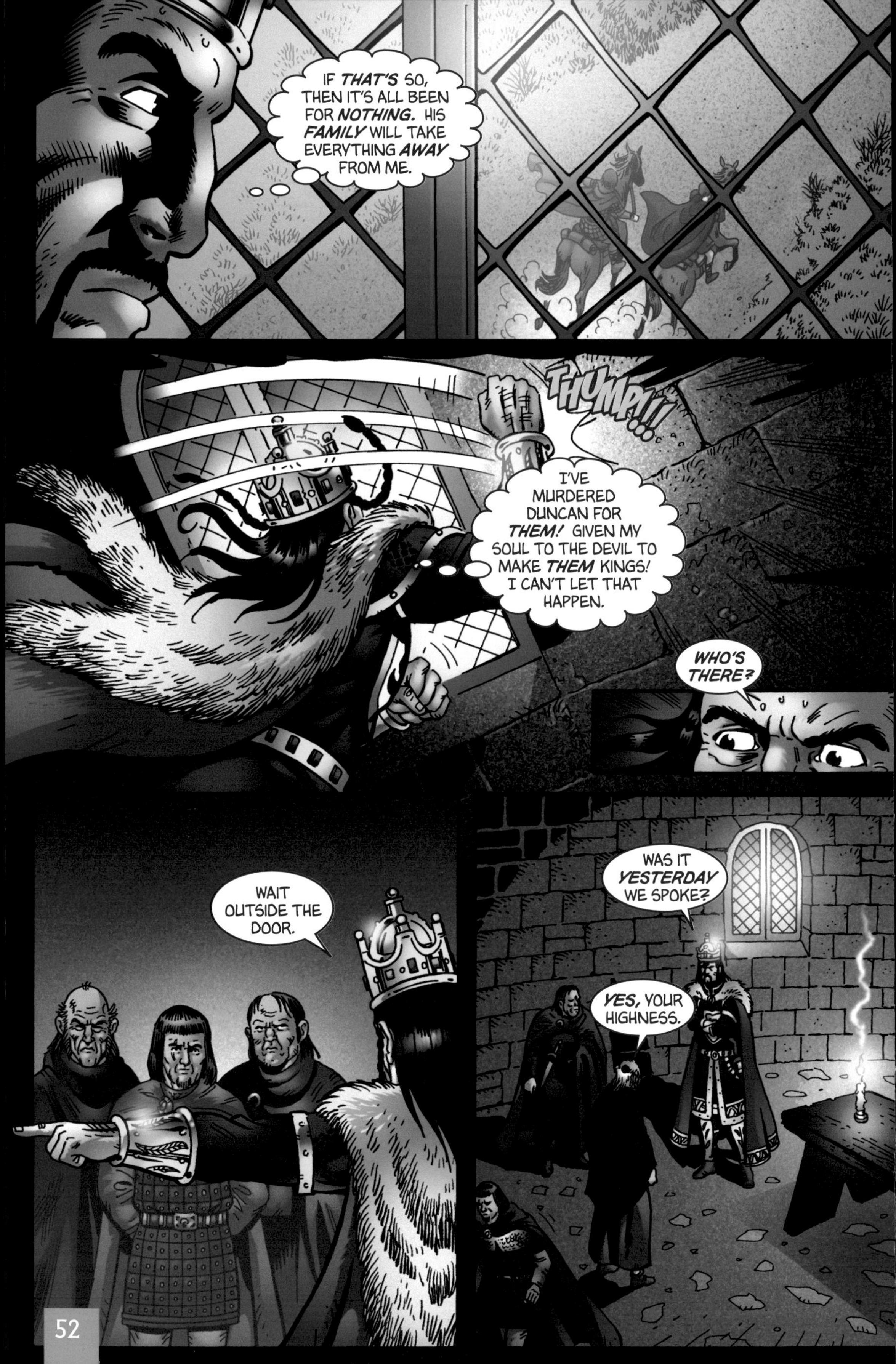
IF THAT'S SO, THEN IT'S ALL BEEN FOR NOTHING. HIS FAMILY WILL TAKE EVERYTHING AWAY FROM ME.
THUMP!!!
I'VE MURDERED DUNCAN FOR THEM! GIVEN MY SOUL TO THE DEVIL TO MAKE THEM KINGS! I CAN'T LET THAT HAPPEN.
WHO'S THERE?
WAIT OUTSIDE THE DOOR.
WAS IT YESTERDAY WE SPOKE?
YES, YOUR HIGHNESS.

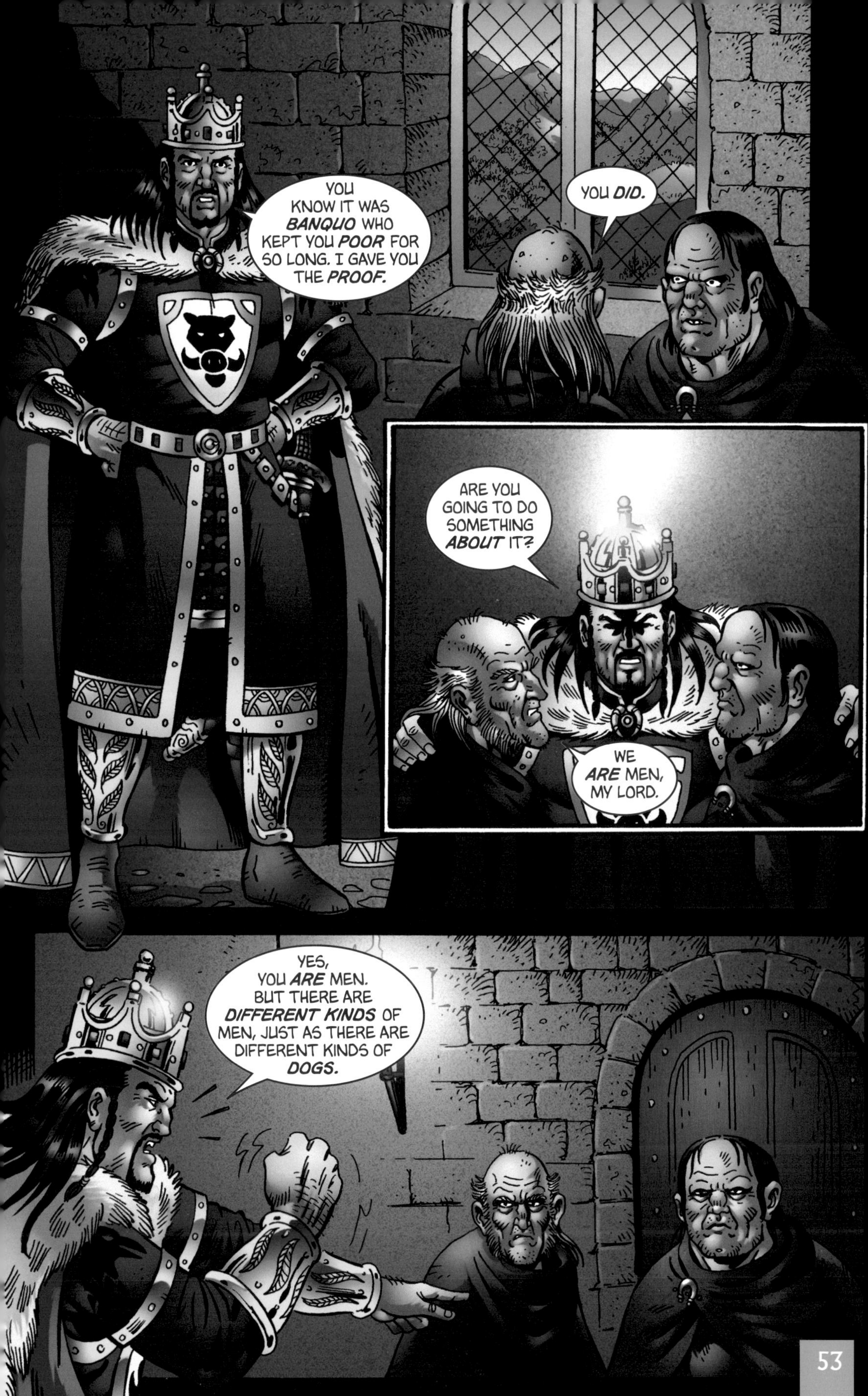
YOU KNOW IT WAS BANQUO WHO KEPT YOU POOR FOR SO LONG. I GAVE YOU THE PROOF.
YOU DID.
ARE YOU GOING TO DO SOMETHING ABOUT IT?
WE ARE MEN, MY LORD.
YES, YOU ARE MEN. BUT THERE ARE DIFFERENT KINDS OF MEN, JUST AS THERE ARE DIFFERENT KINDS OF DOGS.

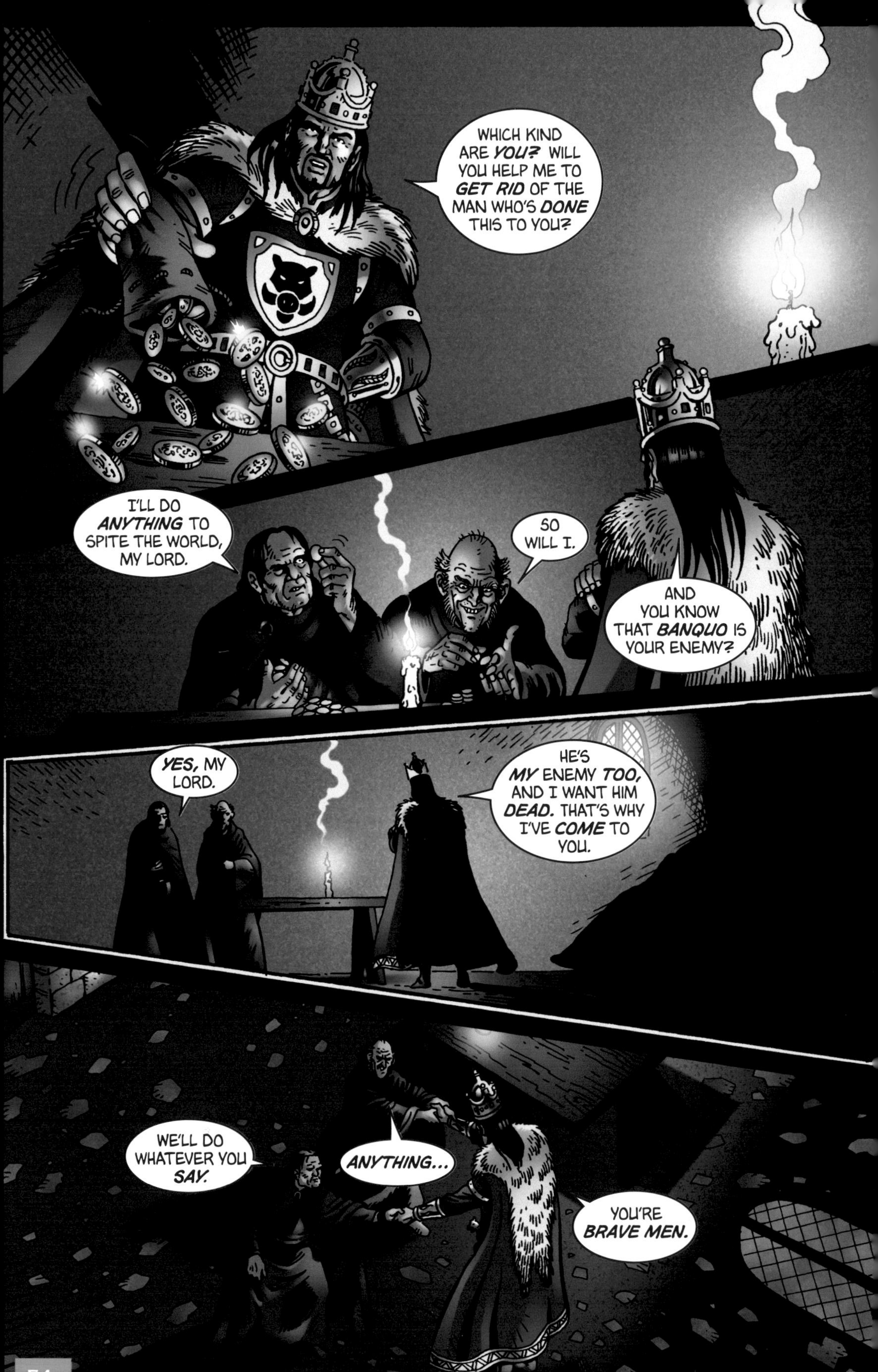
WHICH KIND ARE YOU? WILL YOU HELP ME TO GET RID OF THE MAN WHO'S DONE THIS TO YOU?
I'LL DO ANYTHING TO SPITE THE WORLD, MY LORD.
SO WILL I.
AND YOU KNOW THAT BANQUO IS YOUR ENEMY?
YES, MY LORD.
HE'S MY ENEMY TOO, AND I WANT HIM DEAD. THAT'S WHY I'VE COME TO YOU.
WE'LL DO WHATEVER YOU SAY.
ANYTHING...
YOU'RE BRAVE MEN.

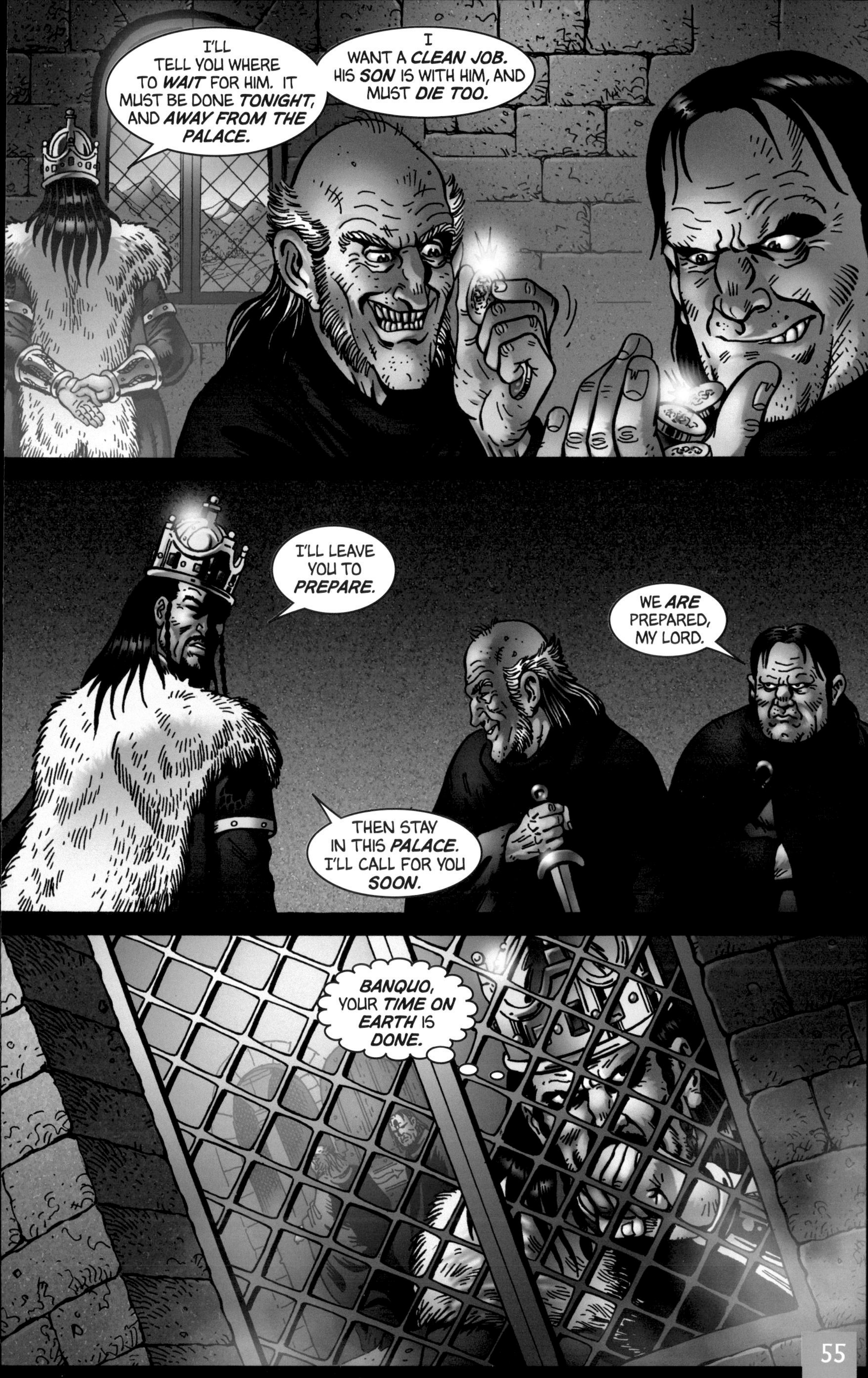
I'LL TELL YOU WHERE TO WAIT FOR HIM. IT MUST BE DONE TONIGHT, AND AWAY FROM THE PALACE.
I WANT A CLEAN JOB. HIS SON IS WITH HIM, AND MUST DIE TOO.
I'LL LEAVE YOU TO PREPARE.
WE ARE PREPARED, MY LORD.
THEN STAY IN THIS PALACE. I'LL CALL FOR YOU SOON.
BANQUO, YOUR TIME ON EARTH IS DONE.

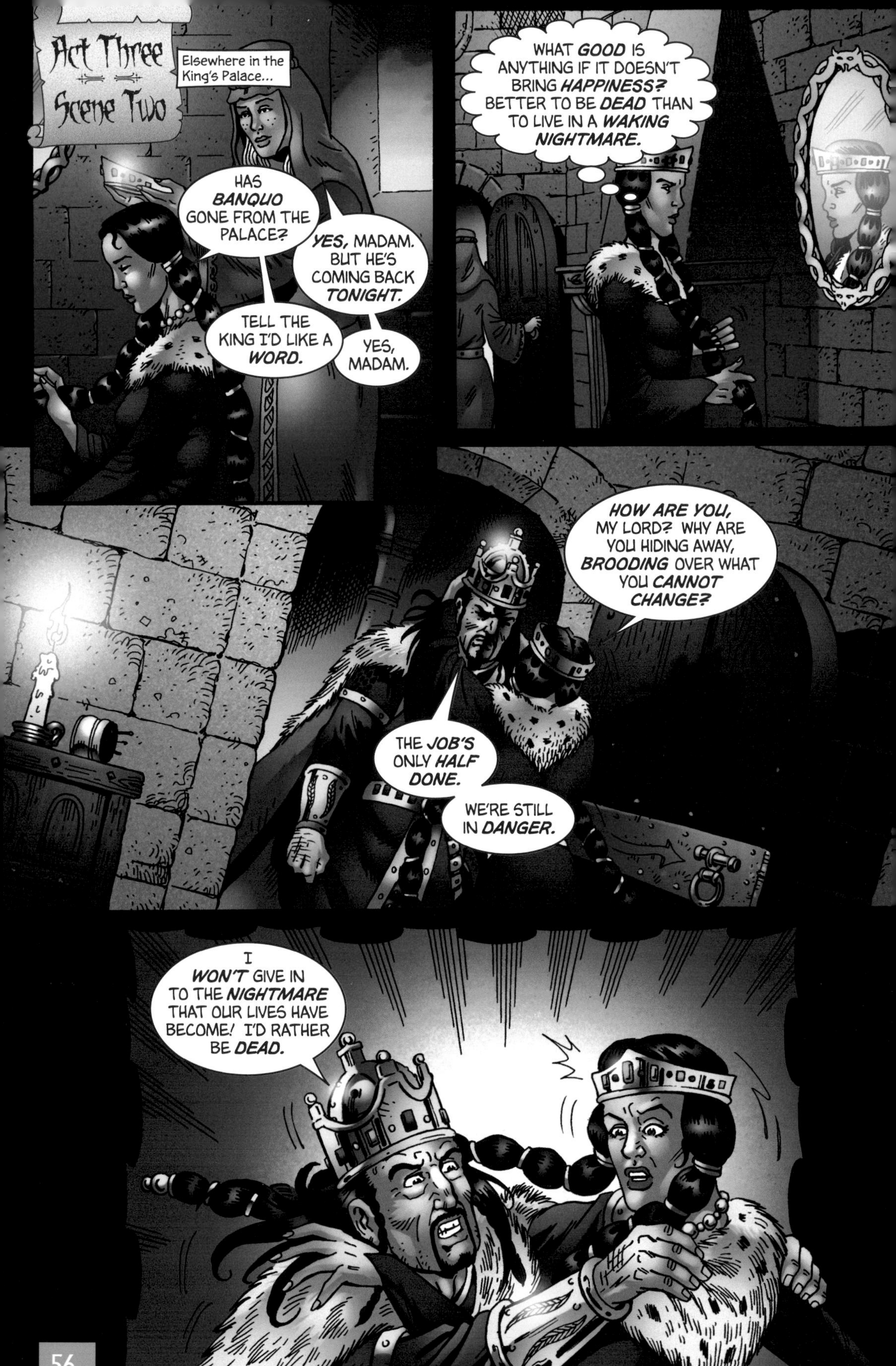
Act Three
Scene Two
Elsewhere in the King's Palace...
HAS BANQUO GONE FROM THE PALACE?
YES, MADAM. BUT HE'S COMING BACK TONIGHT.
TELL THE KING I'D LIKE A WORD.
YES, MADAM.
WHAT GOOD IS ANYTHING IF IT DOESN'T BRING HAPPINESS? BETTER TO BE DEAD THAN TO LIVE IN A WAKING NIGHTMARE.
HOW ARE YOU, MY LORD? WHY ARE YOU HIDING AWAY, BROODING OVER WHAT YOU CANNOT CHANGE?
THE JOB'S ONLY HALF DONE.
WE'RE STILL IN DANGER.
I WON'T GIVE IN TO THE NIGHTMARE THAT OUR LIVES HAVE BECOME! I'D RATHER BE DEAD.

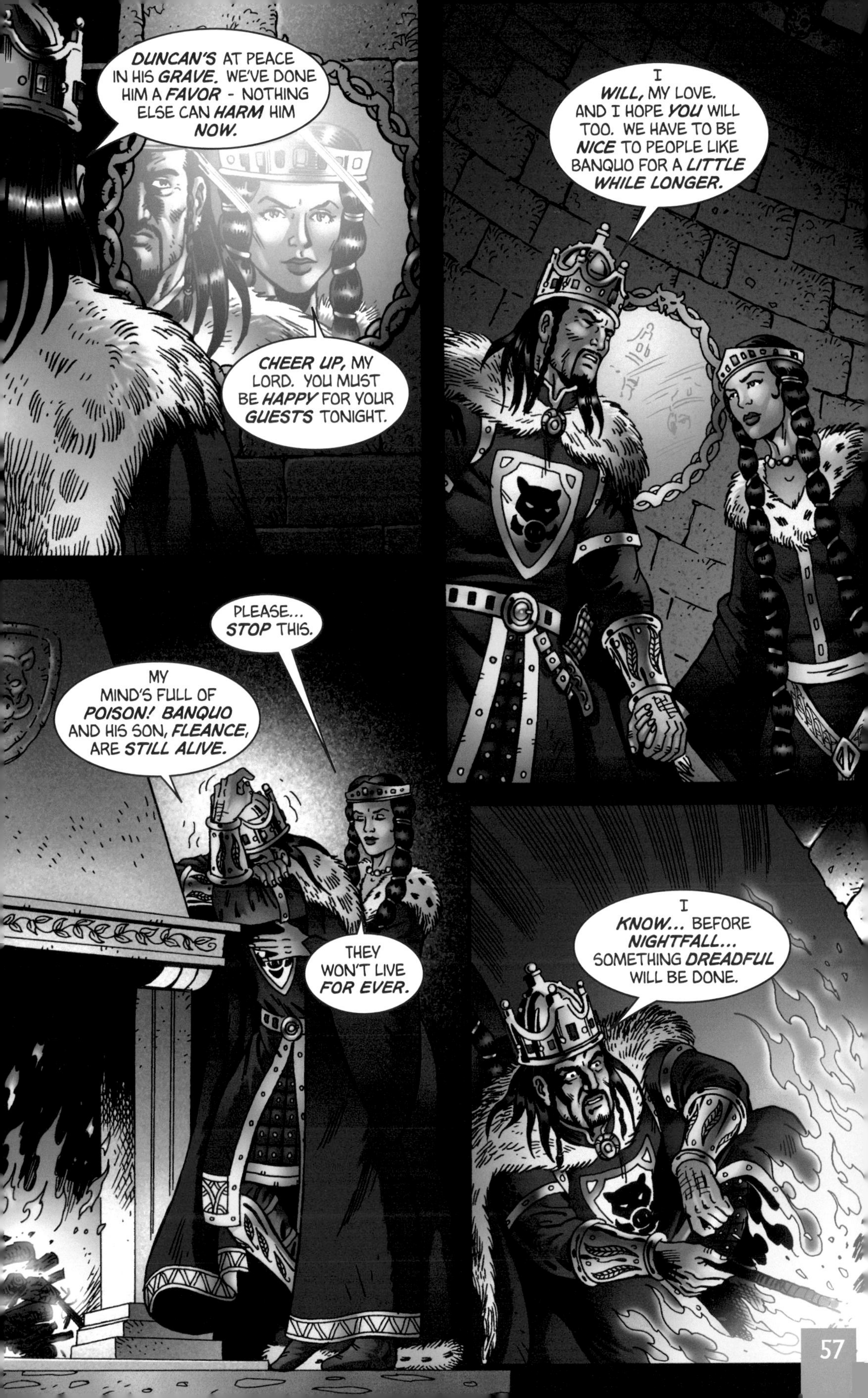
DUNCAN'S AT PEACE IN HIS GRAVE. WE'VE DONE HIM A FAVOR - NOTHING ELSE CAN HARM HIM NOW.
CHEER UP, MY LORD. YOU MUST BE HAPPY FOR YOUR GUESTS TONIGHT.
I WILL, MY LOVE. AND I HOPE YOU WILL TOO. WE HAVE TO BE NICE TO PEOPLE LIKE BANQUO FOR A LITTLE WHILE LONGER.
PLEASE... STOP THIS.
MY MIND'S FULL OF POISON! BANQUO AND HIS SON, FLEANCE, ARE STILL ALIVE.
THEY WON'T LIVE FOR EVER.
I KNOW... BEFORE NIGHTFALL... SOMETHING DREADFUL WILL BE DONE.

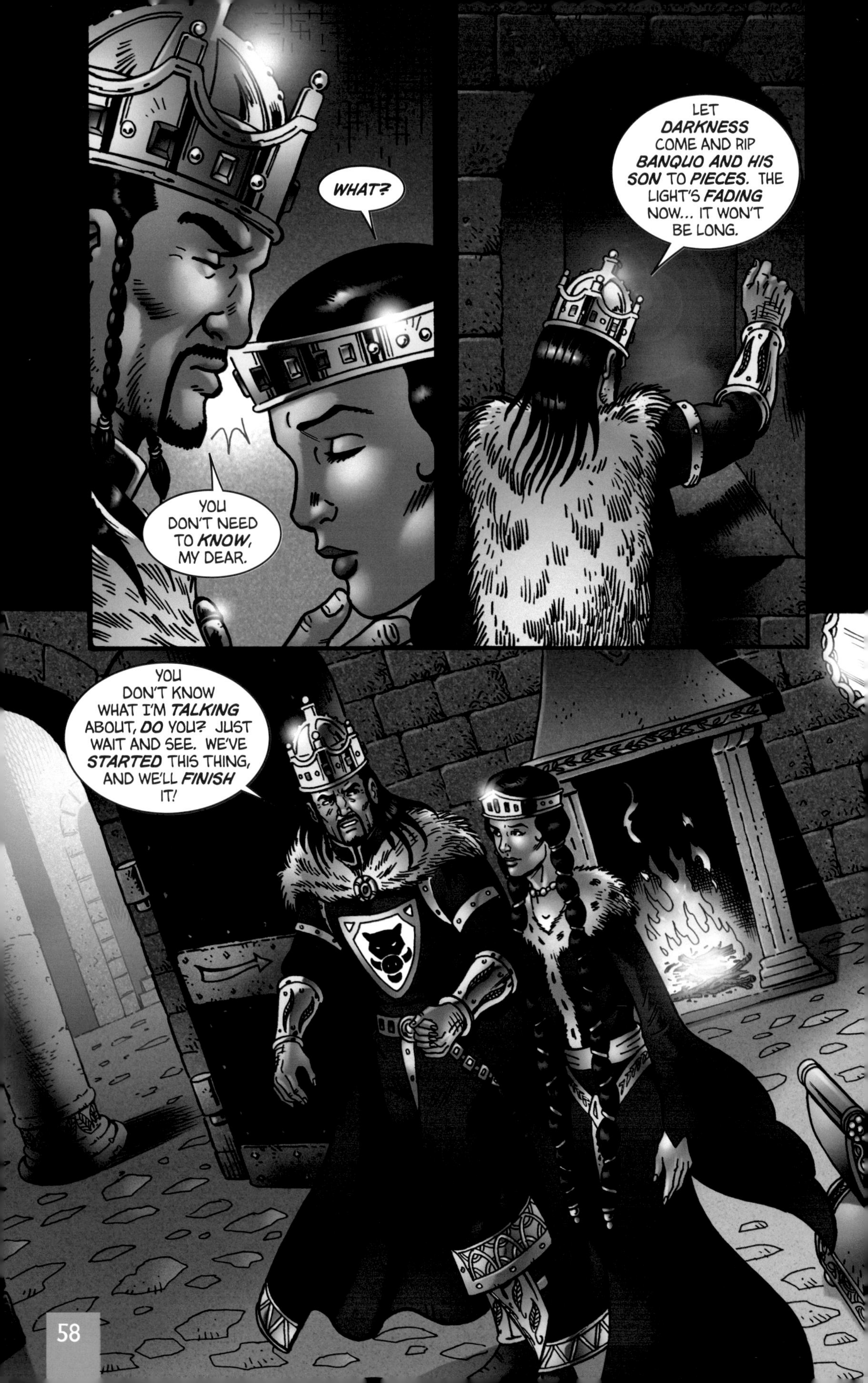
WHAT?
YOU DON'T NEED TO KNOW, MY DEAR.
LET DARKNESS COME AND RIP BANQUO AND HIS SON TO PIECES. THE LIGHT'S FADING NOW... IT WON'T BE LONG.
YOU DON'T KNOW WHAT I'M TALKING ABOUT, DO YOU? JUST WAIT AND SEE. WE'VE STARTED THIS THING, AND WE'LL FINISH IT!

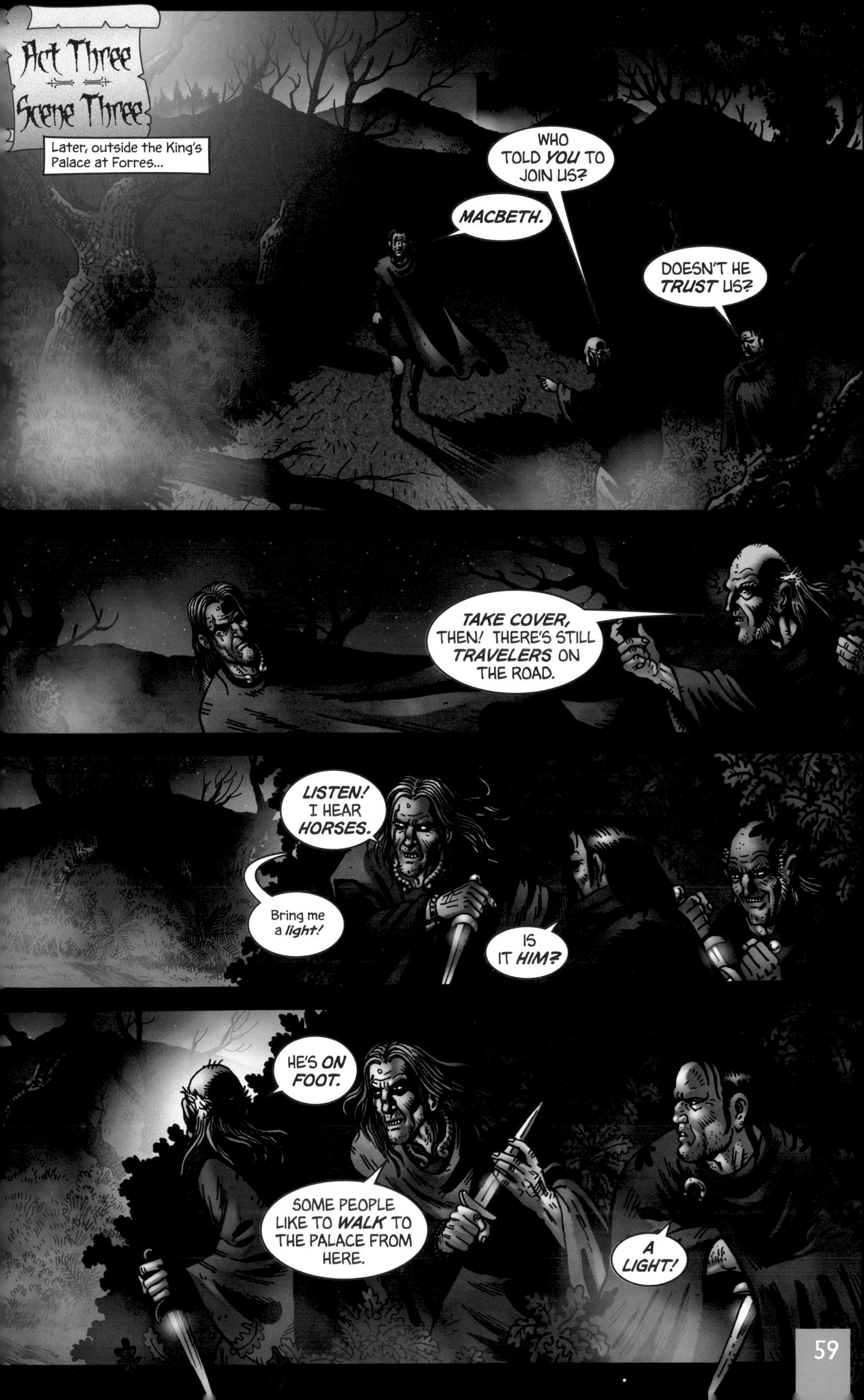
Act Three
Scene Three
Later, outside the King's Palace at Forres...
WHO TOLD *YOU* TO JOIN US?
MACBETH.
DOESN'T HE *TRUST* US?
TAKE COVER, THEN! THERE'S STILL *TRAVELERS* ON THE ROAD.
LISTEN! I HEAR *HORSES.*
Bring me a *light!*
IS IT *HIM?*
HE'S *ON FOOT.*
SOME PEOPLE LIKE TO *WALK* TO THE PALACE FROM HERE.
A LIGHT!

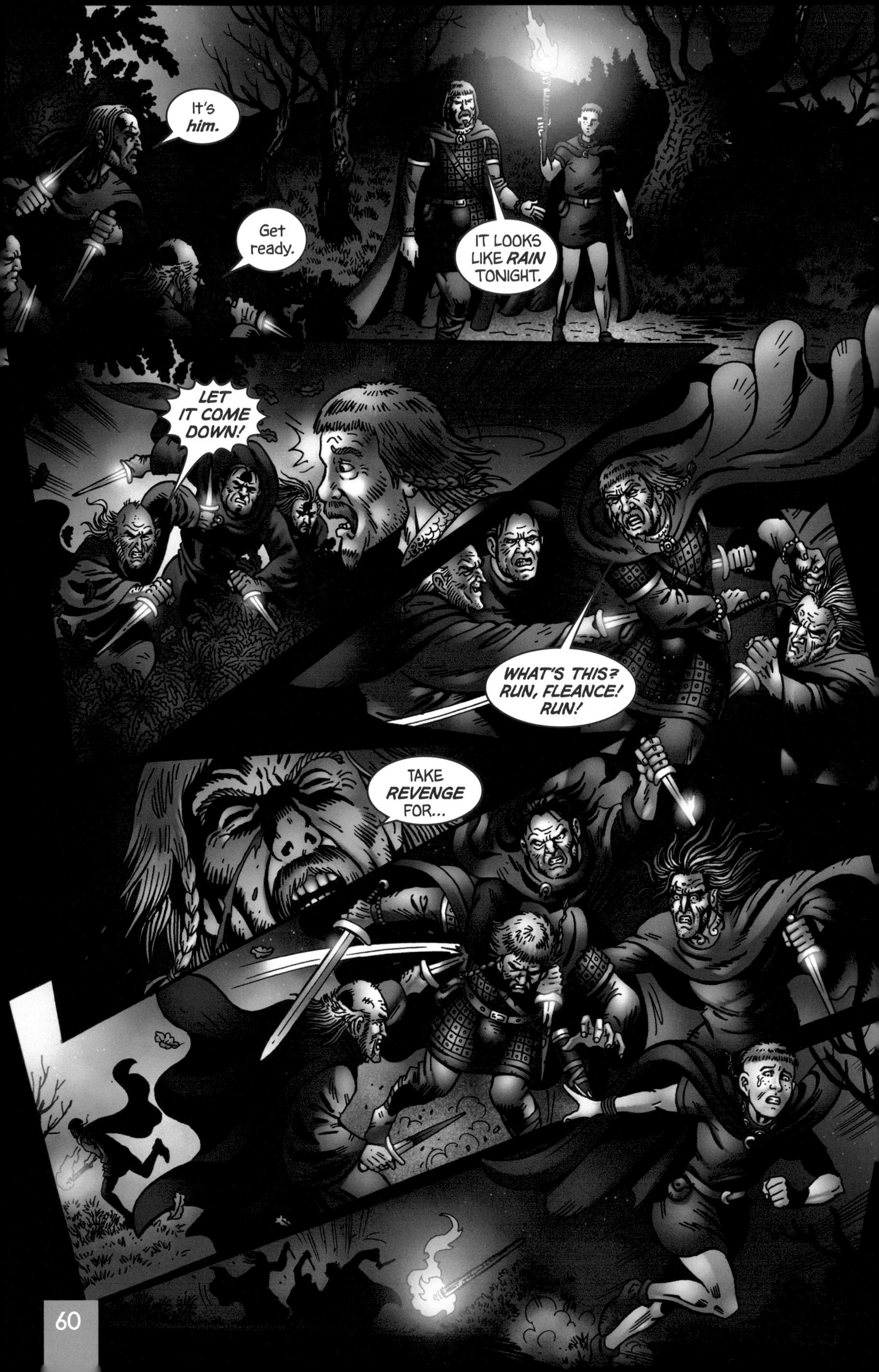
It's *him.*
Get ready.
IT LOOKS LIKE *RAIN* TONIGHT.
LET IT COME DOWN!
WHAT'S THIS? RUN, FLEANCE! RUN!
TAKE *REVENGE* FOR...

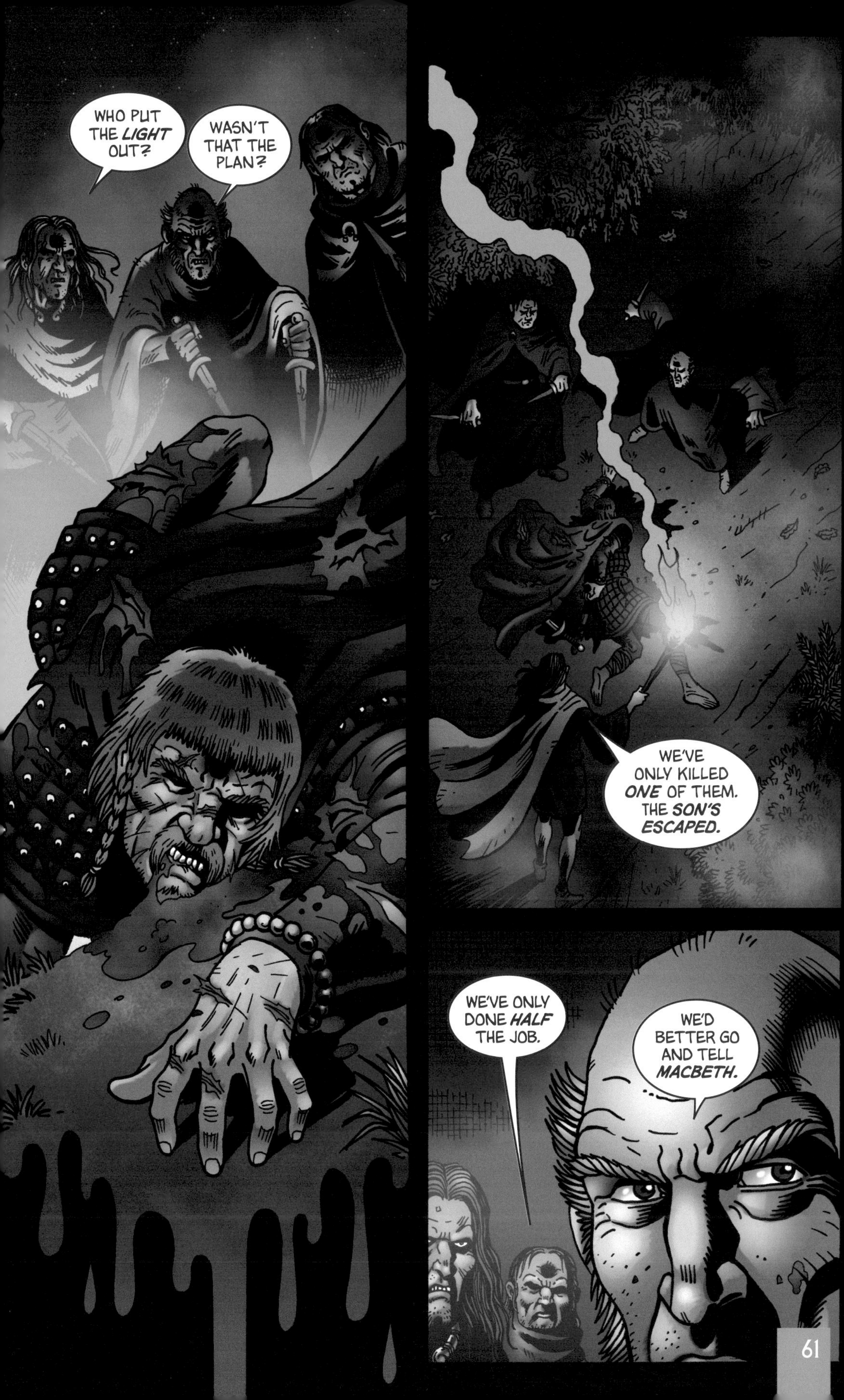

WHO PUT THE *LIGHT* OUT?
WASN'T THAT THE PLAN?
WE'VE ONLY KILLED *ONE* OF THEM. THE *SON'S ESCAPED.*
WE'VE ONLY DONE *HALF* THE JOB.
WE'D BETTER GO AND TELL *MACBETH.*

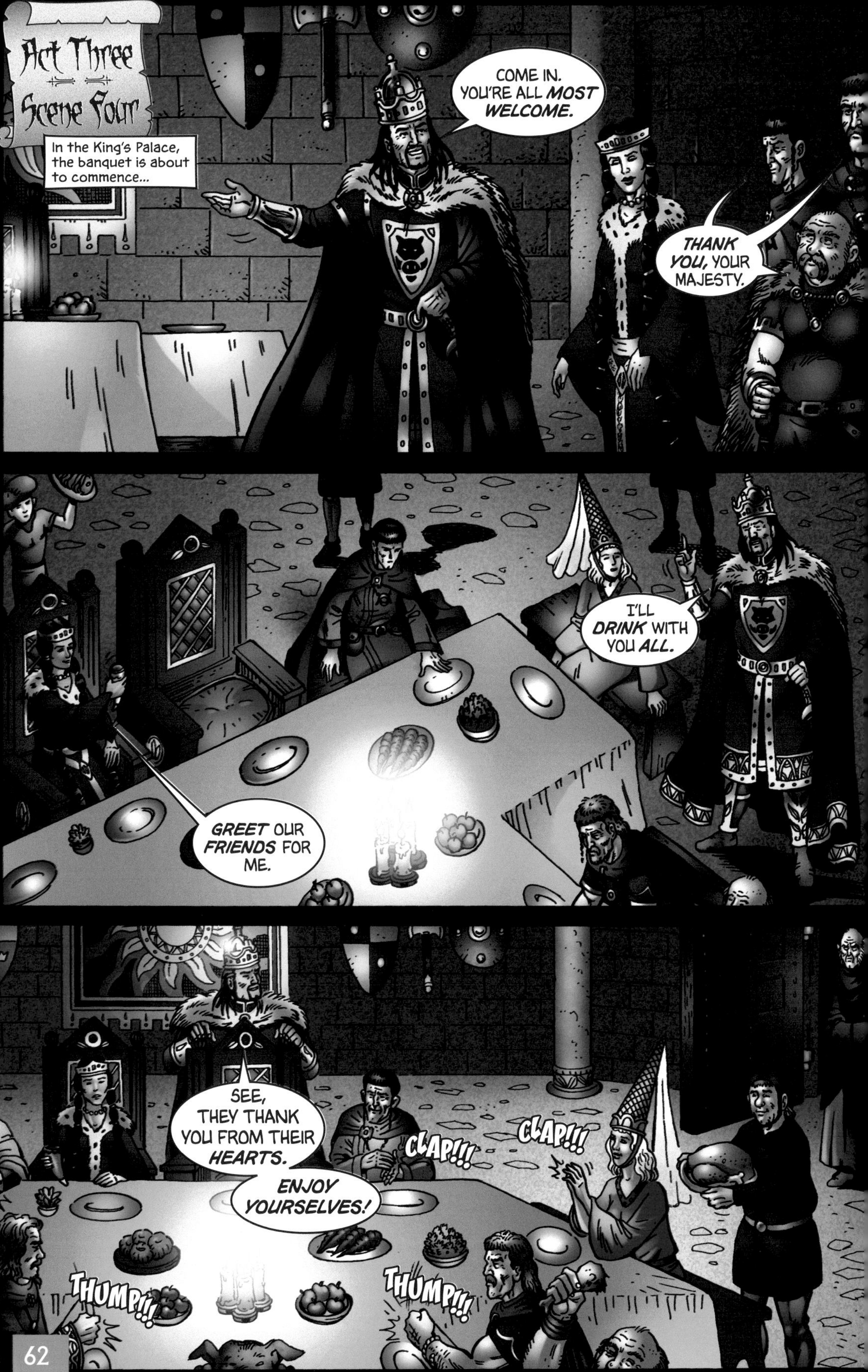
Act Three
Scene Four
In the King's Palace, the banquet is about to commence...
COME IN. YOU'RE ALL MOST WELCOME.
THANK YOU, YOUR MAJESTY.
I'LL DRINK WITH YOU ALL.
GREET OUR FRIENDS FOR ME.
SEE, THEY THANK YOU FROM THEIR HEARTS.
ENJOY YOURSELVES!
CLAP!!!
CLAP!!!
THUMP!!!
THUMP!!!

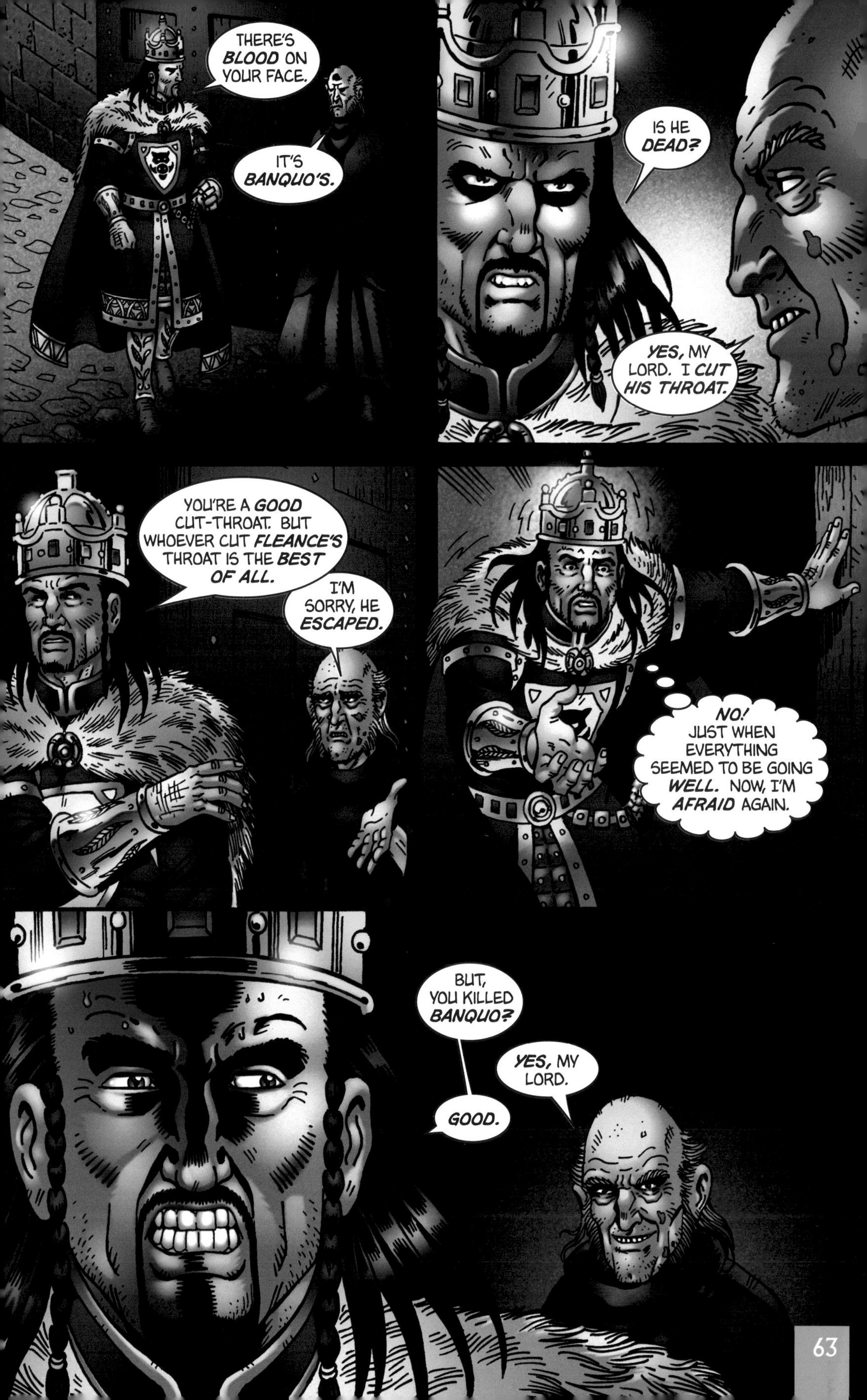
THERE'S BLOOD ON YOUR FACE.
IT'S BANQUO'S.
IS HE DEAD?
YES, MY LORD. I CUT HIS THROAT.
YOU'RE A GOOD CUT-THROAT. BUT WHOEVER CUT FLEANCE'S THROAT IS THE BEST OF ALL.
I'M SORRY, HE ESCAPED.
NO! JUST WHEN EVERYTHING SEEMED TO BE GOING WELL. NOW, I'M AFRAID AGAIN.
BUT, YOU KILLED BANQUO?
YES, MY LORD.
GOOD.

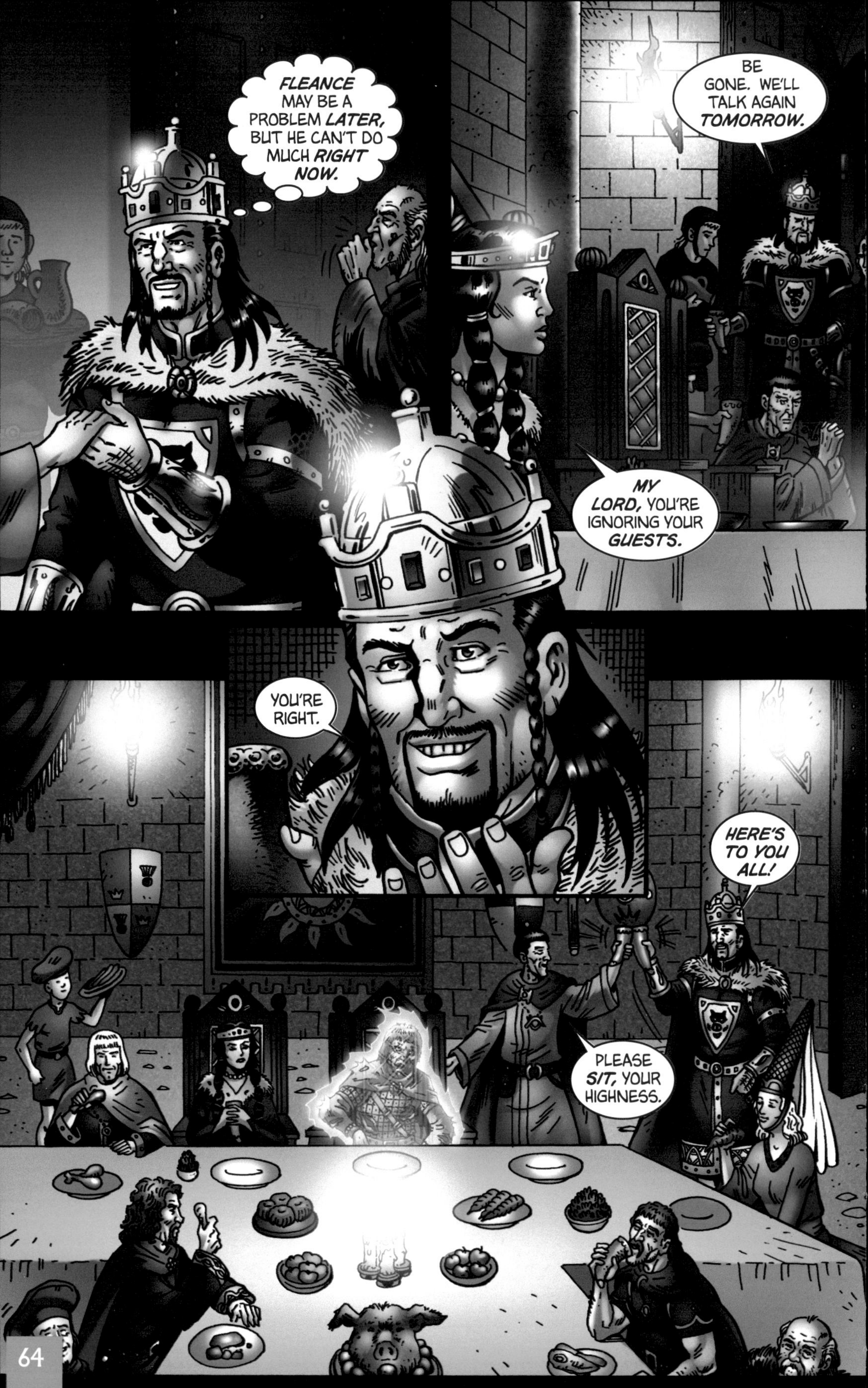
FLEANCE MAY BE A PROBLEM LATER, BUT HE CAN'T DO MUCH RIGHT NOW.
BE GONE. WE'LL TALK AGAIN TOMORROW.
MY LORD, YOU'RE IGNORING YOUR GUESTS.
YOU'RE RIGHT.
HERE'S TO YOU ALL!
PLEASE SIT, YOUR HIGHNESS.

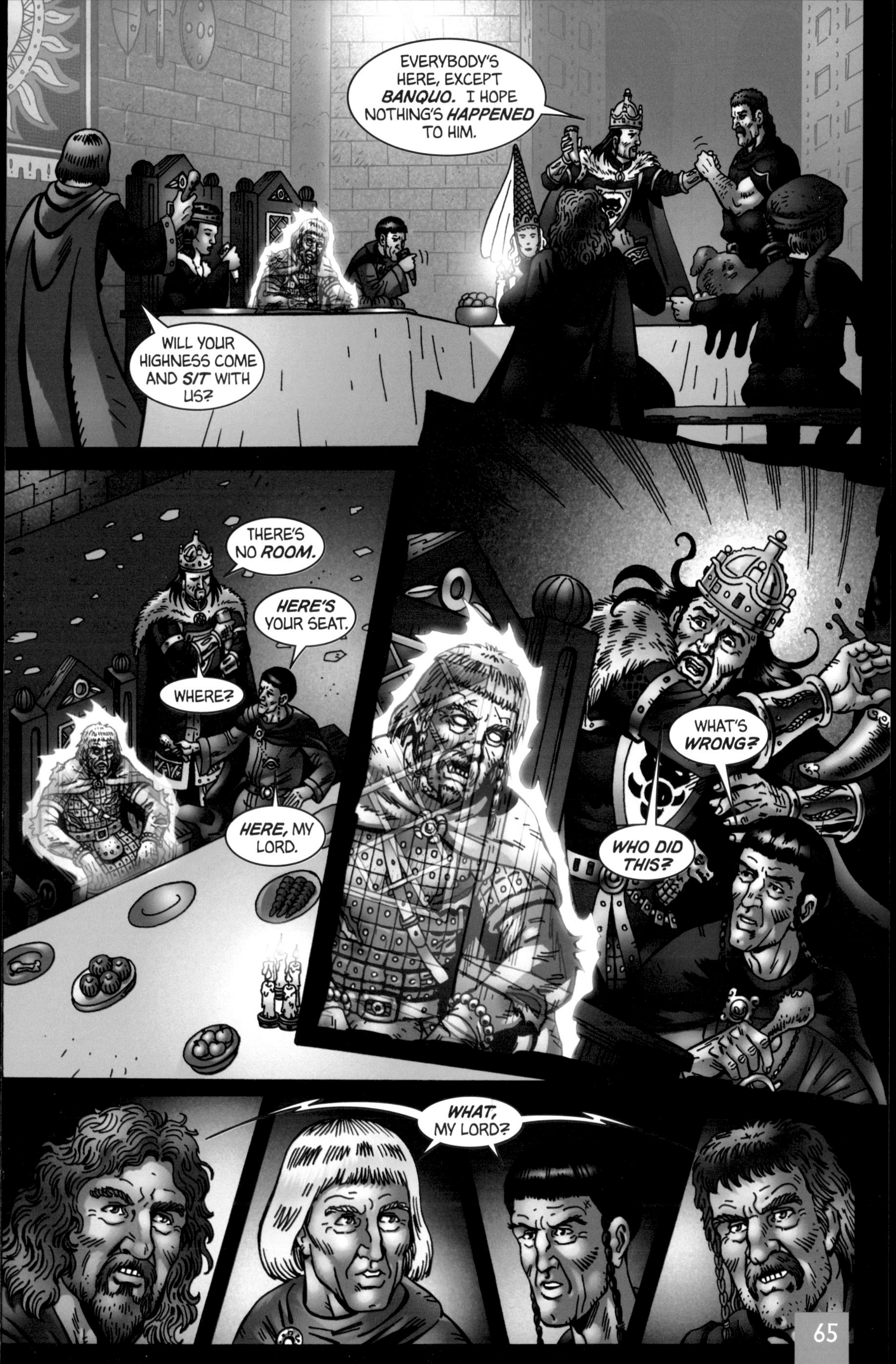
EVERYBODY'S HERE, EXCEPT BANQUO. I HOPE NOTHING'S HAPPENED TO HIM.
WILL YOUR HIGHNESS COME AND SIT WITH US?
THERE'S NO ROOM.
HERE'S YOUR SEAT.
WHERE?
HERE, MY LORD.
WHAT'S WRONG?
WHO DID THIS?
WHAT, MY LORD?

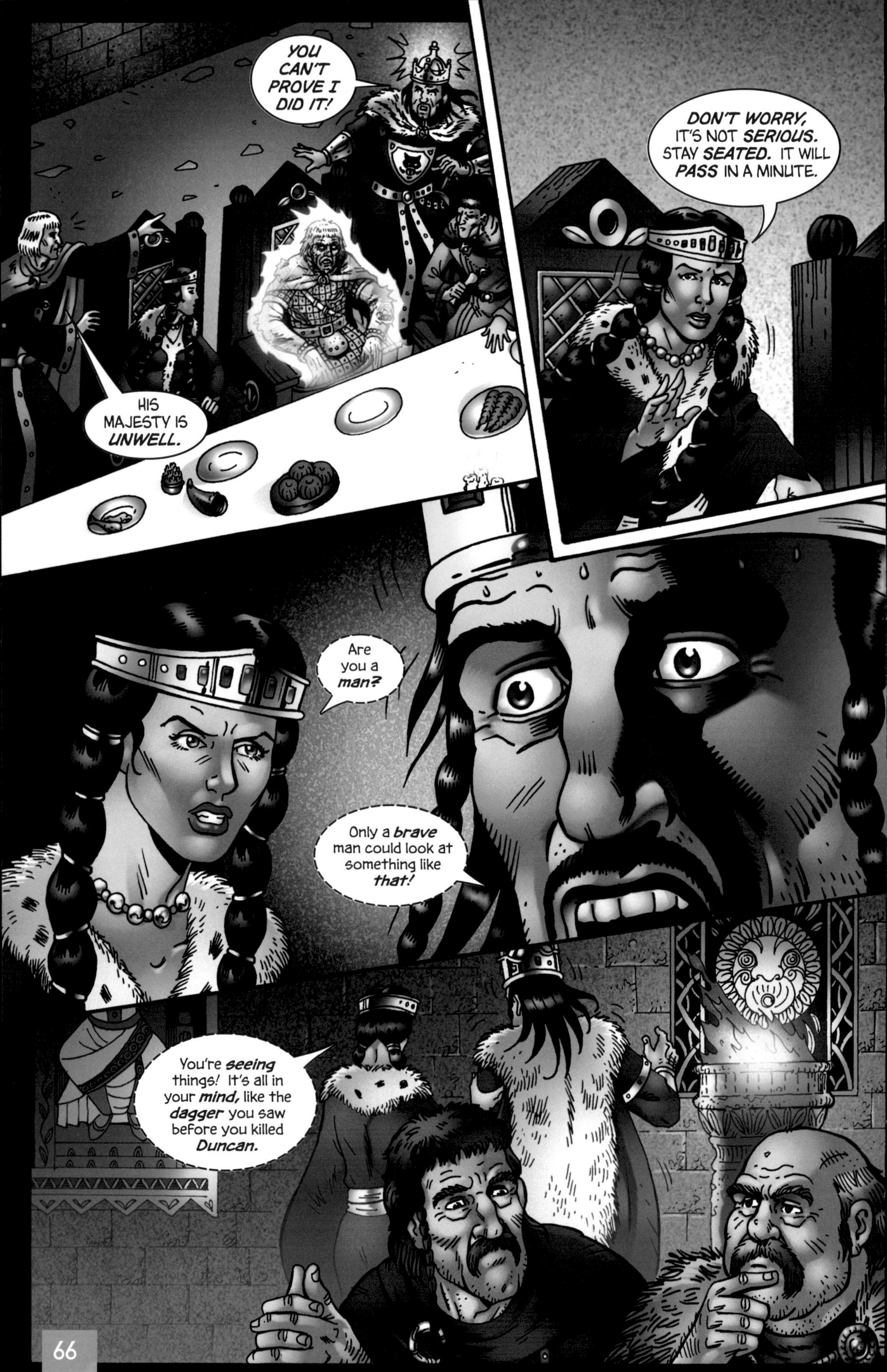
YOU CAN'T PROVE I DID IT!
HIS MAJESTY IS UNWELL.
DON'T WORRY, IT'S NOT SERIOUS. STAY SEATED. IT WILL PASS IN A MINUTE.
Are you a man?
Only a brave man could look at something like that!
You're seeing things! It's all in your mind, like the dagger you saw before you killed Duncan.

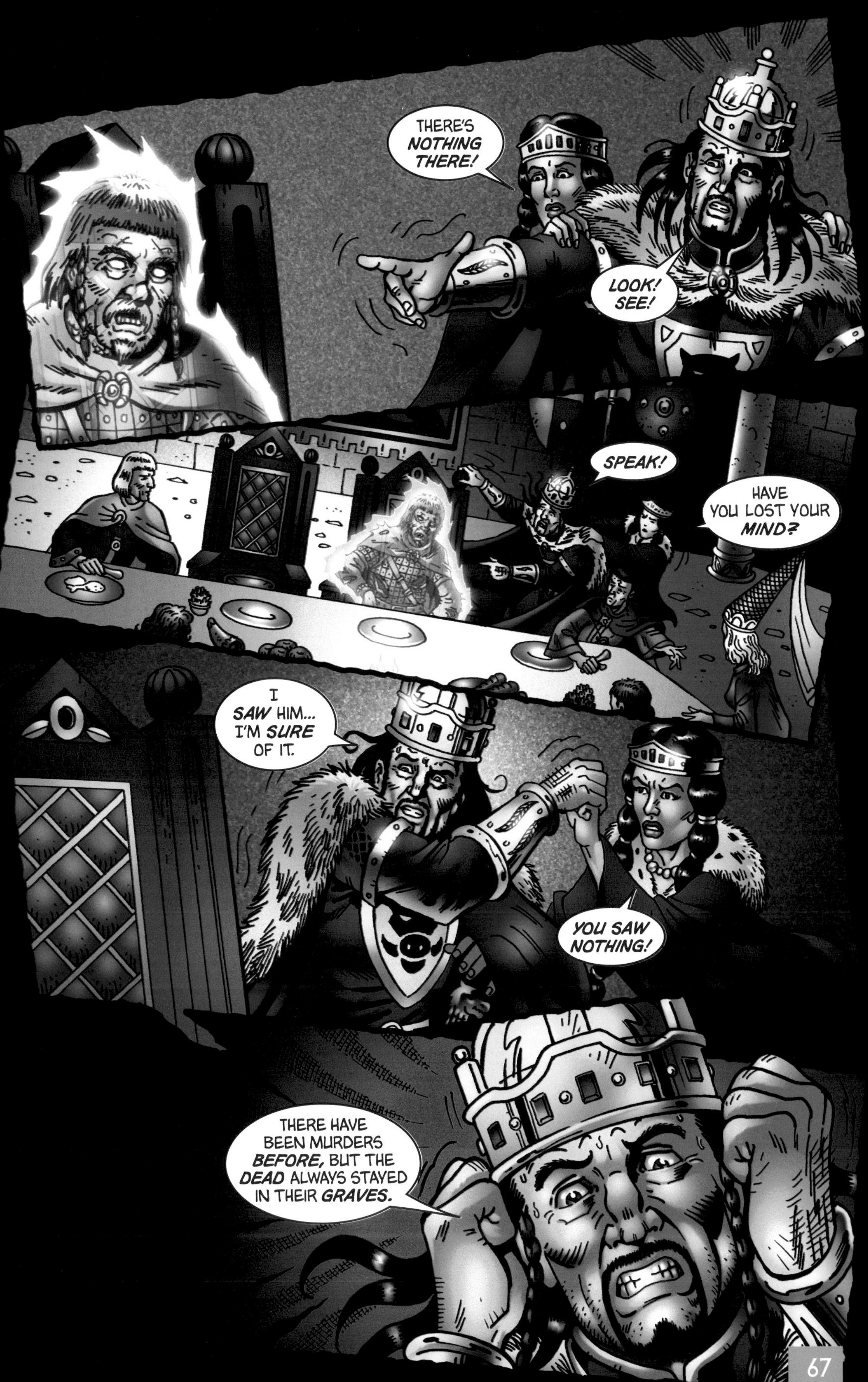
THERE'S NOTHING THERE!
LOOK! SEE!
SPEAK!
HAVE YOU LOST YOUR MIND?
I SAW HIM... I'M SURE OF IT.
YOU SAW NOTHING!
THERE HAVE BEEN MURDERS BEFORE, BUT THE DEAD ALWAYS STAYED IN THEIR GRAVES.

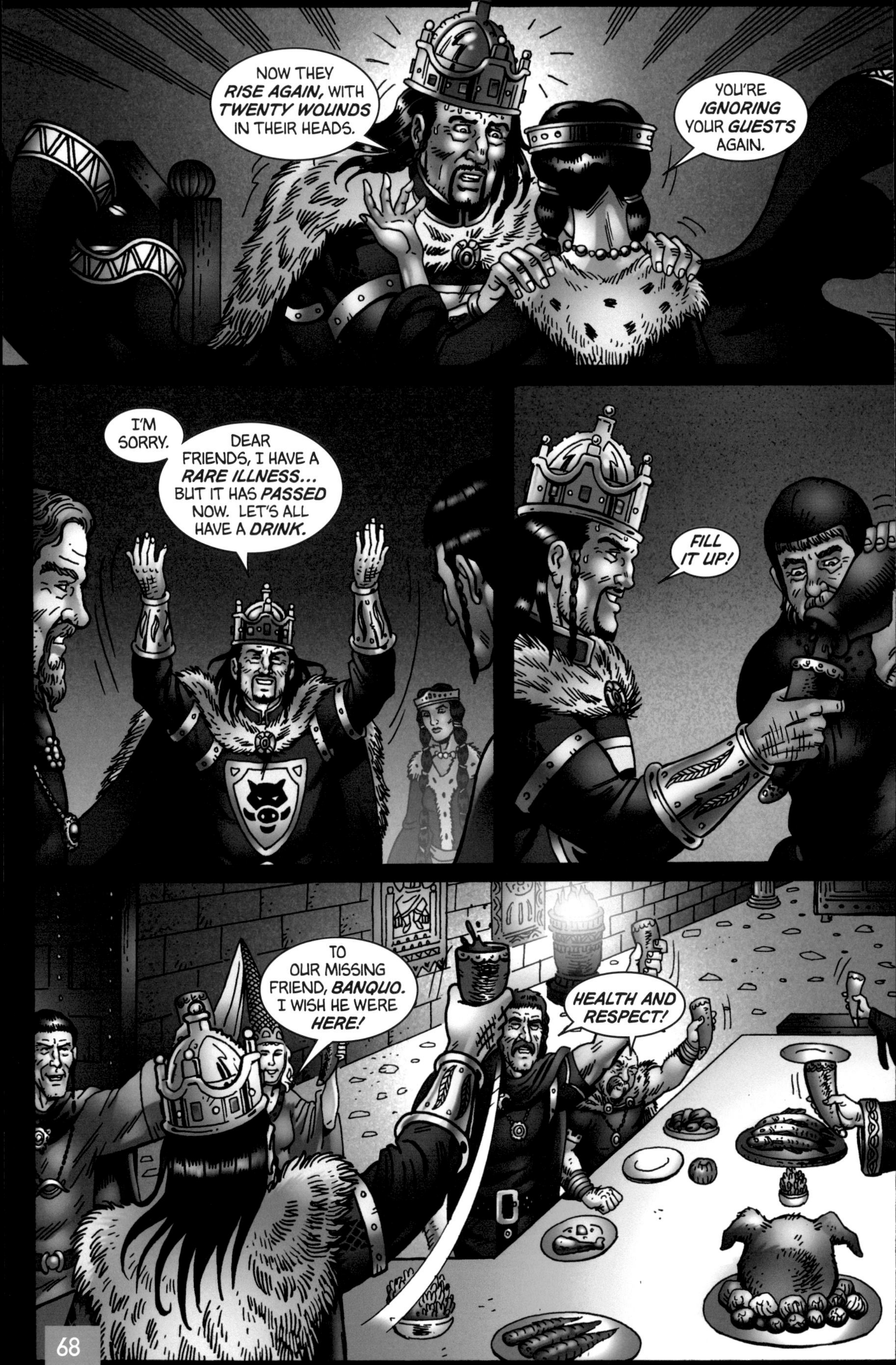
NOW THEY RISE AGAIN, WITH TWENTY WOUNDS IN THEIR HEADS.
YOU'RE IGNORING YOUR GUESTS AGAIN.
I'M SORRY.
DEAR FRIENDS, I HAVE A RARE ILLNESS... BUT IT HAS PASSED NOW. LET'S ALL HAVE A DRINK.
FILL IT UP!
TO OUR MISSING FRIEND, BANQUO. I WISH HE WERE HERE!
HEALTH AND RESPECT!

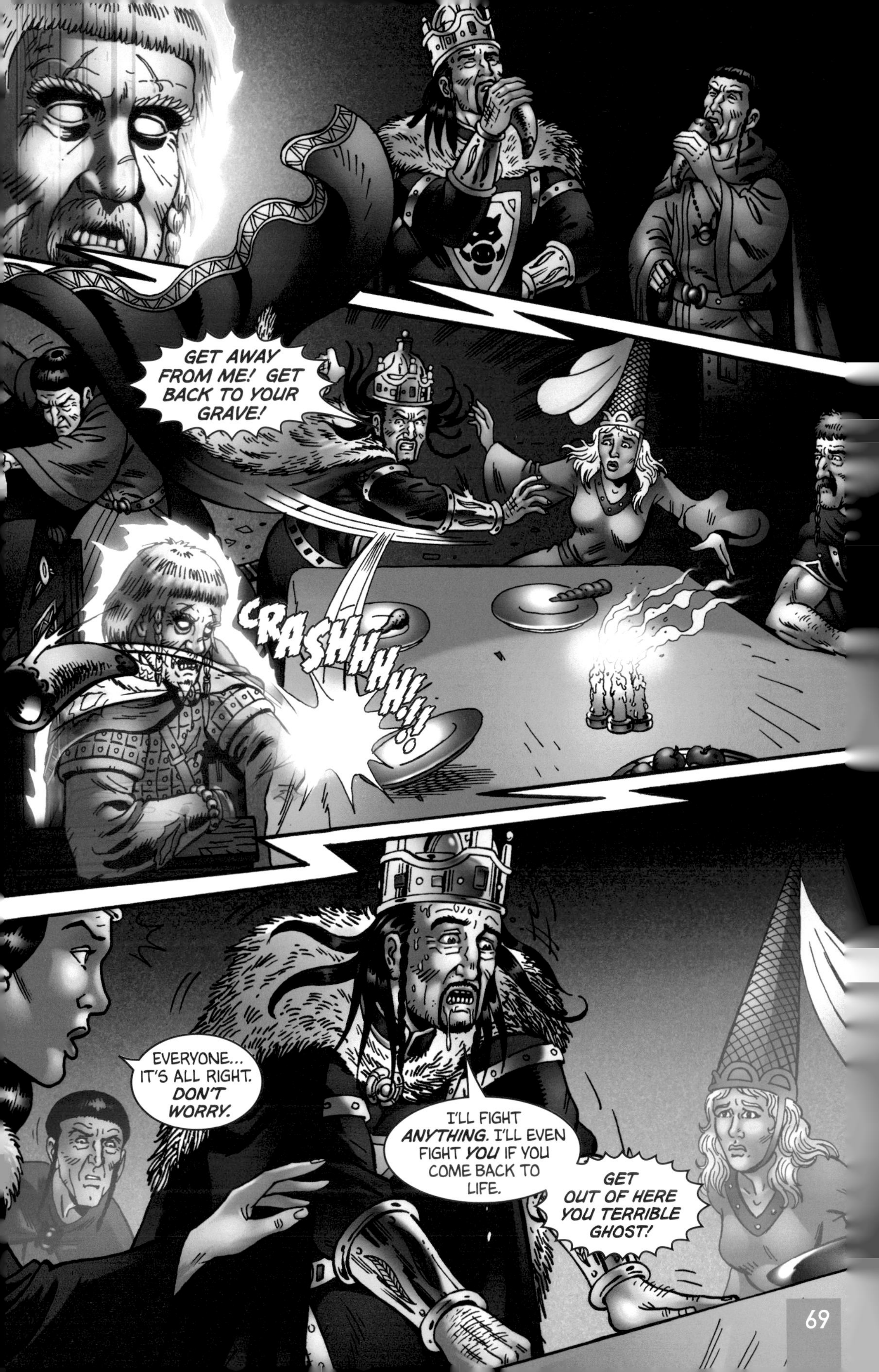
GET AWAY FROM ME! GET BACK TO YOUR GRAVE!
CRASHHHH!!!!
EVERYONE... IT'S ALL RIGHT. DON'T WORRY.
I'LL FIGHT ANYTHING. I'LL EVEN FIGHT YOU IF YOU COME BACK TO LIFE.
GET OUT OF HERE YOU TERRIBLE GHOST!

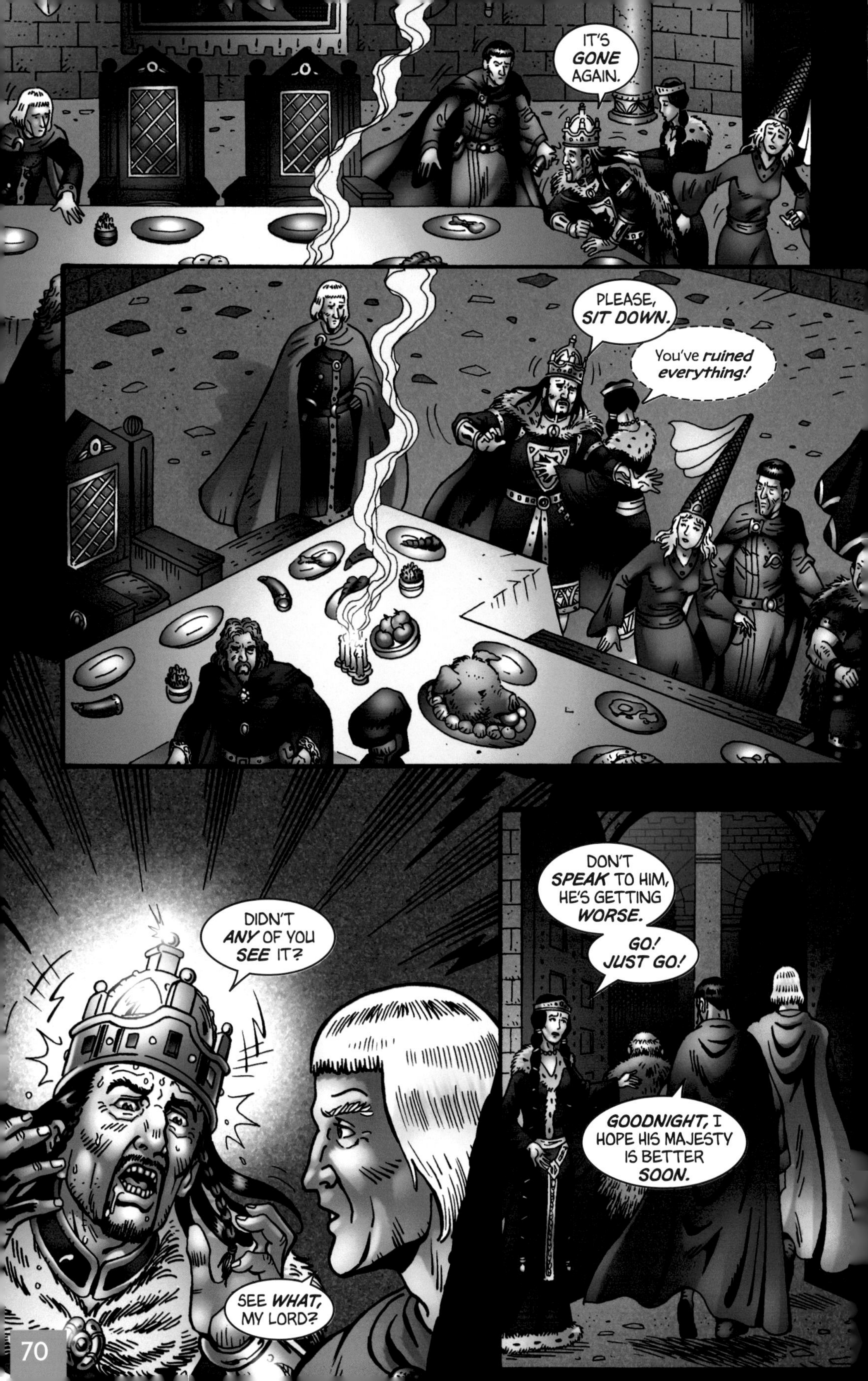
IT'S GONE AGAIN.
PLEASE, SIT DOWN.
You've ruined everything!
DIDN'T ANY OF YOU SEE IT?
SEE WHAT, MY LORD?
DON'T SPEAK TO HIM, HE'S GETTING WORSE.
GO! JUST GO!
GOODNIGHT, I HOPE HIS MAJESTY IS BETTER SOON.

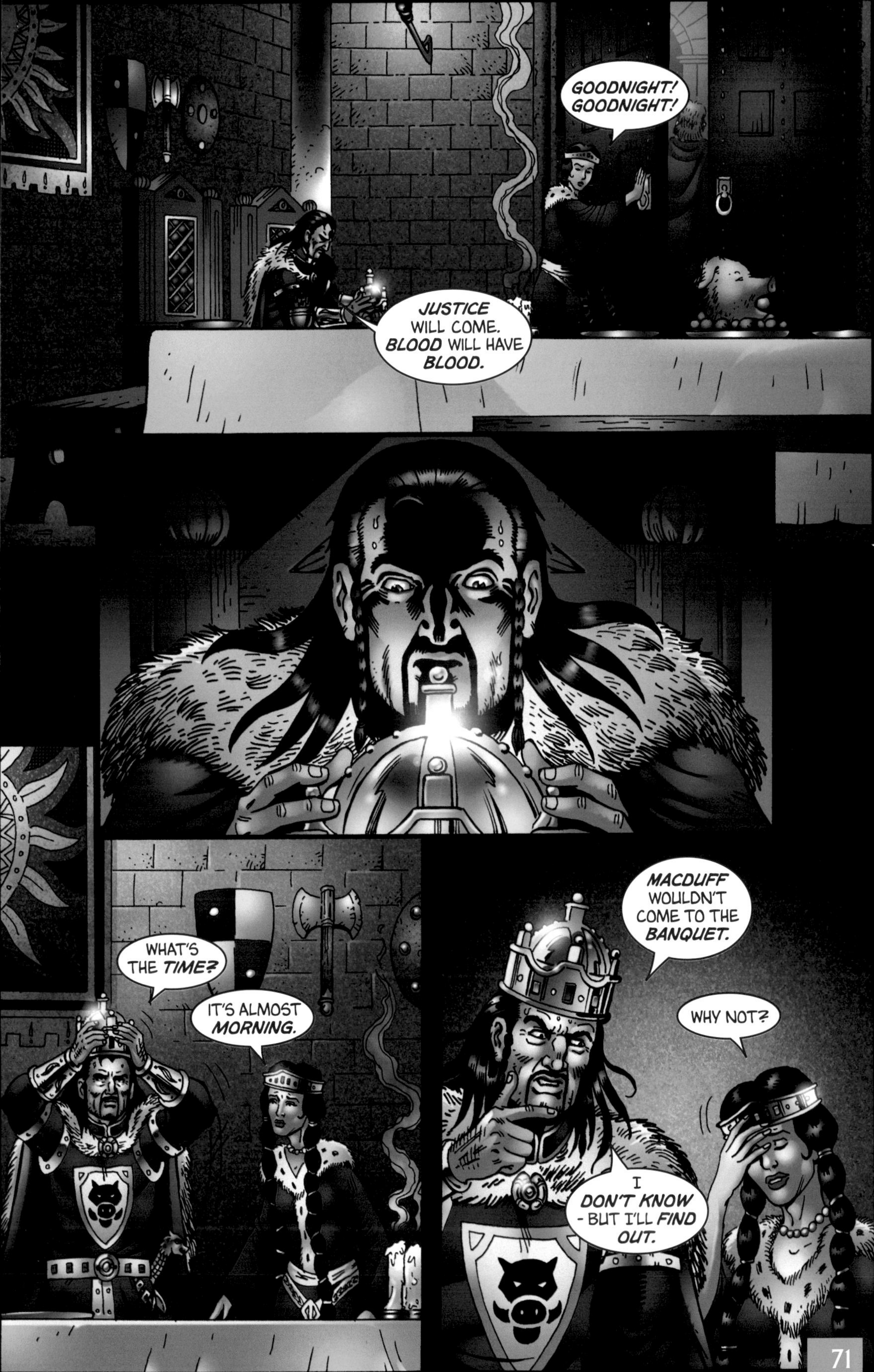
GOODNIGHT! GOODNIGHT!
JUSTICE WILL COME. BLOOD WILL HAVE BLOOD.
WHAT'S THE TIME?
IT'S ALMOST MORNING.
MACDUFF WOULDN'T COME TO THE BANQUET.
WHY NOT?
I DON'T KNOW - BUT I'LL FIND OUT.

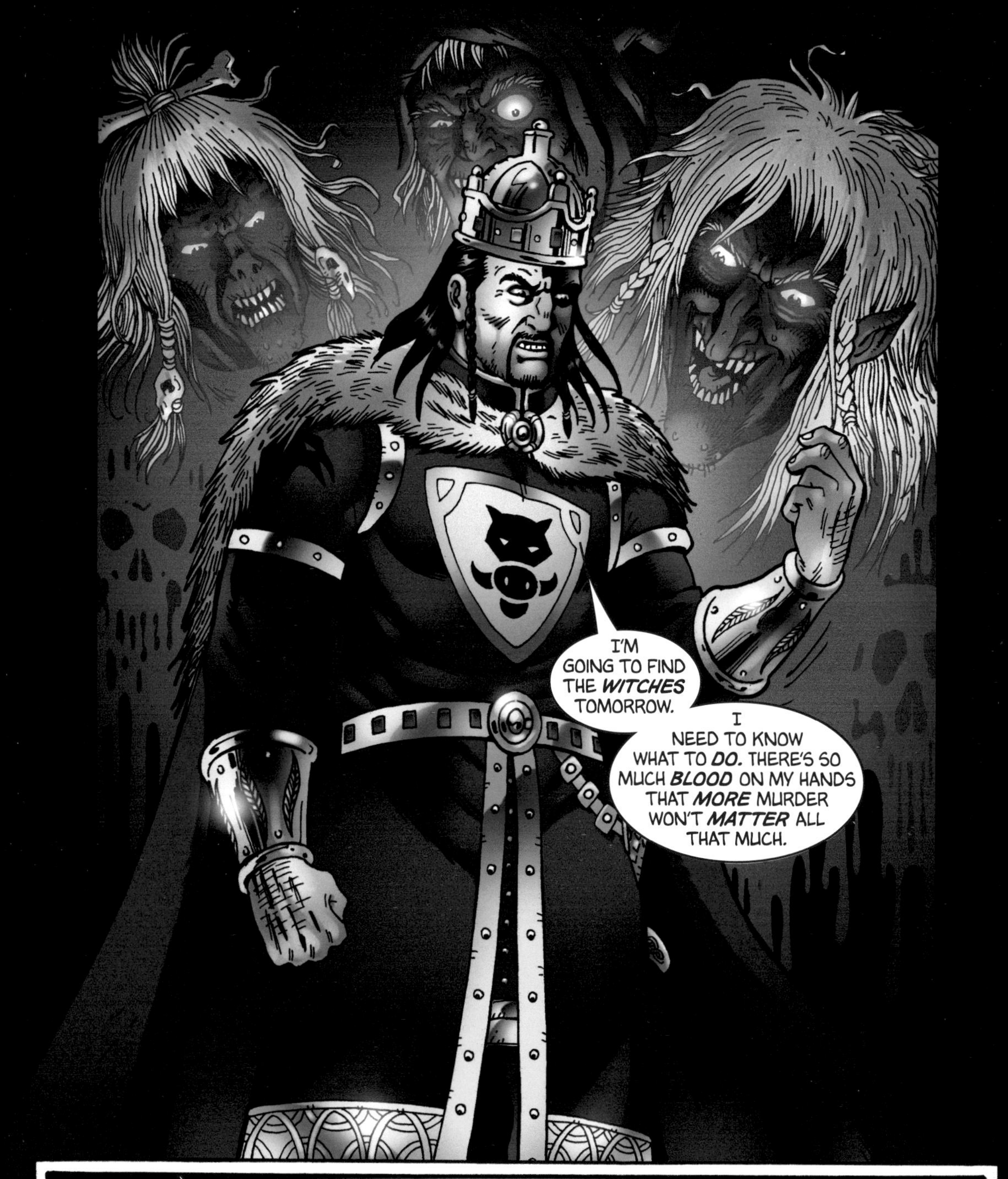
I'M GOING TO FIND THE *WITCHES* TOMORROW.
I NEED TO KNOW WHAT TO *DO.* THERE'S SO MUCH *BLOOD* ON MY HANDS THAT *MORE* MURDER WON'T *MATTER* ALL THAT MUCH.

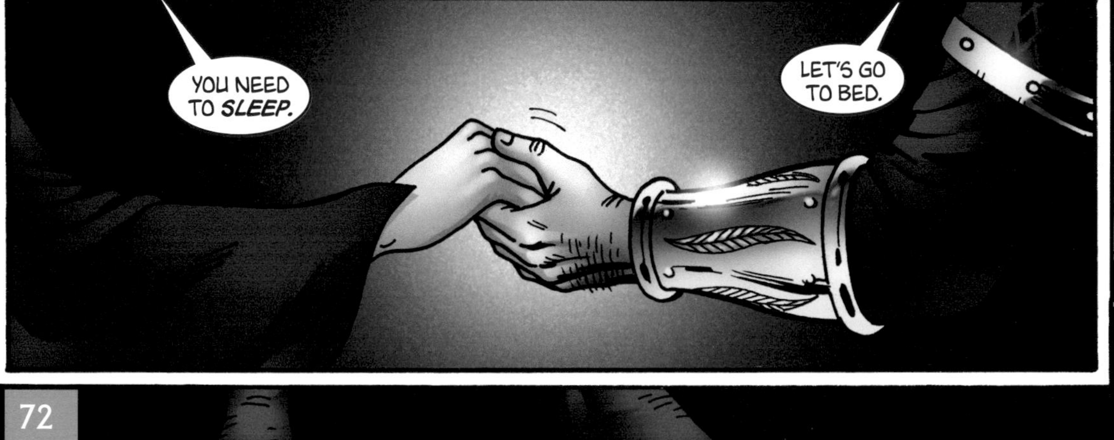
YOU NEED TO *SLEEP.*
LET'S GO TO BED.

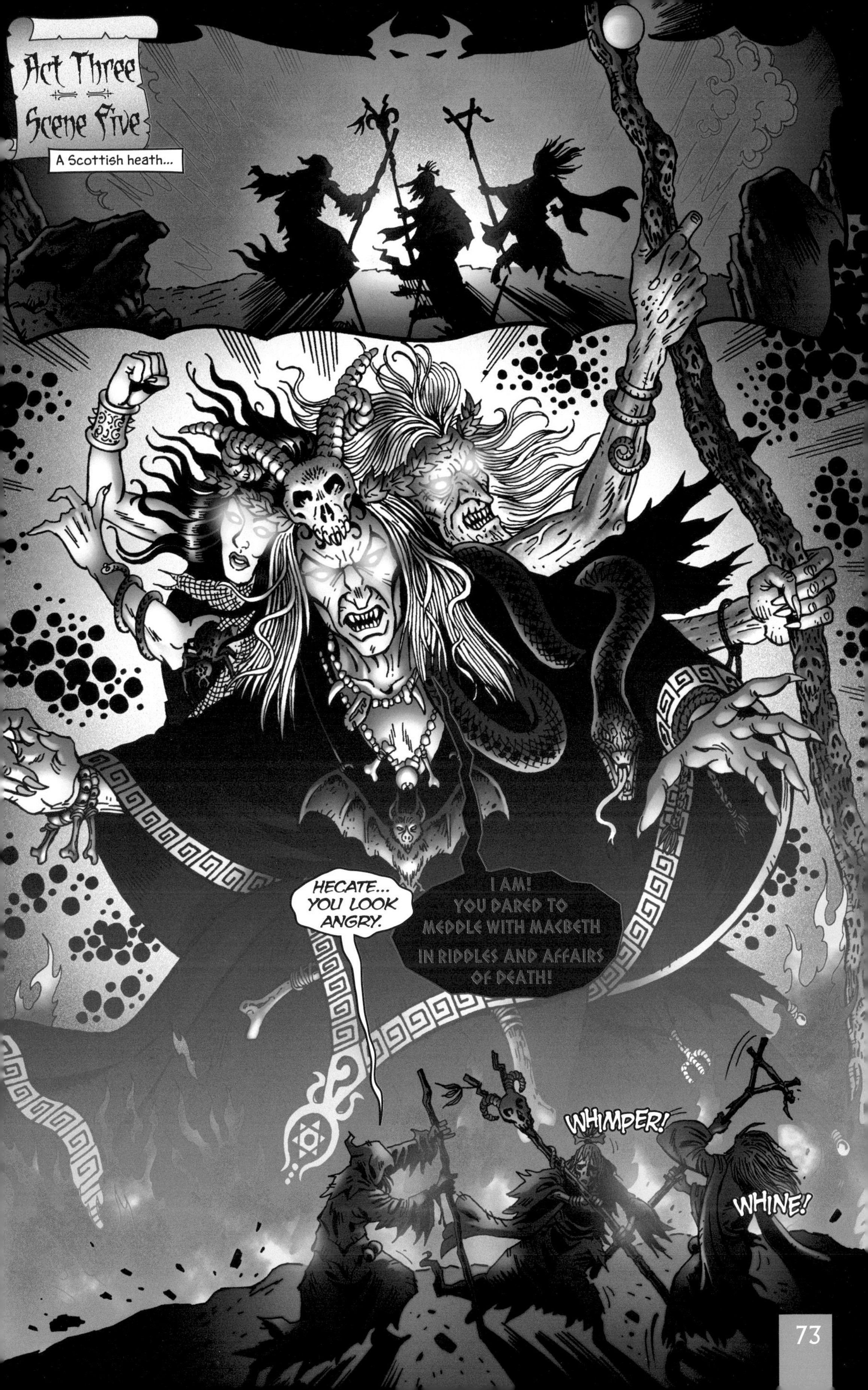

Act Three
Scene Five
A Scottish heath...
HECATE... YOU LOOK ANGRY.
I AM! YOU DARED TO MEDDLE WITH MACBETH
IN RIDDLES AND AFFAIRS OF DEATH!
WHIMPER!
WHINE!

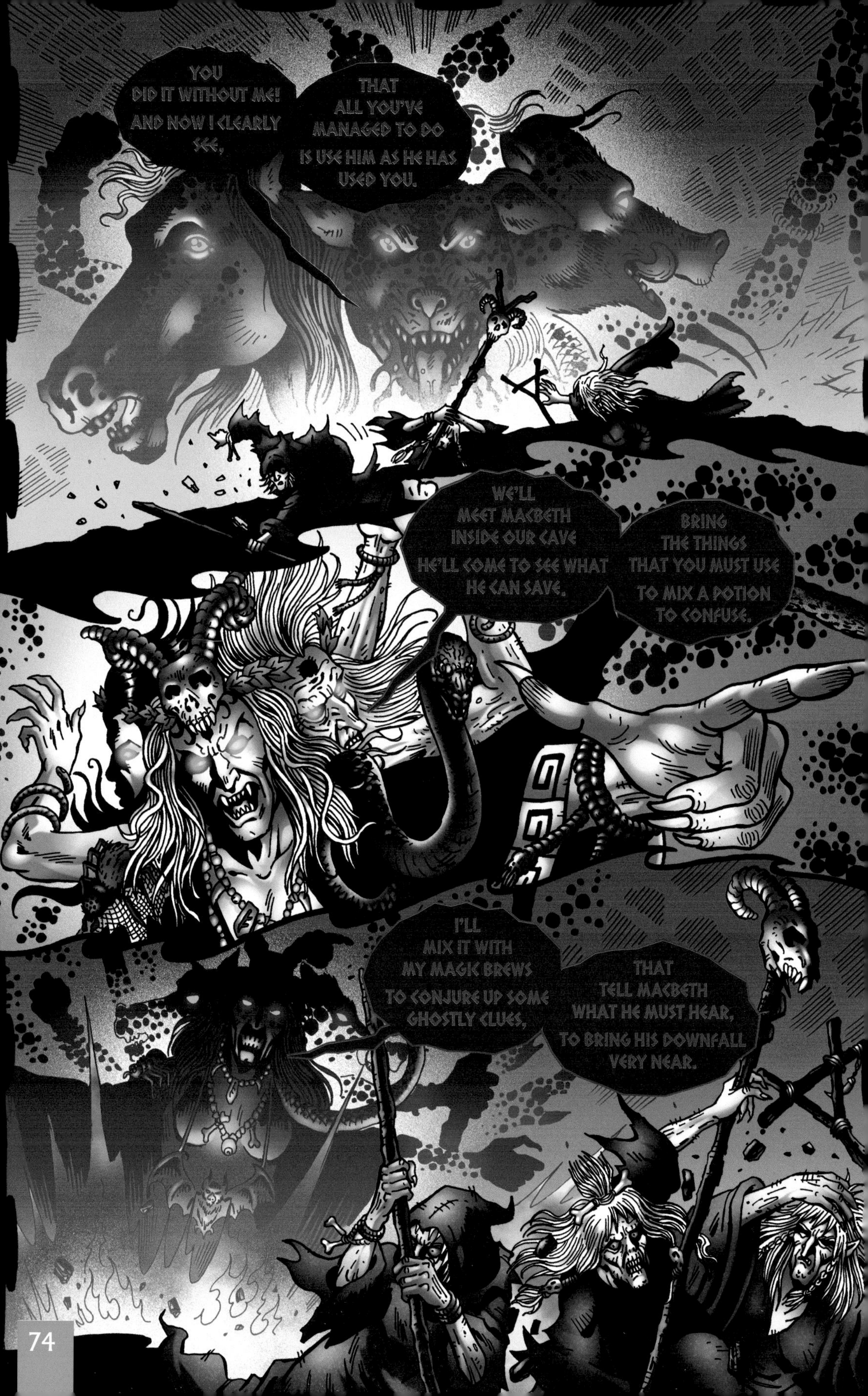
YOU DID IT WITHOUT ME! AND NOW I CLEARLY SEE,
THAT ALL YOU'VE MANAGED TO DO IS USE HIM AS HE HAS USED YOU.
WE'LL MEET MACBETH INSIDE OUR CAVE
HE'LL COME TO SEE WHAT HE CAN SAVE.
BRING THE THINGS THAT YOU MUST USE TO MIX A POTION TO CONFUSE.
I'LL MIX IT WITH MY MAGIC BREWS
TO CONJURE UP SOME GHOSTLY CLUES,
THAT TELL MACBETH WHAT HE MUST HEAR,
TO BRING HIS DOWNFALL VERY NEAR.

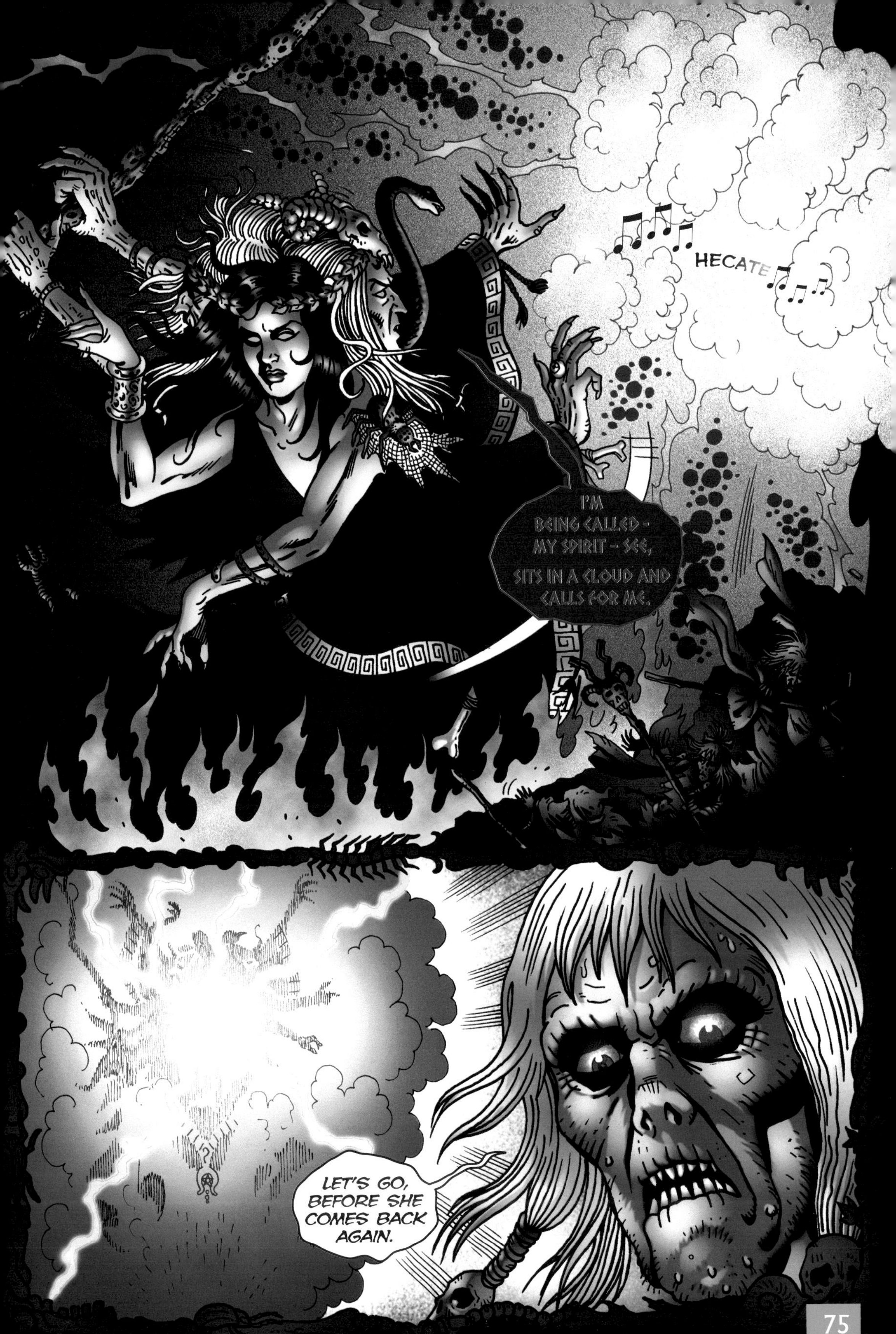
HECATE
I'M BEING CALLED - MY SPIRIT - SEE, SITS IN A CLOUD AND CALLS FOR ME.
LET'S GO, BEFORE SHE COMES BACK AGAIN.

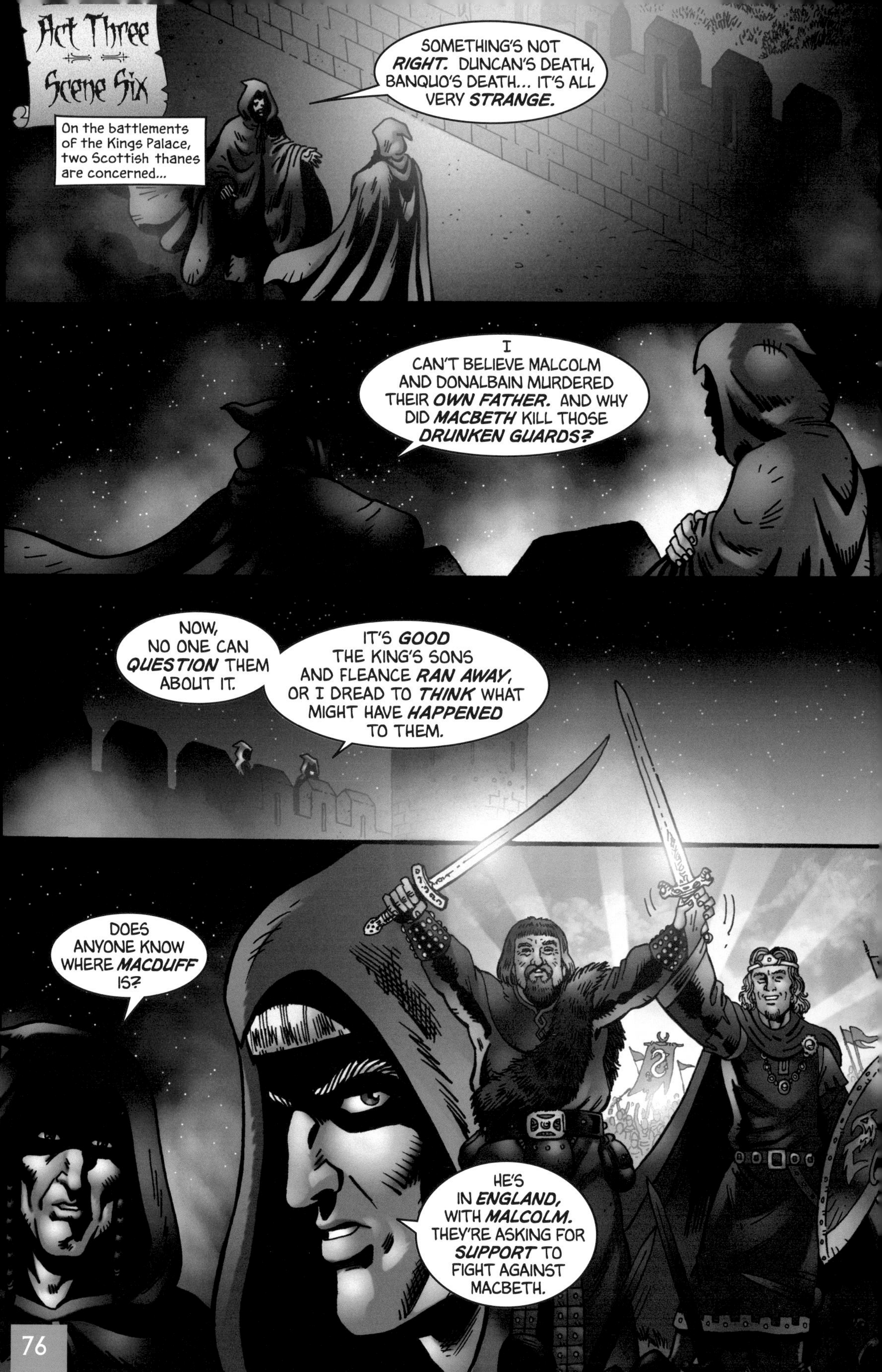
Act Three
Scene Six
On the battlements of the Kings Palace, two Scottish thanes are concerned...
SOMETHING'S NOT RIGHT. DUNCAN'S DEATH, BANQUO'S DEATH... IT'S ALL VERY STRANGE.
I CAN'T BELIEVE MALCOLM AND DONALBAIN MURDERED THEIR OWN FATHER. AND WHY DID MACBETH KILL THOSE DRUNKEN GUARDS?
NOW, NO ONE CAN QUESTION THEM ABOUT IT.
IT'S GOOD THE KING'S SONS AND FLEANCE RAN AWAY, OR I DREAD TO THINK WHAT MIGHT HAVE HAPPENED TO THEM.
DOES ANYONE KNOW WHERE MACDUFF IS?
HE'S IN ENGLAND, WITH MALCOLM. THEY'RE ASKING FOR SUPPORT TO FIGHT AGAINST MACBETH.

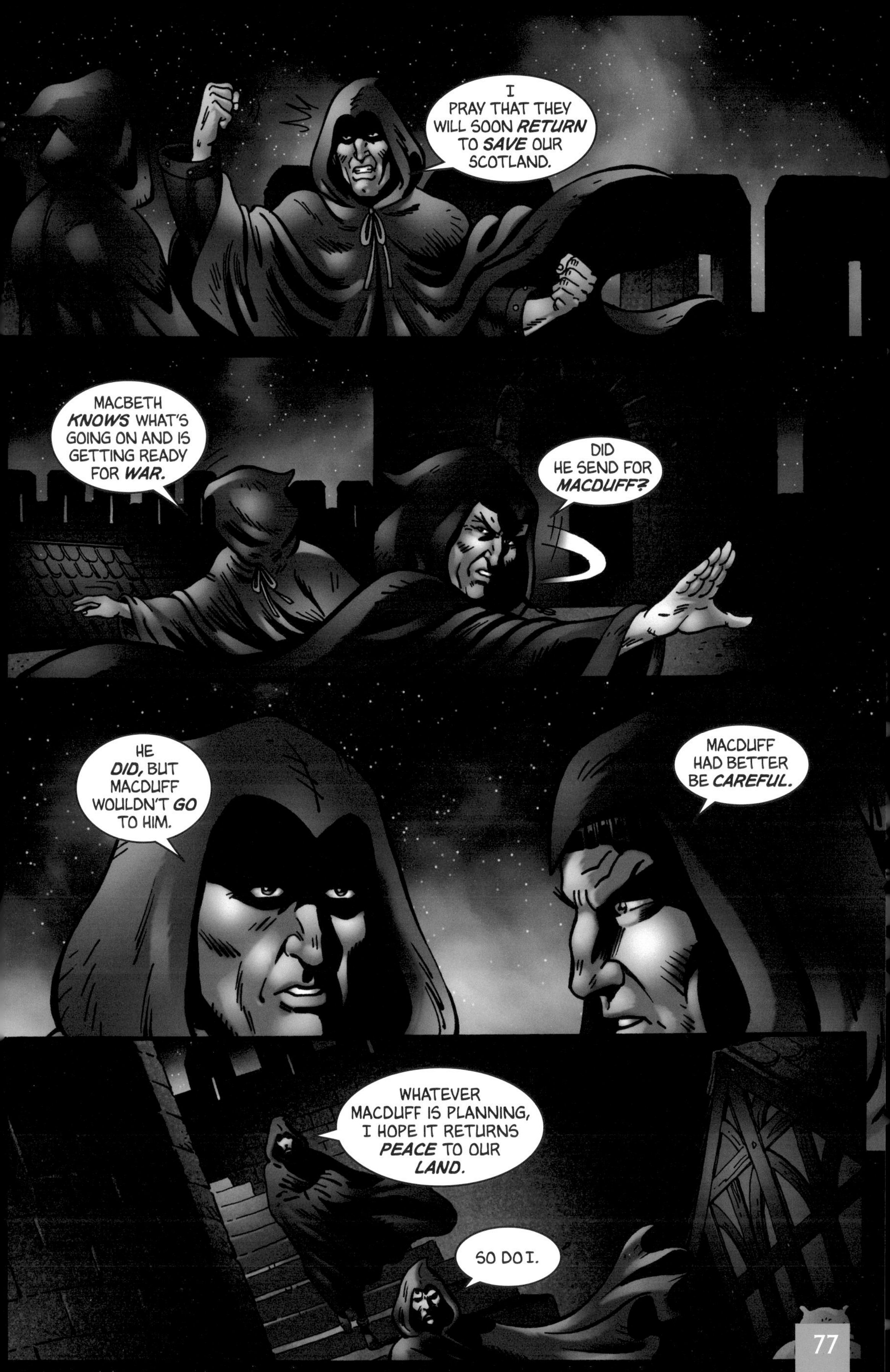
I PRAY THAT THEY WILL SOON RETURN TO SAVE OUR SCOTLAND.
MACBETH KNOWS WHAT'S GOING ON AND IS GETTING READY FOR WAR.
DID HE SEND FOR MACDUFF?
HE DID, BUT MACDUFF WOULDN'T GO TO HIM.
MACDUFF HAD BETTER BE CAREFUL.
WHATEVER MACDUFF IS PLANNING, I HOPE IT RETURNS PEACE TO OUR LAND.
SO DO I.

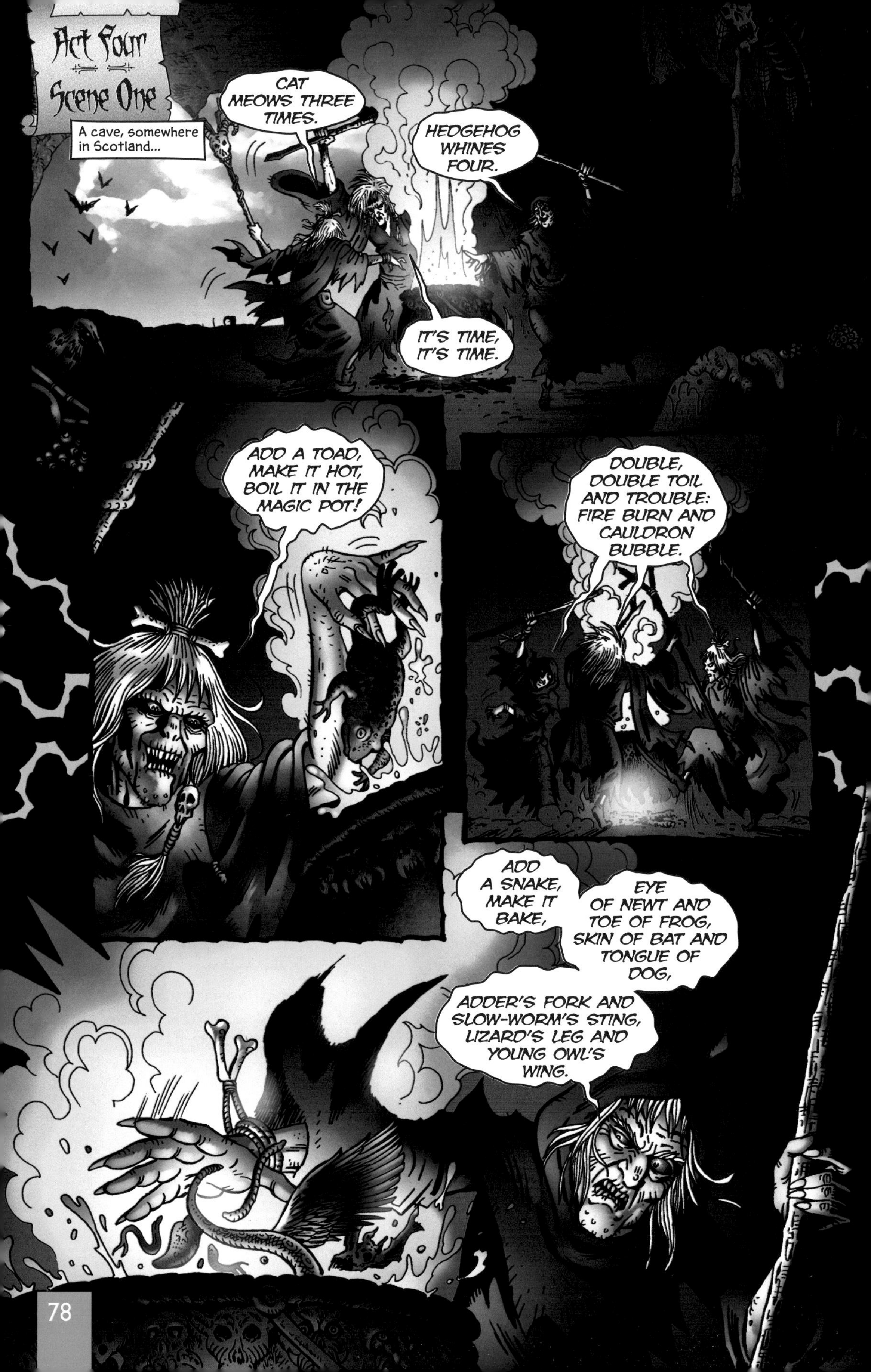
Act Four
Scene One
A cave, somewhere in Scotland...
CAT MEOWS THREE TIMES.
HEDGEHOG WHINES FOUR.
IT'S TIME, IT'S TIME.
ADD A TOAD, MAKE IT HOT, BOIL IT IN THE MAGIC POT!
DOUBLE, DOUBLE TOIL AND TROUBLE: FIRE BURN AND CAULDRON BUBBLE.
ADD A SNAKE, MAKE IT BAKE,
EYE OF NEWT AND TOE OF FROG, SKIN OF BAT AND TONGUE OF DOG,
ADDER'S FORK AND SLOW-WORM'S STING, LIZARD'S LEG AND YOUNG OWL'S WING.

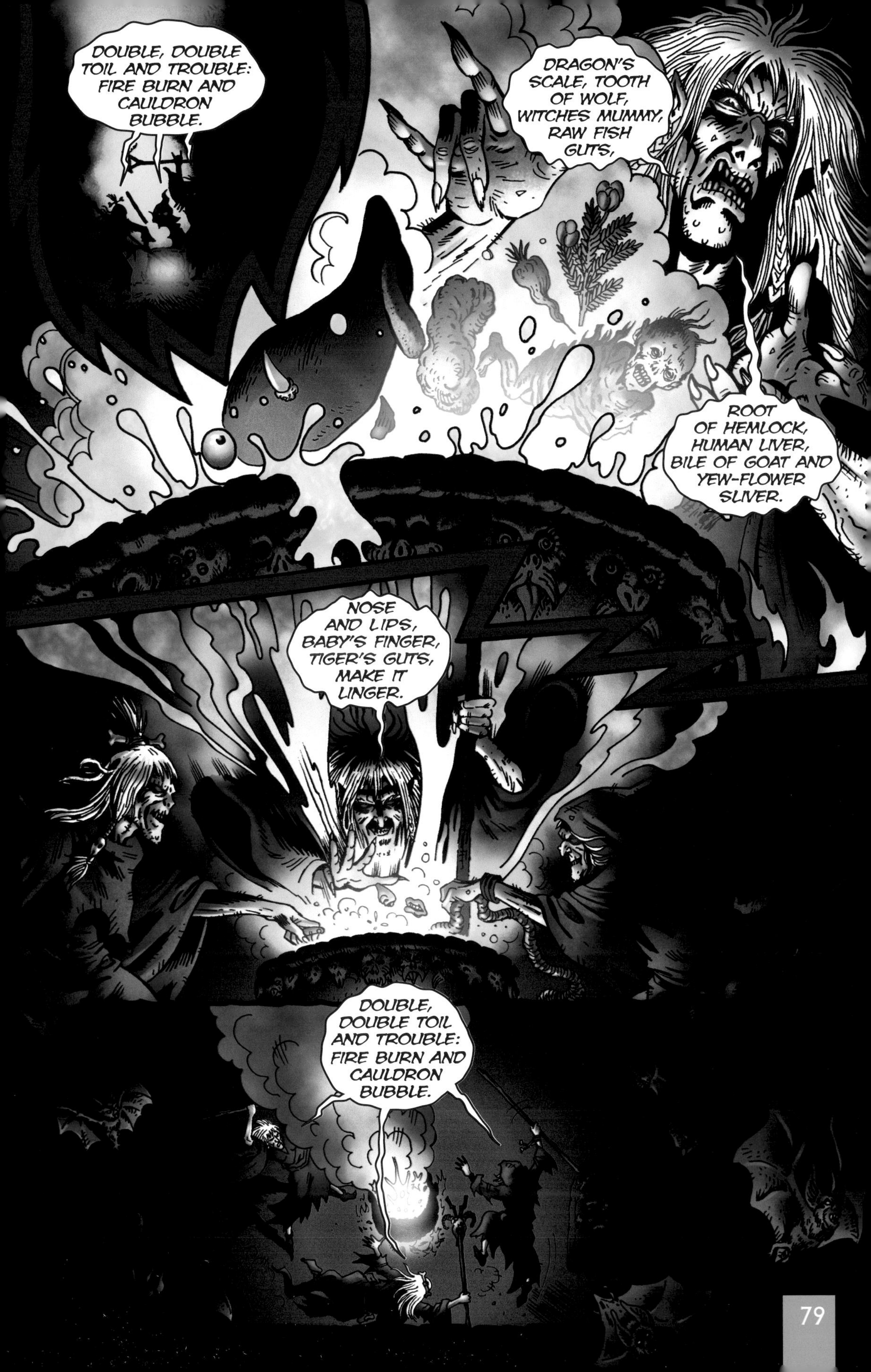
DOUBLE, DOUBLE TOIL AND TROUBLE: FIRE BURN AND CAULDRON BUBBLE.
DRAGON'S SCALE, TOOTH OF WOLF, WITCHES MUMMY, RAW FISH GUTS,
ROOT OF HEMLOCK, HUMAN LIVER, BILE OF GOAT AND YEW-FLOWER SLIVER.
NOSE AND LIPS, BABY'S FINGER, TIGER'S GUTS, MAKE IT LINGER.
DOUBLE, DOUBLE TOIL AND TROUBLE: FIRE BURN AND CAULDRON BUBBLE.

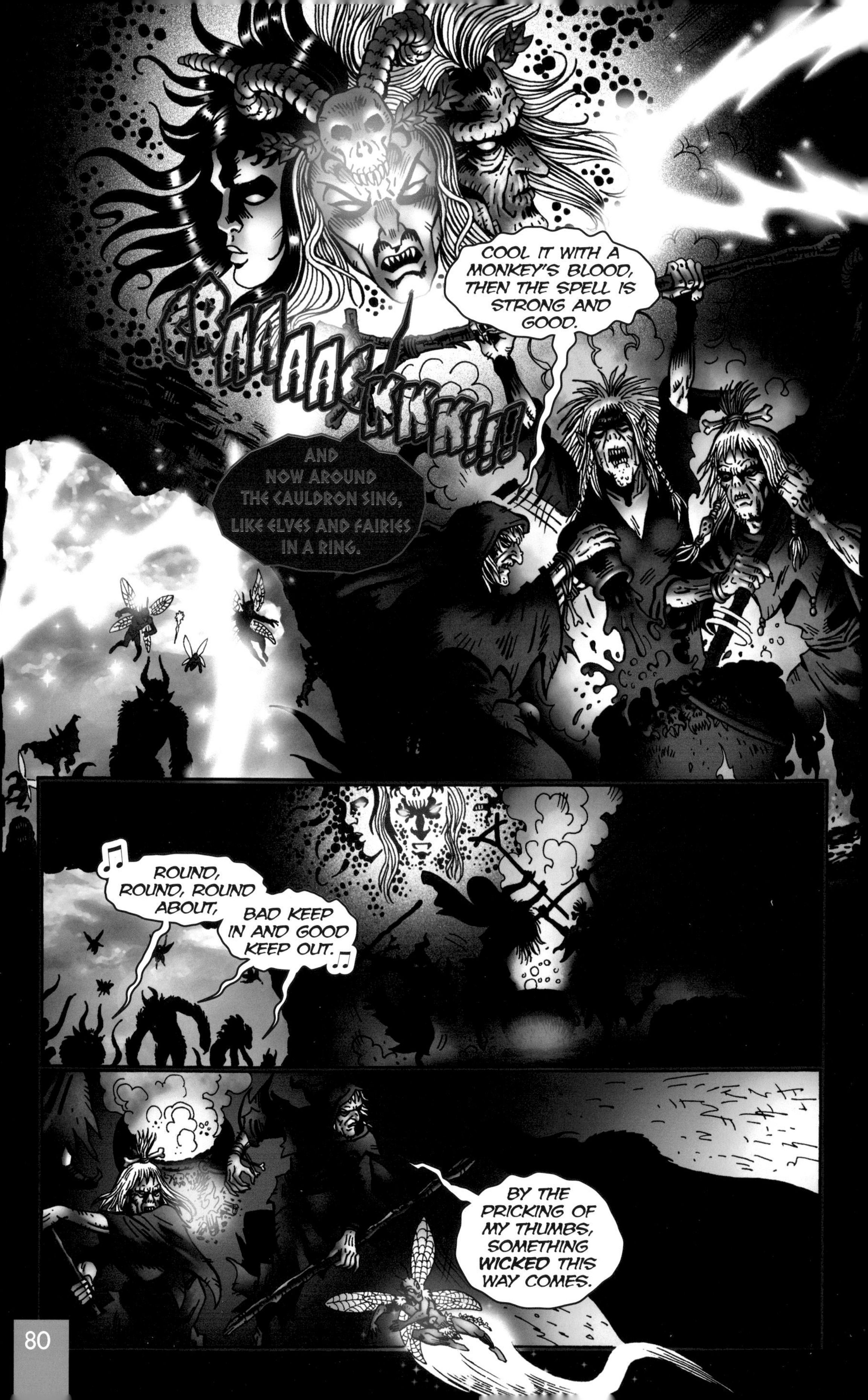
COOL IT WITH A MONKEY'S BLOOD, THEN THE SPELL IS STRONG AND GOOD.
CRAAAACKKKK!!!
AND NOW AROUND THE CAULDRON SING, LIKE ELVES AND FAIRIES IN A RING.
ROUND, ROUND, ROUND ABOUT,
BAD KEEP IN AND GOOD KEEP OUT.
BY THE PRICKING OF MY THUMBS, SOMETHING WICKED THIS WAY COMES.

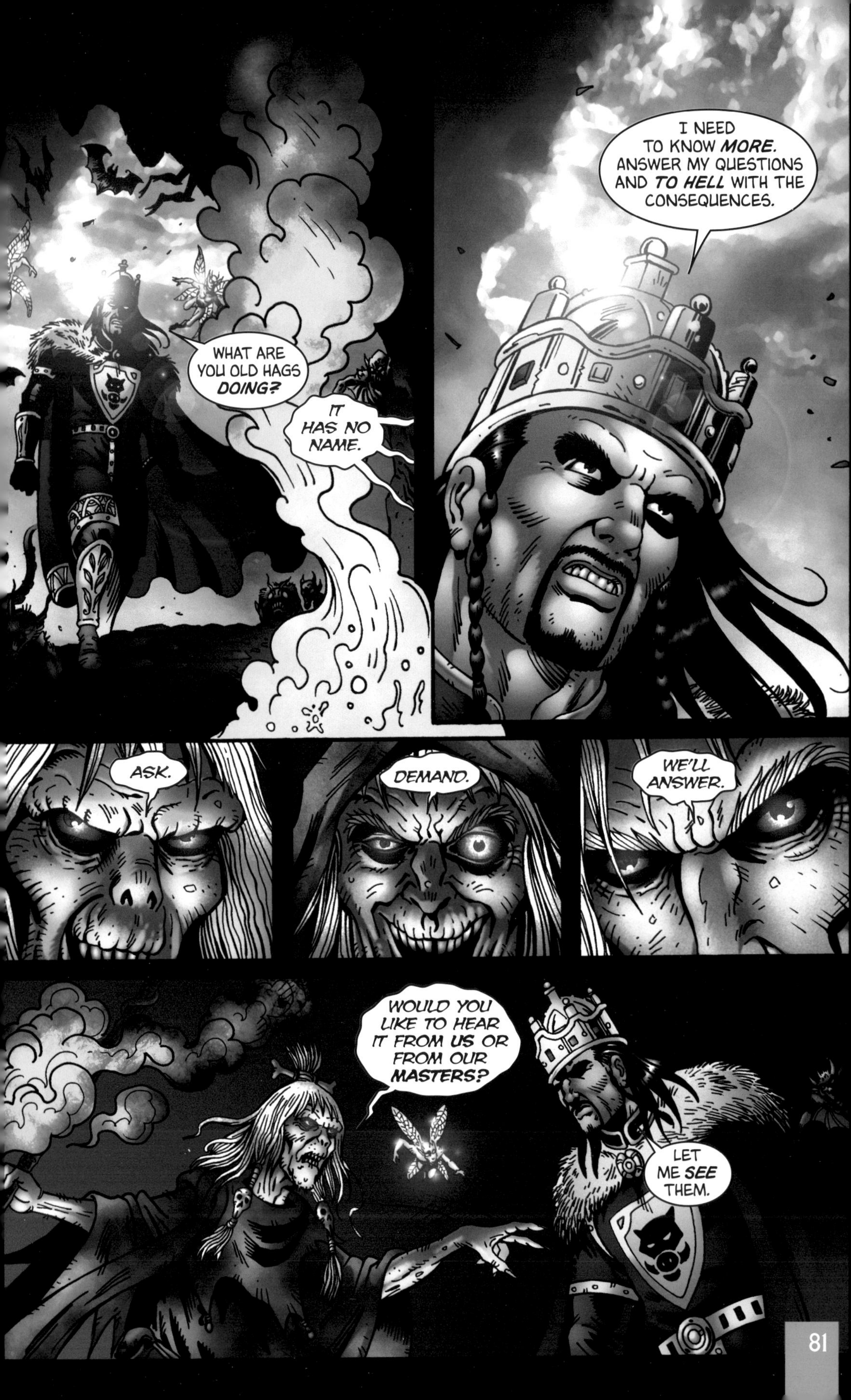
WHAT ARE YOU OLD HAGS DOING?
IT HAS NO NAME.
I NEED TO KNOW MORE. ANSWER MY QUESTIONS AND TO HELL WITH THE CONSEQUENCES.
ASK.
DEMAND.
WE'LL ANSWER.
WOULD YOU LIKE TO HEAR IT FROM US OR FROM OUR MASTERS?
LET ME SEE THEM.

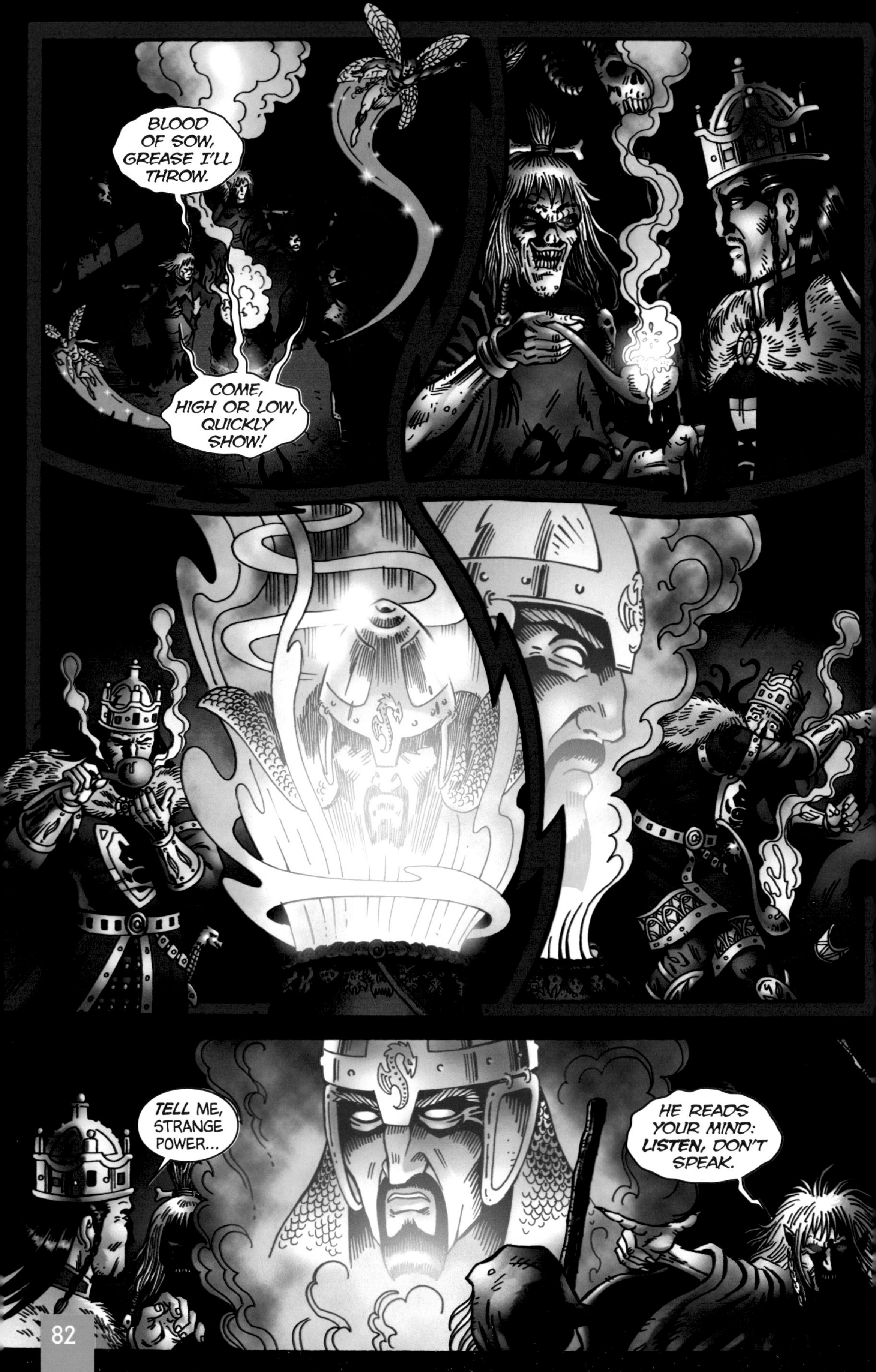
BLOOD OF SOW, GREASE I'LL THROW.
COME, HIGH OR LOW, QUICKLY SHOW!
TELL ME, STRANGE POWER...
HE READS YOUR MIND: LISTEN, DON'T SPEAK.

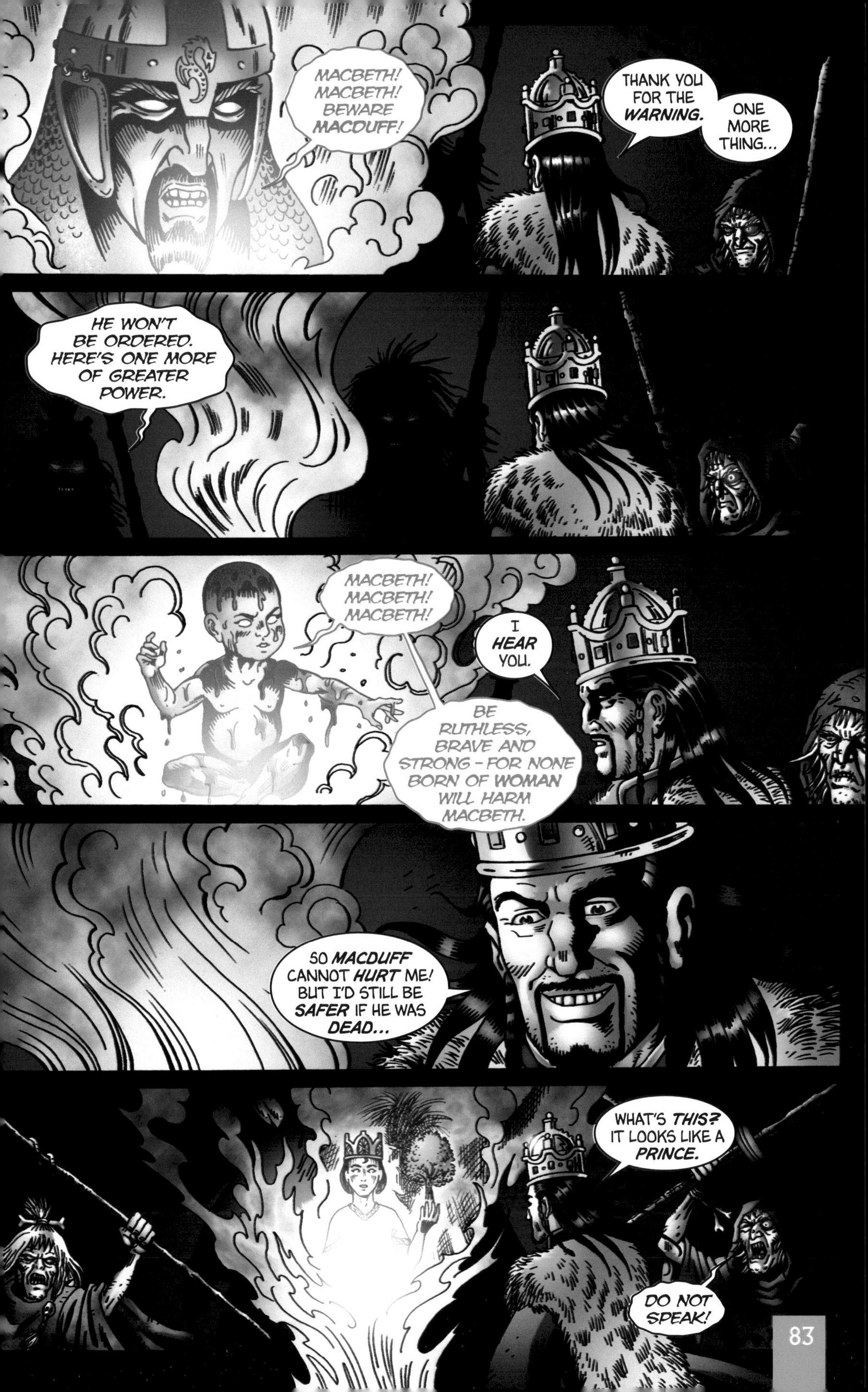
MACBETH! MACBETH! BEWARE MACDUFF!
THANK YOU FOR THE WARNING.
ONE MORE THING...
HE WON'T BE ORDERED. HERE'S ONE MORE OF GREATER POWER.
MACBETH! MACBETH! MACBETH!
I HEAR YOU.
BE RUTHLESS, BRAVE AND STRONG - FOR NONE BORN OF WOMAN WILL HARM MACBETH.
SO MACDUFF CANNOT HURT ME! BUT I'D STILL BE SAFER IF HE WAS DEAD...
WHAT'S THIS? IT LOOKS LIKE A PRINCE.
DO NOT SPEAK!

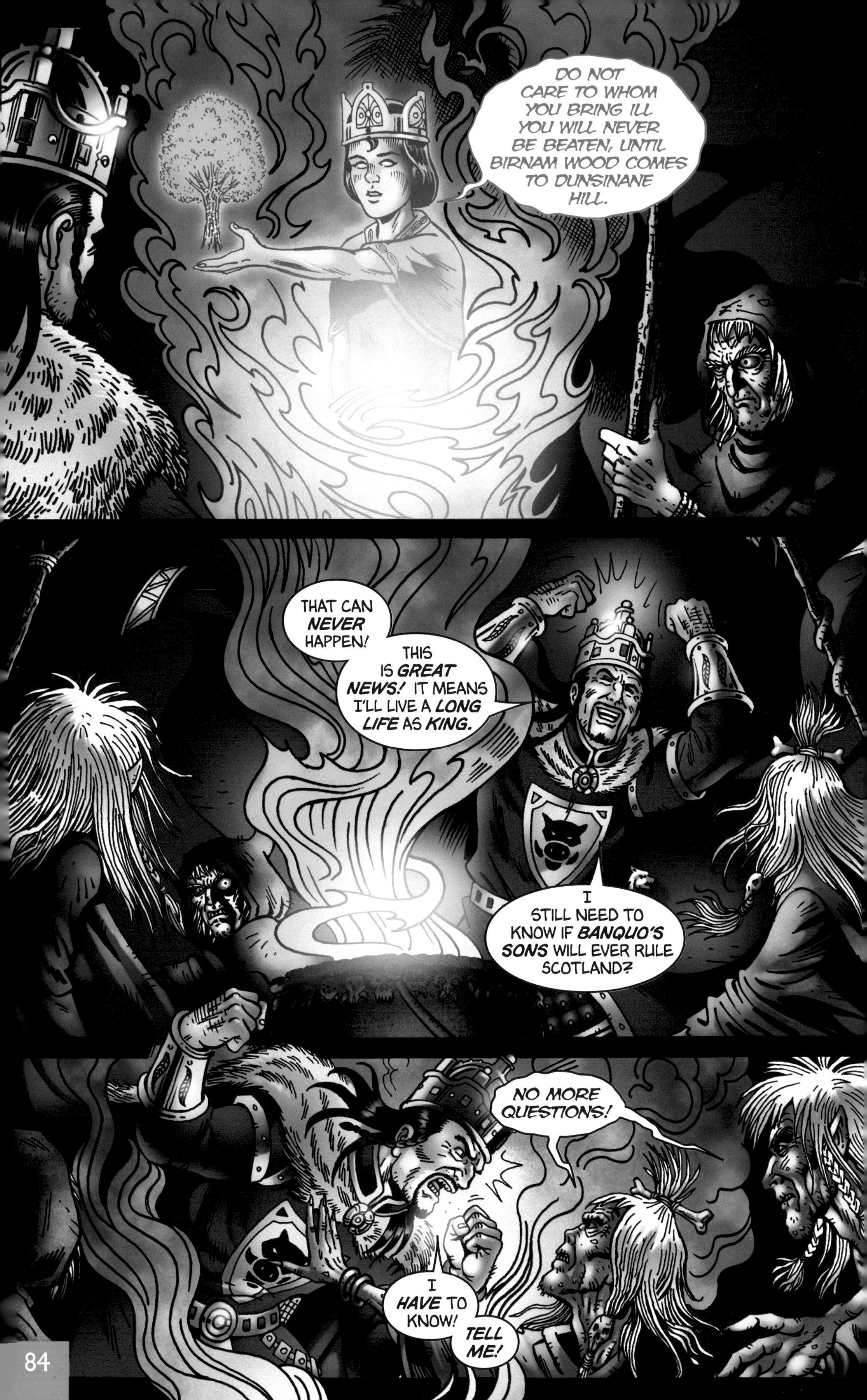
DO NOT CARE TO WHOM YOU BRING ILL YOU WILL NEVER BE BEATEN, UNTIL BIRNAM WOOD COMES TO DUNSINANE HILL.
THAT CAN *NEVER* HAPPEN!
THIS IS *GREAT NEWS!* IT MEANS I'LL LIVE A *LONG LIFE* AS *KING.*
I STILL NEED TO KNOW IF *BANQUO'S SONS* WILL EVER RULE SCOTLAND?
NO MORE QUESTIONS!
I *HAVE* TO KNOW!
TELL ME!

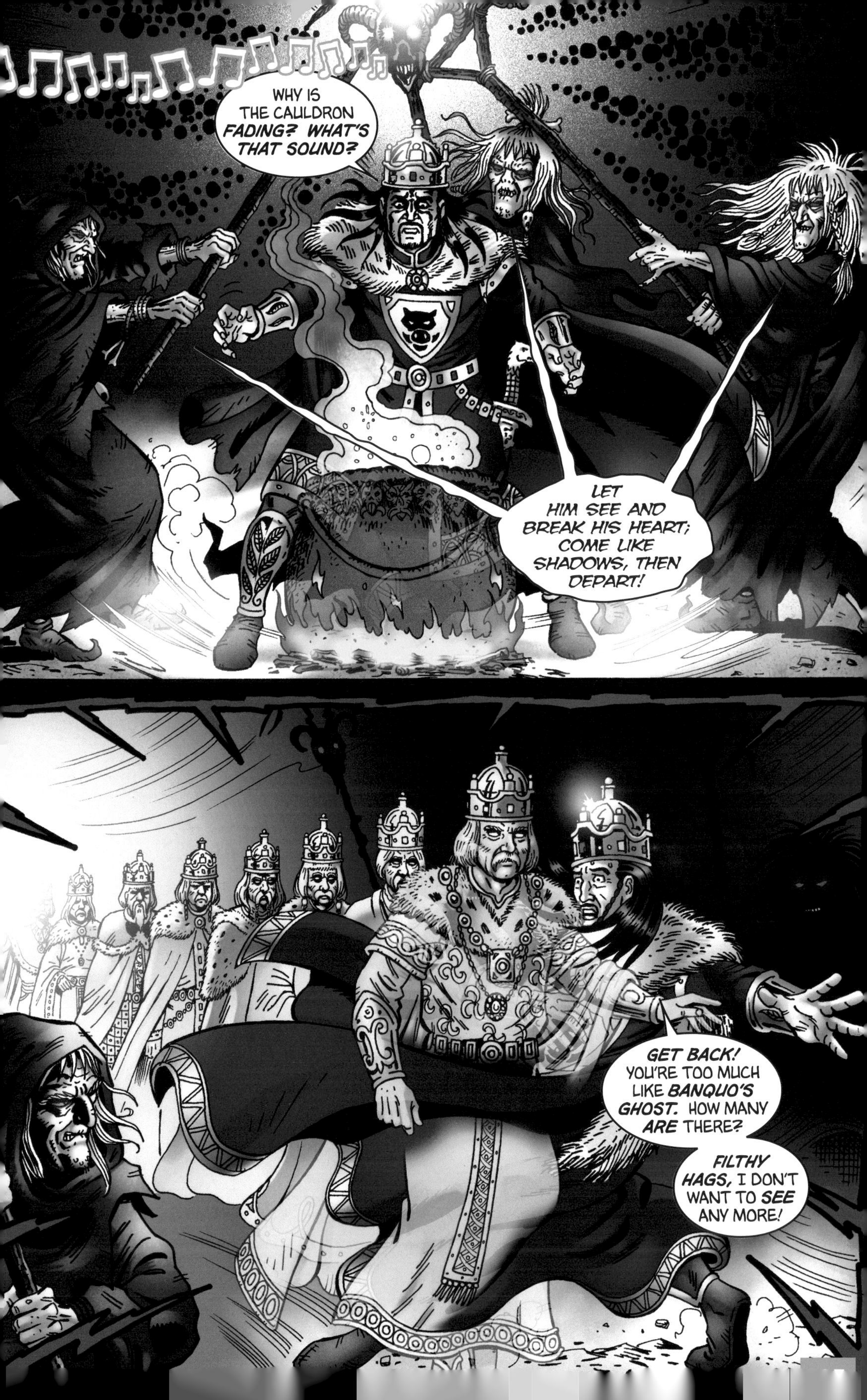
WHY IS THE CAULDRON FADING? WHAT'S THAT SOUND?
LET HIM SEE AND BREAK HIS HEART; COME LIKE SHADOWS, THEN DEPART!
GET BACK! YOU'RE TOO MUCH LIKE BANQUO'S GHOST. HOW MANY ARE THERE?
FILTHY HAGS, I DON'T WANT TO SEE ANY MORE!

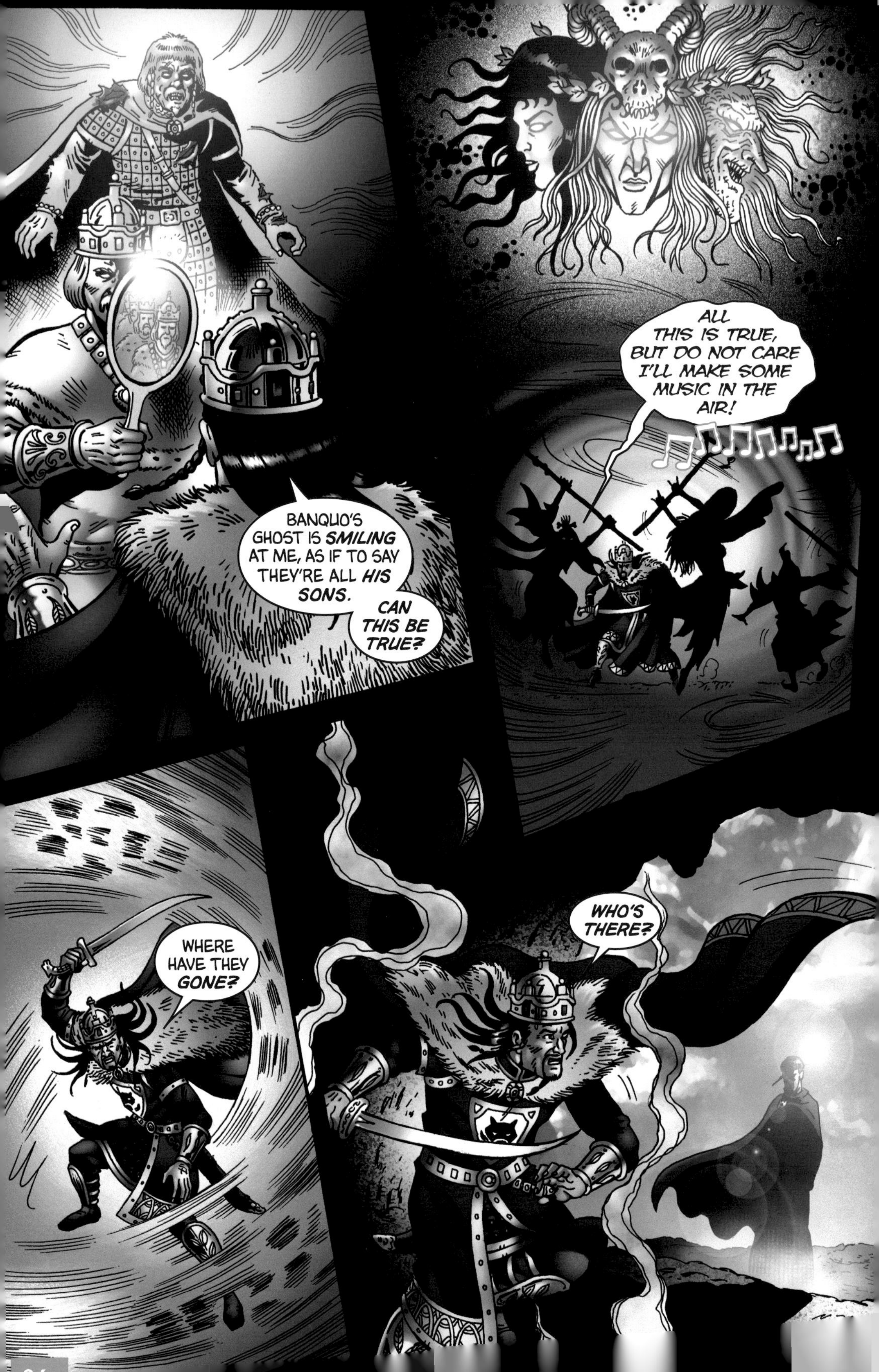
BANQUO'S GHOST IS SMILING AT ME, AS IF TO SAY THEY'RE ALL HIS SONS.
CAN THIS BE TRUE?
ALL THIS IS TRUE, BUT DO NOT CARE I'LL MAKE SOME MUSIC IN THE AIR!
WHERE HAVE THEY GONE?
WHO'S THERE?

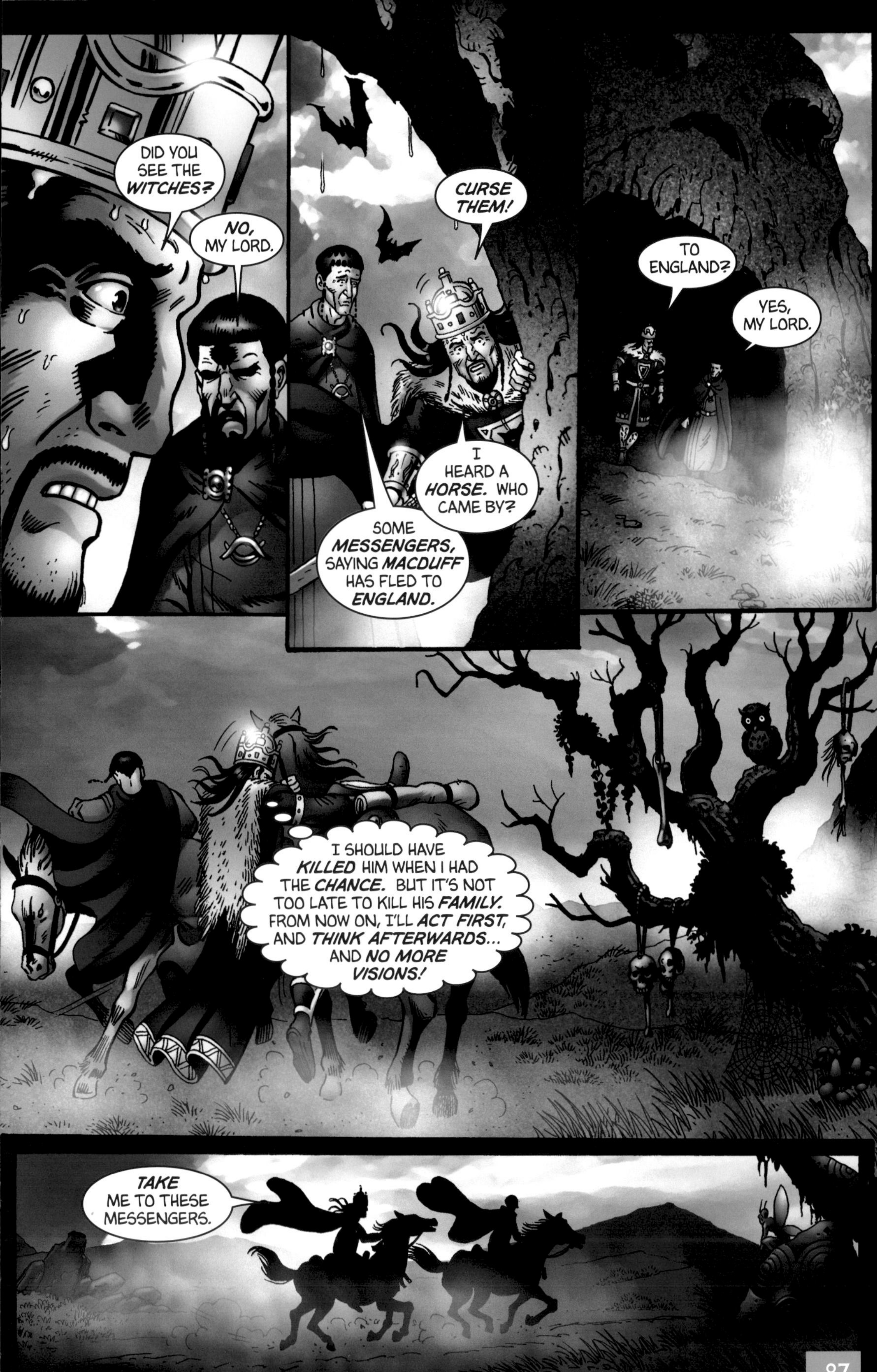
DID YOU SEE THE WITCHES?
NO, MY LORD.
CURSE THEM!
I HEARD A HORSE. WHO CAME BY?
SOME MESSENGERS, SAYING MACDUFF HAS FLED TO ENGLAND.
TO ENGLAND?
YES, MY LORD.
I SHOULD HAVE KILLED HIM WHEN I HAD THE CHANCE. BUT IT'S NOT TOO LATE TO KILL HIS FAMILY. FROM NOW ON, I'LL ACT FIRST, AND THINK AFTERWARDS... AND NO MORE VISIONS!
TAKE ME TO THESE MESSENGERS.

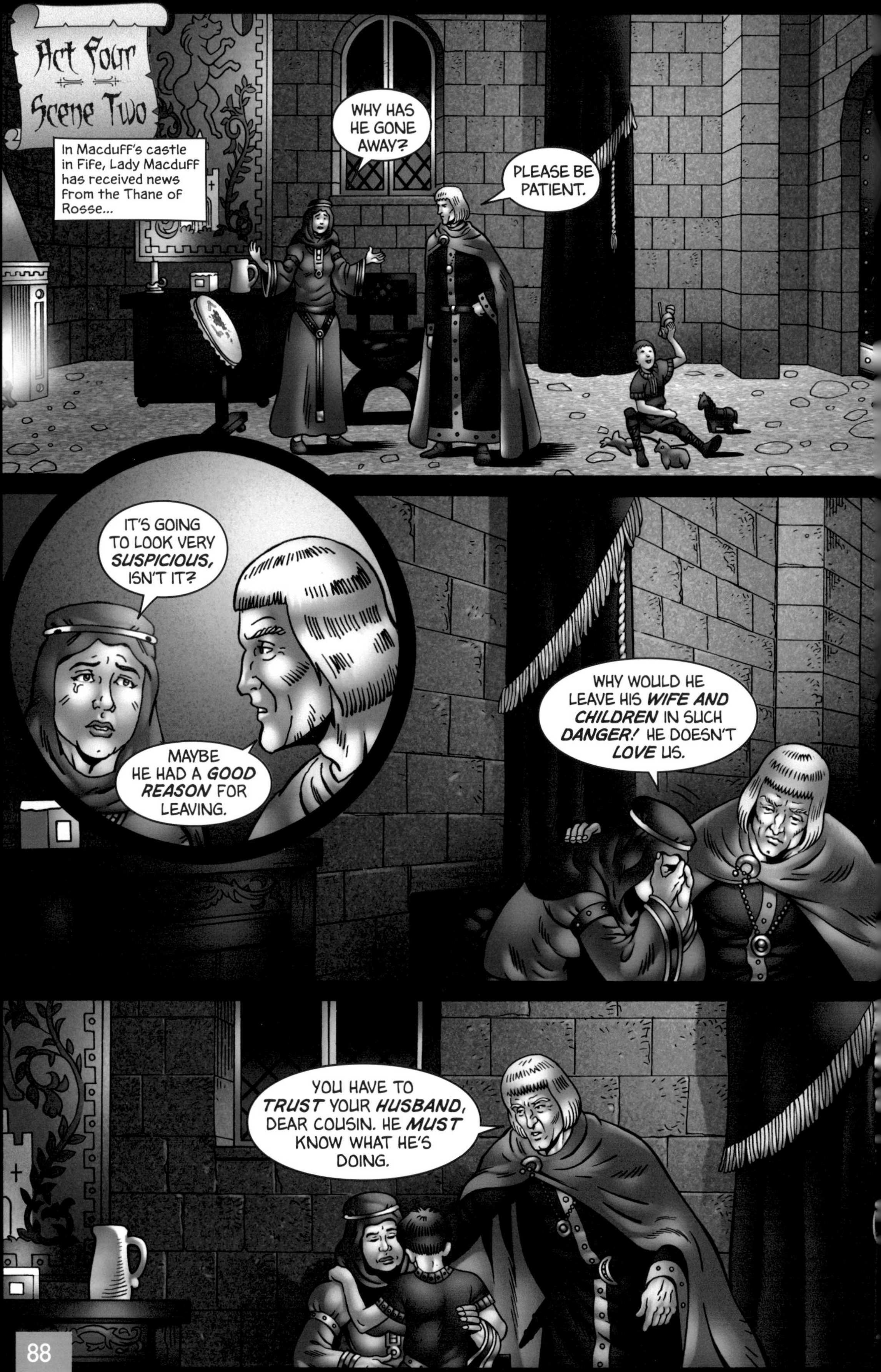

Act Four
Scene Two
In Macduff's castle in Fife, Lady Macduff has received news from the Thane of Rosse...
WHY HAS HE GONE AWAY?
PLEASE BE PATIENT.
IT'S GOING TO LOOK VERY SUSPICIOUS, ISN'T IT?
MAYBE HE HAD A GOOD REASON FOR LEAVING.
WHY WOULD HE LEAVE HIS WIFE AND CHILDREN IN SUCH DANGER! HE DOESN'T LOVE US.
YOU HAVE TO TRUST YOUR HUSBAND, DEAR COUSIN. HE MUST KNOW WHAT HE'S DOING.

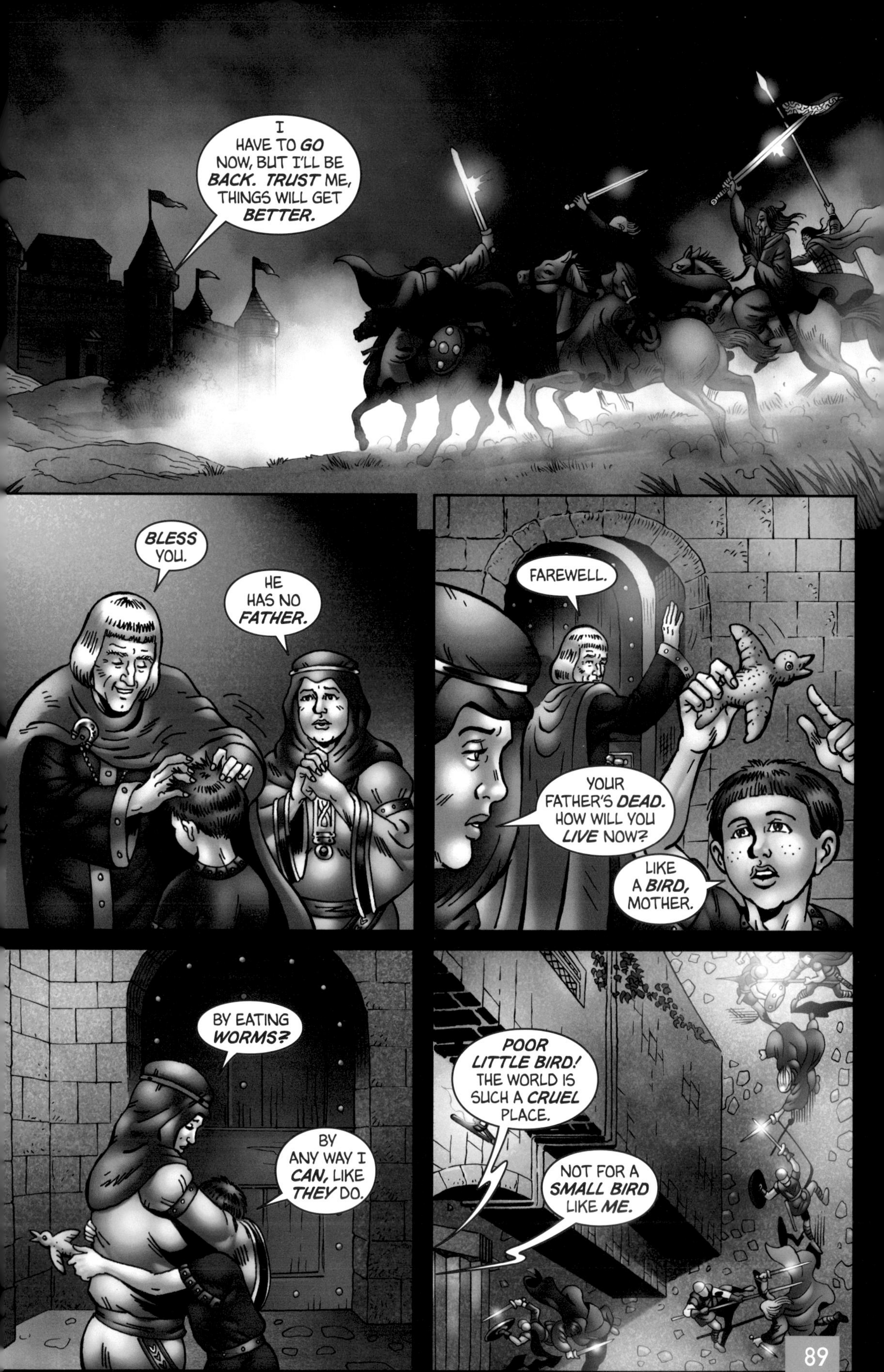
I HAVE TO GO NOW, BUT I'LL BE BACK. TRUST ME, THINGS WILL GET BETTER.
BLESS YOU.
HE HAS NO FATHER.
FAREWELL.
YOUR FATHER'S DEAD. HOW WILL YOU LIVE NOW?
LIKE A BIRD, MOTHER.
BY EATING WORMS?
BY ANY WAY I CAN, LIKE THEY DO.
POOR LITTLE BIRD! THE WORLD IS SUCH A CRUEL PLACE.
NOT FOR A SMALL BIRD LIKE ME.

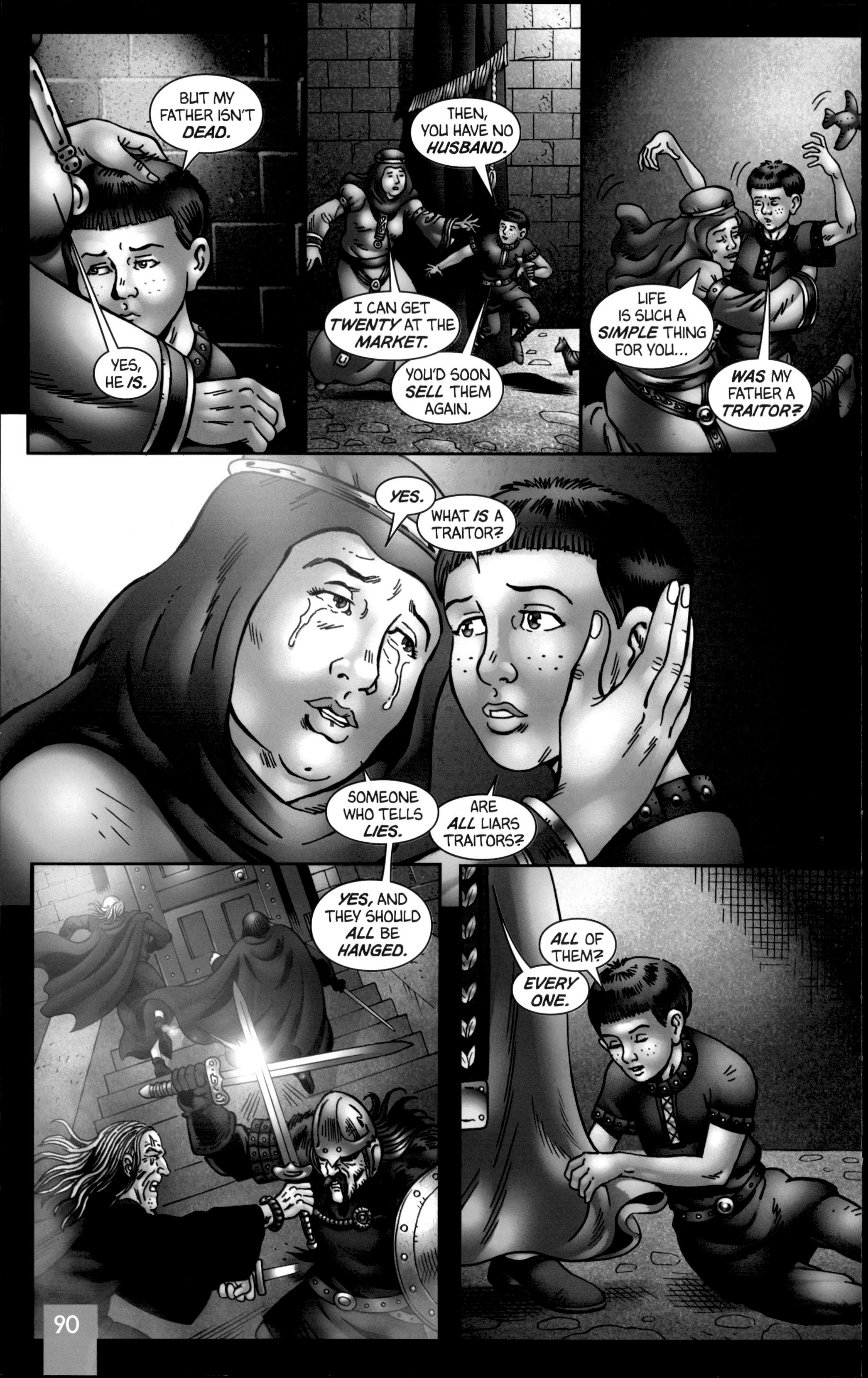
BUT MY FATHER ISN'T DEAD.
YES, HE IS.
THEN, YOU HAVE NO HUSBAND.
I CAN GET TWENTY AT THE MARKET.
YOU'D SOON SELL THEM AGAIN.
LIFE IS SUCH A SIMPLE THING FOR YOU...
WAS MY FATHER A TRAITOR?
YES.
WHAT IS A TRAITOR?
SOMEONE WHO TELLS LIES.
ARE ALL LIARS TRAITORS?
YES, AND THEY SHOULD ALL BE HANGED.
ALL OF THEM?
EVERY ONE.

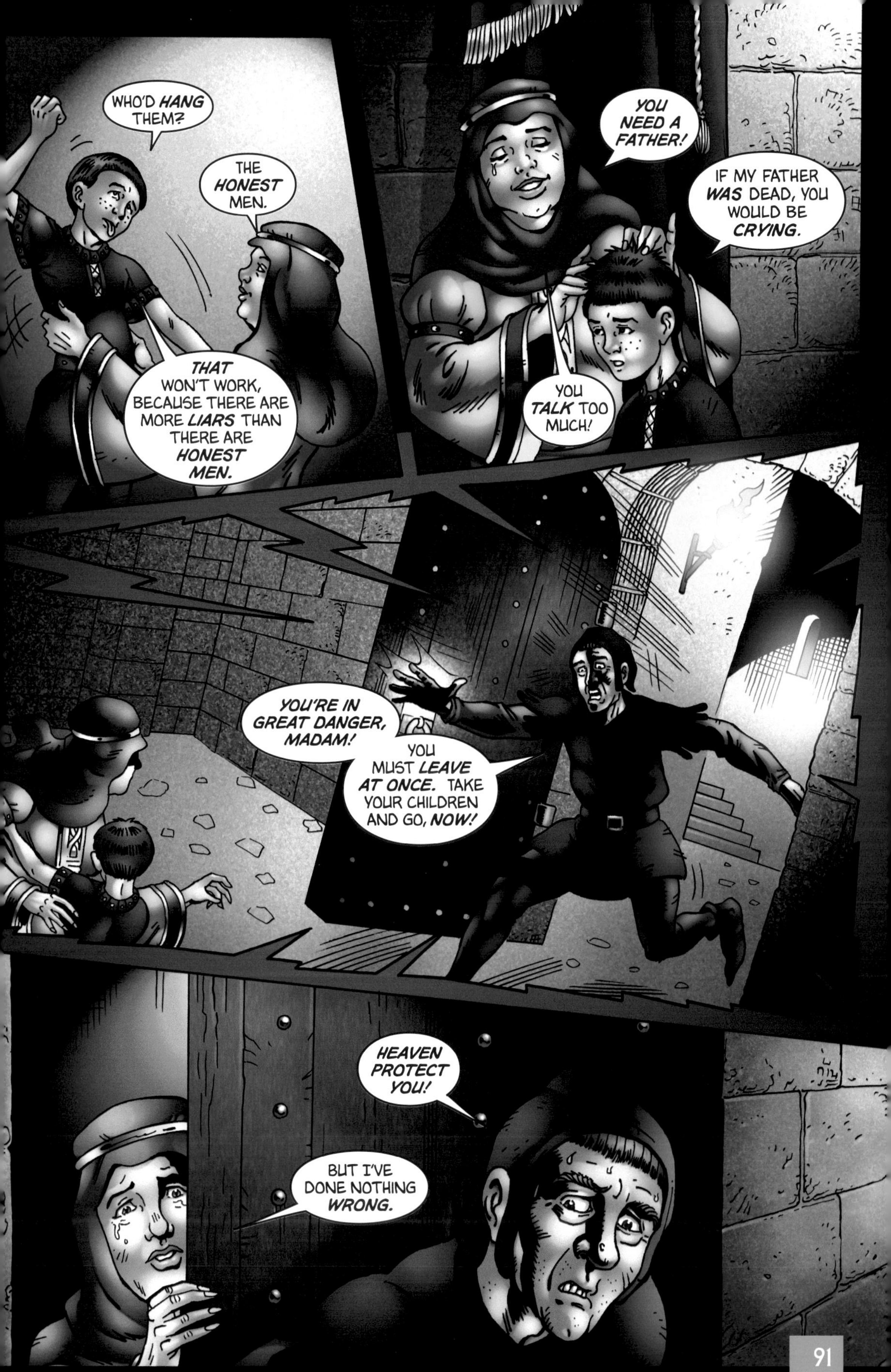
WHO'D HANG THEM?
THE HONEST MEN.
THAT WON'T WORK, BECAUSE THERE ARE MORE LIARS THAN THERE ARE HONEST MEN.
YOU NEED A FATHER!
IF MY FATHER WAS DEAD, YOU WOULD BE CRYING.
YOU TALK TOO MUCH!
YOU'RE IN GREAT DANGER, MADAM!
YOU MUST LEAVE AT ONCE. TAKE YOUR CHILDREN AND GO, NOW!
HEAVEN PROTECT YOU!
BUT I'VE DONE NOTHING WRONG.

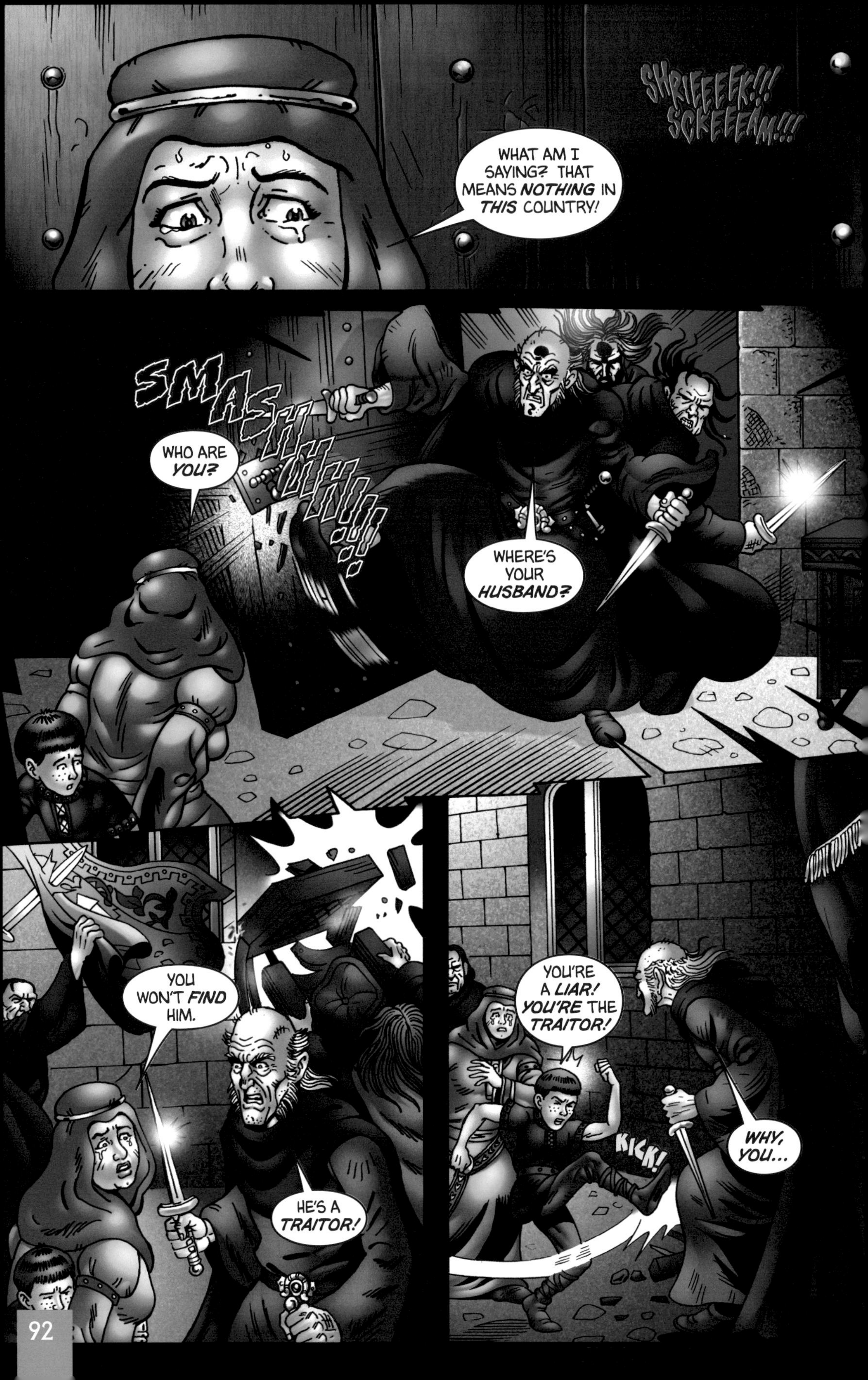
SHRIEEEEK!!!
SCKEEEAM!!!
WHAT AM I SAYING? THAT MEANS *NOTHING* IN *THIS* COUNTRY!
SMASHHH!!!
WHO ARE *YOU?*
WHERE'S YOUR *HUSBAND?*
YOU WON'T *FIND* HIM.
HE'S A *TRAITOR!*
YOU'RE A *LIAR! YOU'RE* THE *TRAITOR!*
KICK!
WHY, YOU...

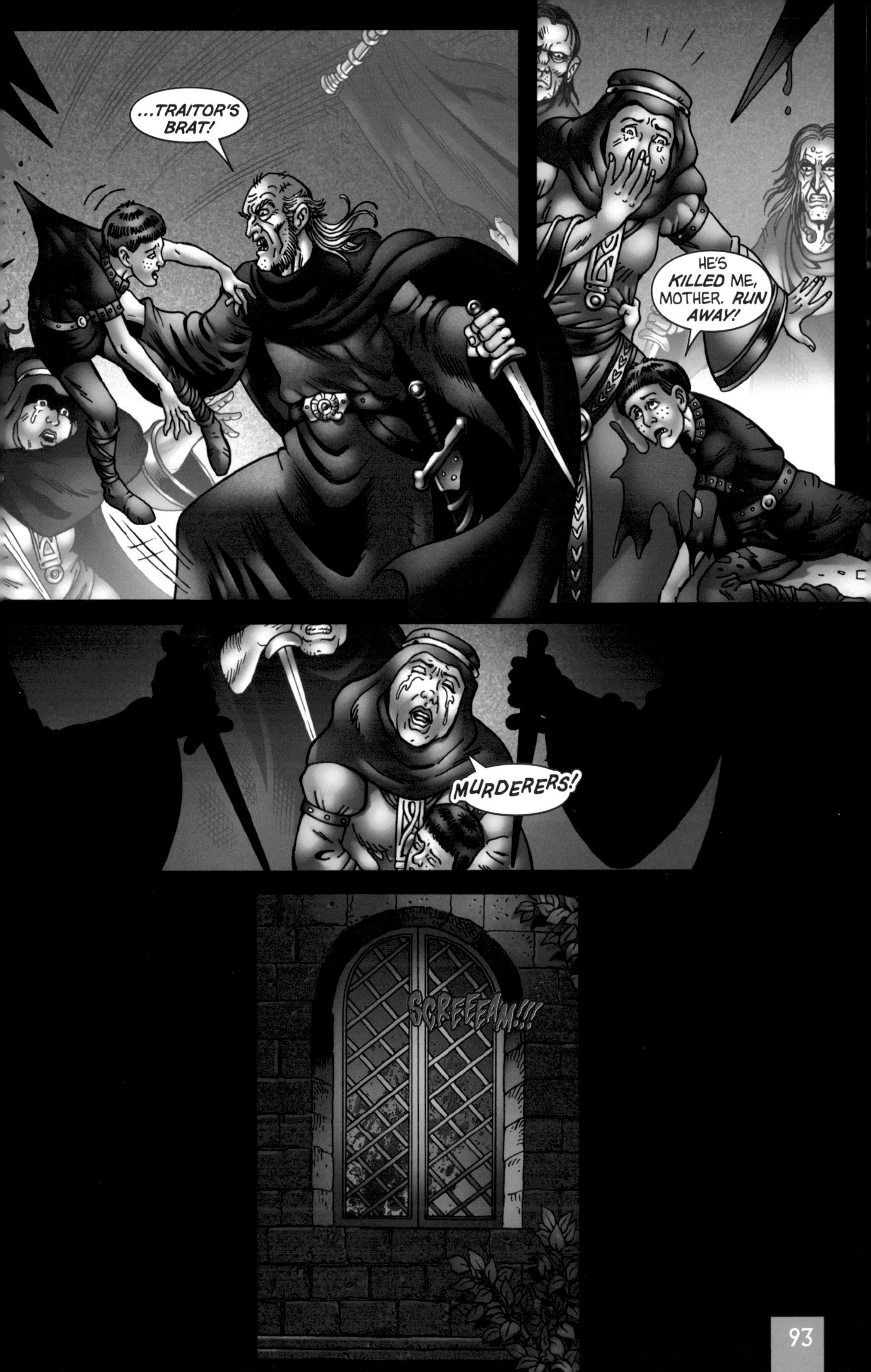
...TRAITOR'S BRAT!
HE'S KILLED ME, MOTHER. RUN AWAY!
MURDERERS!
SCREEEAM!!!

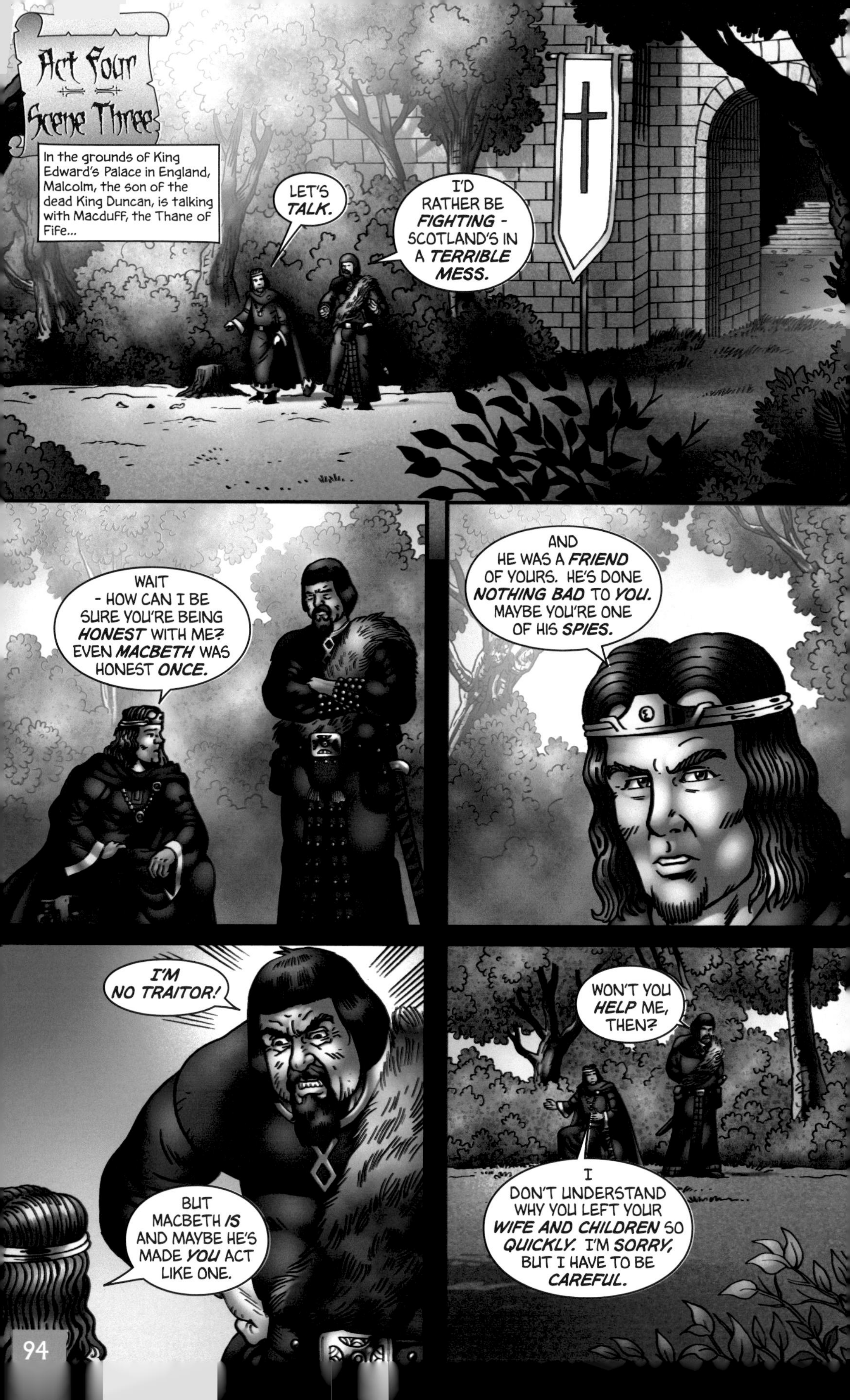
Act Four
Scene Three
In the grounds of King Edward's Palace in England, Malcolm, the son of the dead King Duncan, is talking with Macduff, the Thane of Fife...
LET'S TALK.
I'D RATHER BE FIGHTING - SCOTLAND'S IN A TERRIBLE MESS.
WAIT - HOW CAN I BE SURE YOU'RE BEING HONEST WITH ME? EVEN MACBETH WAS HONEST ONCE.
AND HE WAS A FRIEND OF YOURS. HE'S DONE NOTHING BAD TO YOU. MAYBE YOU'RE ONE OF HIS SPIES.
I'M NO TRAITOR!
BUT MACBETH IS AND MAYBE HE'S MADE YOU ACT LIKE ONE.
WON'T YOU HELP ME, THEN?
I DON'T UNDERSTAND WHY YOU LEFT YOUR WIFE AND CHILDREN SO QUICKLY. I'M SORRY, BUT I HAVE TO BE CAREFUL.

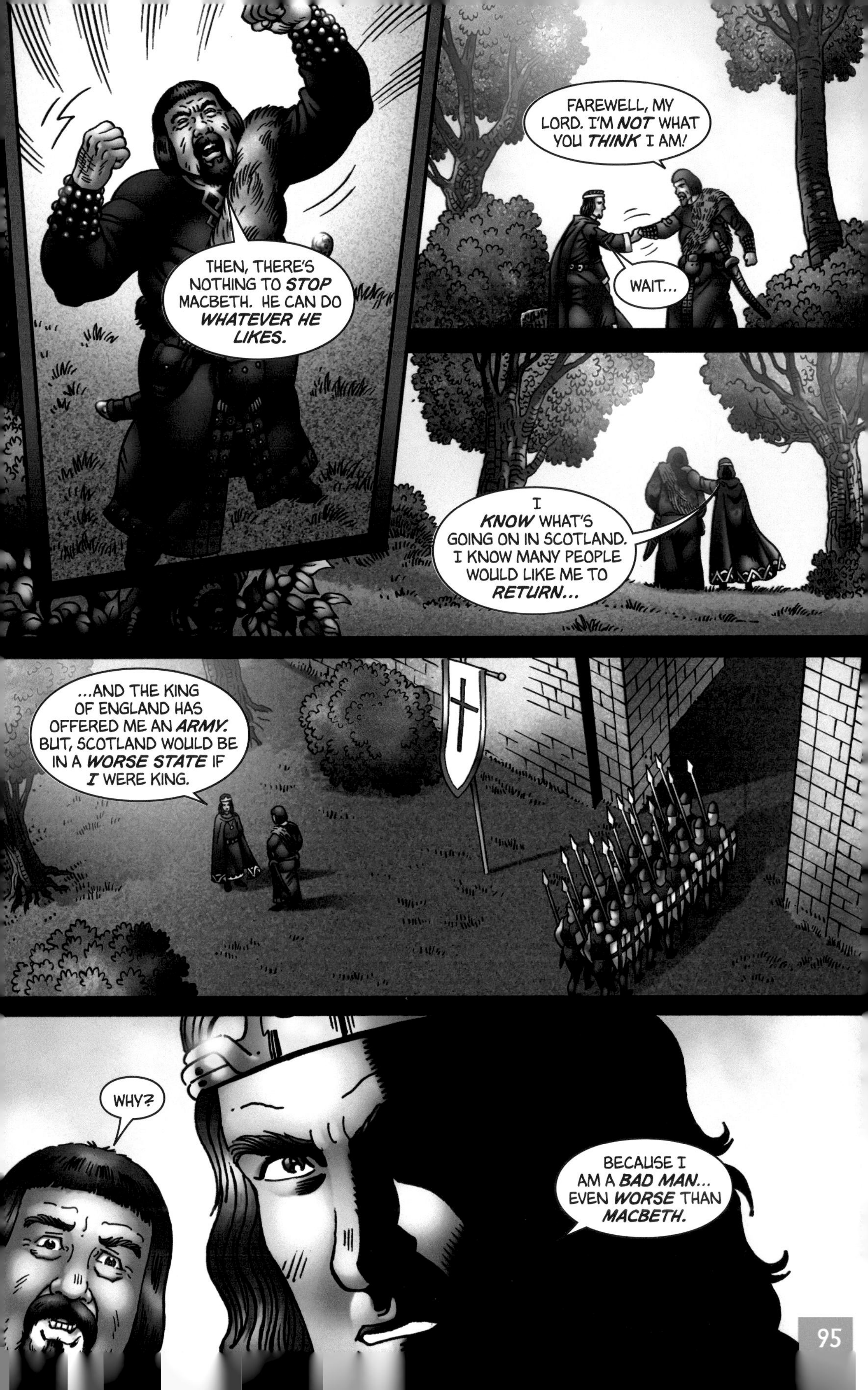
THEN, THERE'S NOTHING TO STOP MACBETH. HE CAN DO WHATEVER HE LIKES.
FAREWELL, MY LORD. I'M NOT WHAT YOU THINK I AM!
WAIT...
I KNOW WHAT'S GOING ON IN SCOTLAND. I KNOW MANY PEOPLE WOULD LIKE ME TO RETURN...
...AND THE KING OF ENGLAND HAS OFFERED ME AN ARMY. BUT, SCOTLAND WOULD BE IN A WORSE STATE IF I WERE KING.
WHY?
BECAUSE I AM A BAD MAN... EVEN WORSE THAN MACBETH.

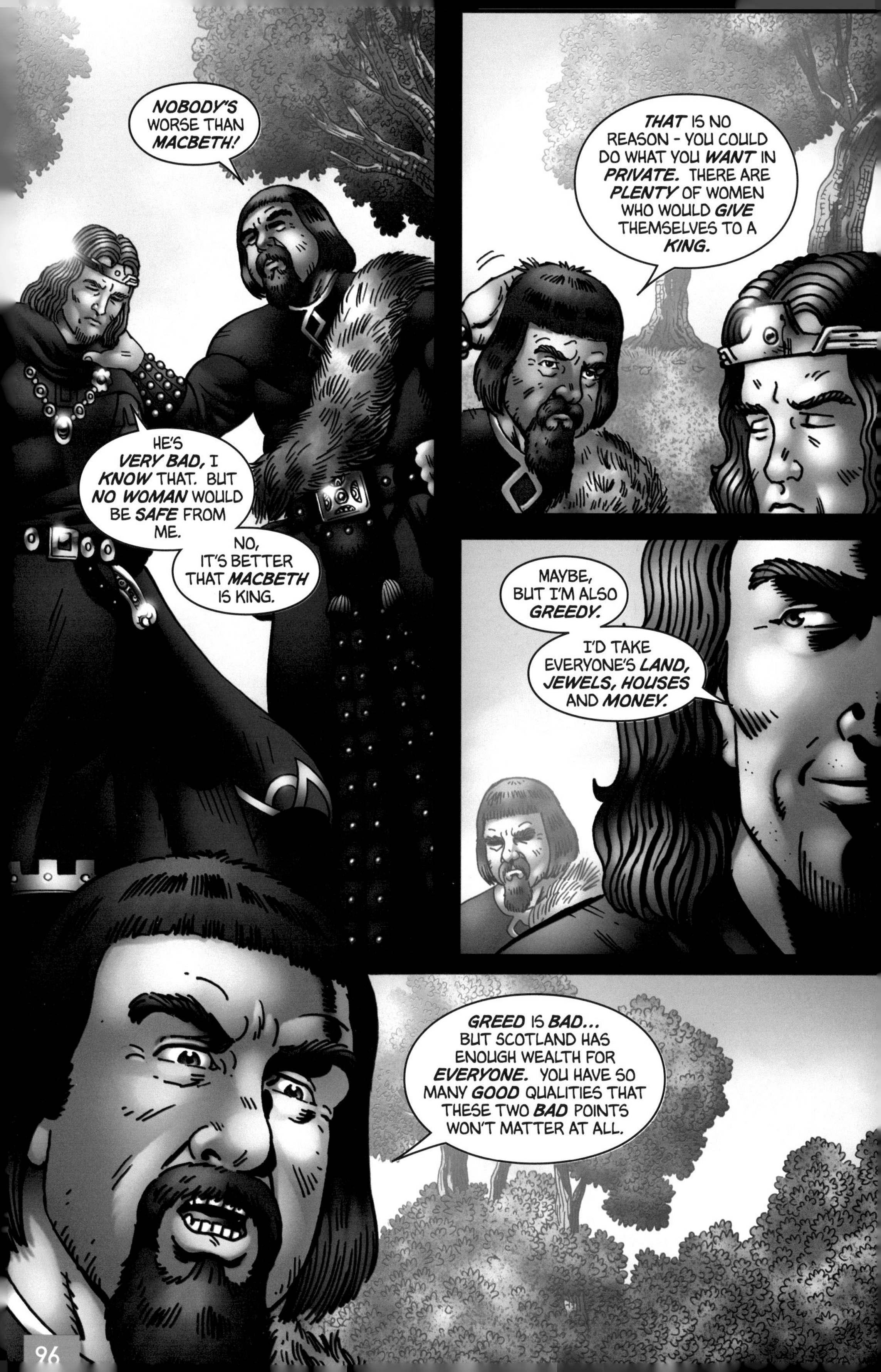
NOBODY'S WORSE THAN MACBETH!
HE'S VERY BAD, I KNOW THAT. BUT NO WOMAN WOULD BE SAFE FROM ME.
NO, IT'S BETTER THAT MACBETH IS KING.
THAT IS NO REASON - YOU COULD DO WHAT YOU WANT IN PRIVATE. THERE ARE PLENTY OF WOMEN WHO WOULD GIVE THEMSELVES TO A KING.
MAYBE, BUT I'M ALSO GREEDY.
I'D TAKE EVERYONE'S LAND, JEWELS, HOUSES AND MONEY.
GREED IS BAD... BUT SCOTLAND HAS ENOUGH WEALTH FOR EVERYONE. YOU HAVE SO MANY GOOD QUALITIES THAT THESE TWO BAD POINTS WON'T MATTER AT ALL.

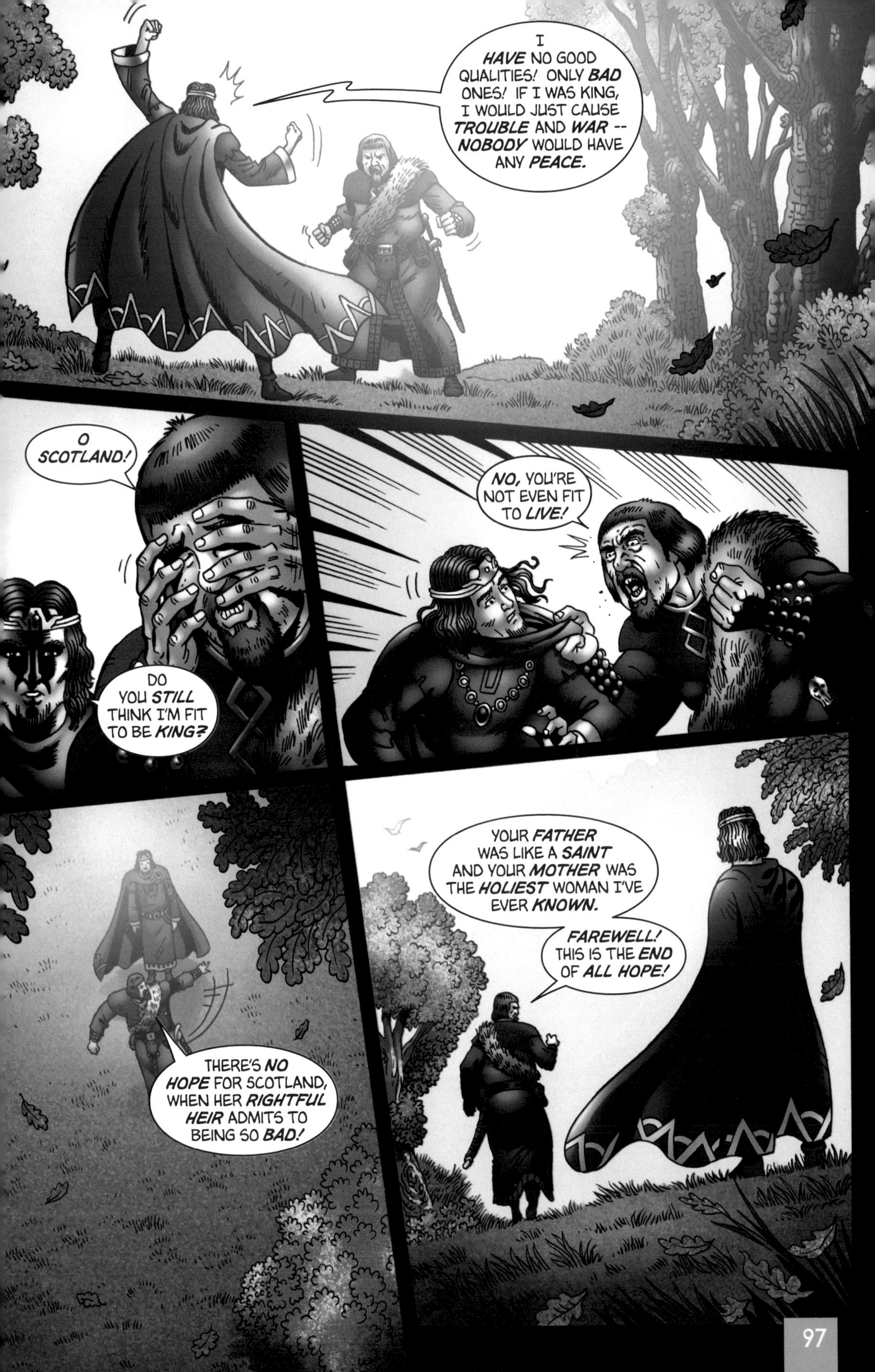
I HAVE NO GOOD QUALITIES! ONLY BAD ONES! IF I WAS KING, I WOULD JUST CAUSE TROUBLE AND WAR -- NOBODY WOULD HAVE ANY PEACE.
O SCOTLAND!
DO YOU STILL THINK I'M FIT TO BE KING?
NO, YOU'RE NOT EVEN FIT TO LIVE!
THERE'S NO HOPE FOR SCOTLAND, WHEN HER RIGHTFUL HEIR ADMITS TO BEING SO BAD!
YOUR FATHER WAS LIKE A SAINT AND YOUR MOTHER WAS THE HOLIEST WOMAN I'VE EVER KNOWN.
FAREWELL! THIS IS THE END OF ALL HOPE!

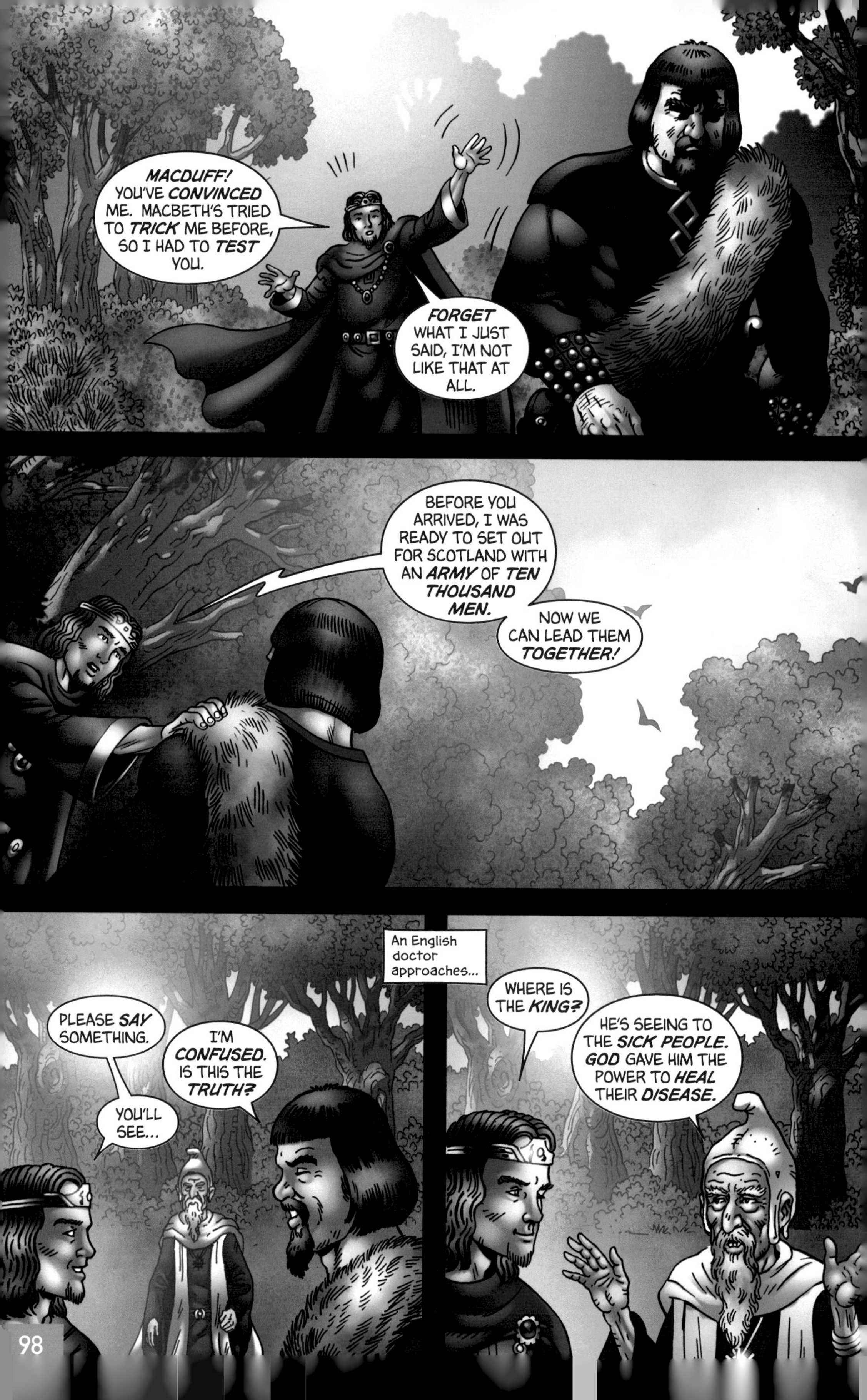
MACDUFF! YOU'VE CONVINCED ME. MACBETH'S TRIED TO TRICK ME BEFORE, SO I HAD TO TEST YOU.
FORGET WHAT I JUST SAID, I'M NOT LIKE THAT AT ALL.
BEFORE YOU ARRIVED, I WAS READY TO SET OUT FOR SCOTLAND WITH AN ARMY OF TEN THOUSAND MEN.
NOW WE CAN LEAD THEM TOGETHER!
PLEASE SAY SOMETHING.
I'M CONFUSED. IS THIS THE TRUTH?
YOU'LL SEE...
An English doctor approaches...
WHERE IS THE KING?
HE'S SEEING TO THE SICK PEOPLE. GOD GAVE HIM THE POWER TO HEAL THEIR DISEASE.

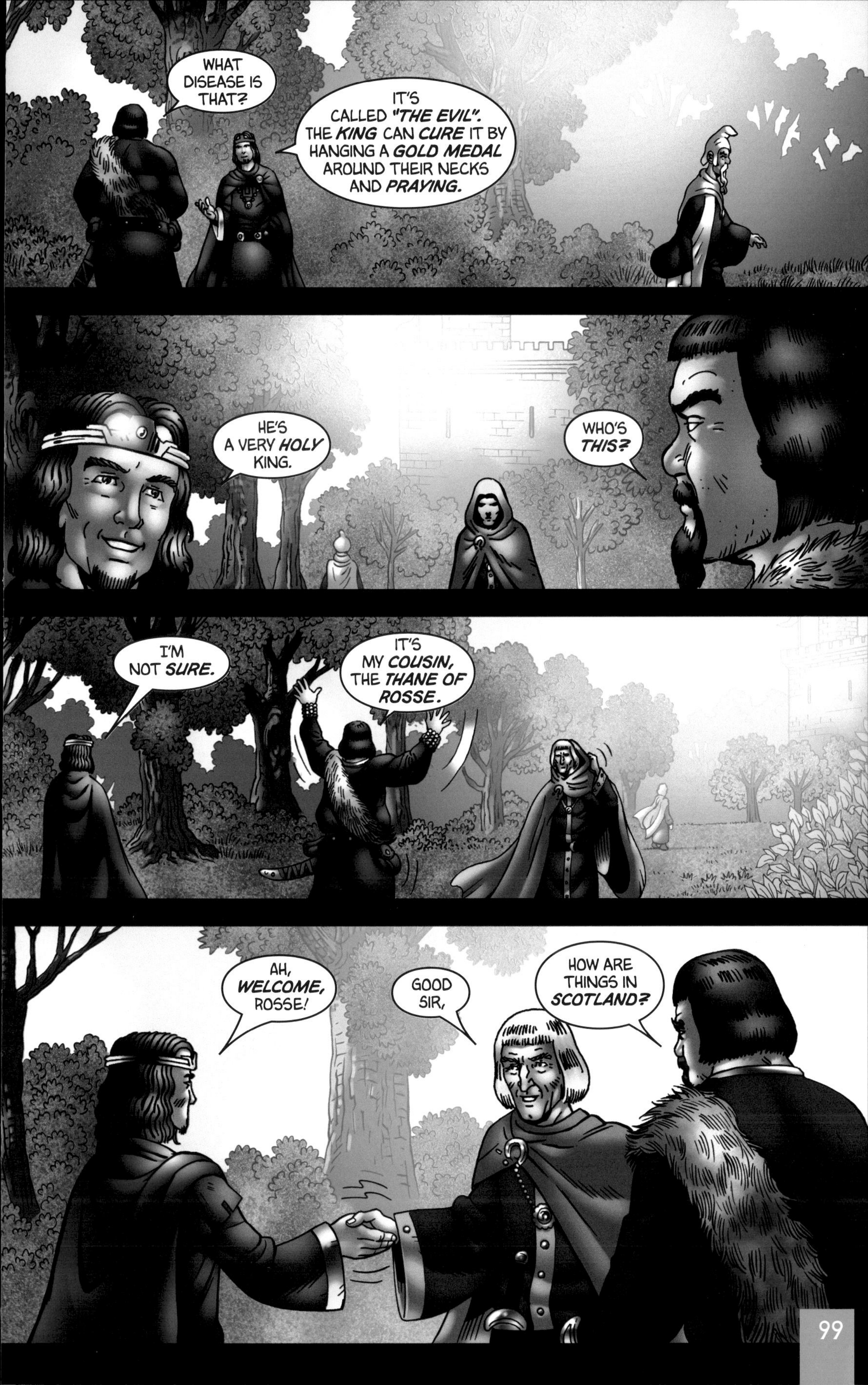
WHAT DISEASE IS THAT?
IT'S CALLED "THE EVIL". THE KING CAN CURE IT BY HANGING A GOLD MEDAL AROUND THEIR NECKS AND PRAYING.
HE'S A VERY HOLY KING.
WHO'S THIS?
I'M NOT SURE.
IT'S MY COUSIN, THE THANE OF ROSSE.
AH, WELCOME, ROSSE!
GOOD SIR,
HOW ARE THINGS IN SCOTLAND?

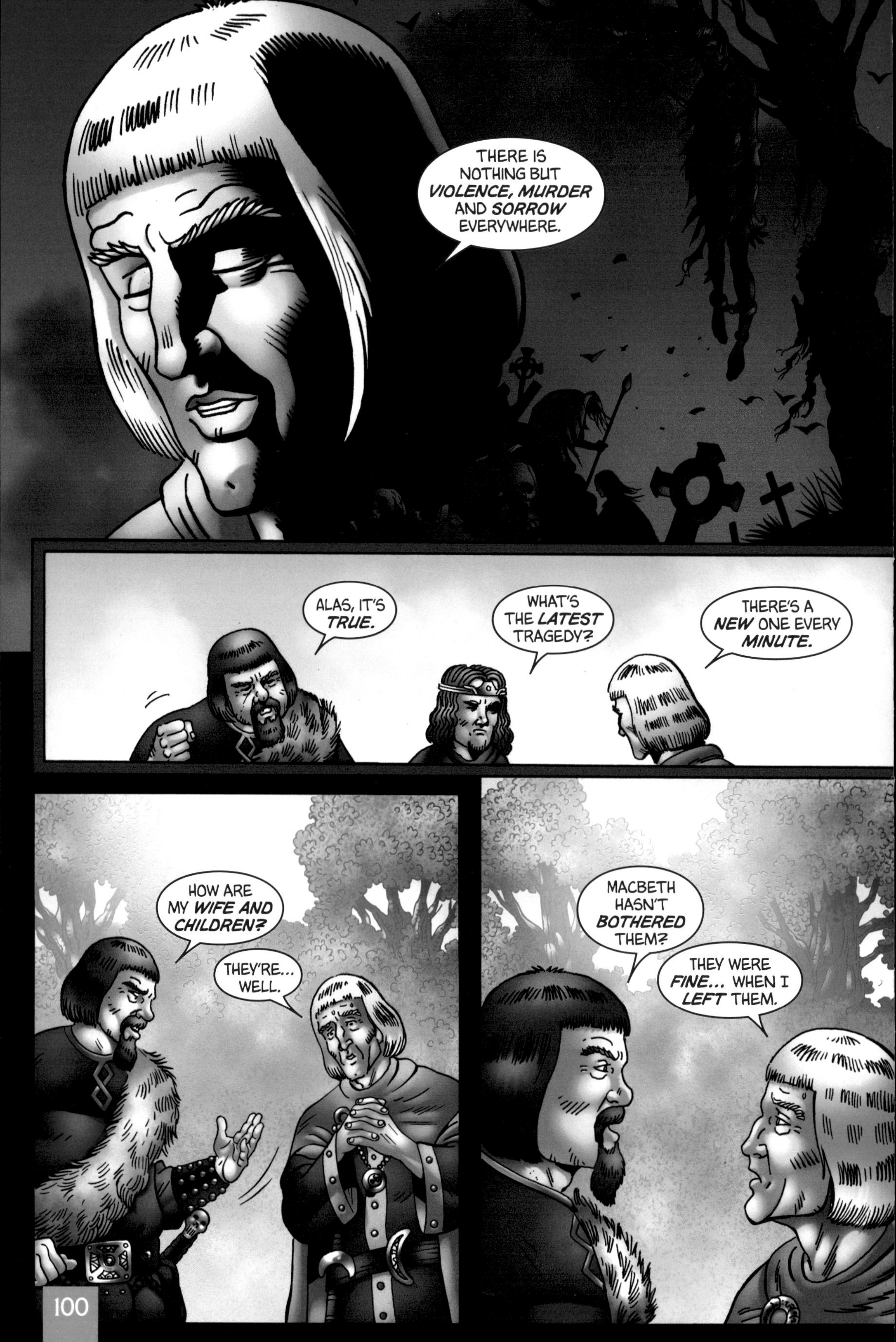
THERE IS NOTHING BUT VIOLENCE, MURDER AND SORROW EVERYWHERE.
ALAS, IT'S TRUE.
WHAT'S THE LATEST TRAGEDY?
THERE'S A NEW ONE EVERY MINUTE.
HOW ARE MY WIFE AND CHILDREN?
THEY'RE... WELL.
MACBETH HASN'T BOTHERED THEM?
THEY WERE FINE... WHEN I LEFT THEM.

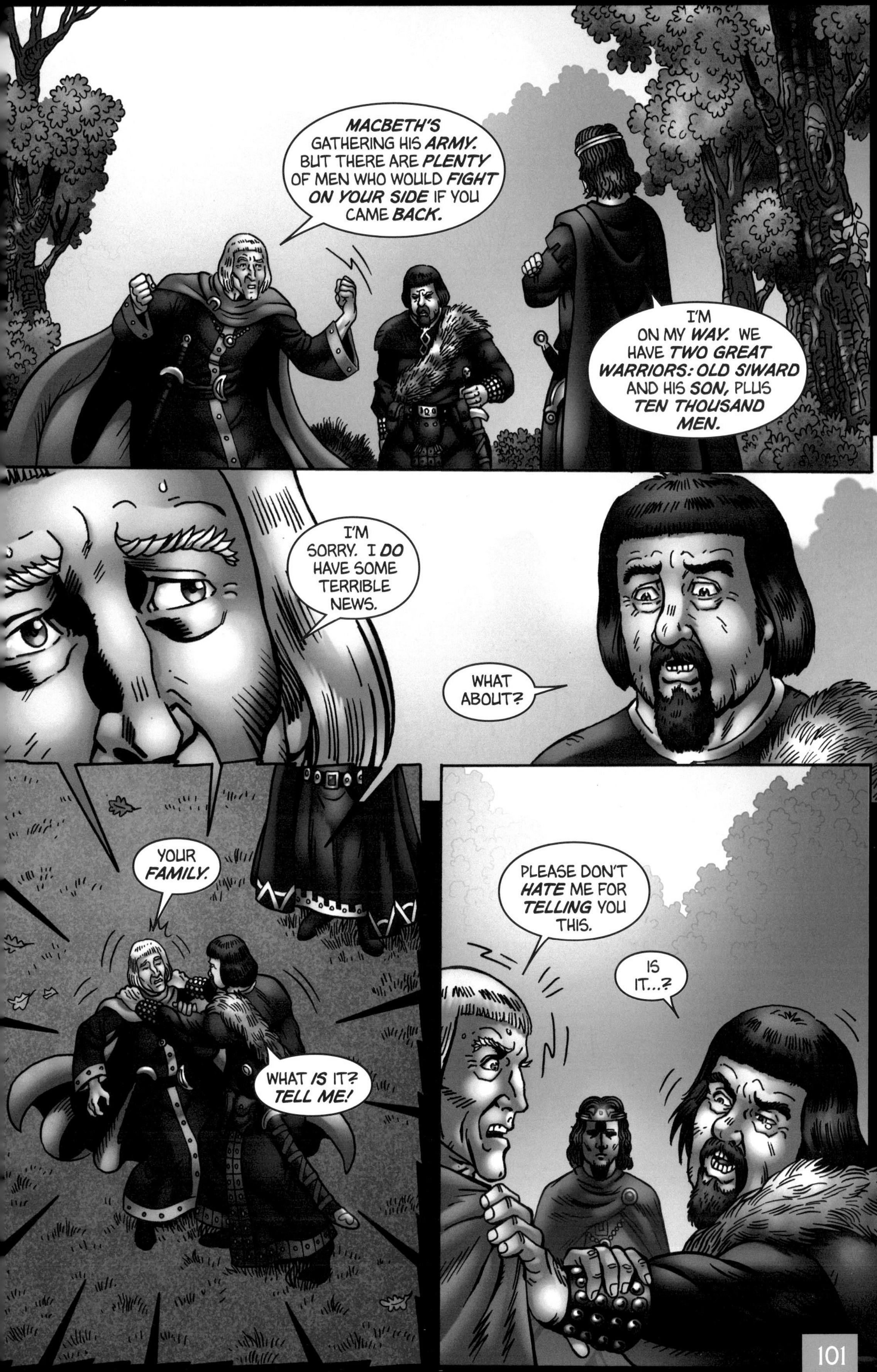
MACBETH'S GATHERING HIS ARMY. BUT THERE ARE PLENTY OF MEN WHO WOULD FIGHT ON YOUR SIDE IF YOU CAME BACK.
I'M ON MY WAY. WE HAVE TWO GREAT WARRIORS: OLD SIWARD AND HIS SON, PLUS TEN THOUSAND MEN.
I'M SORRY. I DO HAVE SOME TERRIBLE NEWS.
WHAT ABOUT?
YOUR FAMILY.
WHAT IS IT? TELL ME!
PLEASE DON'T HATE ME FOR TELLING YOU THIS.
IS IT...?

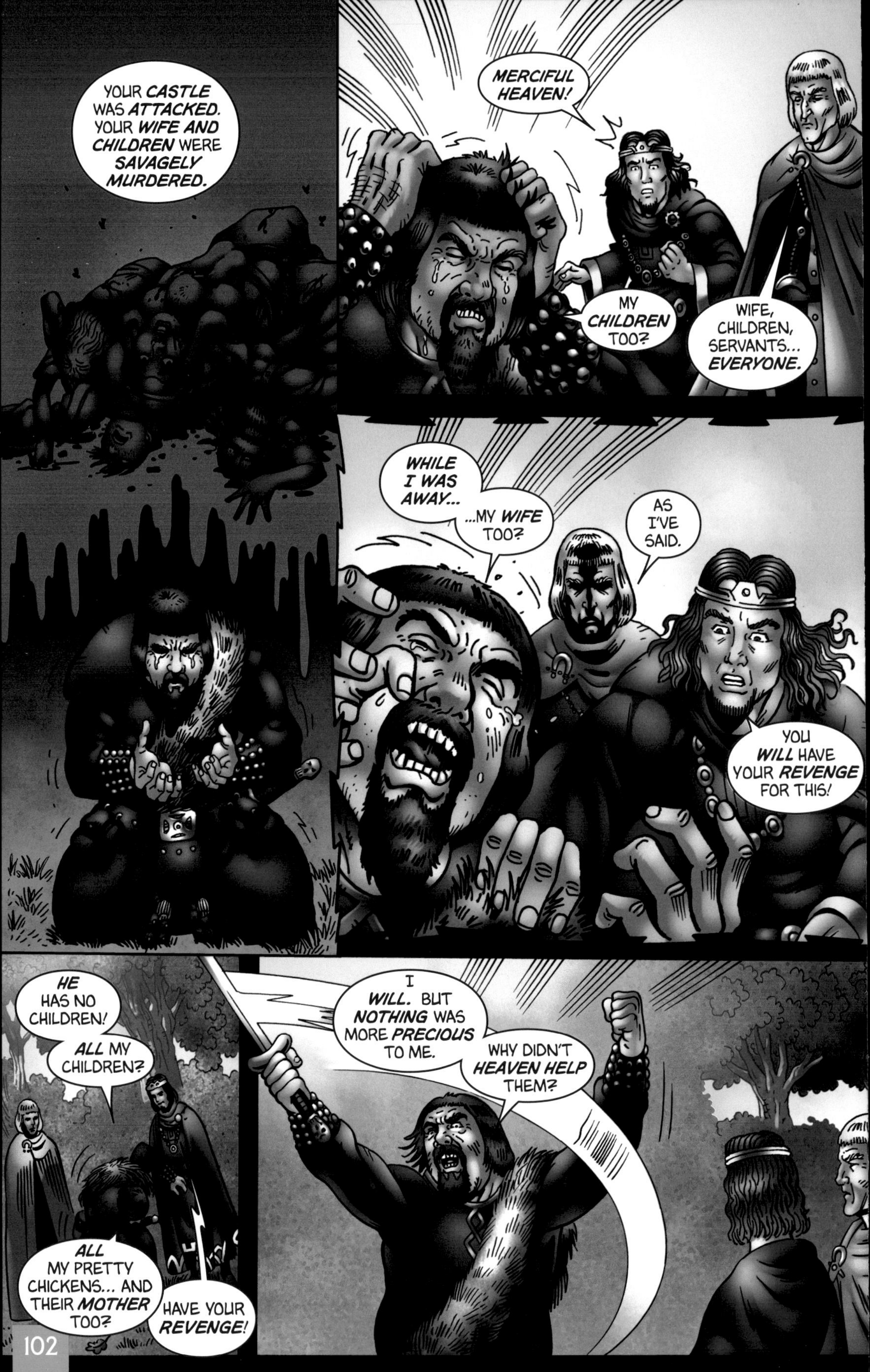
YOUR CASTLE WAS ATTACKED. YOUR WIFE AND CHILDREN WERE SAVAGELY MURDERED.
MERCIFUL HEAVEN!
MY CHILDREN TOO?
WIFE, CHILDREN, SERVANTS... EVERYONE.
WHILE I WAS AWAY...
...MY WIFE TOO?
AS I'VE SAID.
YOU WILL HAVE YOUR REVENGE FOR THIS!
HE HAS NO CHILDREN!
ALL MY CHILDREN?
ALL MY PRETTY CHICKENS... AND THEIR MOTHER TOO?
HAVE YOUR REVENGE!
I WILL. BUT NOTHING WAS MORE PRECIOUS TO ME.
WHY DIDN'T HEAVEN HELP THEM?

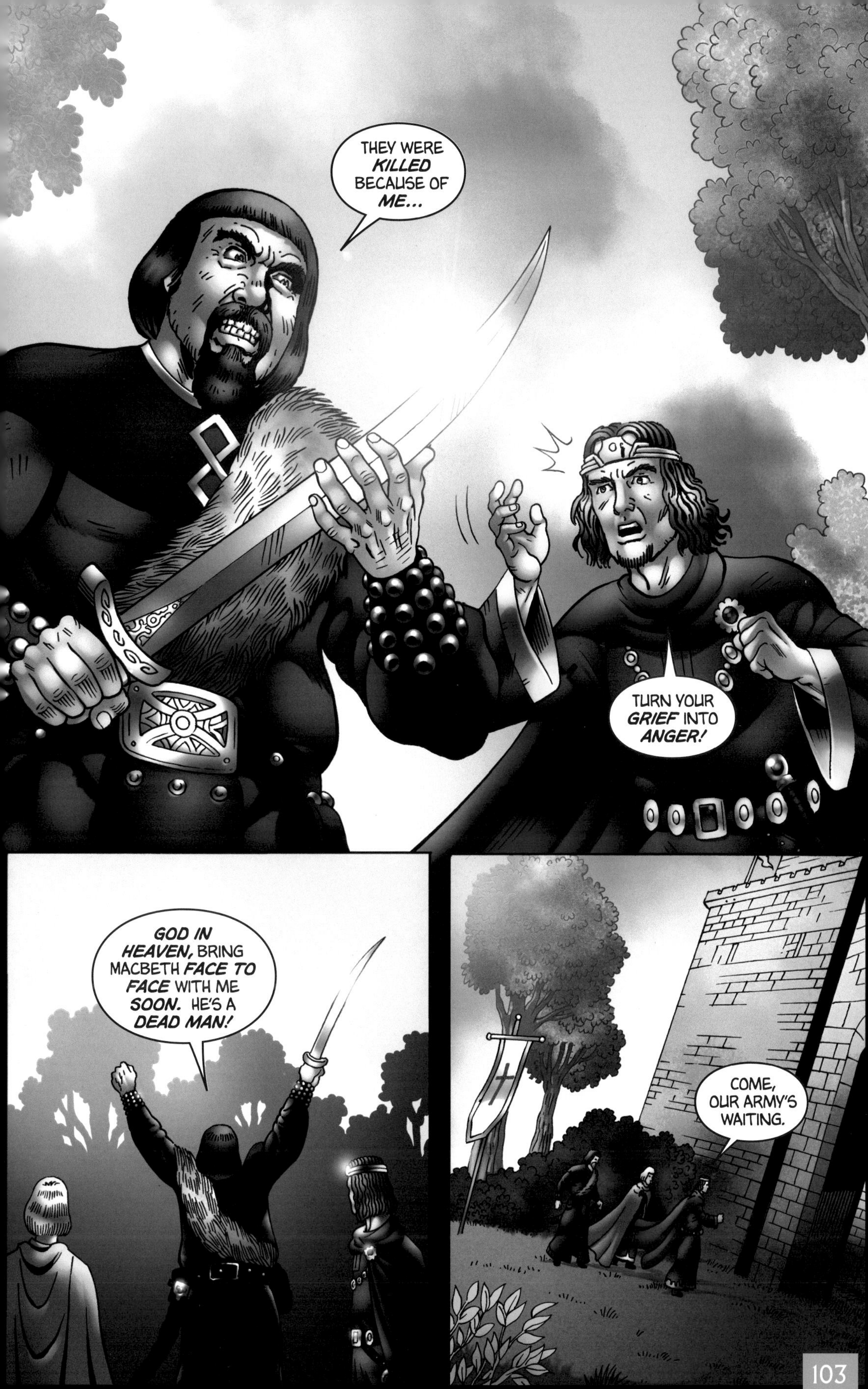
THEY WERE KILLED BECAUSE OF ME...
TURN YOUR GRIEF INTO ANGER!
GOD IN HEAVEN, BRING MACBETH FACE TO FACE WITH ME SOON. HE'S A DEAD MAN!
COME, OUR ARMY'S WAITING.

Late at night in Dunsinane Castle...

NOTHING FOR *TWO NIGHTS* - I'M STARTING TO *DOUBT* YOUR *STORY*.

SINCE THE *KING* WENT TO *WAR*, I HAVE SEEN HER *GET OUT OF BED* AND SLEEPWALK.

DOES SHE *SAY* ANYTHING?

NOTHING I CAN *REPEAT*.

YOU CAN TELL *ME*.

NO SIR, I'LL TELL *NO ONE*.

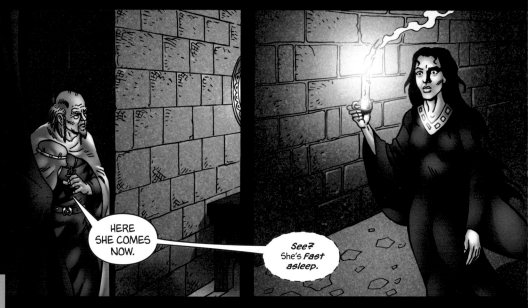

HERE SHE COMES NOW.

See? She's *fast* asleep.

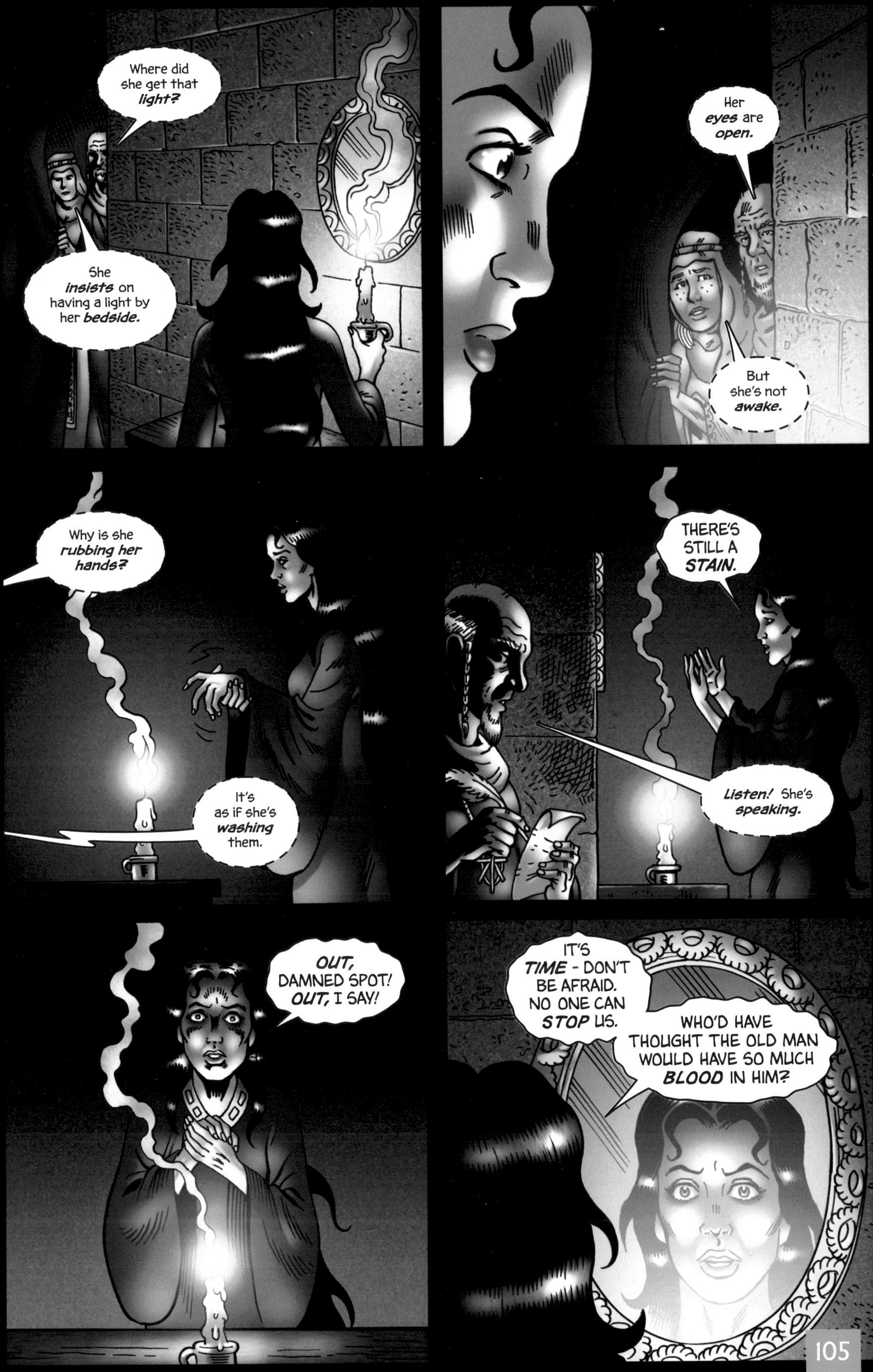
Where did she get that light?
She insists on having a light by her bedside.
Her eyes are open.
But she's not awake.
Why is she rubbing her hands?
It's as if she's washing them.
THERE'S STILL A STAIN.
Listen! She's speaking.
OUT, DAMNED SPOT! OUT, I SAY!
IT'S TIME - DON'T BE AFRAID. NO ONE CAN STOP US.
WHO'D HAVE THOUGHT THE OLD MAN WOULD HAVE SO MUCH BLOOD IN HIM?

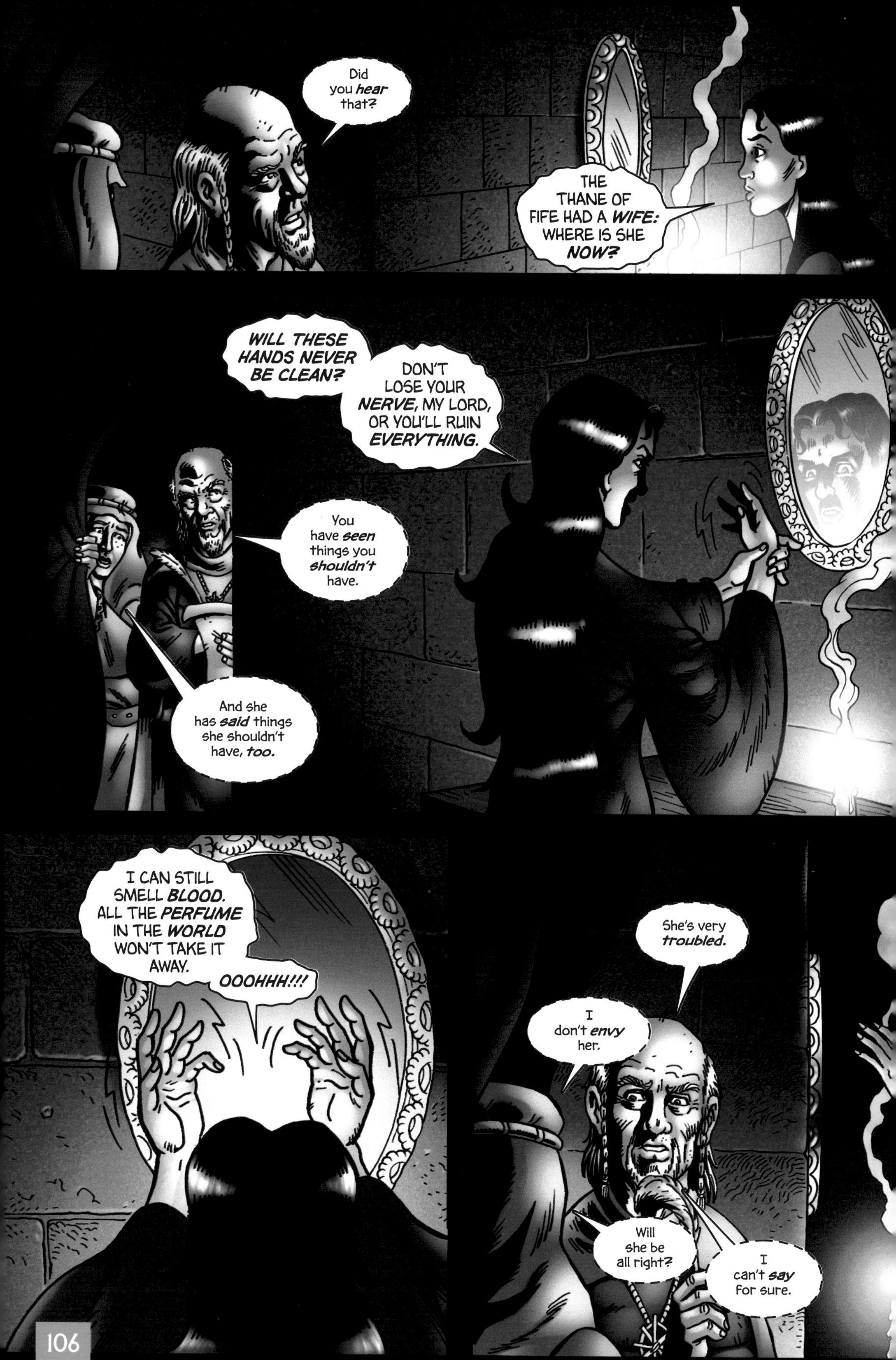
Did you *hear* that?
THE THANE OF FIFE HAD A *WIFE:* WHERE IS SHE *NOW?*
WILL THESE HANDS NEVER BE CLEAN?
DON'T LOSE YOUR *NERVE,* MY LORD, OR YOU'LL RUIN *EVERYTHING.*
You have *seen* things you *shouldn't* have.
And she has *said* things she shouldn't have, *too.*
I CAN STILL SMELL *BLOOD.* ALL THE *PERFUME* IN THE *WORLD* WON'T TAKE IT AWAY.
OOOHHH!!!
She's very *troubled.*
I don't *envy* her.
Will she be all right?
I can't *say* for sure.

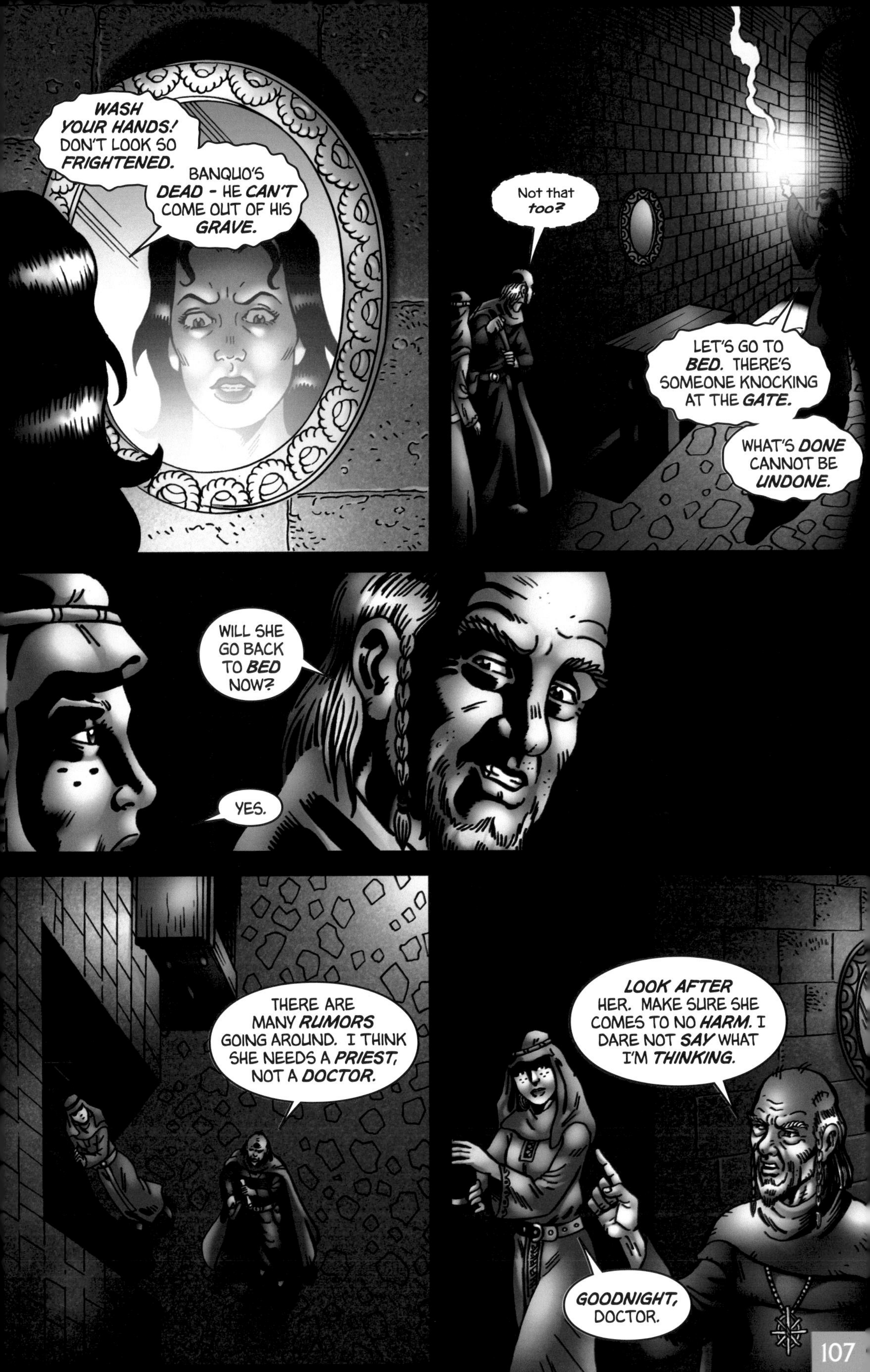
WASH YOUR HANDS! DON'T LOOK SO FRIGHTENED.
BANQUO'S DEAD - HE CAN'T COME OUT OF HIS GRAVE.
Not that too?
LET'S GO TO BED. THERE'S SOMEONE KNOCKING AT THE GATE.
WHAT'S DONE CANNOT BE UNDONE.
WILL SHE GO BACK TO BED NOW?
YES.
THERE ARE MANY RUMORS GOING AROUND. I THINK SHE NEEDS A PRIEST, NOT A DOCTOR.
LOOK AFTER HER. MAKE SURE SHE COMES TO NO HARM. I DARE NOT SAY WHAT I'M THINKING.
GOODNIGHT, DOCTOR.

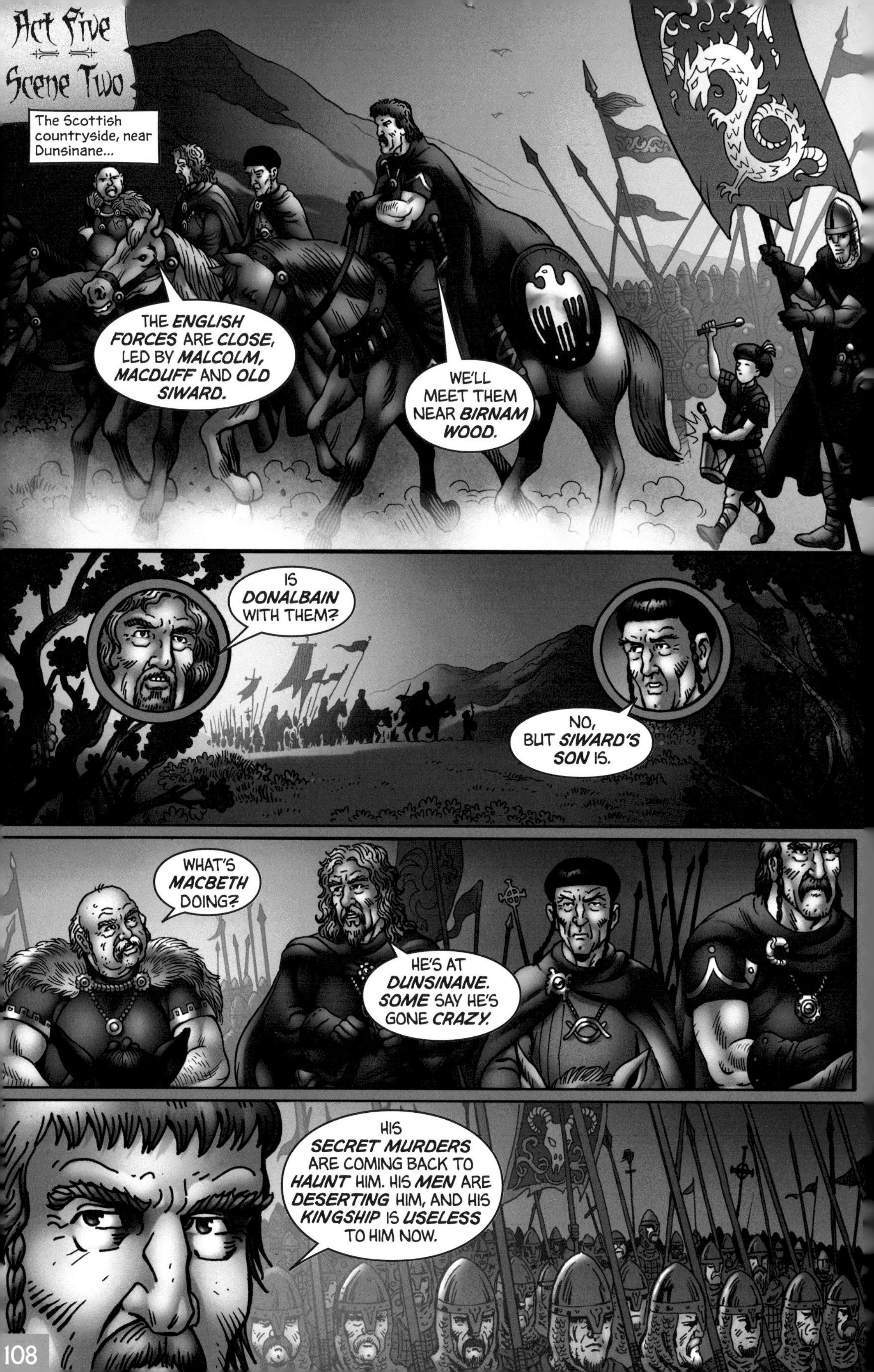
Act Five
Scene Two
The Scottish countryside, near Dunsinane...
THE ENGLISH FORCES ARE CLOSE, LED BY MALCOLM, MACDUFF AND OLD SIWARD.
WE'LL MEET THEM NEAR BIRNAM WOOD.
IS DONALBAIN WITH THEM?
NO, BUT SIWARD'S SON IS.
WHAT'S MACBETH DOING?
HE'S AT DUNSINANE. SOME SAY HE'S GONE CRAZY.
HIS SECRET MURDERS ARE COMING BACK TO HAUNT HIM. HIS MEN ARE DESERTING HIM, AND HIS KINGSHIP IS USELESS TO HIM NOW.

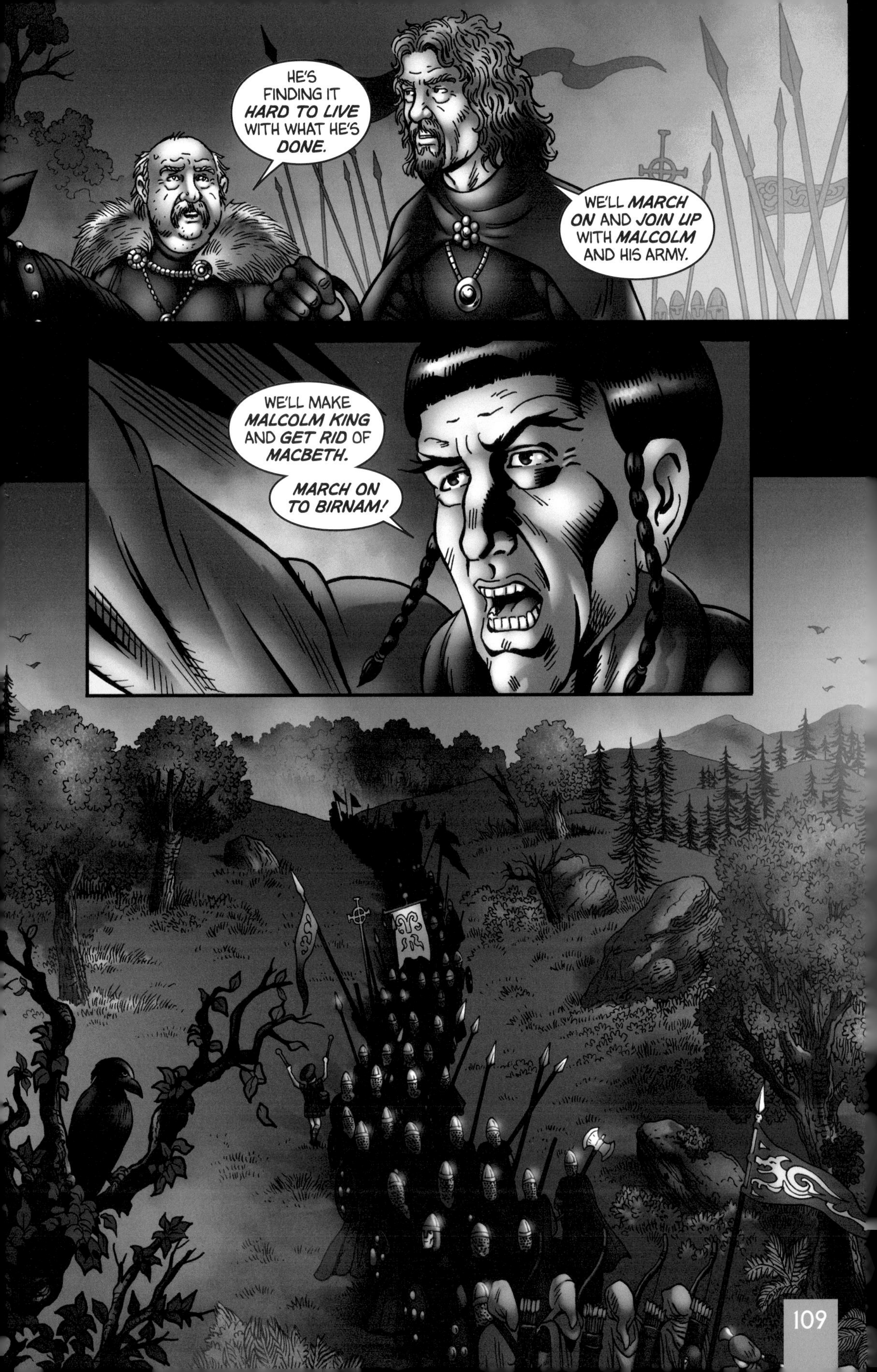
HE'S FINDING IT HARD TO LIVE WITH WHAT HE'S DONE.
WE'LL MARCH ON AND JOIN UP WITH MALCOLM AND HIS ARMY.
WE'LL MAKE MALCOLM KING AND GET RID OF MACBETH.
MARCH ON TO BIRNAM!

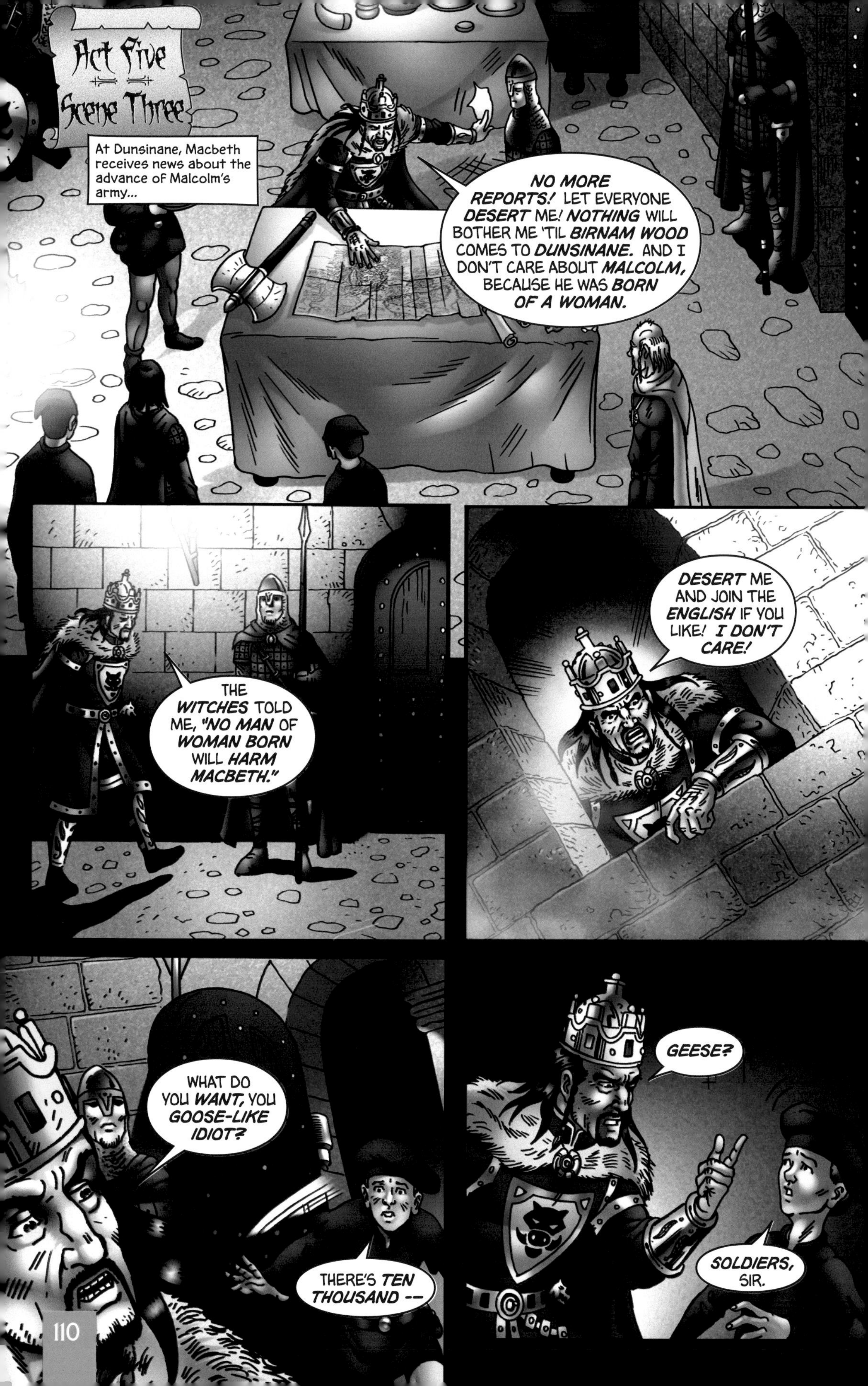
Act Five
Scene Three
At Dunsinane, Macbeth receives news about the advance of Malcolm's army...
NO MORE REPORTS! LET EVERYONE DESERT ME! NOTHING WILL BOTHER ME 'TIL BIRNAM WOOD COMES TO DUNSINANE. AND I DON'T CARE ABOUT MALCOLM, BECAUSE HE WAS BORN OF A WOMAN.
THE WITCHES TOLD ME, "NO MAN OF WOMAN BORN WILL HARM MACBETH."
DESERT ME AND JOIN THE ENGLISH IF YOU LIKE! I DON'T CARE!
WHAT DO YOU WANT, YOU GOOSE-LIKE IDIOT?
THERE'S TEN THOUSAND --
GEESE?
SOLDIERS, SIR.

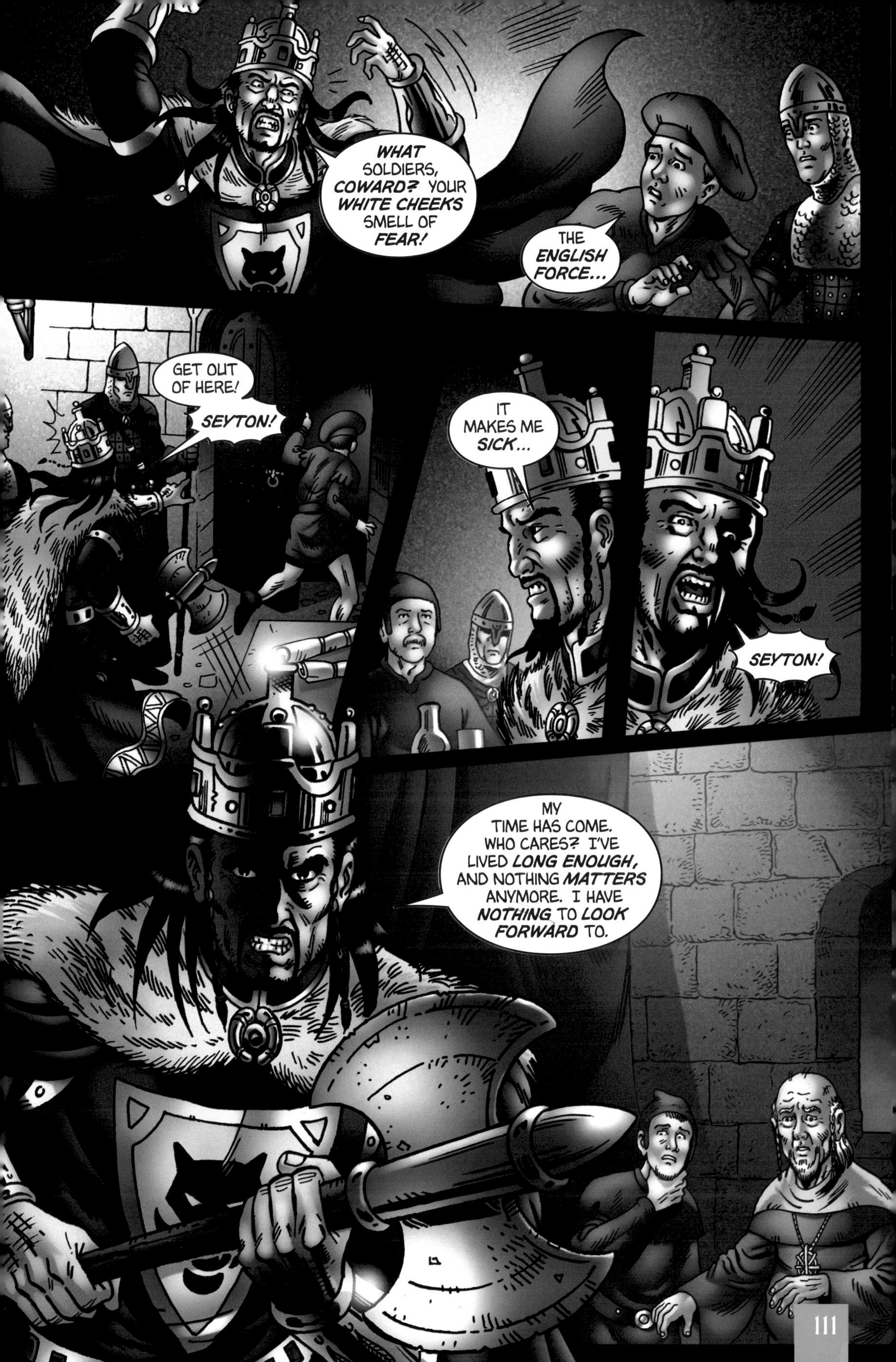
WHAT SOLDIERS, COWARD? YOUR WHITE CHEEKS SMELL OF FEAR!
THE ENGLISH FORCE...
GET OUT OF HERE!
SEYTON!
IT MAKES ME SICK...
SEYTON!
MY TIME HAS COME. WHO CARES? I'VE LIVED LONG ENOUGH, AND NOTHING MATTERS ANYMORE. I HAVE NOTHING TO LOOK FORWARD TO.

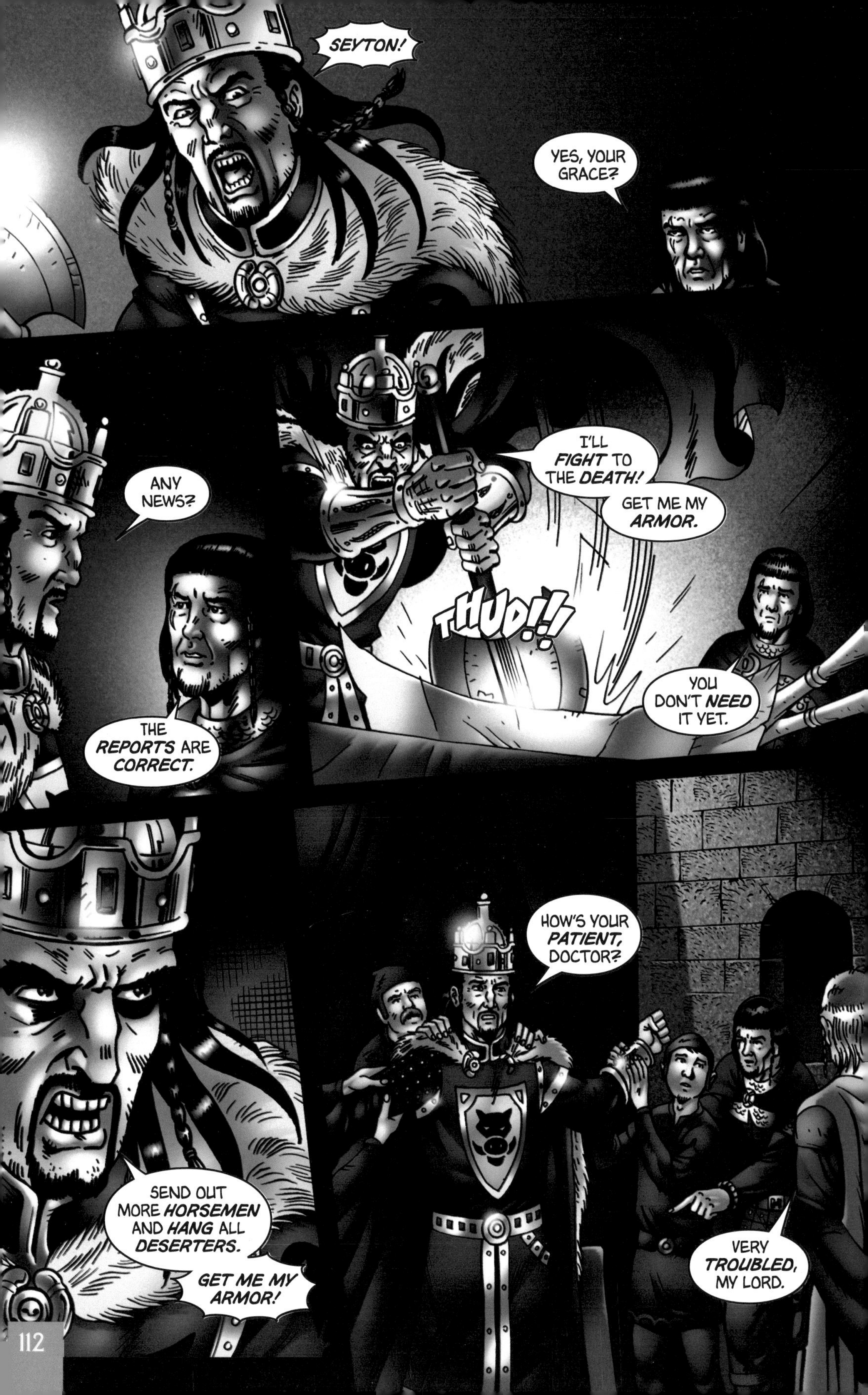
SEYTON!
YES, YOUR GRACE?
ANY NEWS?
THE REPORTS ARE CORRECT.
I'LL FIGHT TO THE DEATH!
GET ME MY ARMOR.
THUD!!!
YOU DON'T NEED IT YET.
SEND OUT MORE HORSEMEN AND HANG ALL DESERTERS.
GET ME MY ARMOR!
HOW'S YOUR PATIENT, DOCTOR?
VERY TROUBLED, MY LORD.

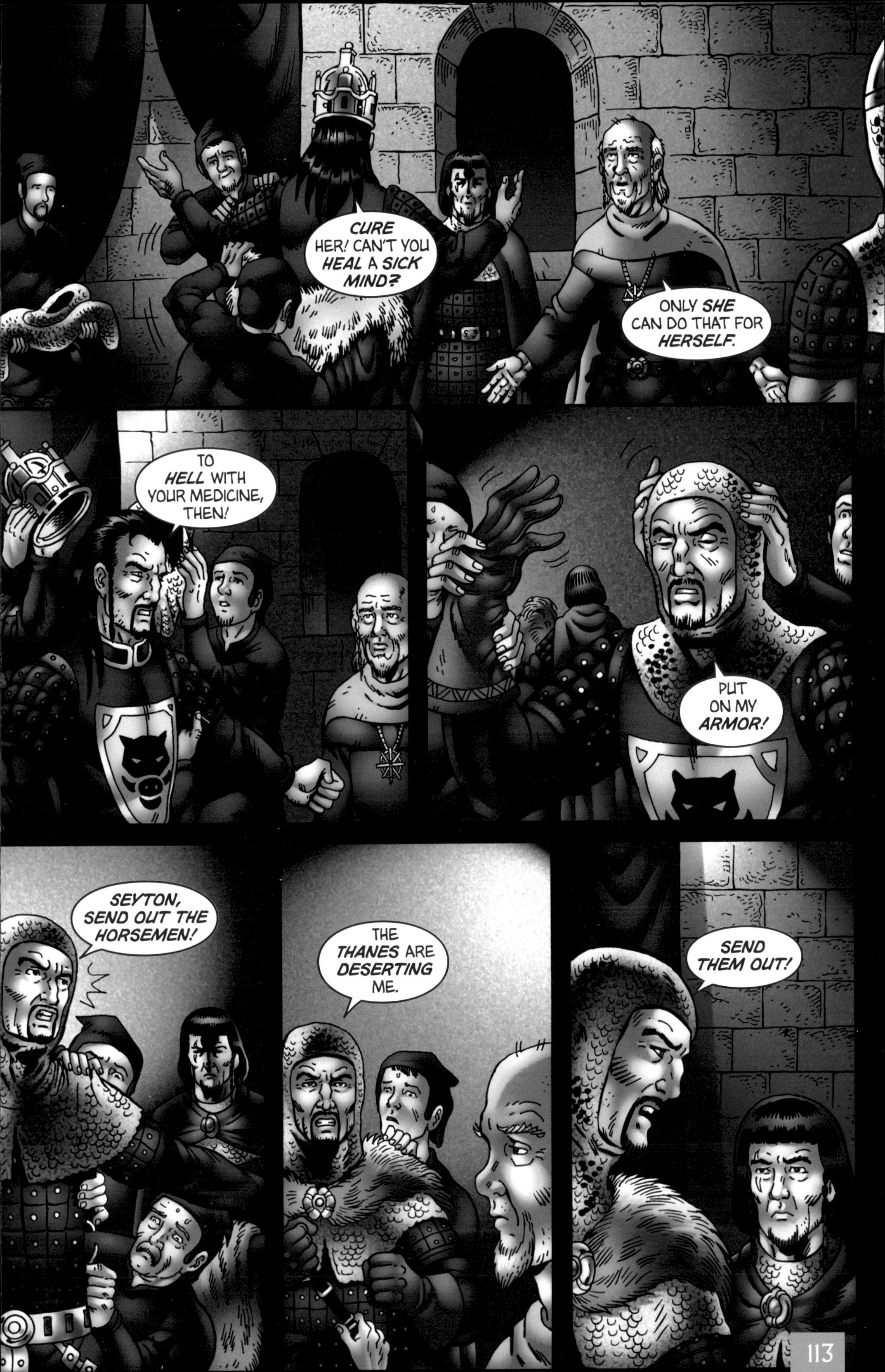
CURE HER! CAN'T YOU HEAL A SICK MIND?
ONLY SHE CAN DO THAT FOR HERSELF.
TO HELL WITH YOUR MEDICINE, THEN!
PUT ON MY ARMOR!
SEYTON, SEND OUT THE HORSEMEN!
THE THANES ARE DESERTING ME.
SEND THEM OUT!

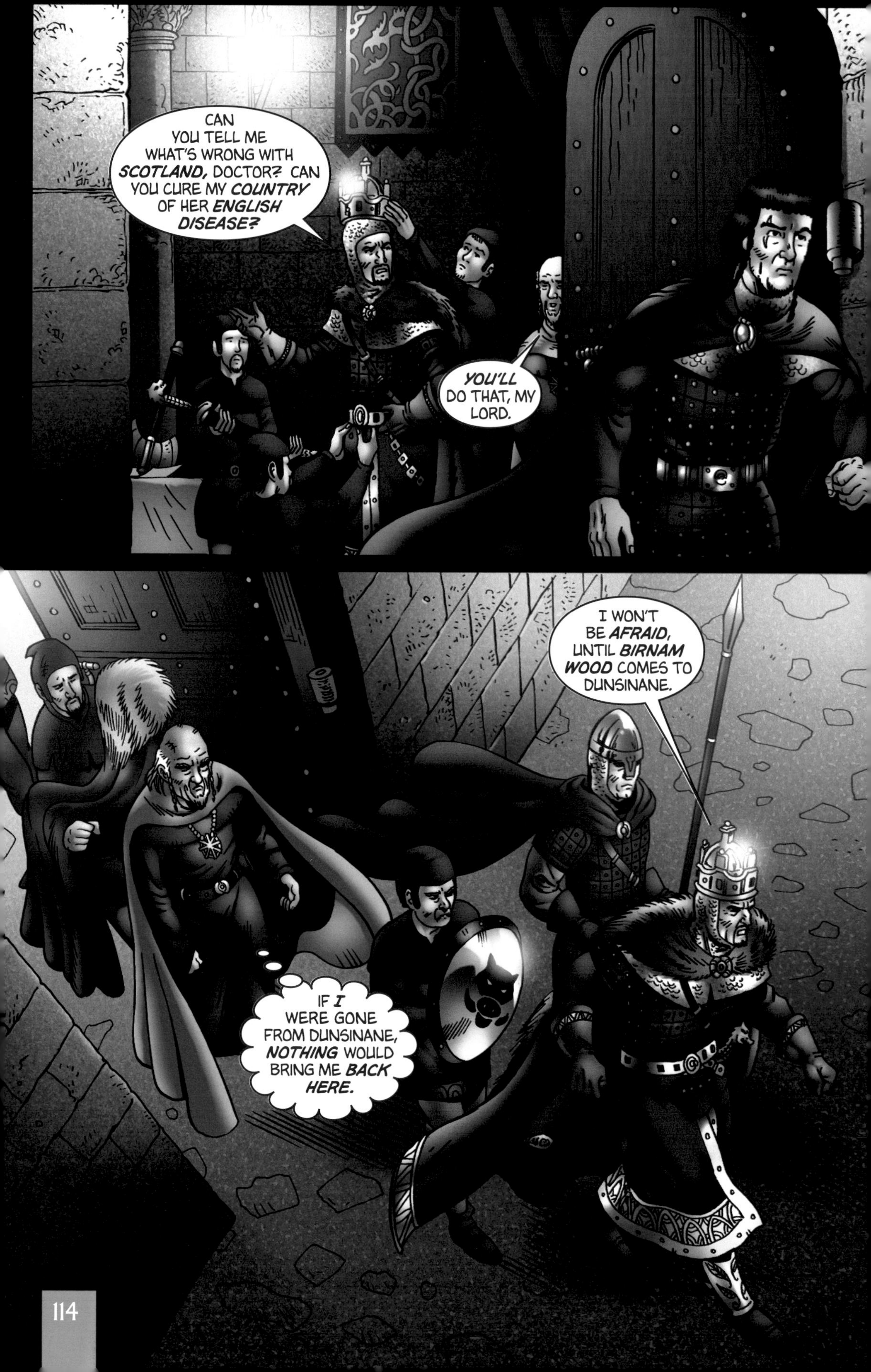
CAN YOU TELL ME WHAT'S WRONG WITH SCOTLAND, DOCTOR? CAN YOU CURE MY COUNTRY OF HER ENGLISH DISEASE?
YOU'LL DO THAT, MY LORD.
I WON'T BE AFRAID, UNTIL BIRNAM WOOD COMES TO DUNSINANE.
IF I WERE GONE FROM DUNSINANE, NOTHING WOULD BRING ME BACK HERE.

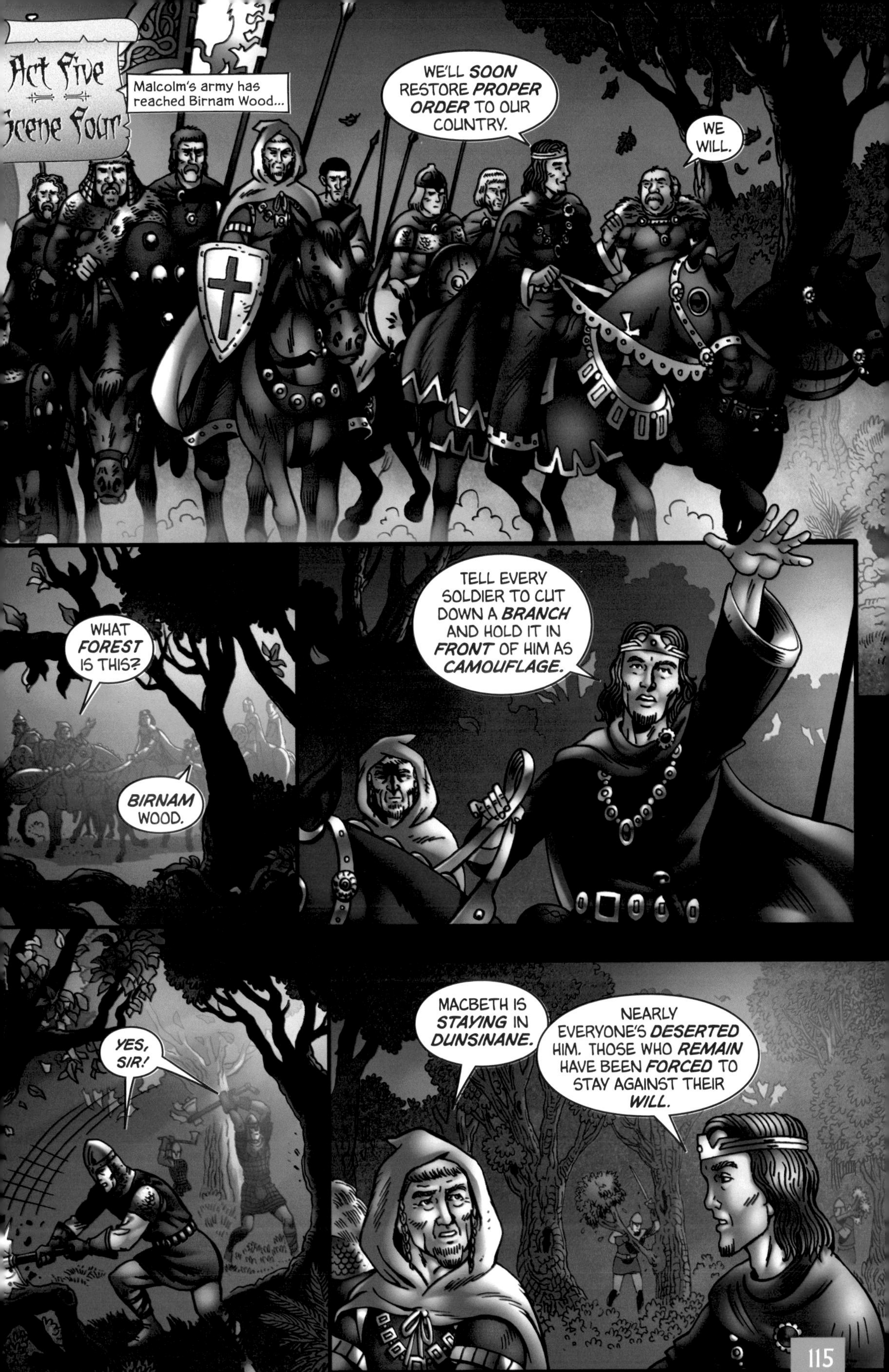
Act Five
Scene Four
Malcolm's army has reached Birnam Wood...
WE'LL SOON RESTORE PROPER ORDER TO OUR COUNTRY.
WE WILL.
WHAT FOREST IS THIS?
BIRNAM WOOD.
TELL EVERY SOLDIER TO CUT DOWN A BRANCH AND HOLD IT IN FRONT OF HIM AS CAMOUFLAGE.
YES, SIR!
MACBETH IS STAYING IN DUNSINANE.
NEARLY EVERYONE'S DESERTED HIM. THOSE WHO REMAIN HAVE BEEN FORCED TO STAY AGAINST THEIR WILL.

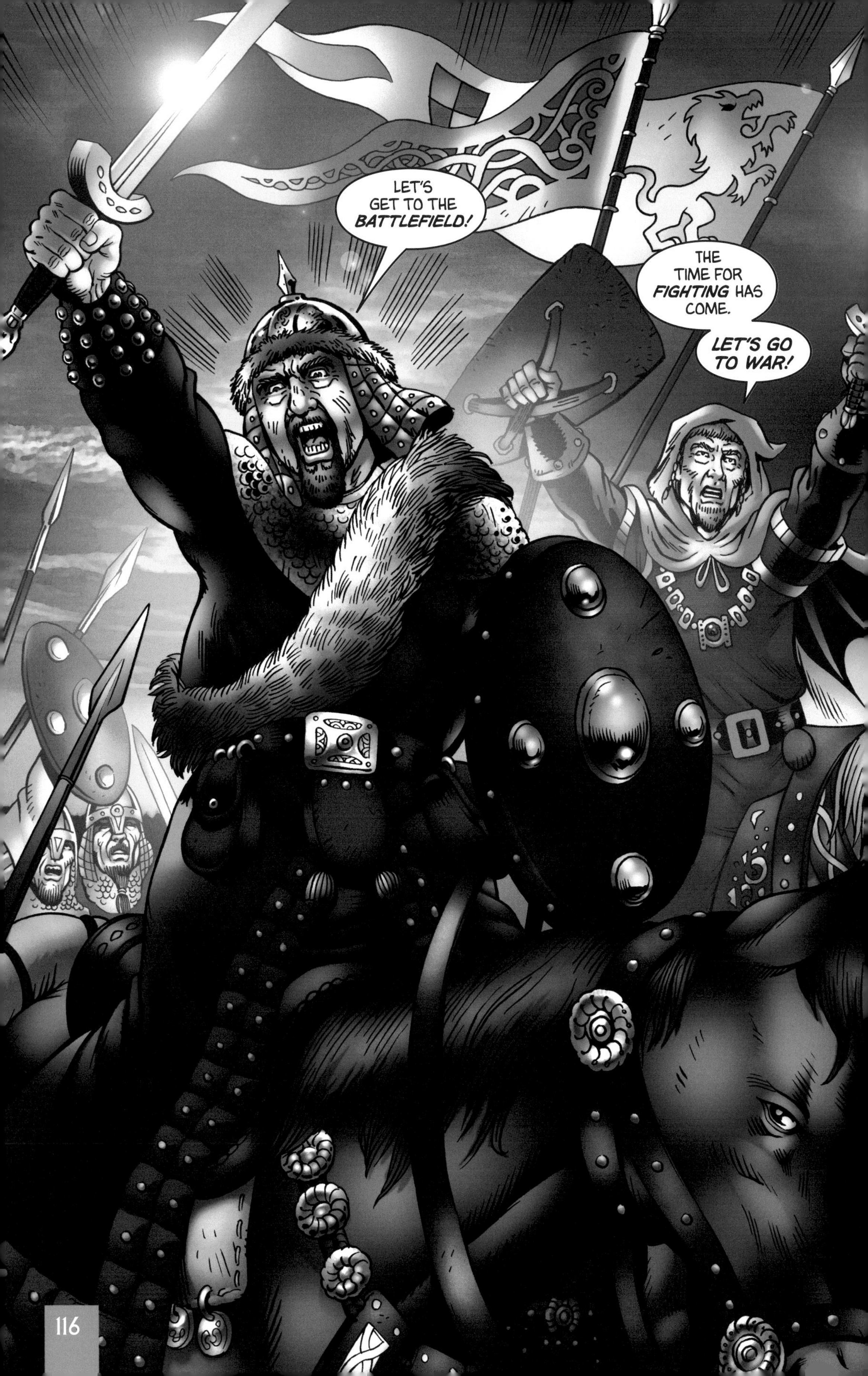
LET'S GET TO THE *BATTLEFIELD!*
THE TIME FOR *FIGHTING* HAS COME.
LET'S GO TO WAR!

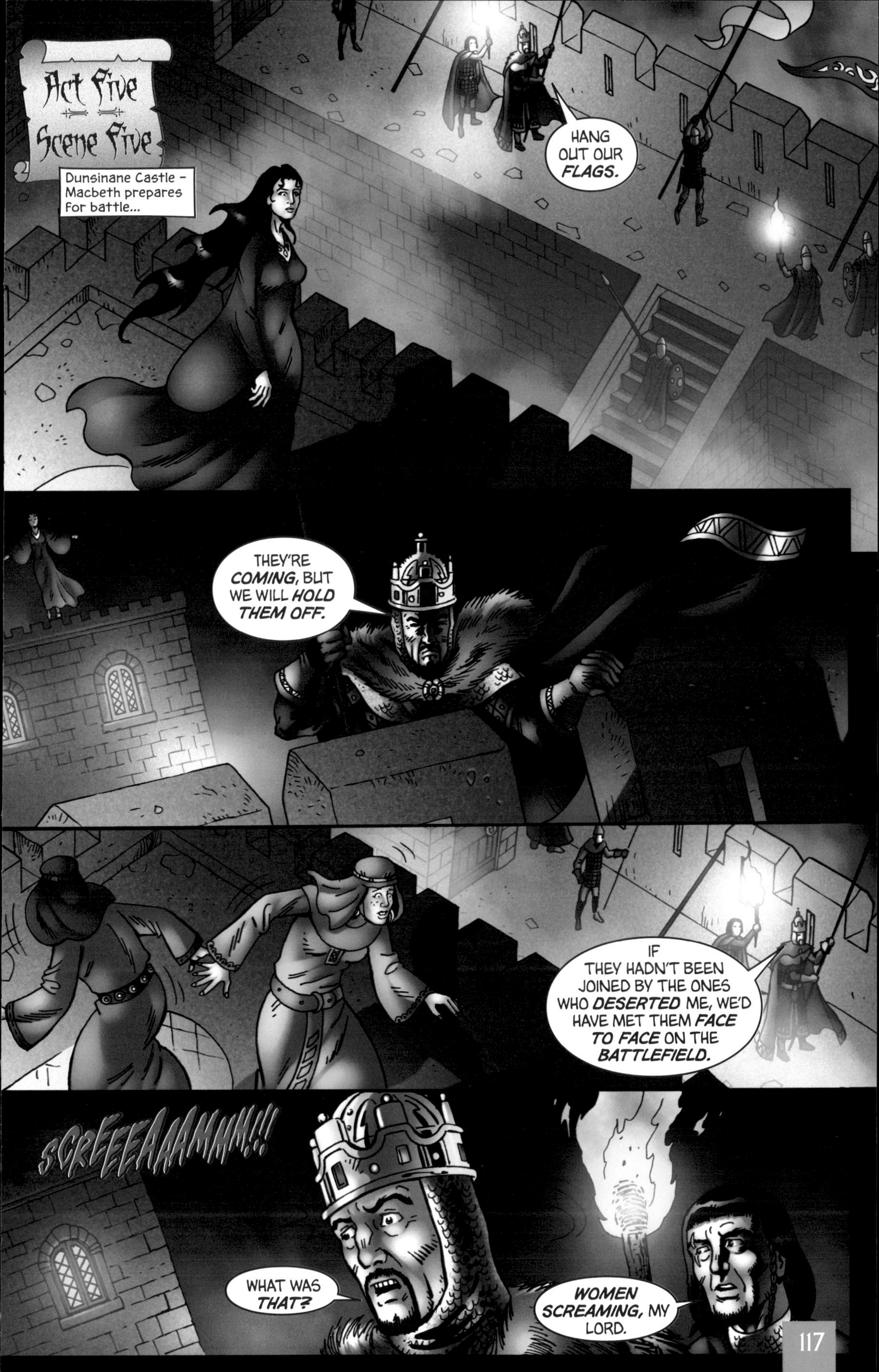
Act Five
Scene Five
Dunsinane Castle – Macbeth prepares for battle...
HANG OUT OUR FLAGS.
THEY'RE COMING, BUT WE WILL HOLD THEM OFF.
IF THEY HADN'T BEEN JOINED BY THE ONES WHO DESERTED ME, WE'D HAVE MET THEM FACE TO FACE ON THE BATTLEFIELD.
SCREEEAAAMMM!!
WHAT WAS THAT?
WOMEN SCREAMING, MY LORD.

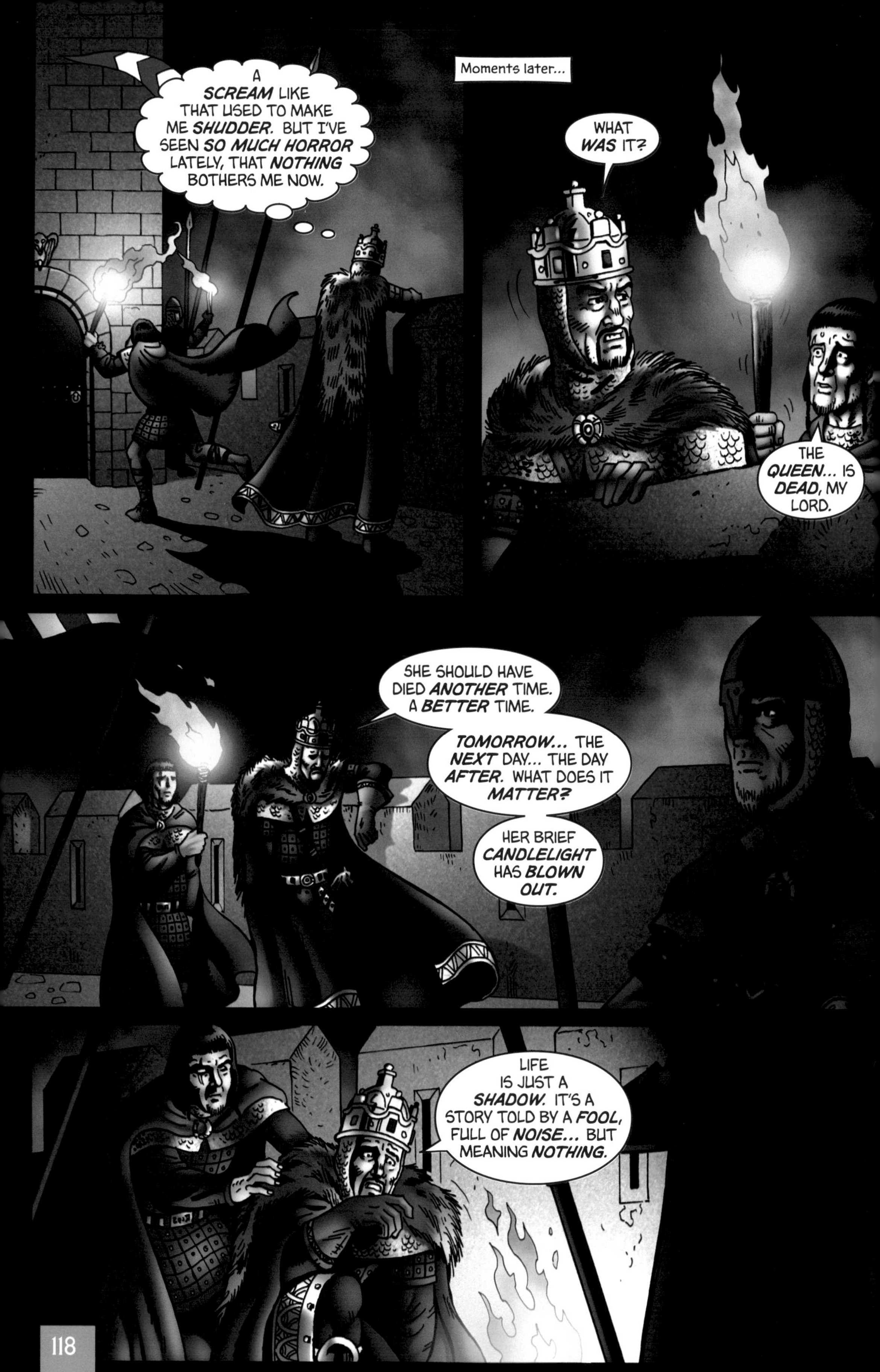
A SCREAM LIKE THAT USED TO MAKE ME SHUDDER. BUT I'VE SEEN SO MUCH HORROR LATELY, THAT NOTHING BOTHERS ME NOW.
Moments later...
WHAT WAS IT?
THE QUEEN... IS DEAD, MY LORD.
SHE SHOULD HAVE DIED ANOTHER TIME. A BETTER TIME.
TOMORROW... THE NEXT DAY... THE DAY AFTER. WHAT DOES IT MATTER?
HER BRIEF CANDLELIGHT HAS BLOWN OUT.
LIFE IS JUST A SHADOW. IT'S A STORY TOLD BY A FOOL, FULL OF NOISE... BUT MEANING NOTHING.

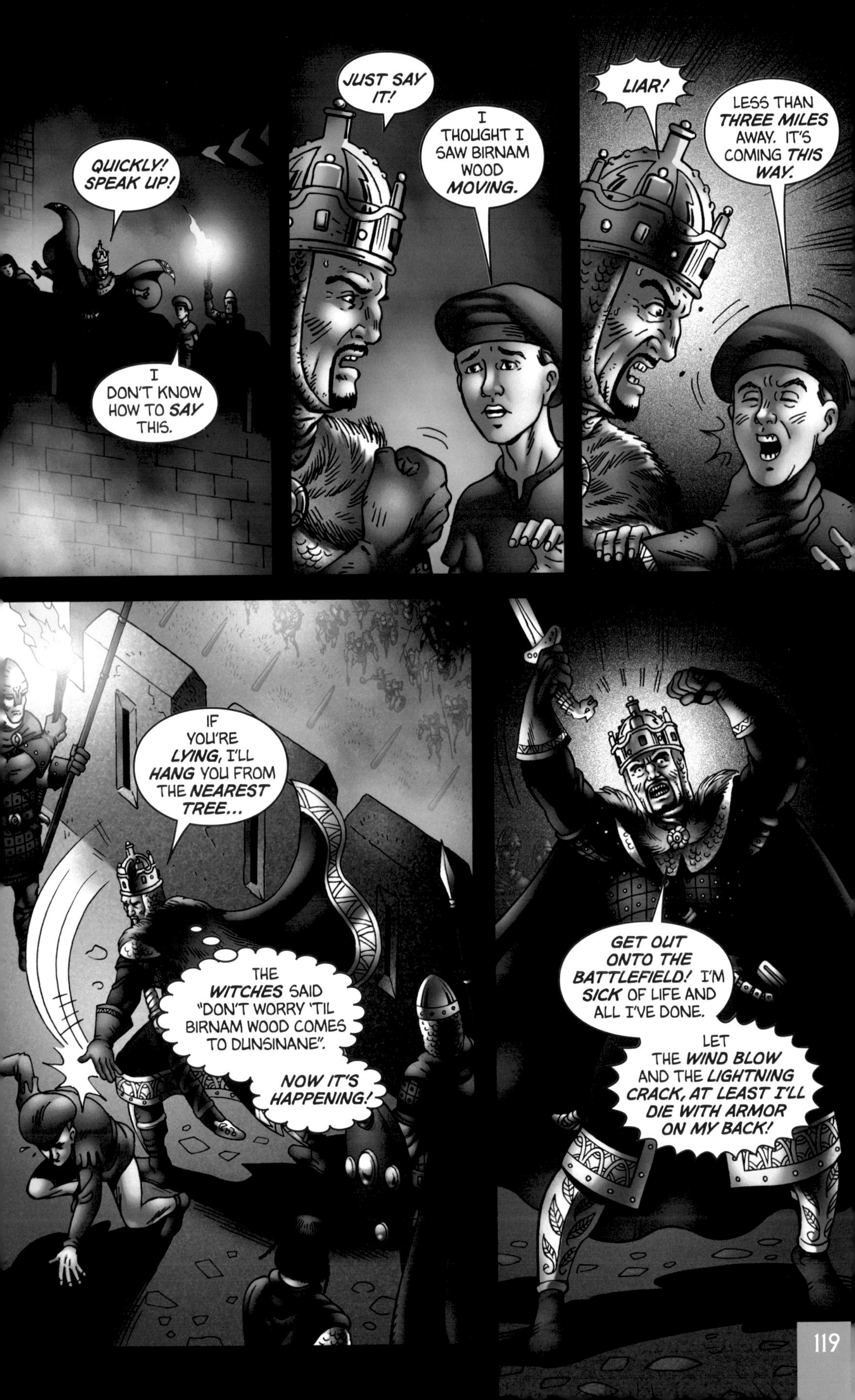
QUICKLY! SPEAK UP!
I DON'T KNOW HOW TO SAY THIS.
JUST SAY IT!
I THOUGHT I SAW BIRNAM WOOD MOVING.
LIAR!
LESS THAN THREE MILES AWAY. IT'S COMING THIS WAY.
IF YOU'RE LYING, I'LL HANG YOU FROM THE NEAREST TREE...
THE WITCHES SAID "DON'T WORRY 'TIL BIRNAM WOOD COMES TO DUNSINANE".
NOW IT'S HAPPENING!
GET OUT ONTO THE BATTLEFIELD! I'M SICK OF LIFE AND ALL I'VE DONE.
LET THE WIND BLOW AND THE LIGHTNING CRACK, AT LEAST I'LL DIE WITH ARMOR ON MY BACK!

Act Five
Scene Six

Malcolm's army has reached Dunsinane...

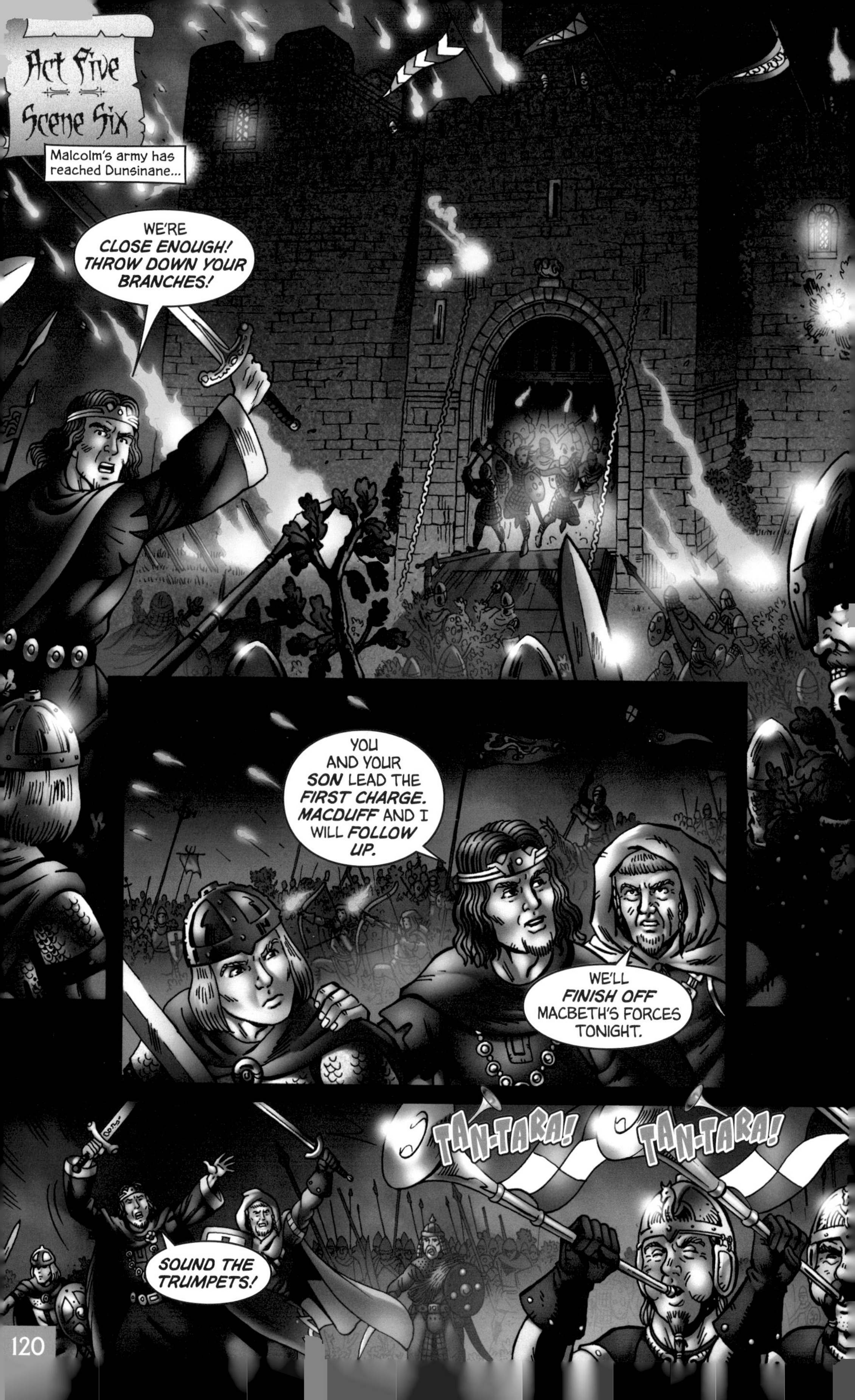
WE'RE CLOSE ENOUGH! THROW DOWN YOUR BRANCHES!
YOU AND YOUR SON LEAD THE FIRST CHARGE. MACDUFF AND I WILL FOLLOW UP.
WE'LL FINISH OFF MACBETH'S FORCES TONIGHT.
SOUND THE TRUMPETS!
TAN-TARA!
TAN-TARA!

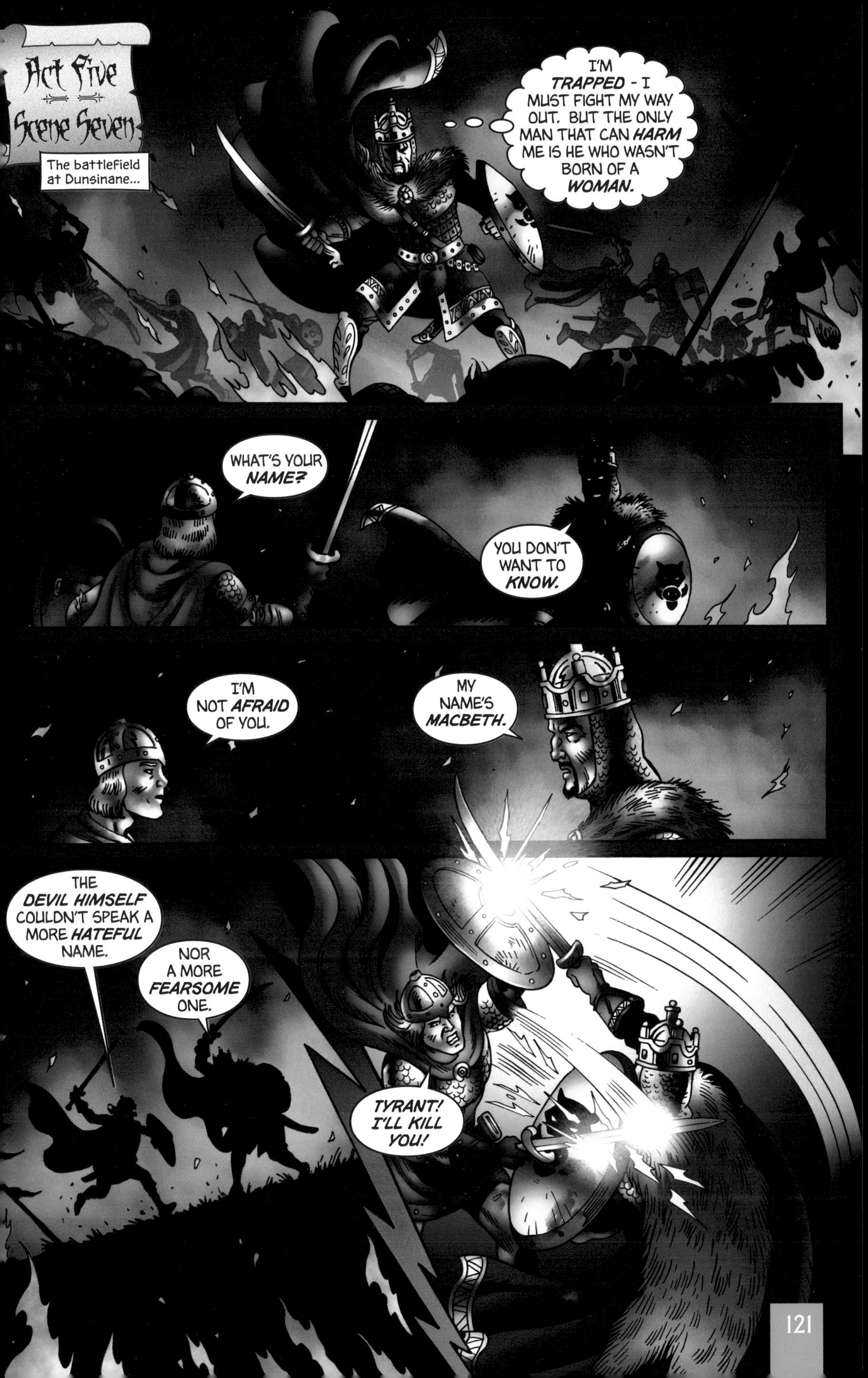
Act Five
Scene Seven
The battlefield at Dunsinane...
I'M TRAPPED - I MUST FIGHT MY WAY OUT. BUT THE ONLY MAN THAT CAN HARM ME IS HE WHO WASN'T BORN OF A WOMAN.
WHAT'S YOUR NAME?
YOU DON'T WANT TO KNOW.
I'M NOT AFRAID OF YOU.
MY NAME'S MACBETH.
THE DEVIL HIMSELF COULDN'T SPEAK A MORE HATEFUL NAME.
NOR A MORE FEARSOME ONE.
TYRANT! I'LL KILL YOU!

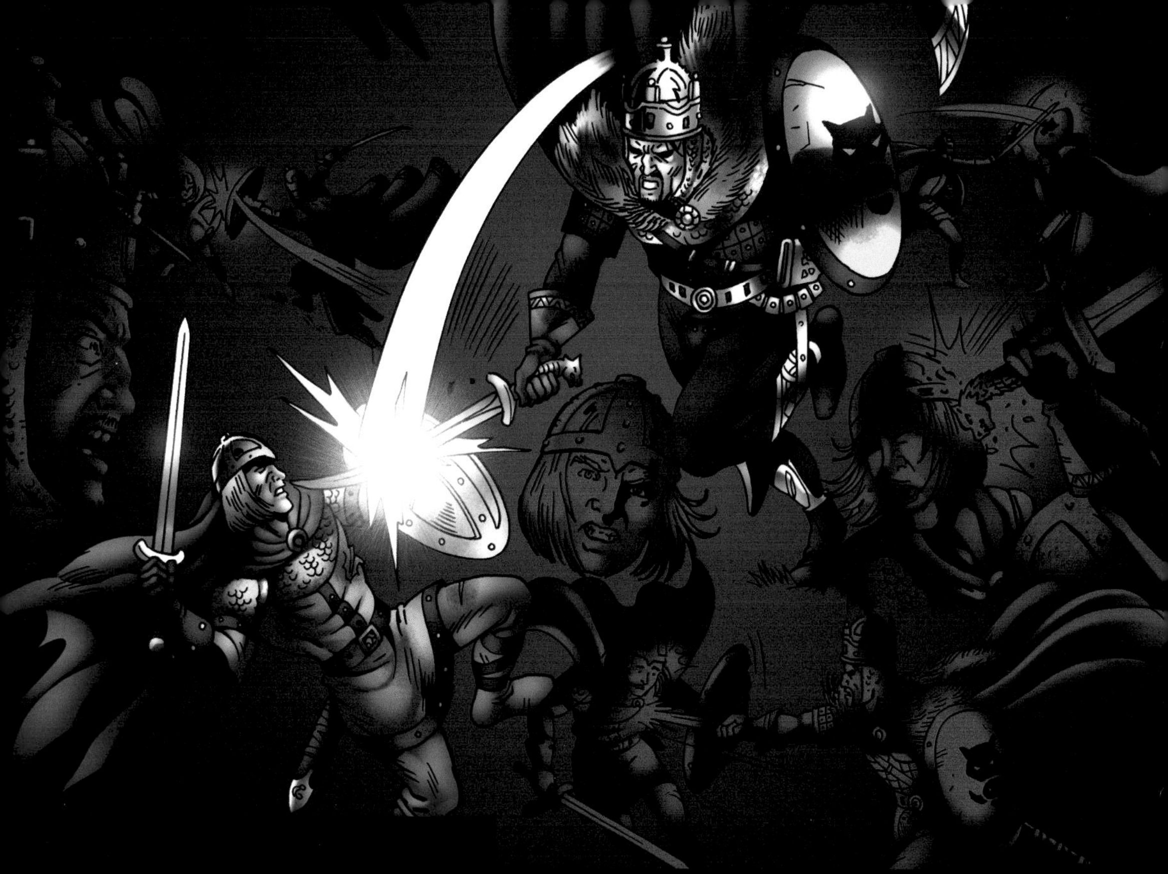

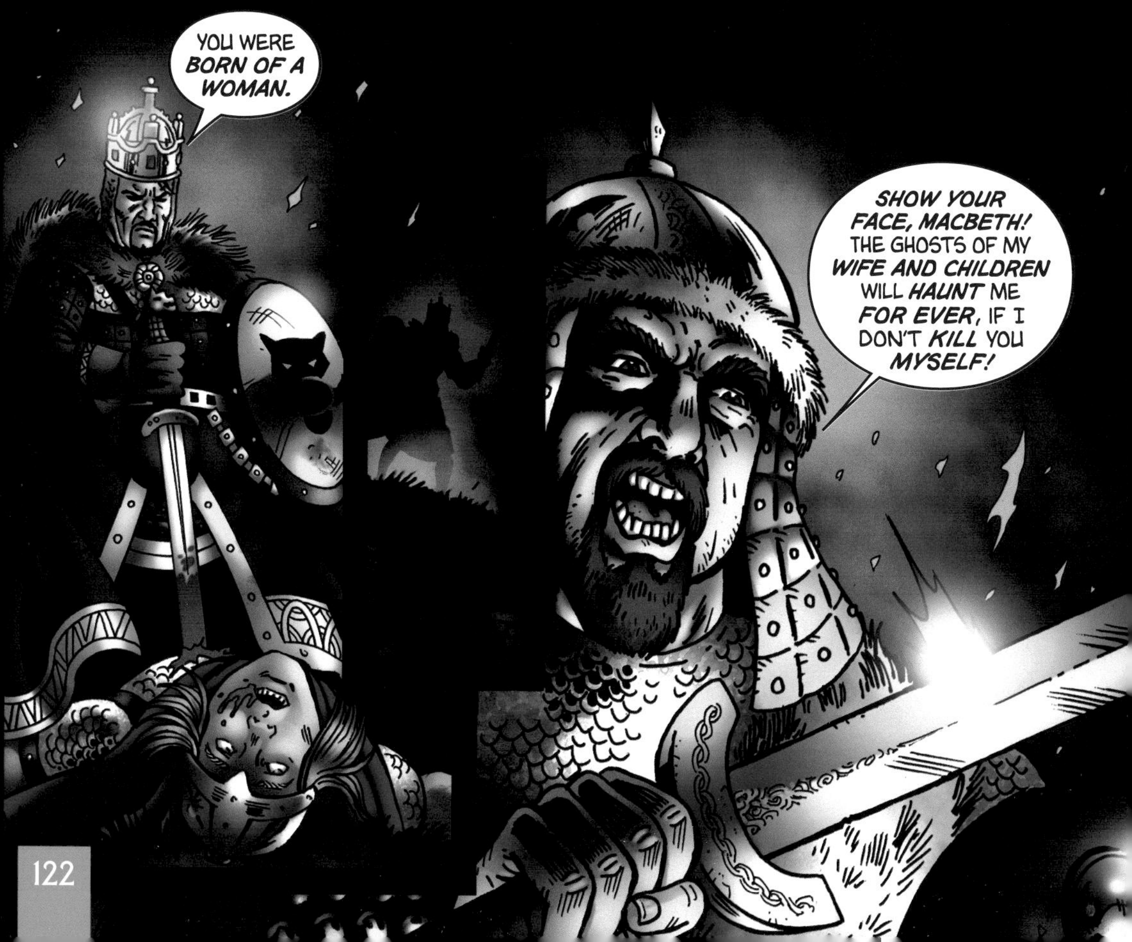
YOU WERE BORN OF A WOMAN.
SHOW YOUR FACE, MACBETH! THE GHOSTS OF MY WIFE AND CHILDREN WILL HAUNT ME FOR EVER, IF I DON'T KILL YOU MYSELF!

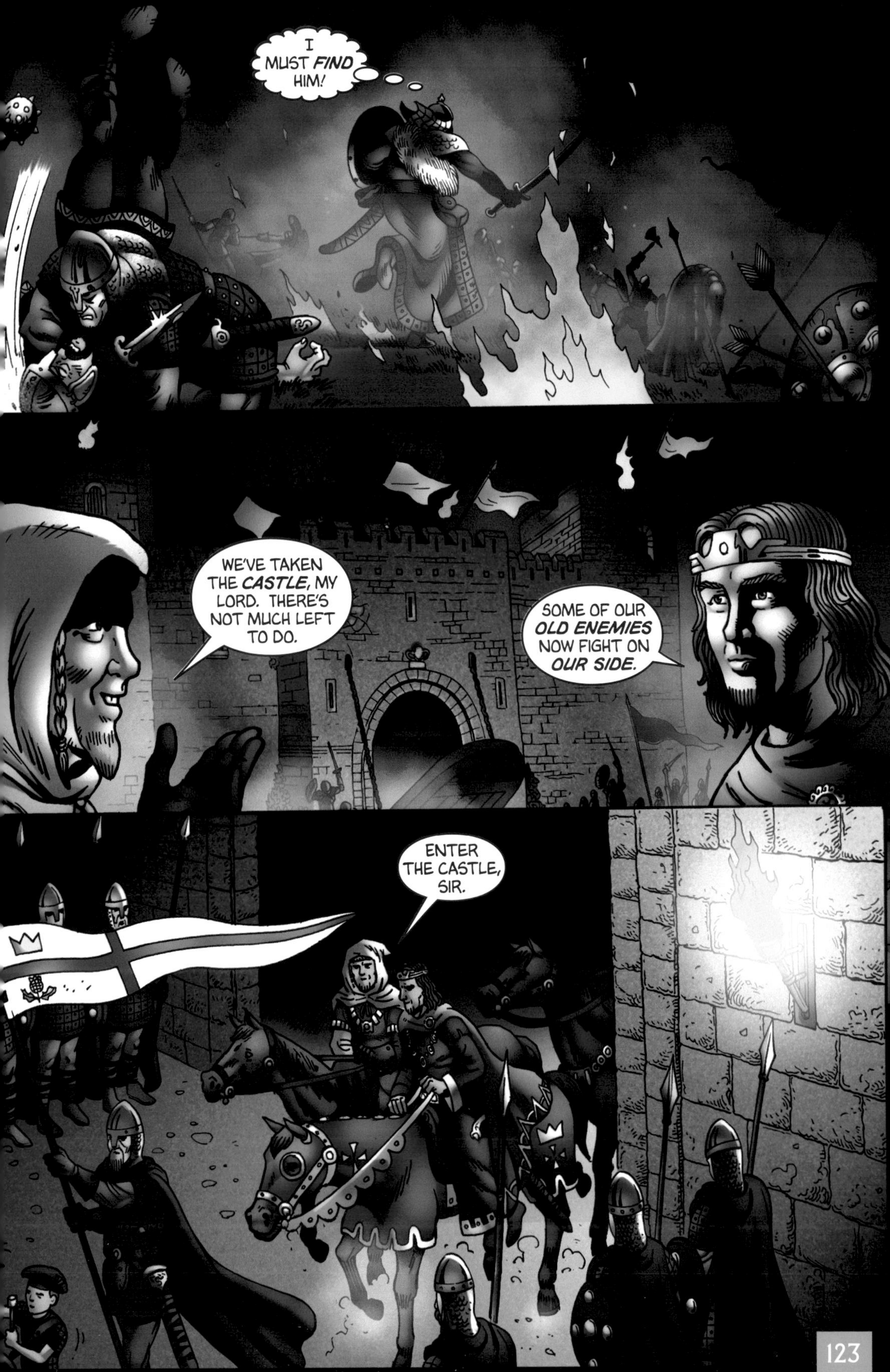
I MUST FIND HIM!
WE'VE TAKEN THE CASTLE, MY LORD. THERE'S NOT MUCH LEFT TO DO.
SOME OF OUR OLD ENEMIES NOW FIGHT ON OUR SIDE.
ENTER THE CASTLE, SIR.

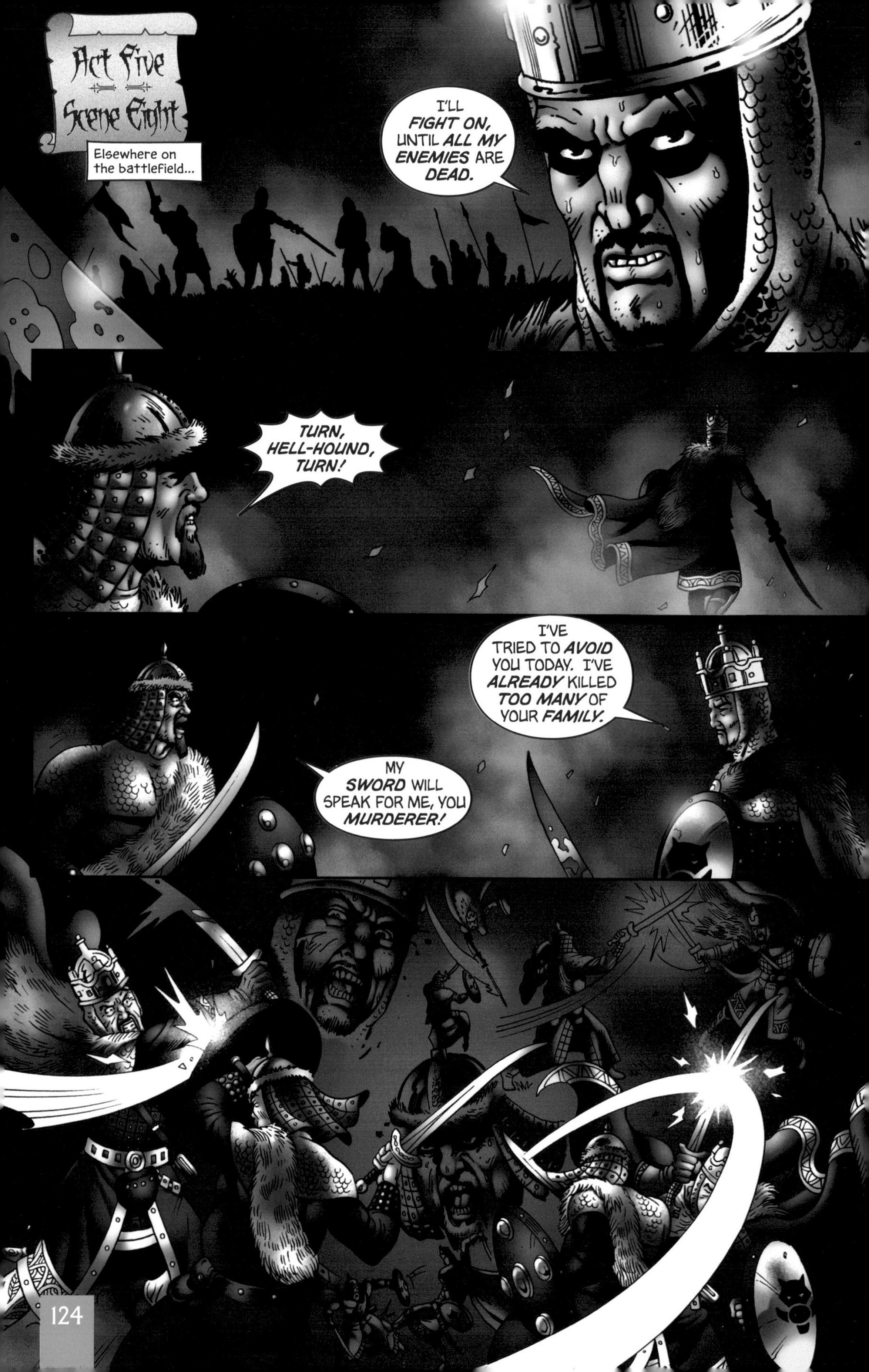
Act Five
Scene Eight
Elsewhere on the battlefield...
I'LL FIGHT ON, UNTIL ALL MY ENEMIES ARE DEAD.
TURN, HELL-HOUND, TURN!
I'VE TRIED TO AVOID YOU TODAY. I'VE ALREADY KILLED TOO MANY OF YOUR FAMILY.
MY SWORD WILL SPEAK FOR ME, YOU MURDERER!

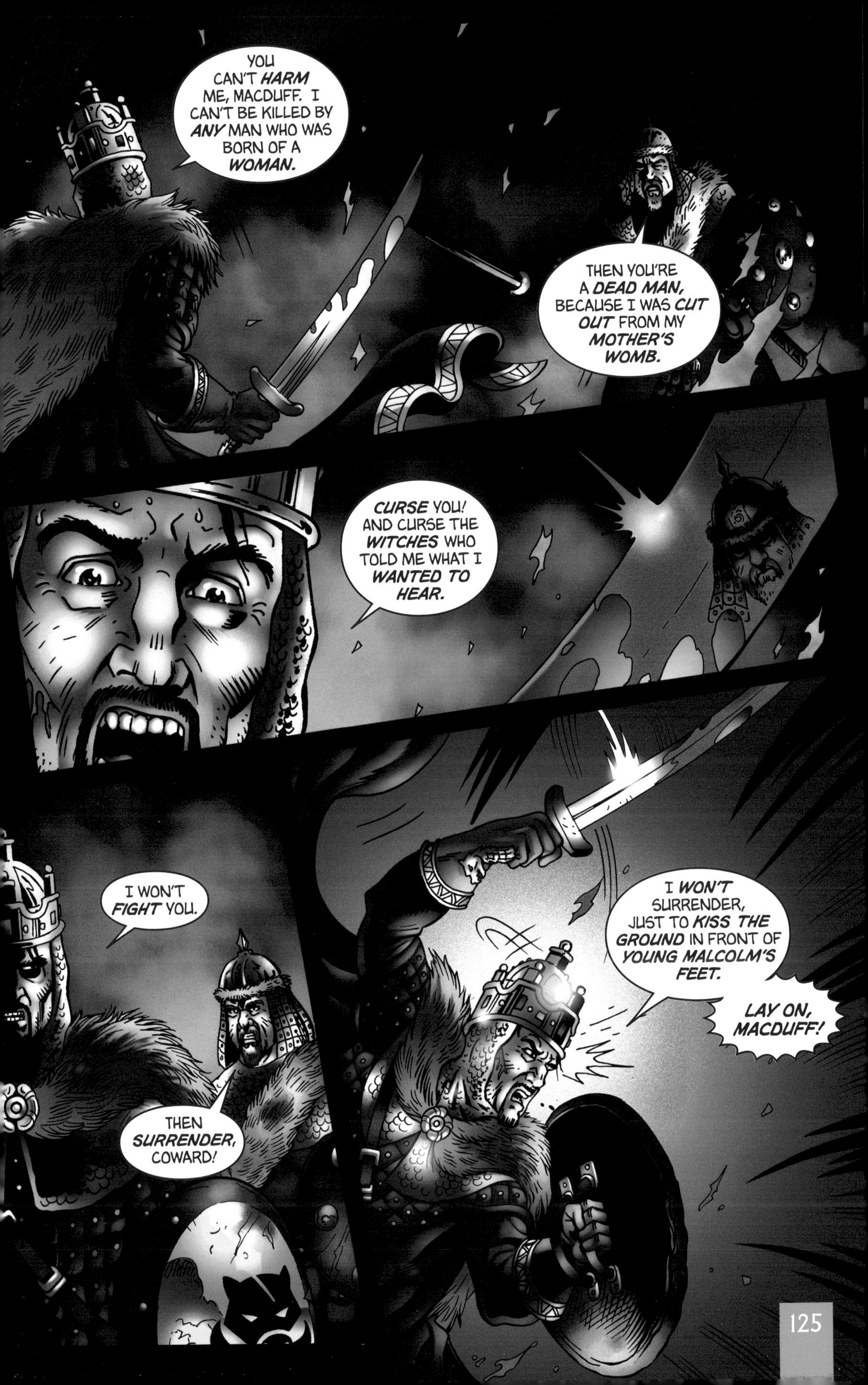
YOU CAN'T HARM ME, MACDUFF. I CAN'T BE KILLED BY ANY MAN WHO WAS BORN OF A WOMAN.
THEN YOU'RE A DEAD MAN, BECAUSE I WAS CUT OUT FROM MY MOTHER'S WOMB.
CURSE YOU! AND CURSE THE WITCHES WHO TOLD ME WHAT I WANTED TO HEAR.
I WON'T FIGHT YOU.
THEN SURRENDER, COWARD!
I WON'T SURRENDER, JUST TO KISS THE GROUND IN FRONT OF YOUNG MALCOLM'S FEET.
LAY ON, MACDUFF!

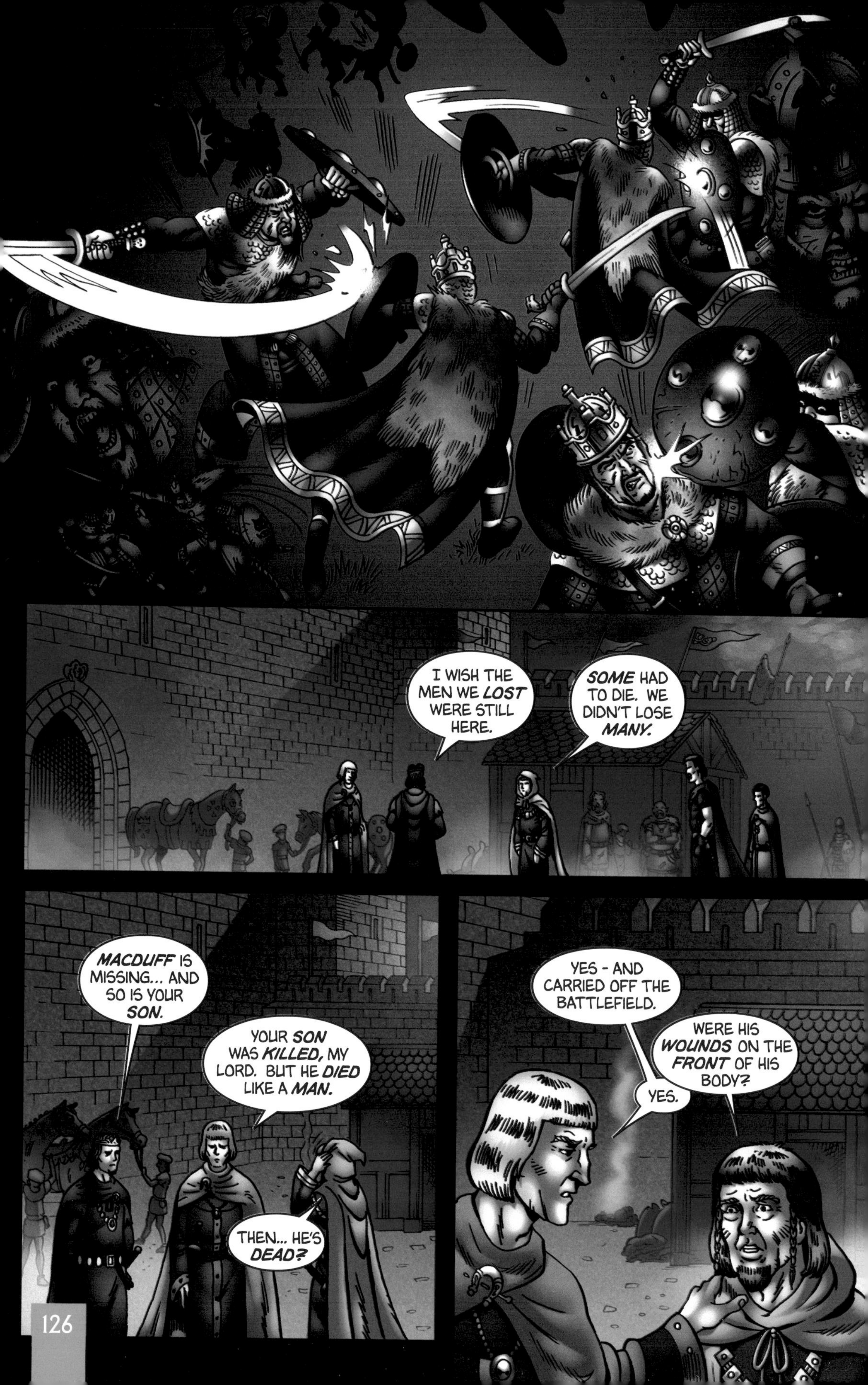
I WISH THE MEN WE LOST WERE STILL HERE.
SOME HAD TO DIE. WE DIDN'T LOSE MANY.
MACDUFF IS MISSING... AND SO IS YOUR SON.
YOUR SON WAS KILLED, MY LORD. BUT HE DIED LIKE A MAN.
THEN... HE'S DEAD?
YES - AND CARRIED OFF THE BATTLEFIELD.
WERE HIS WOUNDS ON THE FRONT OF HIS BODY?
YES.

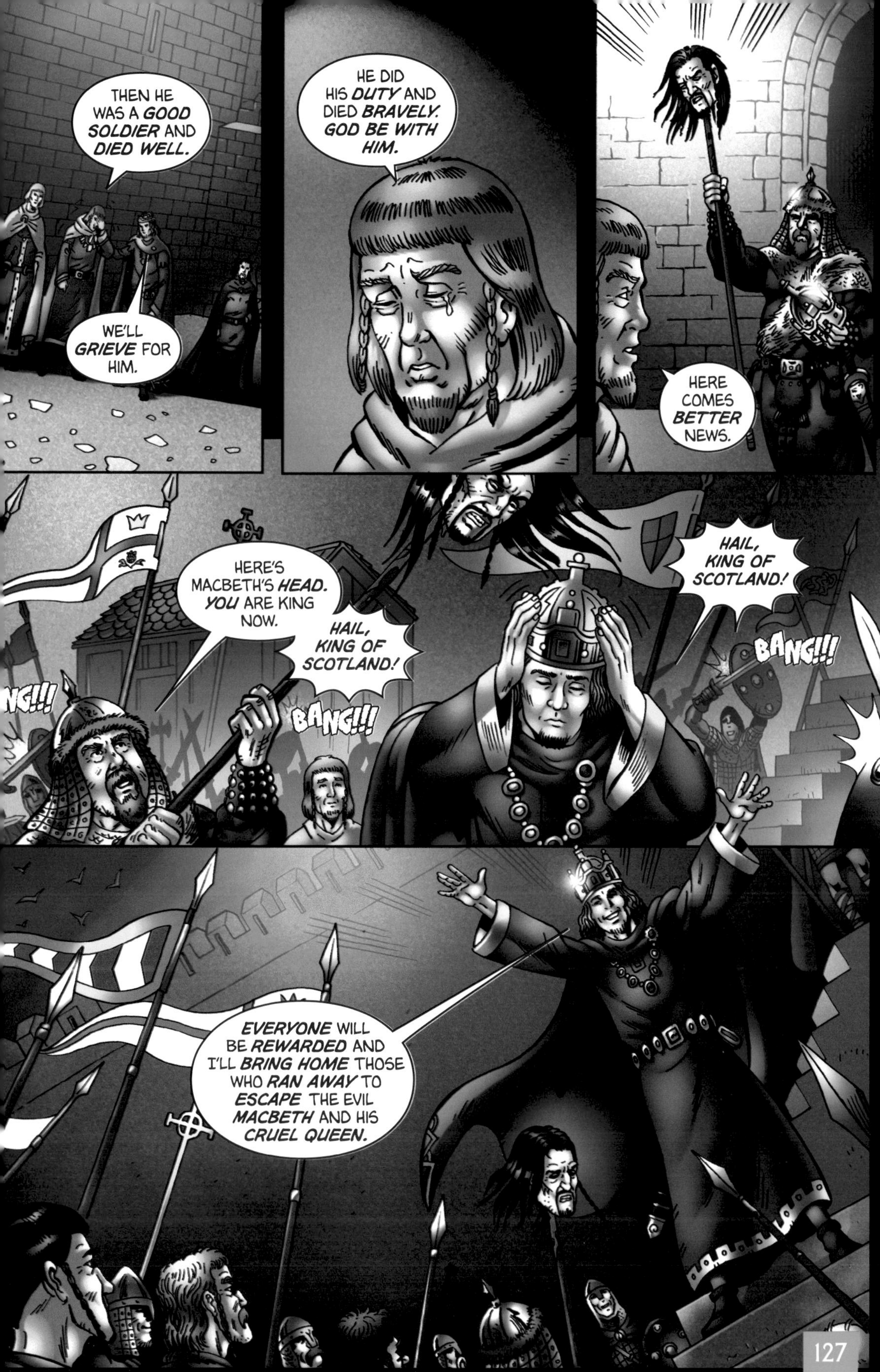
THEN HE WAS A GOOD SOLDIER AND DIED WELL.
WE'LL GRIEVE FOR HIM.
HE DID HIS DUTY AND DIED BRAVELY. GOD BE WITH HIM.
HERE COMES BETTER NEWS.
HERE'S MACBETH'S HEAD. YOU ARE KING NOW.
HAIL, KING OF SCOTLAND!
BANG!!!
HAIL, KING OF SCOTLAND!
BANG!!!
EVERYONE WILL BE REWARDED AND I'LL BRING HOME THOSE WHO RAN AWAY TO ESCAPE THE EVIL MACBETH AND HIS CRUEL QUEEN.

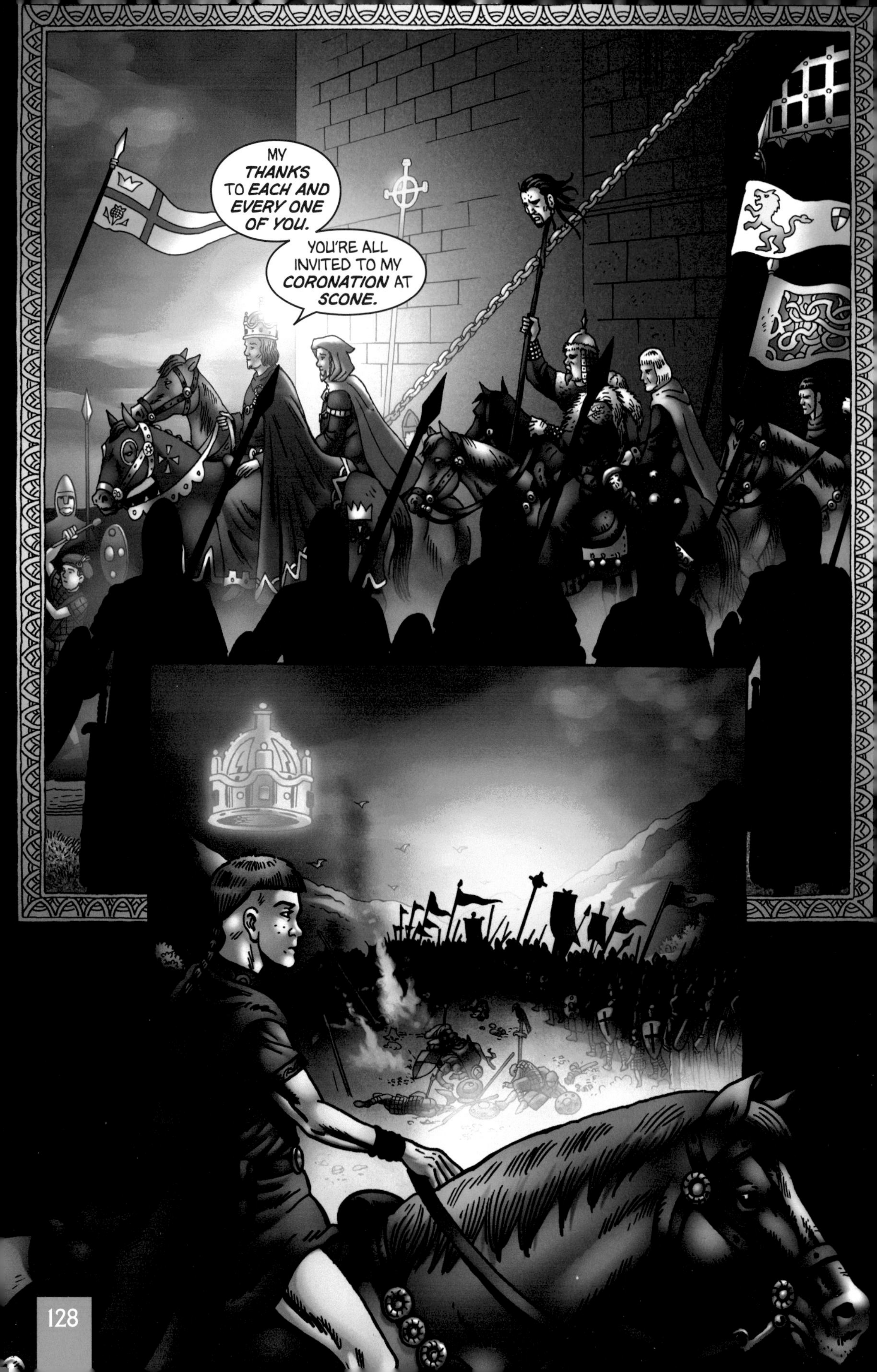
MY THANKS TO EACH AND EVERY ONE OF YOU.
YOU'RE ALL INVITED TO MY CORONATION AT SCONE.

Macbeth

End

William Shakespeare

(c.1564 - 1616 AD)

National Portrait Gallery, London

William Shakespeare is one of the most widely read authors and possibly the best dramatist ever to live. The actual date of his birth is not known, but April 23, 1564 (St George's Day) has traditionally been his accepted birthday, as this was three days before his baptism. He died on the same date in 1616, at the age of fifty-two.

The life of William Shakespeare can be divided into three acts. The first twenty years of his life were spent in Stratford-upon-Avon, where he grew up, went to school, got married and became a father. The next twenty-five years he spent as an actor and playwright in London. He spent his last few years back in Stratford-upon-Avon, where he enjoyed his retirement in moderate wealth gained from his successful years in the theater.

William, the third of eight children, was the eldest son of tradesman John Shakespeare and Mary Arden. His father was later elected mayor of Stratford, which was the highest post a man in civic politics could attain. In sixteenth-century England, William was lucky to survive into adulthood: syphilis, scurvy, smallpox, tuberculosis, typhus and dysentery shortened life expectancy at the time to approximately thirty-five years. The Bubonic Plague took the lives of many and was believed to have been the cause of death for three of William's seven siblings.

Little is known of William's childhood, but he is thought to have attended the local grammar school, where he studied Latin and English Literature. In 1582, at the age of eighteen, William married a local farmer's daughter, Anne Hathaway, who was eight years his senior and three months pregnant. During their marriage they had three children: Susanna, born on May 26, 1583, and twins, Hamnet and Judith, born on February 2, 1585. Hamnet, William's only son, caught Bubonic Plague and died at the age of eleven.

Five years into his marriage, in 1587, William's wife and children stayed in Stratford, while he moved to London. He appeared as an actor at "The Theatre" (England's first permanent theater), and gave public recitals of his own poems; but he quickly became famous for his playwriting. His fame soon spread far and wide. When Queen Elizabeth I died in 1603, the new King James I (who was already King James VI of Scotland) gave royal consent for Shakespeare's acting company, "The Lord Chamberlain's Men" to be called "The King's Men" in return for entertaining the court. This association was to shape a number of plays, such as *Macbeth*, which was written to please the Scottish King.

William Shakespeare is attributed with writing and collaborating on 38 plays, 154 sonnets and 5 poems, in just twenty-three years between 1590 and 1613. No original manuscript exists for any of his plays, making it hard to accurately date any of them.

However, from their contents and reports at the time, it is believed that his first play was *The Taming of the Shrew* and that his last complete work was *Two Noble Kinsmen*, written two years before he died. The cause of his death remains unknown.

He was buried on April 25, 1616, two days after his death, at the Church of the Holy Trinity (the same Church where he had been baptized fifty-two years earlier). His gravestone bears these words, believed to have been written by William himself:-

"Good friend for Jesus sake forbear,
To dig the dust enclosed here!
Blest be the man that spares these stones,
And curst be he that moves my bones"

At the time of his death, William had substantial properties, which he bestowed on his family and associates from the theater. Most went to his eldest daughter, Susanna. Curiously, all he left to his wife Anne was his second-best bed!

William Shakespeare's last direct descendant died in 1670. She was his granddaughter, Elizabeth.

The Real Macbeth

(c.1005 - 1057 AD)

Macbeth is one of Shakespeare's most famous characters. It is a name that's known the whole world over, but many people don't realize that the story is linked to actual historical events — even if those events have been heavily embellished and altered for the sake of entertainment.

Shakespeare obtained his information about the real Macbeth from Raphael Holinshed's book *The Chronicles of England, Scotland and Ireland*, published in 1574 (which Shakespeare used as a primary resource for all of his historical plays). Holinshed himself derived his information from a variety of sources, most notably Andrew of Wyntoun's *Orygynale Cronykil* (Original Chronicle) which traces a history of Scotland from Biblical times, and Hector Boece's

Scotorum Historiae (Scottish History), published in 1526 and translated from Latin into English by John Bellenden in 1535.

Macbeth, or Mac Bethad as he would have been called, was King of Scotland from 1040 to 1057 (although in Shakespeare's play, his reign is made to appear significantly less than seventeen years). The name "Mac Bethad" means

"son of life" and is actually Irish, rather than Scottish, in origin.

Eleventh-century Scotland was a barbaric land where war and ruthless slaughter were a fact of life. Survival depended on having a strong and capable local ruler or chieftain to protect both life and property. Such a leader would provide a strong paternalistic rule, guarding the family, community and land from all enemies.

Some of these enemies could be, and often were, collections of distant family members challenging the current leadership.

A number of local rulers would often unite under the nominal leadership of one "king" to promote their common interests and to wage war on more distant clans. Interestingly, in those times, kings and rulers could name their own successor – it wasn't a privilege that was handed down from parent to eldest child as the English monarchy operates today. However, family linkage tended to be respected, and the title usually passed to a relative of the king, selected as being the one most suitable for immediate rule and not necessarily the natural heir. Understandably, this selection process would have been challenged, especially by those individuals who felt that they had a greater right to become king than the person taking on the title. Such grievances were often dealt with or pre-empted by the murdering of family members judged unsuitable for power, to ensure that the "favorite" won the race.

Macbeth was the son of Findláech mac Ruaidrí (who was a High Steward of Moray) in the north of Scotland, around 1005. His mother's name is unknown, and indeed her own parentage is inaccurately recorded. It is uncertain whether she was the daughter of King Kenneth II or King Malcolm II. However, that is largely immaterial as whichever man was Macbeth's grandfather would be a strong enough family link for him to make a claim for the throne.

In 1020, Macbeth's father Findláech died. It is thought that he was killed, most probably by his brother Máel Brigté's son Máel Coluim (Malcolm). Findláech's title of High Steward went to his nephew Gille Coemgáin. In 1032, Gille Coemgáin and fifty other people were burned to death as punishment for the murder of Findláech. This act of retribution could well have been carried out by

Macbeth and his allies. Following Gille Coemgáin's death, Macbeth took the title of High Steward of Moray.

It was around this time that he married Gille Coemgáin's widow, Gruoch, and became step-father to her son, Lulach (which explains why Shakespeare has Lady Macbeth talk about motherhood, whereas at no time does Macbeth make any reference to being a father. Moreover, Macduff states that Macbeth has no children in Act IV Scene III (page 102)). Macbeth's marriage to Gruoch was significant, because she was the grand-daughter of Kenneth III. Therefore through their combined ancestors, the marriage ensured that Macbeth had a strong claim to the throne.

Within a very short space of time, Macbeth's rival Gille Coemgáin had not only lost his life, but his title and his widowed wife had gone swiftly to Macbeth.

While Macbeth was a high-ranking lord of Moray, the King at the time was Donnchad mac Crináin (King Duncan I). Duncan succeeded to the throne when his grandfather, King Malcolm II, died at Glamis. It is thought likely that Malcolm had engineered the succession through the tactical assassination of any family members who might have felt they had a stronger claim to the crown.

Given the circumstances, it would have been a sensible course of action for Duncan to make peace with his remaining family, in particular his cousin Thorfinn the Mighty (Earl of Orkney), his cousin Macbeth, and the person closest to his throne in terms of lineage, namely Gruoch, the wife of Macbeth. Duncan appears to have been unsuccessful in uniting the "royal family", and Macbeth pressed his own claim to the throne with the help of that same cousin and ally, Earl Thorfinn of Orkney. He eventually won the crown by slaying Duncan at Bothgowanan near Elgin in 1040.

Macbeth has been judged by history to be a more able king than his predecessor. Under his rule the kingdom became relatively stable and reasonably prosperous, so much so, that by 1050 he was confident enough to leave the country for a number of months and make a pilgrimage to Rome. At this time he was said to have been so wealthy that he "scattered alms like seed corn". As Wyntoun's *Orygynale Cronykil* says:-
"In pilgrimage þidder he come,
And in almus he sew siluer"

All was not peaceful, however, and in 1054 Duncan I's son, Máel Coluim mac Donnchada (Malcolm Canmore, nicknamed "big head"), challenged Macbeth for the throne of Scotland. He did so in alliance with Siward, Earl of Northumbria (who also happened to be the cousin of Duncan's widow) and they took control of much of southern Scotland. Three years later, on August 15, 1057, Macbeth's army was finally defeated at the Battle of Lumphanan, in Aberdeenshire. Macbeth was killed in battle. He is believed to be buried in the graveyard at Saint Oran's Chapel on the Isle of Iona, the last of many Kings of Alba and Dalriada to be laid to rest there. This site is also supposed to be the final resting place of King Duncan I.

Unlike in Shakespeare's play, the killing of Macbeth didn't result in the crown going straight to Duncan's son Malcolm. It first went to Macbeth's step-son Lulach, on the basis that Kenneth III was his maternal great-grandfather. Lulach was a weak king, and people called him "Lulach the Simple" or "Lulach the Fool". After a few months of rule, he was murdered, and Malcolm, son of Duncan I, became King Malcolm III of Scotland.

No-one knows what happened to Lady Macbeth. Dramatically, Shakespeare has her losing her sanity and taking her own life – however, there is no record of that happening, or even of her falling to a bloody death. Having lived through the murder of her first husband, the killing of her second husband in battle, and the murder of her son, even if she was to outlive them all, it's unlikely that she enjoyed any form of happiness.

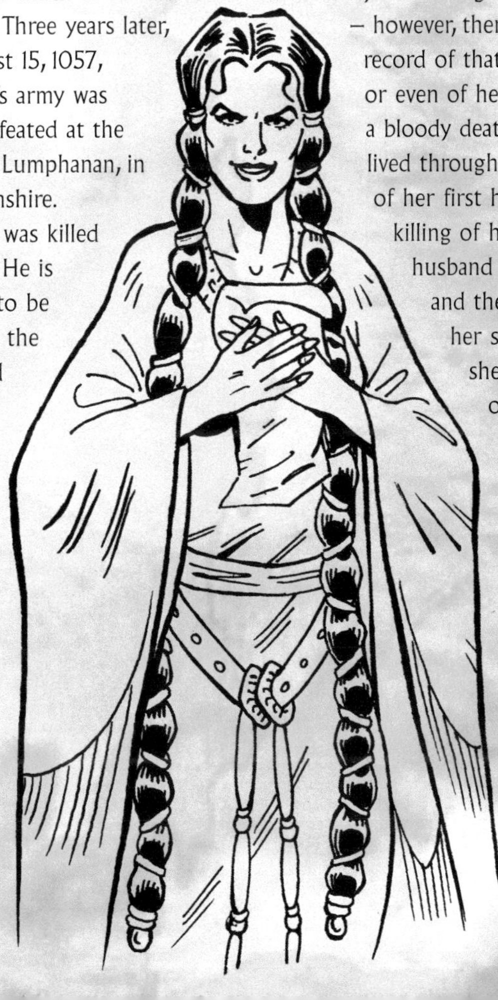

Macbeth and the Kings of Scotland

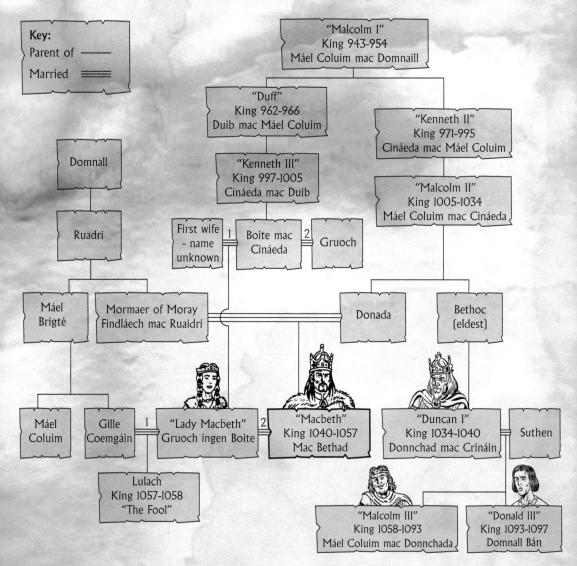

Key:
Parent of ———
Married ═══

"Malcolm I"
King 943-954
Máel Coluim mac Domnaill

"Duff"
King 962-966
Duib mac Máel Coluim

"Kenneth II"
King 971-995
Cináeda mac Máel Coluim

Domnall

"Kenneth III"
King 997-1005
Cináeda mac Duib

"Malcolm II"
King 1005-1034
Máel Coluim mac Cináeda

Ruadri

First wife - name unknown 1 Boite mac Cináeda 2 Gruoch

Máel Brigté

Mormaer of Moray
Findláech mac Ruaidrí

Donada

Bethoc [eldest]

Máel Coluim

Gille Coemgáin 1 "Lady Macbeth"
Gruoch ingen Boite 2 "Macbeth"
King 1040-1057
Mac Bethad

"Duncan I"
King 1034-1040
Donnchad mac Crináin

Suthen

Lulach
King 1057-1058
"The Fool"

"Malcolm III"
King 1058-1093
Máel Coluim mac Donnchada

"Donald III"
King 1093-1097
Domnall Bán

The Macbeth Murder Trail

1020 — Macbeth's father Findláech died — thought to have been killed by his own nephew, Máel Coluim. His title of High Steward went to Máel Coluim's brother, Gille Coemgáin.

1032 — Gille Coemgáin and 50 other people were burned to death as punishment for the killing of Findláech. This may have been carried out by Macbeth and his allies as retribution for killing his father. Macbeth then took Coemgáin's title (that had belonged to Macbeth's father) and took Gille Coemgáin's widow, Gruoch, for his wife. There is also a theory that Gille Coemgáin killed Boite mac Cináeda because he had made his wife the heiress to his estate. As retaliation for this murder, Boite's wife,

Gruoch (the stepmother of the Gruoch that married Gille Coemgáin and later Macbeth), mustered an army to kill Gille Coemgáin.

1040 — Macbeth killed King Duncan I at Bothgowanan.

1050 — Macbeth went on a pilgrimage to Rome.

1054 — Máel Coluim mac Donnchada (Malcolm, son of King Duncan I) staked his claim to the throne and challenged Macbeth in the first of a series of battles.

1057 — Macbeth's army was finally defeated by Malcolm's army at the Battle of Lumphanan. Macbeth was killed in battle. Macbeth's step-son Lulach then became King.

1057 — After only a few months of rule, Malcolm killed Lulach to become King Malcolm III of Scotland.

The History of Shakespeare's Macbeth

When comparing the play to the actual historical events, it is clear that those events were merely inspiration for Shakespeare's own take on the story. It is unlikely that he deliberately intended to misrepresent the facts; however, it is important to recognize that as a playwright, Shakespeare had a responsibility to entertain his audience with his works. Therefore, what takes place on the stage is an artistic modification of what took place in history; to give the best portrayal of the plots and motives of the characters in order to arrive at a worthy spectacle. Among other things, Shakespeare possessed good business sense – and a successful play would draw in the fee-paying public to provide him and his troupe with an income.

But money was not his sole concern. His position in society was paramount, and of prime importance was the need to pander to the monarch.

Macbeth is thought to have been written to be performed in honor of a royal visit by the King of Denmark to King James I in 1606. King James I became King of England in 1603 when Elizabeth I died. He was already King of Scotland (King James VI of Scotland). Interestingly, James I was a keen scholar and had such a deep interest in witchcraft that in 1597 he wrote a book on the subject, which he called *Daemonologie*. In it he advocated severe punishment for witches. In addition, he was a keen supporter of the arts, having the title of "The King's Men" bestowed upon Shakespeare's acting company soon after his coronation. In return, The King's Men were expected to perform at court whenever they were asked, which amounted to around a dozen performances each year.

Setting the play in Scotland and including elements of witchcraft appears to be a deliberate attempt by Shakespeare to please the new King. But he can't take the credit for including witchcraft in the tale of *Macbeth*: we have Holinshed to thank for that. Raphael Holinshed's *Chronicles of England, Scotland and Ireland*, first published in 1574, was a primary source of reference for a number of Shakespeare's plays, and *Macbeth* is no exception. The following extract from Holinshed's *Chronicles* demonstrates just how closely Shakespeare borrowed from his version of events:

"It fortuned as Makbeth and Banquho iournied towards Fores, where the king then laie, they went sporting by the waie togither without other company saue onelie themselues, passing thorough the woods and fields, when suddenlie in the middest of a laund, there met them three women in strange and wild apparell, resembling creatures of the elder world, whome when they attentiuelie beheld, woondering much at the sight, the first of them spake and said: All haile Makbeth, thane of Glammis (for he had latelie entered into that dignitie and office by the death of his father Sinell). The second of them said: Haile Makbeth thane of Cawder. But the third said: All haile Makbeth that heereafter shalt be king of Scotland.

Then Banquho: What manner of women (saith he) are you, that seeme so little fauourable vnto me, whereas to my fellow heere, besides high offices, ye assigne also the kingdome, appointing foorth nothing for me at all? Yes, (saith the first of them) we promise greater benefits vnto thee, than vnto him, for he shall reigne in deed, but with an vnluckie end: neither shall he leaue anie issue behind him to succeed in his place, where contrarilie thou in deed shalt not reigne at all, but of thee those shall be borne which shall gouern the Scotish kingdome by long order of continuall descent. Herewith the foresaid women vanished immediatlie out of their sight."

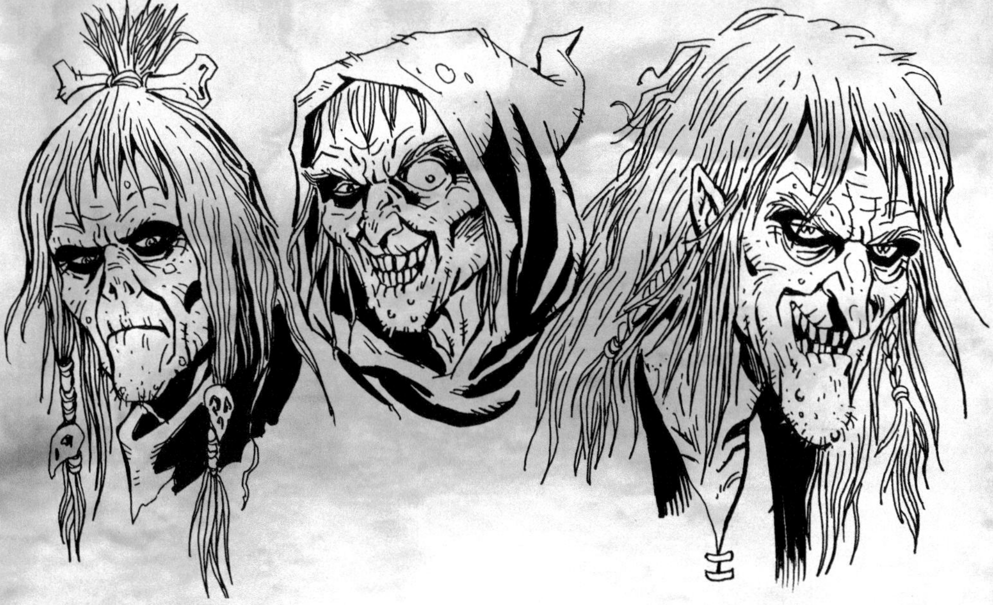

In those days, the Stuart Kings of Scotland (King James I was a Stuart) were believed to have descended from Banquo (this is unproven but may have some truth in it). The witches "predicted" a long line of kings, and this is dealt with in the play verbally in Act I Scene III (page 15) and visually in Act IV Scene I (page 85), when Macbeth is shown a large number of kings in a line, all of whom bear a resemblance to Banquo. The "bloodline" is only made possible by Fleance escaping when his father is attacked. Holinshed describes how Walter Steward, the founder of the Stuart royal family who married the daughter of Robert Bruce, was a descendent of Fleance and therefore Banquo. This ancestral connection must have been behind a change that Shakespeare made to Holinshed's accounts, namely that in Holinshed, Banquo was an accomplice in Duncan's murder; to portray an ancestor of the King as murderous would have been rather foolhardy on Shakespeare's part. Other pandering includes the reference to the English King (Edward the Confessor) having God-given powers to cure "the evil" in Act IV Scene III (page 99), also known as Scrofula. Edward was believed to have that power, and King James I revived the custom of sufferers being "touched" by the monarch as a cure for it.

But it is with his portrayal of the witches where Shakespeare really aimed to please the King. In his book, King James denounced witchcraft absolutely. It was his belief that witches were mostly women who had masculine features such as facial hair. They were in league with the devil, could summon up spirits, and could even curse images of people to control their destiny. These were early days in the understanding of witchcraft, and the very subject was a threat to King James' belief of divine right of kingship. In his world, witchcraft was a devil-based display of evil that was an ever-present challenge to the sanctity of his God-given rule. It is a general fear of witchcraft, then, that is the possible reason why neither Holinshed nor Shakespeare ever refers to the women as witches. In fact, the elements of witchcraft that exist in the play, particularly the spells and the appearance of Hecate, are now believed to be later additions, made by Thomas Middleton following on from his own play, ***The Witch***. The term only appears once, in Act I Scene III (page 12*), and even then it could be an insult being reported by the speaker.

Beyond the belief that it was written for the visit of the King of Denmark in 1606, a number of other elements point towards it being authored in that year. The Porter's ramblings in Act II Scene III (page 38*) make mention of equivocation:

*Original Text version only

The line "O, come in, equivocator" may refer to the verbal cunning displayed by Father Garnet, one of the Gunpowder Plot conspirators in the trial of 1606. Also that year, a ship called The Tiger returned to England after a terrible two year voyage, and that ship is named in Act I Scene III (page 12*). However, as the first printed version of the play didn't appear until the Folio printing in 1623, the true dating and authenticity of each of the parts of the play are difficult to establish. For certain, a version of the play was first performed at The Globe Theatre in April 1611.

The Scottish Play

Macbeth is steeped in superstition, so much so that actors consider it the height of bad luck to even utter the name, unless they are rehearsing it at the time. Often, people will make references to "The Bard's Play" or "The Scottish Play" simply to avoid saying the "M"-word. There are a number of theories about the origins of the "curse" of *Macbeth*:

- It is thought that the witches' incantations are taken from real rituals and are believed to cast actual spells on the players.
- Legend has it that in 1606, Hal Berridge, the boy playing Lady Macbeth (remember that all the parts, male and female, were played by males at the time) died backstage.
- Another gruesome legend reports that in 1672 an actor playing the part of Macbeth substituted a real dagger for the blunt stage one, and actually killed the actor playing King Duncan in full view of the audience.

The more rational explanations are easier to accept.

- The majority of the play takes place in darkly lit scenes, and this tended to lead to a lot of accidents backstage.
- Because *Macbeth* is a short play, and so well known, theater groups would perform the play when they were in some financial trouble. Of course, a single play is rarely enough to save an ailing company, and therefore the performance of *Macbeth* became associated with failure, misery, and being out of work.

Whether any of those reasons are true or not is open to much speculation; what is beyond any doubt is that the story of *Macbeth* is a powerful, timeless tale of ambition, of the evil that is embedded in ill-gotten gains, and a question that lies at the heart of life itself — are we all the subjects of fate and destiny? Or do we carve out our own existence on this planet?

137

Page Creation

In order to create three versions of the same book, the play is first adapted into three scripts: Original Text, Plain Text and Quick Text. While the degree of complexity changes for the dialogue in each script, the artwork remains the same for all three books.

ACT 3 SCENE 5
SWIRLING MIST
BLACK BALLOON WITH RED LETTERING

On the left is a rough thumbnail sketch of page 73 created from the script (below). Once the rough sketch is approved, it is redrawn as a clean finished pencil sketch (right).

HOT HOT HOTTER THAN HELL..
HECATE BRIGHT GREEN EYES HER WORD BALLOON BLACK WITH RED GREEK TYPE FACE

ACT 3 – SCENE 5

249. Somewhere far beyond the light of the sun, the three Witches huddle. Strange weather and strange landscapes surround them. They sense the approach of Hecate, the Queen of Darkness and they're frightened.

250. BIG. Suddenly she's there! Hecate appears as a triple goddess, with three heads (women's in this frame, all identical, harsh-looking, but not ugly) and three bodies, standing back-to-back. She towers over the three Witches, piercing the gloom with her fierce stare. They cringe and make frightened animal noises.

	QUICK TEXT	PLAIN ENGLISH TEXT	ORIGINAL TEXT
WITCHES (2 & 3)	WHIMPER! WHINE!	WHIMPER! WHINE!	WHIMPER! WHINE!
1ST WITCH	Hecate…you look angry.	Hecate! You look so angry.	Why, how now, Hecate! you look angerly.
HECATE	I am! You dared to meddle with Macbeth In riddles and affairs of death	Have I not reason, chaos that you are, Impertinent and rash? How did you dare To trade and traffic with Macbeth, In riddles, and affairs of death;	Have I not reason, beldams as you are, Saucy, and overbold? How did you dare To trade and traffic with Macbeth, In riddles, and affairs of death;

251. BIGish. The Witches scuttle round Hecate like dogs round their master. Hecate's three heads metamorphose into the heads of a horse, a dog and a boar.

HECATE	You did it without me! And now I clearly see That all you've managed to do Is use him as he has used you.	And I, the mistress of your charms, The true instrument of all harms, Was never called to play my part, Or show the glory of our art? And, which is worse, all you have done Was only for a wayward son, Spiteful, and hateful; who, as others do, Wants all he can get and nought for you.	And I, the mistress of your charms, The close contriver of all harms, Was never call'd to bear my part, Or show the glory of our art? And, which is worse, all you have done Hath been but for a wayward son, Spiteful, and wrathful; who, as others do, Loves for his own ends, not for you.

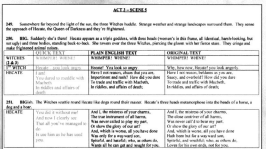

From the pencil sketch, an inked version of the same page is created (right).

HOT HOT HOTTER THAN HELL..
HECATE BRIGHT GREEN EYES HER WORD BALLOON BLACK WITH RED GREEK TYPE FACE

Inking is not simply tracing over the pencil sketch; it is the process of using black ink to fill in the shaded areas and to add clarity, cohesion, depth and texture to the "pencils".

The "inks" give us the final outline, which is checked for accuracy before being passed on to the colorist.

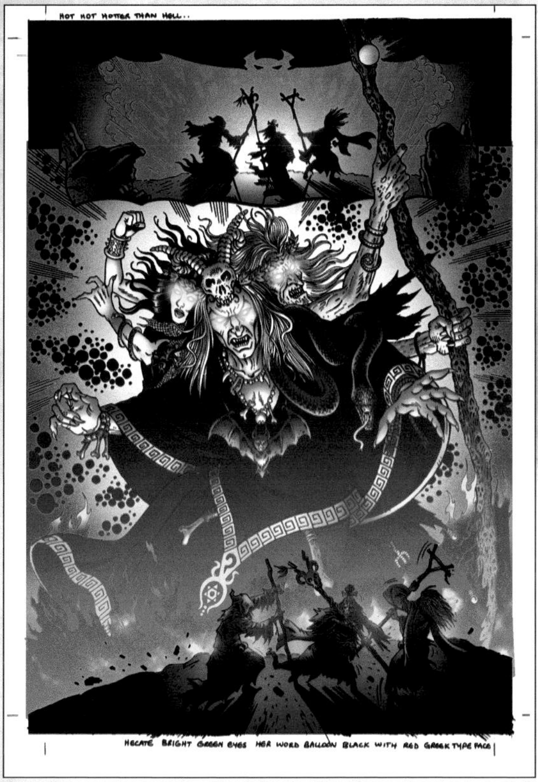
HOT HOT HOTTER THAN HELL..
HECATE BRIGHT GREEN EYES HER WORD BALLOON BLACK WITH RED GREEK TYPE FACE

Adding color brings the page and its characters to life.

Each character has a detailed Character Study. This is useful for the artists to refer to and ensures continuity throughout the book.

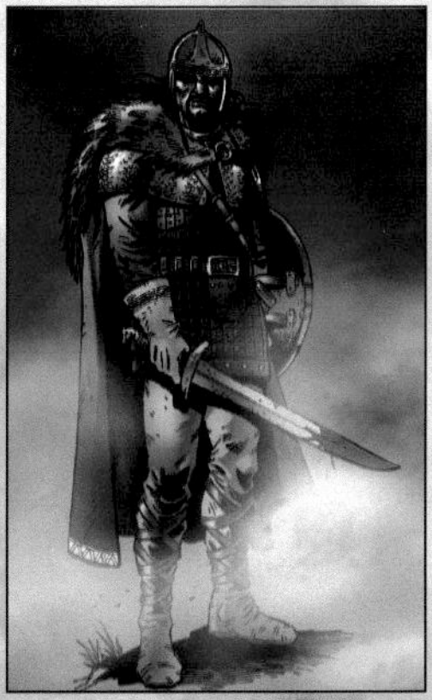

Macbeth character study

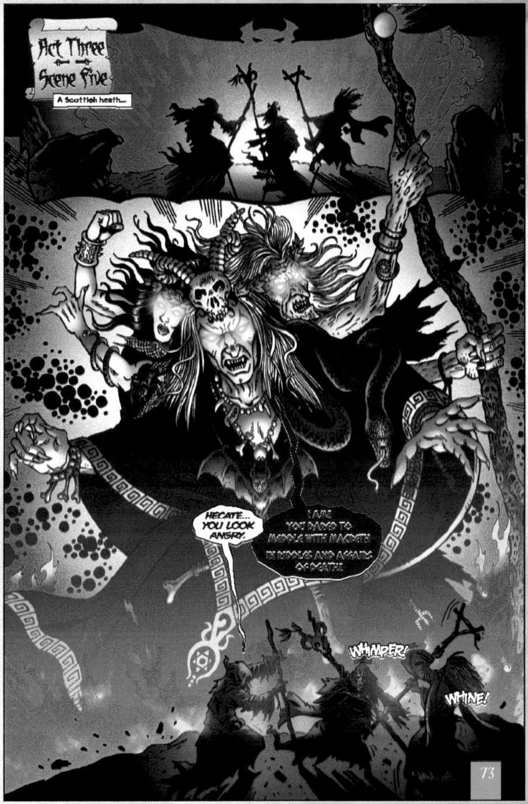
Act Three
Scene Five
A Scottish heath...
HECATE... YOU LOOK ANGRY.
I AM! YOU DARED TO MEDDLE WITH MACBETH IN RIDDLES AND AFFAIRS OF DEATH!
WHIMPER!
WHINE!
73

The last stage of page creation is to add the speech bubbles and any sound effects.

Speech bubbles are created from the words in the script and are laid over the finished, colored artwork.

Three versions of lettering are produced for the three different versions of ***Macbeth***. These are then saved as final artwork pages and compiled into separate books for printing.

Original Text

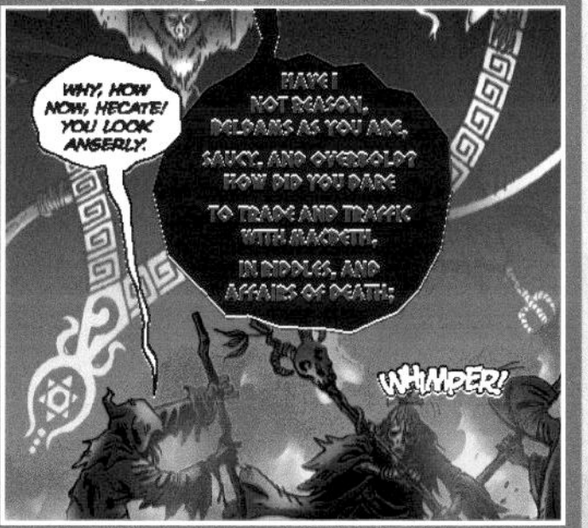
WHY, HOW NOW, HECATE! YOU LOOK ANGERLY.
HAVE I NOT REASON, BELDAMS AS YOU ARE, SAUCY, AND OVERBOLD? HOW DID YOU DARE TO TRADE AND TRAFFIC WITH MACBETH, IN RIDDLES, AND AFFAIRS OF DEATH;
WHIMPER!

Plain Text

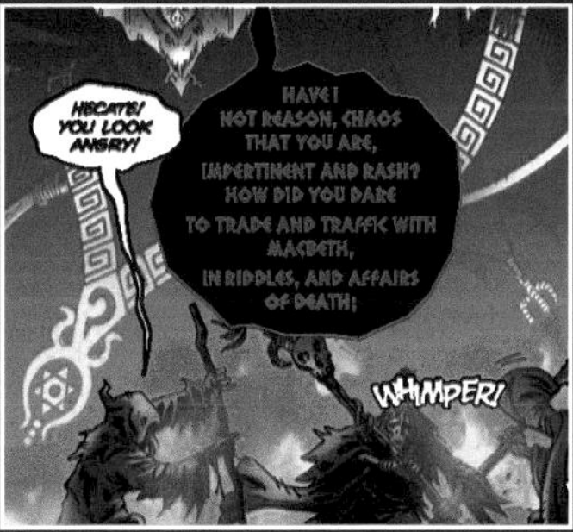
HECATE! YOU LOOK ANGRY!
HAVE I NOT REASON, CHAOS THAT YOU ARE, IMPERTINENT AND RASH? HOW DID YOU DARE TO TRADE AND TRAFFIC WITH MACBETH, IN RIDDLES, AND AFFAIRS OF DEATH;
WHIMPER!

Quick Text

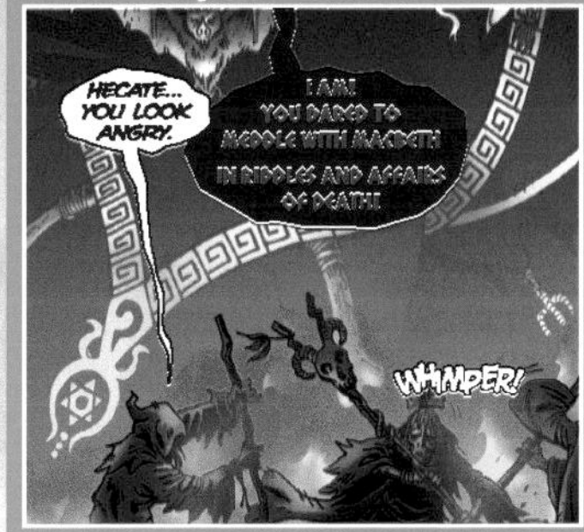
HECATE... YOU LOOK ANGRY.
I AM! YOU DARED TO MEDDLE WITH MACBETH IN RIDDLES AND AFFAIRS OF DEATH!
WHIMPER!

Shakespeare Around the Globe

The Globe Theatre and Shakespeare

It is hard to appreciate today how theaters were actually a new idea in William Shakespeare's time. The very first theater in Elizabethan London to show only plays, aptly called "The Theatre," was introduced by an entrepreneur by the name of James Burbage. In fact, "The Globe Theatre," possibly the most famous theater of that era, was built from the timbers of "The Theatre." The landlord of "The Theatre" was Giles Allen, a Puritan who disapproved of theatrical entertainment. When he decided to enforce a huge rent increase in the winter of 1598, the theater members dismantled the building piece by piece and shipped it across the Thames to Southwark for reassembly. Allen was powerless to do anything, as the company owned the wood - although he spent three years in court trying to sue the perpetrators!

The report of the dismantling party (written by Schoenbaum)

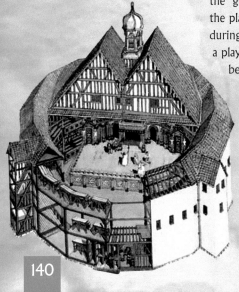

says: "ryotous... armed... with divers and manye unlawfull and offensive weapons... in verye ryotous outragious and forcyble manner and contrarye to the lawes of your highnes Realme... and there pulling breaking and throwing downe the sayd Theater in verye outragious violent and riotous sort to the great disturbance and terrefyeing not onlye of your subjectes... but of divers others of your majesties loving subjectes there neere inhabitinge."

William Shakespeare became a part owner of this new Globe Theatre in 1599. It was one of four major theaters in the area, along with the Swan, the Rose, and the Hope. The exact physical structure of the Globe is unknown, although scholars are fairly sure of some details through drawings from the period. The theater itself was a closed structure with an open courtyard where the stage stood. Tiered galleries around the open area accommodated the wealthier patrons who could afford seats, and those of the lower classes - the "groundlings" - stood around the platform or "thrust" stage during the performance of a play. The space under and behind the stage was used for special effects, storage and costume changes. Surprisingly, although the entire structure was not very big by modern standards, it is known to have accommodated fairly large crowds - as many as 3,000 people - during a single performance.

The Globe II

In 1613, the original Globe Theatre burned to the ground when a cannon shot during a performance of *Henry VIII* set fire to the thatched roof of the gallery. Undeterred, the company completed a new Globe (this time with a tiled roof) on the foundations of its predecessor. Shakespeare didn't write any new plays for this theater. He retired to Stratford-Upon-Avon that year, and died two years later. Performances continued until 1642, when the Puritans closed down all theaters and places of entertainment. Two years later, the Puritans razed the building to the ground in order to build tenements upon the site. No more was to be seen of the Globe for 352 years.

Shakespeare's Globe

Led by the vision of the late Sam Wanamaker, work began on the construction of a new Globe in 1993, close to the site of the original theater. It was completed three years later, and Queen Elizabeth II officially opened the New Globe Theatre on June 12th 1997 with a production of *Henry V.*

The New Globe Theatre is as faithful a reproduction as possible to the Elizabethan theater, given that the details of the original are only known from sketches of the time. The building can accommodate 1,500 people between the galleries and the "groundlings."

www.shakespeares-globe.org

Shakespeare Birthplace Trust

As so few relics survive from Shakespeare's life, it is amazing that the house where he was born and raised remains intact. It is owned and cared for by the Shakespeare Birthplace Trust, which looks after a number of houses in the area:

Shakespeare's Birthplace

- Shakespeare's Birthplace.
- Mary Arden's Farm: The childhood home of Shakespeare's mother.
- Anne Hathaway's Cottage: The childhood home of Shakespeare's wife.
- Hall's Croft: The home of Shakespeare's eldest daughter, Susanna.
- New Place: Only the grounds exist of the house where Shakespeare died in 1616.
- Nash's House: The home of Shakespeare's granddaughter.

www.shakespeare.org.uk

Martin Droeshout's engraving of Shakespeare

Formed in 1847, the Trust also works to promote Shakespeare around the world. In early 2009, it announced that it had found a new Shakespeare portrait, believed to have been painted within his lifetime, with a trail of provenance that links it to Shakespeare himself.

It is accepted that Martin Droeshout's engraving (left) that appears on the First Folio of 1623 is an authentic likeness of Shakespeare because the people involved in its publication would have personally known him. This new portrait (once owned by Henry Wriothesley, 3rd Earl of Southampton, one of Shakespeare's most loyal supporters) is so similar in all facial aspects that it is now suspected to have been the source that Droeshout used for his famous engraving. www.shakespearefound.org.uk

TEACHING RESOURCE PACKS NOW AVAILABLE TO ACCOMPANY THE SERIES

Macbeth
978-1-907127-73-1

Romeo & Juliet
978-1-907127-74-8

Henry V
978-1-906332-53-2

The Tempest
978-1-906332-77-8

A Midsummer Night's Dream
978-1-907127-76-2

Jane Eyre
978-1-906332-55-6

A Christmas Carol
978-1-906332-57-0

Frankenstein
978-1-907127-77-9

INCLUDES CD-ROM

- 100+ photocopiable pages.
- Electronic version included for whole-class teaching and digital printing.
- Cross-curricular topics and activities.
- Ideal for differentiated teaching.
- Includes CD-ROM with pages in PDF format for direct digital printing.

HELPING YOU PREPARE MOTIVATING AND STIMULATING LESSONS

MORE TITLES AVAILABLE FROM

Shakespeare's plays in a choice of 3 text versions. Simply choose the text version to match your reading level.

Original Text	SHAKESPEARE'S ENTIRE PLAY AS A FULL COLOR GRAPHIC NOVEL!
Plain Text	THE ENTIRE PLAY TRANSLATED INTO PLAIN ENGLISH!
Quick Text	THE ENTIRE PLAY IN QUICK MODERN ENGLISH FOR A FAST-PACED READ!

2010 WINNER
aep
DISTINGUISHED ACHIEVEMENT

Romeo & Juliet: The Graphic Novel (William Shakespeare)

• Script Adaptation: John McDonald • Linework: Will Volley
• Colors: Jim Devlin • Letters: Jim Campbell • 168 Pages

HE JESTS AT SCARS THAT NEVER FELT A WOUND.
BUT SOFT! WHAT LIGHT THROUGH YONDER WINDOW BREAKS?
IT IS THE EAST, AND JULIET IS THE SUN. ARISE, FAIR SUN, AND KILL THE ENVIOUS MOON, WHO IS ALREADY SICK AND PALE WITH GRIEF THAT THOU HER MAID ARE FAR MORE FAIR THAN SHE.

ISBN: 978-1-906332-61-7

ONLY THOSE WHO HAVE NEVER BEEN IN LOVE MAKE JOKES ABOUT A BROKEN HEART.
- BUT, SOFT! WHAT LIGHT THROUGH YONDER WINDOW BREAKS?
IT IS THE EAST, AND JULIET IS THE SUN. RISE, LOVELY SUN, AND KILL THAT OLD JEALOUS MOON! IT IS PALE AND SAD BECAUSE JULIET IS MORE BEAUTIFUL.

ISBN: 978-1-906332-62-4

LET THEM MAKE THEIR JOKES --
WHAT LIGHT THROUGH YONDER WINDOW BREAKS?
IT MUST BE THE EAST, AND JULIET IS THE RISING SUN.

ISBN: 978-1-906332-63-1

A Midsummer Night's Dream: The Graphic Novel (William Shakespeare)

• Script Adaptation: John McDonald • Characters & Artwork: Kat Nicholson & Jason Cardy
• Letters: Jim Campbell • 144 Pages

AND NOW THEY NEVER MEET IN GROVE, OR GREEN, BY FOUNTAIN CLEAR, OR SPANGLED STARLIGHT SHEEN,
BUT THEY DO SQUARE; THAT ALL THEIR ELVES, FOR FEAR, CREEP INTO ACORN CUPS, AND HIDE THEM THERE.

ISBN: 978-1-907127-28-1

NOW THEY WON'T MEET IN WOODS OR GREEN, BY WATERFALLS OR IN SKY SO CLEAN.
INSTEAD, THEY ARGUE WHEN THEY ARE NEAR, WHILE THEIR ELVES ALL HIDE AWAY IN FEAR.

ISBN: 978-1-907127-29-8

BUT TITANIA, SHE LOVES THE BOY. HE REALLY IS HER PRIDE AND JOY!
AND NOW, WHENEVER THEY MEET OR ARE NEAR, THEY ARGUE SO MUCH, THEIR ELVES HIDE IN FEAR.

ISBN: 978-1-907127-30-4

IP

The Tempest: The Graphic Novel (William Shakespeare)

• Script Adaptation: John McDonald • Pencils: Jon Haward
• Inks: Gary Erskine • Colors: & Letters: Nigel Dobbyn • 144 Pages

BUT THIS ROUGH MAGIC I HERE ABJURE; AND, WHEN I HAVE REQUIR'D SOME HEAVENLY MUSIC, (WHICH EVEN NOW I DO), TO WORK MINE END UPON THEIR SENSES, THAT THIS AIRY CHARM IS FOR, I'LL BREAK MY STAFF, BURY IT CERTAIN FATHOMS IN THE EARTH, AND, DEEPER THAN DID EVER PLUMMET SOUND, I'LL DROWN MY BOOK.

ISBN: 978-1-906332-69-3

BUT THE TIME HAS COME FOR ME TO GIVE UP THAT MAGIC. AFTER I CONJURE UP SOME UNEARTHLY MUSIC TO CAST ONE FINAL SPELL, THAT WILL MAKE THEM DO AS I COMMAND, I'LL BREAK MY STAFF AND BURY IT DEEP IN THE EARTH. I'LL ALSO SEND MY BOOK OF SPELLS DEEPER INTO THE SEA THAN ANY ANCHOR EVER SANK.

ISBN: 978-1-906332-70-9

BUT THE TIME HAS COME TO STOP - I MUST CONJURE UP ONE FINAL SPELL.

ISBN: 978-1-906332-71-6

Recognizing Excellence in Independent Publishing
INDEPENDENT PUBLISHER
IP
BOOK AWARDS
SILVER

Henry V: The Graphic Novel (William Shakespeare)

• Script Adaptation: John McDonald • Pencils: Neill Cameron • Inks: Bambos
• Colors: Jason Cardy & Kat Nicholson • Letters: Nigel Dobbyn • 144 Pages

WE DOUBT NOT OF A FAIR AND LUCKY WAR, SINCE GOD SO GRACIOUSLY HATH BROUGHT TO LIGHT THIS DANGEROUS TREASON LURKING IN OUR WAY TO HINDER OUR BEGINNINGS. WE DOUBT NOT NOW BUT EVERY RUB IS SMOOTHED ON OUR WAY.
THEN FORTH, DEAR COUNTRYMEN! LET US DELIVER OUR PUISSANCE INTO THE HAND OF GOD, PUTTING IT STRAIGHT IN EXPEDITION. CHEERLY TO SEA! THE SIGNS OF WAR ADVANCE!
NO KING OF ENGLAND, IF NOT KING OF FRANCE!

ISBN: 978-1-906332-41-9

THERE'S NO DOUBT NOW THAT ALL OBSTACLES HAVE BEEN REMOVED. SO, MY COUNTRYMEN, LET'S GO!
LET'S DELIVER OUR ARMY INTO THE HAND OF GOD AND BEGIN OUR EXPEDITION IMMEDIATELY. AWAY TO SEA, WITH OUR WARLIKE ADVANCE!
I WON'T BE KING OF ENGLAND, IF I'M NOT ALSO KING OF FRANCE!

ISBN: 978-1-906332-42-6

THERE'S NOTHING ELSE IN OUR WAY, SO LET'S ADVANCE.
I WON'T BE KING OF ENGLAND, IF I'M NOT ALSO KING OF FRANCE!

ISBN: 978-1-906332-43-3

OUR AWARD-WINNING RANGE

Classic Literature in a choice of 2 text versions. Simply choose the text version to match your reading level.

Original Text	THE CLASSIC NOVEL BROUGHT TO LIFE IN FULL COLOR!
Quick Text	THE FULL STORY IN QUICK MODERN ENGLISH FOR A FAST-PACED READ!

Dracula: The Graphic Novel (Bram Stoker)

- Script Adaptation: Jason Cobley • Linework: Staz Johnson
- Colors: James Offredi • Letters: Jim Campbell

WELCOME TO MY HOUSE! ENTER FREELY AND OF YOUR OWN WILL! COME FREELY. GO SAFELY.
I AM DRACULA. AND I BID YOU WELCOME, MR. HARKER, TO MY HOUSE.
COME IN; THE NIGHT AIR IS CHILL, AND YOU MUST NEED TO EAT AND REST. IT IS LATE, AND MY PEOPLE ARE NOT AVAILABLE.
LET ME SEE TO YOUR COMFORT MYSELF.

ISBN: 978-1-906332-67-9

WELCOME TO MY HOUSE!
I AM DRACULA, AND I BID YOU WELCOME.
YOU MUST NEED TO EAT AND REST. IT IS LATE, AND MY PEOPLE ARE NOT AVAILABLE. LET ME LOOK AFTER YOU.

ISBN: 978-1-906332-68-6

"I went down into the vaults. There lay the Count! He was either dead or asleep, I could not say which."

• 152 Pages

DRACULA
THE GRAPHIC NOVEL
DRACULA

An Inspector Calls: The Graphic Novel (J. B. Priestley)

- Script Adaptation: Jason Cobley • Linework: Will Volley
- Colors: Alejandro Sanchez • Letters: Jim Campbell

I'D LIKE SOME INFORMATION, IF YOU DON'T MIND, MR. BIRLING.
TWO HOURS AGO A YOUNG WOMAN DIED IN THE INFIRMARY. SHE'D BEEN TAKEN THERE THIS AFTERNOON BECAUSE SHE'D SWALLOWED A LOT OF STRONG DISINFECTANT. BURNT HER INSIDE OUT, OF COURSE.

ISBN: 978-1-907127-23-6

TWO HOURS AGO, A YOUNG WOMAN DIED IN THE INFIRMARY.
SHE HAD SWALLOWED A LOT OF STRONG DISINFECTANT THAT BURNT HER INSIDES.

ISBN: 978-1-907127-24-3

"But don't you see, if all that's come out tonight is true, then it doesn't much matter who it was who made us confess."

• 144 Pages

An Inspector Calls
THE GRAPHIC NOVEL
An Inspector Calls

Sweeney Todd: The Graphic Novel (Anonymous)

- Script Adaptation: Seán Michael Wilson • Linework: Declan Shalvey
- Colors: Jason Cardy & Kat Nicholson • Letters: Jim Campbell

I'LL CUT YOUR THROAT FROM EAR TO EAR, IF YOU REPEAT ONE WORD OF WHAT PASSES IN THIS SHOP, OR DARE TO MAKE ANY SUPPOSITION, OR DRAW ANY CONCLUSION FROM ANYTHING YOU MAY SEE, OR HEAR, OR FANCY YOU SEE OR HEAR.
I'LL CUT YOUR THROAT FROM EAR TO EAR - DO YOU UNDERSTAND ME?

ISBN: 978-1-907127-09-0

I WILL CUT YOUR THROAT IF YOU TELL ANYONE WHAT GOES ON HERE - DO YOU UNDERSTAND?

ISBN: 978-1-907127-10-6

"Oh! to be sure, he came here, and I shaved him and polished him off."

• 168 Pages

SWEENEY TODD
THE DEMON BARBER OF FLEET STREET
THE GRAPHIC NOVEL

Wuthering Heights: The Graphic Novel (Emily Brontë)

- Script Adaptation: Seán Michael Wilson • Artwork: John M. Burns
- Letters: Jim Campbell

IF I WERE IN HEAVEN, NELLY, I SHOULD BE EXTREMELY MISERABLE. I DREAMT ONCE THAT I WAS THERE.
HEAVEN DID NOT SEEM TO BE MY HOME; AND I BROKE MY HEART WITH WEEPING TO COME BACK TO EARTH; AND THE ANGELS WERE SO ANGRY THAT THEY FLUNG ME OUT INTO THE MIDDLE OF THE HEATH ON THE TOP OF WUTHERING HEIGHTS; WHERE I WOKE SOBBING FOR JOY.
THAT WILL DO TO EXPLAIN MY SECRET, AS WELL AS THE OTHER.

ISBN: 978-1-907127-11-3

I DREAMT THAT I WAS IN HEAVEN, BUT I WAS NOT HAPPY THERE AND I WEPT TO COME BACK TO EARTH.
THE ANGELS WERE SO ANGRY THAT THEY FLUNG ME OUT INTO THE MIDDLE OF THE MOORS, WHERE I WOKE CRYING WITH JOY.

ISBN: 978-1-907127-12-0

"That minx, Catherine Linton, or Earnshaw, or however she was called – wicked little soul!"

• 160 Pages

Wuthering Heights
THE GRAPHIC NOVEL

To see the complete range, and to view samples online, go to www.classicalcomics.com

AVAILABLE IN THREE TEXT VERSIONS

Macbeth:
The Graphic Novel
Original Text

ISBN:
978-1-906332-44-0

THE ENTIRE PLAY TRANSLATED INTO PLAIN ENGLISH!

THE ENTIRE SHAKESPEARE PLAY - AS A GRAPHIC NOVEL

Macbeth:
The Graphic Novel
Plain Text

ISBN:
978-1-906332-45-7

THE ENTIRE PLAY IN QUICK MODERN ENGLISH FOR A FAST-PACED READ!

Macbeth:
The Graphic Novel
Quick Text

ISBN:
978-1-906332-46-4

CHOOSE FROM ONE OF THREE TEXT VERSIONS, ALL USING THE SAME HIGH QUALITY ARTWORK:

Original Text

UPON MY HEAD THEY PLAC'D A *FRUITLESS CROWN,* AND PUT A *BARREN SCEPTRE* IN MY GRIPE, THENCE TO BE WRENCH'D WITH AN *UNLINEAL HAND,* NO SON OF MINE SUCCEEDING. IF 'T BE SO, FOR *BANQUO'S ISSUE* HAVE I FIL'D MY MIND;

This is the full, original script - just as The Bard intended.
This version is ideal for purists, students and for readers who want to experience the unaltered text: all of the text, all of the excitement!

Plain Text

SO... THEY'VE PUT A *USELESS CROWN* ON MY HEAD AND AN *EMPTY SCEPTRE* IN MY HAND. IT WILL ALL BE TAKEN AWAY BY *ANOTHER FAMILY* IF NO SON OF MINE *SUCCEEDS ME.* IF THAT'S THE CASE, I'VE CORRUPTED MY OWN SOUL FOR *BANQUO'S* DESCENDANTS.

We take the original script and "convert" it into modern English, verse-for-verse. If you've ever wanted to appreciate the works of Shakespeare fully, but find the original language rather cryptic, then this is the version for you!

Quick Text

IF SO, THEN IT'S ALL BEEN FOR *NOTHING.* HIS *FAMILY* WILL TAKE EVERYTHING *AWAY* FROM ME.

We take the dialogue and reduce it to as few words as possible while retaining the full essence of the story.
This version allows readers to enter into and enjoy the stories quickly.